W9-BKC-862

PRAISE FOR *LAURUS*

'Stylistically ornate and compulsively readable . . . delivered with great aplomb and narrative charm.'

Times Literary Supplement

'A remarkable novel . . . Russia's answer to *The Name of the Rose*.'

Atticus Lish, author of *Preparation for the Next Life*

'Impressive . . . *Laurus* cannot be faulted for its ambition or for its poignant humanity. It is a profound, sometimes challenging, meditation on faith, love and life's mysteries.'

Financial Times

'In *Laurus*, Vodolazkin aims directly at the heart of the Russian religious experience and perhaps even at that maddeningly elusive concept that is cherished to the point of cliché: the Russian soul.'

The New Yorker

'A treasure house of Russian medieval lore and customs . . . a very clever, self-aware contemporary novel . . . a quirky, ambitious book.'

Los Angeles Review of Books

'Vodolazkin explores multifaceted questions of "Russianness" and concludes, like the 19th-century poet Fyodor Tyutchev, that Russia cannot be rationally understood. This is what leads him, with a gradual, but unstoppable momentum, to place faith and the transcendent human spirit at the centre of his powerful worldview.'

Washington Post

'Love, faith and a quest for atonement are the driving themes of [this] epic, prize-winning Russian novel . . . With flavours of Umberto Eco and *The Canterbury Tales*, this affecting, idiosyncratic novel . . . is an impressive achievement.'

Kirkus

'A masterpiece by any standards.'

Huffington Post UK

'A stroke of brilliant storytelling . . . a uniquely lavish, multi-layered work that blends an invented hagiography with the rapturous energy of Dostoevsky's spiritual obsessions.'

Booklist

Also by Eugene Vodolazkin

Laurus
Solovyov and Larionov

THE AVIATOR

EUGENE VODOLAZKIN

Translated from the Russian by
Lisa C. Hayden

ONEWORLD

A Oneworld Book

First published in North America, Great Britain
and Australia by Oneworld Publications, 2018

Originally published in Russian as Авиатор by AST, Elena Shubina imprint, 2016

The publication of the book was negotiated through Banke, Goumen & Smirnova
Literary Agency (www.bgs-agency.com)

ISBN 978-1-78607-271-9 (hardback)
ISBN 978-1-78607-272-6 (ebook)

Published with the support of the Institute for Literary Translation, Russia.

ИНСТИТУТ ПЕРЕВОДА

AD VERBUM

Typeset in 12/16pt Janson MT by Falcon Oast Graphic Art Ltd
Printed and bound in Great Britain by Clays Ltd, St Ives plc

Oneworld Publications
10 Bloomsbury Street
London WC1B 3SR
England

Stay up to date with the latest books,
special offers, and exclusive content from
Oneworld with our newsletter

Sign up on our website
oneworld-publications.com

To my daughter

Contents

'Why is it you keep writing?'

'I'm describing things, sensations. People. I write every day now, hoping to save them from oblivion.'

'God's world is too great to count on success with that.'

'You know, if each person were to describe his own sliver of that world, even if it's a small piece . . . Although why, really, is it small? You can always find someone whose field of view is broad enough.'

'Such as?'

'Such as an aviator.'

— Conversation on an airplane

Part One

I used to tell her: wear a hat when it's cold, otherwise you'll get frostbite on your ears. Have a look, I would say, at how many pedestrians these days don't have ears. She would agree – yes, yes, she'd say, I should – but she didn't wear one. She would laugh at the joke and go around without a hat anyway. That little picture surfaced in my memory just now, though I haven't the faintest idea whom it concerns.

Or perhaps a scandalous scene had come to mind, an outrageous and grueling one. It is unclear where it played out. The shame is that the interaction began well (one might even say good-naturedly) and then one word led to another and everyone quarreled. The main thing is that we were the ones who were surprised later: what was that for, why?

Someone noticed that funeral banquets are often like that: people talk for an hour and a half or so about what a good person the deceased was. And then someone in attendance remembers that, actually, the deceased was not perfect. And here, as if on command, lots of people begin speaking out and adding on, so, little by little, they come to the conclusion that the deceased was basically a first-rate heel.

Or there could be a real phantasmagoria: someone's hit on the head with a piece of sausage and then that person rolls along an inclined plane, rolls and can't stop, and his head spins from the rolling.

My head. Spins. I'm lying on a bed.

Where am I?

Footsteps.

An unfamiliar person in a white lab coat entered. He stood, placing a hand to his lips, and looked at me (someone else's head is in the crack in the door). For my part, I looked at him, but as if I were not showing it. Out from behind eyelids not tightly closed. He noticed their trembling.

'You're awake?'

I opened my eyes. The unfamiliar person approached my bed and extended a hand:

'Geiger. Your doctor.'

I pulled my right hand out from under the blanket and felt Geiger's cautious handshake. This is how people touch when they're afraid of breaking something. He glanced back for an instant and the door slammed shut. Geiger bent toward me without letting go of my hand:

'And you're Innokenty Petrovich Platonov, isn't that so?'

I could not confirm that. If he was saying that, it meant he had grounds to do so. Innokenty Petrovich . . . I silently concealed my hand under the blanket.

'You don't remember anything?' Geiger asked.

I shook my head. Innokenty Petrovich Platonov. Sounds respectable. Perhaps a bit literary.

'Do you remember my coming over to your bed just now? How I introduced myself?'

Why was he like this with me? Or was I truly in sorry shape? I paused and rasped:

'I remember.'

'And before that?'

I felt tears choking me. They had broken out into the open and I began sobbing. Geiger took a napkin from the bedside table and wiped my face.

'Come now, Innokenty Petrovich. There are so few events on this earth that are worth remembering and you're upset.'

'Will my memory be restored?'

'I very much hope so. Your case is one where it's impossible to assert anything for certain.' He placed a thermometer under my arm. 'You know, try recalling as much as you can, your effort is important here. We need you to remember everything yourself.'

I saw hairs in Geiger's nose. There were scratches on his chin from shaving.

He was looking at me calmly. High forehead, straight nose, pince-nez – it was as if someone had drawn him. There are faces so very typical they seem invented.

'Was I in an accident?'

'One might say that.'

In an open vent window, air from the hospital room was mixing with winter air from outside. The air was growing murky, trembling and fusing; a vertical slat on the frame was merging with a tree trunk; and this early dusk – I have already seen it somewhere. And I had seen snowflakes floating in, too. Melting before reaching the windowsill . . . Where?

'I don't remember anything. Only some little things: snowflakes in a hospital window, the coolness of glass if one touches it with a forehead. I don't remember events.'

'I could, of course, remind you about something that occurred, but one can't retell a life in all its fullness. I know only the most sur-face aspects of your life: where you lived, who you interacted with. Beyond that, the history of your thoughts and feelings is unknown to me, do you see?' He pulled the thermometer out from under my arm. 'Thirty-eight point five. Rather high.'

MONDAY

Yesterday, there was still no such thing as time. But today is Monday. Here is what happened. Geiger brought a pencil and a thick notebook. And left. He returned with a writing stand.

'Write down everything that happened during the day. And write down everything you recall from the past, too. This journal is for me. I'll see how quickly we're making progress with what we do.'

'All my events so far are connected with you. Does that mean I should write about you?'

'Abgemacht.[1] Describe and assess me from all angles: my modest persona will begin pulling other threads of your consciousness behind it. And we will gradually broaden your social circle.'

Geiger adjusted the stand over my stomach. It rose slightly, dolefully, with each of my breaths, as if it were breathing, too. Geiger straightened the stand. He opened the notebook and placed the pencil in my fingers; this was, really, a bit much. I may be sick (with what, one might ask?) but I can move my arms and legs. What, in actuality, could I write? Nothing, after all, is happening or being recalled.

The notebook is huge; it would be enough for a novel. I twirl the pencil in my hand. What is my illness, anyway? Doctor, will I live?

'What is today's date, doctor?'

He is silent. I am silent, too. Did I really ask something indecorous?

'Let's do this,' Geiger finally utters, 'let's have you just indicate the days of the week. We'll come to an understanding about time easier that way.'

Geiger is mysteriousness itself. I answer:

'Abgemacht.'

---

1 Agreed (Germ.).

He laughs.

So I went ahead and wrote everything down – about yesterday and about today.

TUESDAY

Today I made the acquaintance of Valentina, the nurse. She's shapely. Not talkative.

I feigned sleep when she entered; this is already becoming a habit. Then I opened one eye and asked:

'What is your name?'

'Valentina. The doctor said you need rest.'

She answered no further questions. She swabbed the floor with a mop, her back to me. A triumph of rhythm. When she bent to rinse the rag in the pail, her underclothes showed through her white coat. What kind of rest could I have ... ?

I'm joking. I have no strength whatsoever. Geiger took my temperature this morning: 38.7, which worries him.

What worries me is that I cannot seem to distinguish recollections from dreams.

Ambiguous impressions from last night. I am lying at home with a temperature – it's influenza. My grandmother's hand is cool; the thermometer is cool. Swirls of snow outside are covering the road to my school, where I did not go today. This means they will come to the letter 'P' in the roll call (a finger, all chalky, will slide through the record book) and call Platonov.

But Platonov is not here, reports the class monitor, he stayed home due to influenza. I dare say they are reading *Robinson Crusoe* to him. It's possible a wall clock is audible at the house. His grand-mother, continues the monitor, is pressing a pince-nez to her nose so her eyes look large and bugged from the lenses. That is an expressive little picture, agrees the teacher, let us call this the apotheosis of reading (animation in the classroom).

In short, the essence of what happened, says the monitor, boils down to the following. A frivolous young man sets off on an ocean journey and is shipwrecked. He is washed up on an uninhabited island where he remains, without means for existence and – the most important thing – without people. There are no people at all. If he had conducted himself sensibly from the very beginning . . . I don't know how to express this, so as not to slip into an instructional tone. It is a sort of parable about a prodigal son.

There is an equation (yesterday's arithmetic) on the classroom chalkboard; the floorboards retain moisture from the morning clean-ing. The teacher vividly imagines Robinson's helpless floundering as he strives to reach the shore. Aivazovsky's painting *The Ninth Wave* helps him see the true scope of the catastrophe. Not one interjection breaks the shaken teacher's silence. Coach wheels are barely audible outside the double windows.

I myself read from *Robinson Crusoe* rather often, but you don't read a whole lot during an illness. Your eyes smart, the lines float. I follow my grandmother's mouth. She raises a finger to her lips before turning a page. Sometimes she gulps cooled tea and then a barely noticeable spray flies on *Robinson Crusoe*. Sometimes there are crumbs from rusks eaten between chapters. After returning to health, I carefully page through what was read and brush out dried, flattened particles of bread.

'I remember many various places and people,' I nervously announced to Geiger. 'I remember some sort of statements. Even if my life depended on it, though, I do not remember exactly who said which words. And where.'

Geiger is calm. He hopes this will pass. He does not consider this consequential.

And maybe this truly is not consequential? Perhaps the only thing that matters is that words were uttered and preserved, so questions of 'where' and 'by whom' are further down the list? I will have to ask Geiger about this; he seems to know everything.

WEDNESDAY

This can happen, too: a picture is completely intact although the words have not been preserved. A person, for example, is sitting in the dusk. He is not switching on the light even though there is already half-darkness in the room: is he economizing or something? A sorrowful immobility. Elbow resting on a table, forehead in repose on palm of hand, little finger sticking out. It is visible even in the darkness that his clothes are in folds, all brownish, to the point of colorlessness, and his face and hand are the only white spot. The person appears to be musing, although in reality he is not thinking about anything, only resting. Maybe he is even saying something but the words are inaudible. In any case, his words are not important to me: who is there for him to talk with, himself? He does not know, after all, that I am observing him and if he happens to be saying anything, it is not to me. His lips move; he looks out the window. Drops on the glass reflect the luminescence of the street and sparkle with glimmers from carriages. The vent window squeaks.

Up until now, I have seen only two people in my room: Geiger and Valentina. A doctor and a nurse; who else, in actuality, is necessary? I gathered my strength, stood, and walked over to the window: the yard was empty, the snow was knee-deep. One time I went outside my room into the corridor, holding on to the wall, but Valentina appeared immediately: you're on a bed-rest regime, go back to your room. A regime . . .

By the way: they both look like they're from the old regime. When Geiger is not wearing a white coat, without fail he wears a three-piece suit. He reminds me of Chekhov . . . I kept thinking: who does he remind me of? Chekhov! And he wears a pince-nez, too. Of those alive today, I think I have only seen one on Stanislavsky, but he is a person of the theater . . . Then again, I would say there is some sort of theatricality in the pair that is treating me. Valentina is every bit the war-time sister of mercy. 1914. I don't know how they'll regard this impression of mine: Geiger will read this, we agreed to that. After all, it was he who asked me to write everything down, openly: what I notice, recall, and think, so that's how I'm writing.

My pencil lead broke today, so I told Valentina. She took something akin to a pencil out of her pocket and held it out to me.

'That's funny,' I say, 'metal lead, I've never seen anything like it.'

Valentina blushed and quickly took the thing back. She brought me another pencil later. Why did she blush? She doesn't blush when she takes me to the toilet or pulls down my drawers for injections, but come now!, this is a just pencil! There are masses of minor riddles in my life right now that I am powerless to unravel . . . But she blushes charmingly, to the tips of her ears. Her ears are delicate, elegant. I admired them yesterday when her white kerchief fell off. More precisely, one of them. With her back to me, Valentina leaned over the lamp and the light shone pink through her ear; I wanted to touch it. But dared not. And had not the strength anyway.

I have the strange sensation that I have been lying in this bed for an entire eternity. There's pain in my muscles when I move an arm or a leg, and my legs feel like jelly if I stand without someone's aid. Then again, my temperature has lowered a bit: 38.3.

I ask Geiger:

'So what happened to me, anyway?'

'That,' he answers, 'is something you need to recall, otherwise my consciousness will replace yours. Do you really want that?'

I myself do not know if I want that. Maybe I will turn out to have a consciousness that could stand replacing.

FRIDAY

Regarding the question of consciousness: I lost mine yesterday. Geiger and Valentina had quite a fright. I saw their perturbed faces when I came to: it seems they would have been sorry to lose me. It's nice when people need you for some reason, even if the reason is nothing personal but only, as they say, pure love of one's fellow man. Geiger did not return my papers to me all day yesterday. He was apparently afraid I had strained myself with my writings the day before. I lay there, watching flakes of snow fall outside the window. I fell asleep watching. The flakes were still falling when I woke up.

Valentina was sitting on a chair beside my bed. She wiped my forehead with a damp sponge. Kiss, I wanted to say, kiss me on the forehead. I did not say that. Because it would have worked out that she had been wiping my forehead before she kissed it. In any case, it's clear who is kissed on the forehead . . . I took her by the hand, though, and she didn't take it away. She just placed our joined hands on my stomach so as not to hold mine hanging. Her palm covered my hand like a little house, the way they teach holding one's hand to play the pianoforte. If I know things like this, most likely I was taught that at one time, too. After turning my hand over, I drew my index finger along the ceiling of that little house and sensed it jolt, collapse, and sprawl over my palm. And I sensed its warmth.

'Lie next to me, Valentina,' I asked of her. 'I have no indecent thoughts and I am completely harmless, you are aware of that. I simply need for someone to be next to me. Right next to me, otherwise I will never warm up. I cannot explain it, but that is how it is.'

With effort, I moved on the wide bed and Valentina lay down alongside me, on top of the blanket. I myself do not know why, but I was certain she would fulfill my request. She inclined her head toward my head. I inhaled her scent: an infusion that joined ironed, starched, and snow-white with the aroma of perfume and a youthful body. She was sharing that with me and I could not breathe in enough of it. Geiger came into view as the doorway opened but Valentina remained lying there. Something tensed in her (I felt it) but she did not stand. She probably blushed; she could not help but blush.

'Very good,' said Geiger without entering. 'Get some rest.'

A wonderful reaction in its own way.

I had not really intended to describe this as it relates not only to me, but since Geiger already saw everything . . . Let him have a proper understanding of the essence of what happened (though of course he understands anyway). I want for this to recur, if only for a few minutes each day.

SUNDAY

After waking, I mentally recited the Lord's Prayer. It turns out that I can reproduce the prayer without hesitation. When I could not go to church on Sundays, I would at least recite 'Our Father' to myself.

I would move my lips in the damp wind. I lived on an island where attending services was not taken for granted. And it was not that the island was uninhabited – there were churches – but somehow it turned out that attending was not simple. I can no longer remember the details.

Church is a great joy, especially during childhood. I'm small, meaning I'm holding on to my mother's skirt. The skirt under her fur jacket is long and the hem rustles along the floor. My mother places a candle by an icon and the skirt rises a tiny bit, my hand in a mitten along with it. She carefully picks me up and carries me toward the icon. I feel her palms on the small of my back, my felt boots and mittens move freely in the air, and it is as if I'm soaring toward the icon. Under me are dozens of candles – holiday candles, wavering – and I look at them, unable to avert my gaze from that brightness. They crackle, wax flowing from them, freezing on the spot in intricate stalactites. Coming to greet me, arms spread, is the Mother of God and I clumsily kiss Her on the hand because I am not in control of my flight and, after kissing, I touch Her with my forehead as one should. I feel the coolness of Her hand for an instant. And I soar around the church like that, I drift through aromatic smoke, over a priest swinging a censer. Over the choir, through its canticles (the slowed flapping of the precentor and his grimaces on the high notes). Over the candle lady and the people filling the church (flowing around the pillars), along windows, outside which there is a snow-covered country. Russia? Bitter cold swirls visibly near a door not tightly shut; there is rime on the handle. The crack widens abruptly and Geiger is in the rectangle that has formed.

'We are in Russia, doctor, are we not?' I ask.

'In a certain sense, yes.'

He is preparing my arm for an intravenous drip.

'Then why are you Geiger?'

He looks at me, surprised:

'Because I'm a Russian German. Deutschrusse. Were you worried that we're in Germany?'

No, I was not worried. Now I can simply consider that I know our location for certain. Essentially, that was not very clear until today.

'And where is Nurse Valentina?'

'She has the day off.'

After putting in the drip, Geiger takes my temperature. It's 38.1.

'And so,' I ask, 'there are no other nurses?'

'You're insatiable.'

I do not need another nurse. I just do not understand what kind of establishment this is where there is one doctor, one nurse, and one patient. Then again, anything is possible in Russia. 'In Russia' ... that must be a common phrase if it has even been preserved in my destroyed memory. It has its own rhythm. I don't know what is behind it, but I do remember the *set phrase*.

I already have a few of these phrases that have surfaced out of nowhere. They probably have their own histories, but I'm uttering them as if for the first time. I feel like Adam. Or a child: children often utter set phrases without yet knowing their meaning. Anything is possible in Russia, uh-huh. There is condemnation in that, perhaps even a verdict. It feels as if it is some sort of disagreeable boundlessness, that everything will head in an all-too-obvious direction. How much does that phrase concern me?

After thinking, I announce the phrase to Geiger, as a German, and ask him to evaluate it. I follow the movement of his lips and brows – people sampling wine look like this. He inhales noisily as if in answer, but he exhales just as noisily after pausing. As a German, he decides to keep silent, in order, let us suppose, not to traumatize me. Instead, he asks me to stick out my tongue, which, in my view, is justified in its own way. My tongue still operates independently to a significant degree: it pronounces what it is accustomed to pronouncing, as happens with talking birds. Geiger has apparently understood everything about my tongue so asks me to stick it out. He shakes his head when I do. My tongue does not gladden him.

Geiger turns as he approaches the door:

'Oh, also . . . If you'd like for Nurse Valentina to lie next to you, even, let us suppose, under the same blanket as you, just say so, don't be shy. That's fine.'

'You know yourself she'll be completely safe.'

'I know. Although,' he snaps his fingers, 'anything is possible in Russia, is it not?'

At the moment, *not* everything . . . I sense that like nobody else.

FRIDAY

I had no strength for all those days. Nor do I have any today. Something strange is spinning in my head: 'Aviator Platonov.' Another *set phrase?*

I ask Geiger:

'Doctor, was I an aviator?'

'As far as I know, no . . .'

Where was I called an aviator? Perhaps in Kuokkala? Precisely! In Kuokkala. I shout to Geiger:

'That moniker is linked to Kuokkala, where I . . . where we . . . Have you been to Kuokkala, doctor?'

'It has a different name now.'

'How is that?'

'Well, now it's called Repino . . . The important thing is to write down your recollection.'

I'll write it down, but tomorrow. I'm tired.

SATURDAY

My cousin Seva and I are on the Gulf of Finland. Seva is my mother's brother's son: that explanation of the kinship sounded terribly complicated to me when I was a child. Even now, I don't say it smoothly. Of course 'cousin' is a little easier to say but it's best of all to say 'Seva'. Seva's parents have a house in Kuokkala.

He and I are flying a kite. In the evenings, we run along the beach at the very edge of the water. Sometimes our bare feet graze the water and the spray sparkles in the setting sun. We imagine that we're aviators. We're flying together, me in the front seat, Seva in the back. It's deserted and lonely there in the cold sky but our friendship warms us. If we perish, at least we are together; that draws us close. We attempt to exchange remarks there, up high, but the wind carries our words away.

'Aviator Platonov,' Seva shouts to me from the back. 'Aviator Platonov, the locality of Kuokkala lies ahead!'

I do not understand why Seva is addressing his colleague so ceremoniously. Maybe in order that Platonov not forget he is an aviator. Seva's high voice (it always remained that way) carries along the entire locality we are flying over. Sometimes it merges with the screeches of seagulls and they become almost indistinguishable from one another. To tell the truth, this shouting of his irritates me very much. Glancing at Seva's happy face, I cannot find the strength within to ask him to be quiet. Essentially, it is thanks to his strange birdlike timbre that I remember him.

They give us hot milk with honey before bed. I don't really like hot milk but it evokes no protest after the flight over the gulf, after the sea breeze in my face. Seva and I – despite the fact that the milk has barely begun cooling – drink it in big, loud mouthfuls. A Finnish milkmaid brings the milk and it truly is very delicious, especially when it's not hot. The Finnish woman gets tangled up in her Russian words as she praises her cow. I imagine that the cow resembles the milkmaid herself: huge and unhurried, with wide-set eyes and a taut udder.

Seva and I share a room in a turret. It has a panoramic view (forest behind, sea ahead), something that is not unimportant for experienced aviators. The weather can be evaluated at any time: fog over the sea means a likelihood of rain, whitecaps on the waves and the rocking of pine-tree tops mean a gale-force wind. The pines and the waves change their appearance in the dusk of a white night. It's not quite that a threat appears in them, no: they simply lose their daytime kindness. It is akin to experiencing anxiety when watching a smiling person who has become pensive.

'Are you already asleep?' Seva whispers.

'No,' I say, 'but I plan to be.'

'I saw a giant outside,' says Seva, pointing at the window opposite the sea.

'It's a pine tree. Go to sleep.'

A few minutes later, I can hear Seva's loud breathing. I look at the window Seva pointed to. And I see a giant.

MONDAY

Monday is a rough day ... That's one more *set phrase* from my poor head. Are there many more of them in there? I wonder. There are no longer people or events, but words remain, there they are. Words are probably the last to disappear, especially the written word. It is possible Geiger himself does not completely understand what a profound idea this writing is. Maybe it's words that will turn out, at some point, to be the thread that will manage to drag out everything that happened? Not just with me but everything there ever was at all. A rough day . . . I, however, am feeling a lightness, even a sort of joy. I think it's because I am expecting to see Valentina. I attempted to stand up but felt dizzy and then the lightness disappeared. The joy did not disappear, though.

Valentina pinched my cheek when she entered, which was very nice. Surprising aromas, completely unfamiliar to me, emanate from her. Perfume, soap? Valentina's natural properties? It is awkward to ask and unnecessary, too. Everything should have its secrets, especially a woman . . . That's a *set phrase*, too. I can sense it is!

Here's another one I liked very much: 'Metal conducts heat quickly.' It may not be the most prevalent phrase, but it's one of the first I heard. We're sitting who'd know where or with whom, stirring tea with little spoons. I'm about five years old, I think, no more, and there's an embroidered pillow on the chair under me (I can't reach the table) and I'm stirring tea like an adult. The glass itself is in a metal holder. The spoon is hot. I drop it into the glass with a jingle and blow on my fingers. 'Metal conducts heat quickly,' says a pleasant voice. Beautifully, scientifically. I repeated that in similar circumstances until I was about twelve.

No, that is not the earliest. 'Go intrepidly,' that is the earliest. We are entering someone's house at Christmas. A taxidermied bear stands on its hind legs by the staircase, holding a tray in its front paws.

'What is the tray for?' I ask.

'For visiting cards,' answers my father.

My fingers plunge into the dense bear fur for a moment. Why does the bear need visiting cards (we're walking up the marble steps) and what are visiting cards? I repeat those two words a few times and slip, but I'm dangling on my father's arm. As I swing, I contemplate the runner rug on the marble: it's fastened with golden rods and it's a little curled on the sides and swinging, too. My father's laughing face. We enter a brightly lit hall. Christmas tree, round dance. My hands are sticky from someone's perspiration; I think it's repulsive, but I cannot unclench my hands and cannot leave the round dance. Someone says I'm the smallest in attendance (we are now already sitting on chairs around the Christmas tree). He somehow knows I can recite poems and asks me to say one. And all the others ask loudly, too. An old man wearing an ancient uniform appears next to me; there are medals under his split beard.

'This,' they say, 'is Terenty Osipovich Dobrosklonov.'

An empty space forms around us. I look silently at Terenty Osipovich. He's standing, leaning on a cane and bending slightly to the side, so the thought even flashes that he could fall. He does not fall.

'Go intrepidly,' Terenty Osipovich advises me.

I run from the invitation, through an enfilade of rooms, my head bending and arms spread wide, noticing how my reflection flashes in the mirrors and crockery clinks in cabinets. A fat cook lady catches me in the final room. She solemnly carries me out to the hall, pressing me to her apron (the nauseating scent of the kitchen). She places me on the floor.

'Go intrepidly,' Terenty Osipovich's instruction sounds again.

I do not even go, I take off, ascending under someone's efforts to a bentwood chair and reciting a poem for those gathered. I remember it was not long at all . . . Then the thunder of applause plus the gift of a teddy bear. What did I recite to them then? Happy, I make my way through a crowd of admirers, my gaze thanking those responsible for my success: the cook and Terenty Osipovich, who fortified me with words.

'I did tell you,' he says, his hand sliding along the two ends of his beard: 'Go intrepidly.'

That was not always how my life worked out.

TUESDAY

Geiger likes my descriptions. He said the almighty god of details is guiding my hand. It's a good image: Geiger can be poetic.

'Maybe I was a writer before I lost my memory?' I say. 'Or a newspaper reporter?'

He shrugs his shoulders.

'Or something else: an artist, for example. I would say your descriptions are very visual.'

'So an artist or a writer?'

'A chronicler of lives. We agreed, after all, that there won't be any hints about the main things.'

'And you reduced the staff to two people for that reason?'

'Yes, so that nobody lets anything slip. The most reliable pair remains.'

He laughs.

Geiger leaves after lunch. I see him in the hallway when Valentina comes in – he is wearing his coat and has his hat in his hands. I hear his steps fade, first on this floor, then on the stairs. I have not asked Valentina to lie down with me for two days, though I have dreamt of it. Despite Geiger's permission (or contrary to it?). But now I ask.

And here she is, already next to me, her hand in my hand. A lock of her hair tickles my ear. The thought that we might be caught at *this* would be difficult for me. Something else – wrong, maybe even indecent – would not be awful since indecent is the first thing that would be expected but at *this* . . . After all, everything is so subtle here, so timid and inexplicable, and the feeling won't leave me that this already happened at some time. I ask Valentina if she has done anything like this before, if she has any blurry recollections on that score, not recollections even, but guesses. No, she answers, I haven't, basically nothing like this has ever happened, where would the recollections come from?

That's how it was for me, after all: I truly had not just thought it up. We had been lying like that on the bed, motionless, hand in hand, temple to temple. I could not swallow my saliva right then; I was afraid she would hear the sound of swallowing, so I purposely coughed to justify that sound; that is how nonmaterial our relations were. I would also be afraid a joint would crack: then all the airiness, all the fragility, of our relations would be ruined immediately. There was nothing bodily about them. Her wrist, her little finger, the nail on that finger – as small as a flake of pearl, smooth, pearlescent – that was enough. I write and my hand shakes. Yes, it is from weakness, from fever, but it is also from the great strain of feelings. And also because my memory is hiding everything else from me. What was that?

'What was that?' I scream at Nurse Valentina, tears flowing hard. 'Why is the happiness of my life not being recalled in full?'

Valentina presses her cool lips to my forehead.

'Perhaps it would stop being happiness then.'

Perhaps. But I must recall everything in order to understand that.

WEDNESDAY

I am recalling. Tram rails on a frozen river. A small electric tram forcing its way from one shore to another; benches along its windows. The tram driver's gaze bores through the snowstorm and dusk, but the other shore is still not visible. Streetlights barely illuminate the way and in their gleaming light, any unevenness in the ice looks to the riders like a crack and a chasm. The tram driver is focused; he will be the last to lose hope. The conductor is also strong of spirit but he does not forget to encourage himself with swallows from a flask – the cold and this lunar landscape could dishearten anyone, and a conductor must remain cheerful. He sells tickets for five kopecks and tears them with icy fingers. There are ten sazhens of water below him and a snowstorm at his sides, but his fragile ark, a yellow light on the ice, is striving for its goal: a huge spire lost in the gloom. I recognize that spire and that river. Now I know what city I lived in.

THURSDAY

I loved Petersburg infinitely, you see. I felt acute happiness upon returning from other places. In my eyes, the city's harmony countered a chaos that has frightened and upset me since childhood. I cannot reestablish the events of my life properly now and remember only that when the waves of that chaos overwhelmed me, what saved me was the thought of Petersburg, of the island the waves would smash upon . . .

Valentina just now gave me an injection in my bottom. Some sort of vitamin. Vitamins are painful; for some reason those syringes are much more unpleasant than syringes with medicine. I lost my train of thought . . .

Ah, yes, harmony. Austerity. So I am with my mother and father: I in the center, they on the sides, holding me by the hands, and we're walking along Teatralnaya Street from the Fontanka River toward the Alexandrinsky Theater, right along the middle of the street. We ourselves are the embodiment of symmetry, of harmony, if you will. And so we are walking and my father tells me that the distance between buildings is equal to the height of the buildings and that the length of the streets is ten times greater than the height of the buildings. The theater is growing, nearing, terrifying. Clouds are speeding up in the sky. And this, too: the street was renamed later, somehow wretchedly labeled. Why?

I recalled a fire, too. Not the fire itself but people riding along Nevsky Prospect in early autumn, toward evening, to extinguish it. Ahead, on a black horse, is a bugler. With a horn to his mouth, like an angel of the Apocalypse. The bugler is trumpeting, preparing the way for a column of firefighting vehicles, and everybody is rushing in all directions. Coachmen are whipping horses, pressing them to the side of the road and waiting, standing, half-facing the firemen. And then a carriage carrying firefighters tears along in the emptiness that has come about on roiling Nevsky. They're sitting back to back on a long bench, wearing brass helmets, with the fire brigade's banner fluttering over them. The fire captain is by the banner, ringing the bell. The firemen are tragic in their impassivity; playing on their faces are reflections of the flame that awaits them, which has already flared up somewhere, as yet unseen.

Flame-yellow leaves from Yekaterinsky Garden, which has its own fire, fall upon the riders. My mother and I are standing, pressed against a cast-iron fence and observing as the weightlessness of the leaves is conveyed to the column of vehicles: the column of leaves slowly lifts away from the paving stones and flies over Nevsky at low altitude. Behind the line of firemen there drifts a two-horse cart carrying crowbars, spools for the hoses, and hook ladders; behind that is another cart with a steam pump (steam from a boiler, smoke from a pipe); behind that is a medical van to save the burned. I cry and my mother tells me not to be afraid, but I am not crying from fear, it is from an abundance of feelings. From admiration for the bravery and great glory of these people, from how majestically they drift past the stilled crowd to the ringing of bells.

I wanted very much to become a fire chief and each time I saw firemen I would direct a soundless request to them to take me into their ranks. Riding along Nevsky on the upper deck of an omnibus, I invariably imagined I was heading to a fire. I comported myself solemnly and a bit sadly, not knowing how everything would turn out amid the raging flame; I caught elated gazes and tilted my head slightly to the side at the crowd's greetings, answering with only my eyes. By all appearances, I did not become a fireman after all, though now, some time later, I do not regret that.

SATURDAY

I underwent tests all day yesterday. That somehow left a rather odd impression . . . No, it wasn't painful or even unpleasant for me. The devices surprised me: I had never seen such things. I, of course, am no specialist in devices and what I can say about them is nothing more than my sense of things, but that sense was unusual.

'Was I unconscious for a long time?' I asked Nurse Valentina later. 'So long that new devices had time to come into being?'

Valentina lay down next to me instead of answering. She stroked my hair.

Anastasia had stroked me like that at some time. Fancy that, a name suddenly surfaced. I don't remember who she is or why she stroked me, but I remember she's Anastasia. Her fingers travelled through my hair, sometimes going still in reverie. They would slide along my cheek toward an ear, softly groping at the contour of the outer ear, and I would hear their improbably loud rustling. Sometimes Anastasia would press her forehead to my forehead and twist locks of her hair and mine into one curl. Light with dark. That wound us up terribly, we were so different.

'What are you thinking about?' Valentina asked me.

'Will you speak to me using the informal "you," please?'

She asked again.

Not about anything, I said. I simply have nothing to think about: I don't remember anything. And all that is left of Anastasia is a name. Her name and the scent of her wheaten hair; I have not forgotten that, either. Though maybe I am perceiving the scent of Valentina's hair as an impression that remains intact in my memory. Or this: the scent of Valentina's hair (also wheaten) reminds me of something that once made me happy.

SUNDAY

Geiger brought me *Robinson Crusoe*. Not the new edition with the simplified orthography but an edition from 1906, before the revolution. It is the same book I read as a child – did he know that or something? I would have recognized it with my eyes closed, by touch, by weight. By scent, like Anastasia's hair. The aroma of printer's ink, emanating from that book's glossy leaves, has remained in my nostrils forever. It was the aroma of wandering. The rustle of those leaves was the rustle of island leaves that protected Robinson from the sun: they were huge, bright green, and they barely fluttered. They had crystalline drops in the mornings. I leafed through the book and recognized page after page. With each line, everything that accompanied the book in my time gone by was resurrected: my grandmother's cough, the clank of a knife that fell in the kitchen and (from the same place) the scent of something fried, and the smoke of my father's cigarette. Judging from information about the book's printing, all the events I have noted occurred no earlier than 1906.

MONDAY

A person is sitting at a table. He is visible through a crack in the door: slumping, cutting sausage into even rounds, placing one after another in his mouth. A sorrowful repast. He sighs and pours some vodka into a mug, swigs it back in one motion, and smacks his lips. Looks out the window from time to time. There, leaves swoop downwards along the diagonal, as if leaden. They would descend smoothly but for the wind, which draws them. And I am observing all this from the corridor, where it is dark. I am observing but I am not right at the door, I have stepped back, hence I am not visible. I am interested in what a person does when he doesn't know he is being watched. But he's not doing anything, only cutting round after round of sausage and sadly washing it down with vodka. He wipes his fingers on newspaper before taking the mug. This is nothing special but — what do you know? — it is engraved in my memory. When and where was that?

My temperature has not exceeded 37.5 for several days now. And I feel better; the weakness is passing little by little. Sometimes I sit on the bed until I tire, and I do still tire quickly. There was this torture: they sat a person on a horizontal beam or on a narrow bench so his feet would not reach the ground. And there was no sleeping; not even slumping, either. Hands on knees. They were forced to sit day and night until their feet swelled. And this was called being sent to the beams. What a mess I have in my head . . .

This is better: there we are in Ligovo, in Polezhayevsky Park. The month of June. There's the Ligovka Brook, not large at all, but in the park it's as wide as a lake. There are carriages by the entrance, landaus in large numbers, and I ask my father if the whole city has assembled here. My father deliberates for several moments about *what* is behind my question: simple-mindedness or irony. He answers cautiously: no, not the whole city. In actuality, my question shines with joy: I love a large assemblage of people. At that time I still love it.

On the grass are picnic blankets, samovars, and gramophones. We don't have a gramophone, and I watch as those sitting near us turn the handle. I don't remember who was sitting there, but I still see the handle rotating. An instant later, music rings out: hoarse and stuttering, but music all the same. Singing. A box filled with small singers ridden with head colds – how I wanted to possess that box! Care for it, cherish it, and place it near the stove in the winter, but the important thing is to wind it up with royal offhandedness, like a person doing something they're long accustomed to. Rotating the handle seemed to me like the simple but (at the same time) unobvious reason for those flowing sounds, like a master key to what is beautiful. There was something Mozartian in the circular motion of the hand, something of a conductor's wave of the baton that enlivens mute instruments and is also not fully explained by earthly laws. I would sometimes conduct when I was by myself, humming melodies I had heard, and that came out fairly well. If not for my dream of becoming a fire captain, of course I would have wanted to be a conductor.

We saw a conductor on that July day, too. He moved away from the shore slowly, along with an orchestra that obeyed his baton. This was not the park orchestra and not a wind orchestra, but a symphony orchestra. They were on a raft – it was unclear how they fit – and their music spilled along the water. Boats and ducks floated around the raft, and both the cracking and creak of oarlocks were audible, but that all merged easily into the music – on the whole, the conductor accepted it favorably. The conductor was surrounded by musicians but was solitary at the same time: there is an unfathomable tragicness in that profession. Perhaps that tragicness is not as vividly expressed as for the fire captain: it is not tied to either fire or outside circumstances at all, though its inner nature burns hearts all the stronger.

TUESDAY

Four categories of people received ration cards: the first was workers. A pound of bread per day. Entirely sufficient.

The second was Soviet office staff, a quarter pound of bread per day.

The third was nonworking intelligentsia, just an eighth.

The fourth was the bourgeoisie. Also an eighth, but every other day. Go ahead, indulge yourself . . .

I asked Geiger if ration cards are used now. He answered that they've already been discontinued. Well, thank God. Redeeming cards is a small pleasure, especially for soap and kerosene.

I found out a new distribution center had opened on Vasilevsky Island, at the corner of 8th Line. I had trudged over there from the Petrograd Side – not everybody knows about new places, so the queues were usually shorter. Wind from the gulf and light snow; it stung my ears. I'd been given my grandmother's shawl to take with me (my grandmother was no longer with us), to wear over my service cap but I, a fool, was ashamed. I had already nearly been blown from Tuchkov Bridge. I took the shawl from my book bag and wound it around my head. And what, one might ask, was I ashamed of? It was such a snowstorm that you could not see anything an arm's length away. And even if you could see, who would recognize me in that shawl? I took it off anyway as I approached 8th Line.

I take my place in the queue. Pelageya Vasilyevna says to me:

'I'm Pelageya Vasilyevna and I'm in front of you but I want to stand in the alcove for a while where there's less wind.'

'Of course,' I answer, 'you go stand in the alcove, Pelageya Vasilyevna, what else can I say?'

'But you won't leave the queue? If you leave, come over to me there in the alcove – she points at it – and warn me.'

I nod but she stays where she is.

'I would stand in the queue,' she says, 'but I have a fever. I don't know what will be left of me after standing like this. But I have nothing to cook on without kerosene.'

Nikolai Kuzmich comes over:

'Go, Pelageya, I'll stand in your place for you, for God's sake, don't you worry.'

She lets him have her place.

'I'm not worried: this is Nikolai Kuzmich.'

Everyone standing in the queue is strewn with snow: hats, shoulders, eyelashes. Some knock one foot against the other. Pelageya peers out of the alcove, glancing distrustfully at Nikolai Kuzmich. He notices Pelageya and shakes his head in reproach.

'Thank you, Nikolai,' she says and vanishes in the alcove.

For the first hour, everybody jokes and talks about how difficult it is to live without kerosene. Kerosene and firewood. As the third hour nears its end, Skvortsov, whom I somehow know, approaches. Contributing to the general topic of conversation, Skvortsov says 1919 is the worst year of his life.

'And how old is your life,' asks someone from the queue, 'only nineteen years in all? Or twenty? What have you seen in that lifetime?'

'Well, in the first place . . .'

As he answers, Skvortsov pretends he's a full-fledged member of the queue and is standing along with me. His voice is steady but the queuers don't believe him.

'Now he,' says Nikolai Kuzmich, pointing at me, 'has been standing here from the very beginning, we remember him. We remember Pelageya Vasilyevna; I'm standing here in her place.' Pelageya emerges from the alcove for a moment. 'Forgive me, but we don't remember you.'

Skvortsov shrugs his shoulders and fallen snow drops from them. Skvortsov merges with the snowstorm a moment later. He leaves readily, without an argument. He leaves my life forever because it seems I never saw him again.

WEDNESDAY

There is a statuette of Themis on a cabinet: it was given to my father the day he graduated from law school. They would point it out to me when I was still an infant, saying: Themis. Later – particularly in the presence of guests – they would ask: where is Themis? I would show them. I did not yet know who Themis was, I thought she was just some nonsense standing on a cabinet. I liked everything about Themis except the scales: they didn't swing. I tolerated that until I was about seven and then attempted to make the scales move: I bent them, knocking them with a hammer. I was sure they had to swing; I thought something had jammed them. Of course the scales broke off.

THURSDAY

Geiger stayed in the room today after my morning exam. He slid a hand along the back of a bentwood chair.

'You once asked Valentina if you were unconscious for a long time . . .'

He pressed both hands on the back of the chair and looked at me. I pulled the blanket up to my chin.

'Is that a secret, too?'

'No, why would it be? Your rehabilitation is moving along successfully and I think certain things can already be explained to you. But only certain things, so it's not everything at once.'

As if she had been awaiting that phrase, Valentina entered the room carrying a tray with three cups. I realized it was coffee even as she was barely stepping foot over the threshold. It was fragrant. When was the last time I drank well-brewed coffee? They helped me get up and a minute later we were all sitting: I on my bed, and Geiger and Valentina on chairs.

'The thing is,' said Geiger, 'that you truly were unconscious for a very long time and there have been changes in the world. I'm going to tell you a little at a time and you'll continue recalling everything that happened to you. Our task – together – is for those two streams to merge painlessly.'

The coffee turned out to be just like its smell, maybe even a tiny bit better. Geiger began talking about conquering outer space. It turns out that we and the Americans have already been flying to outer space for a long time. Well, bearing Tsiolkovsky's ideas in mind, that was to be expected. (What's lacking in my coffee is sugar. I ask if I may have some sugar. Geiger wavers; he says he doesn't know how glucose will behave in my body.) The first in outer space was a Russian, but Americans have been on the moon. I don't know much about outer space or the moon but, to my mind, there's nothing much to do there.

'People have been to the depths of the deepest seas,' Geiger went on.

I nodded.

'Could you have thought about something like this in your time?' Valentina asked.

'Yes,' I answered. 'There were already some thoughts on that score even back then.'

I told about how at fairs there was this toy called the 'Australian Resident'. A small (glass) man with bugged eyes floated in a little glass cylinder of water. A rubber membrane was fastened to the top of the cylinder. If you pressed the membrane, the Australian Resident went to the bottom, spinning on his axis. 'The Australian Resident descends to the ocean's depths, seeking human happiness!' shouted the salesman. Limping slightly on one side and shuffling along, the salesman moved around the fair surprisingly quickly, his voice alternately subsiding and then suddenly somehow appearing alongside you. 'The Australian Resident descends . . .' It amused everyone that these fighters for human happiness looked so unusual. That they were so mobile. It goes without saying that Russian residents, unlike the Australian, were unable to spin with such speed.

Geiger's hand was on Valentina's shoulder. His fingers seemed to be mechanically tugging at a lock of her hair. They were pointing at me. Geiger uttered right into her ear, in a stage whisper:

'This isn't just about conquering the elements, after all: think bigger, it's the problem of happiness . . .'

'It seems the struggle for happiness doesn't inspire you much, does it?' Valentina asked me.

'Basically, only tragedy comes from that,' I said.

Valentina made no attempt to move away from Geiger's hand. She laughed. Was there some kind of relationship between them? I wondered. He treated her in a very proprietary manner.

Geiger also told me something about the technology field but

I didn't retain it all. Yes, people now write with a 'ballpoint pen' (there's a ball in the nib), so anyway, that's what Valentina hid from me a few days ago. She wanted to guard me from the jolt. I will tell you honestly: this did not jolt me.

My temperature went up in the evening and Valentina read to me from *Robinson Crusoe*. She asked what, exactly, to read and I asked her to read wherever the book fell open. It makes no difference to me where to begin: it is very likely that I remember that book by heart. It opened at the story about how Robinson transfers his things from his former ship. He knocks together a raft from spare masts and makes trip after trip, bringing ashore his supply of provisions, carpenter's tools, sails, rope, rifles, gunpowder, and many other things. The raft rocks from the weight of the trunks lowered on it and the reader's heart beats faster because everything Robinson has is his last: there's no replacement for anything. The time that had given birth to him remained somewhere far away; maybe it was even gone forever. He is in a different time now, with his previous experience and previous habits, and he needs either to forget them or recreate an entire lost world, something that's not simple at all.

I don't think there is anything between Geiger and Valentina. They communicate between themselves nonchalantly but that proves nothing. It is a sort of doctor's manner.

FRIDAY

We rented a dacha in Siverskaya. We would arrive on the Warsaw railroad line, second class, in puffs of smoke and steam. The train trip took about two hours, stopping four times: in Alexandrovskaya,

Gatchina, Suida, and, of course, in our own Siverskaya. These are my first place names on earth, the first signs of the inhabited world outside Petersburg. I still had no inkling of the existence of Moscow and knew nothing of Paris, but I knew of Siverskaya. I announced the stations along the Warsaw line from the age of two, that's what my parents told me.

After stopping in Siverskaya, the locomotive would exhale heavily and that was its final exhalation. Something inside it still gurgled and something hissed, but there was no longer any preparedness to carry on further: all that those noises indicated was the inability to go quiet instantly. A racehorse snorts like that after a race when restoring its breathing.

Our many belongings – feather beds, hammocks, dishes, balls, and fishing gear – were unloaded from the baggage car to a cart. We rode in a light coach and the cart trailed slowly behind us. We would stop after crossing the Oredezh River along a mill dam. We observed as the coachman assembled local peasant men to push the cart along the rise, up to the steep riverbank. In actuality he didn't assemble them, he chose them: a whole crowd of them stood there on the dam, waiting, knowing that carts would come from the train and need to be pushed. Each asked for twenty kopecks and wouldn't agree to less: that was enough for two bottles of beer and they drank no less.

After finding myself on the platform, I would inhale the incomparable Siverskaya air. I, a little boy, was not yet able to express what that specialness consisted of (I probably cannot do that now, either) but even then I understood clearly that it had nothing in common with Petersburg air. That perhaps this was not even air but something of an oddity: dense, aromatic, and not so much to be inhaled as to be drunk.

The views were different, too, as were the colors and the sounds. Green and rustling. Brown, bottomless, and splashing. Shifting to light blue on a sunny day. There was the roar of a waterfall on a dam and the tremors of metallic railings from the falling of water, and a rainbow in the mist. Along one side of the dam were fullness and reverie; on the other were churning and strain. And above all that was the fiery ochre of steepness: it was Devonian, if put scientifically, the clay on which bricks were laid for the local stoves.

Nobody called that clay Devonian. Red clay, they said, laying brick after brick. The trowel was all red, the work clothes were all red, noses were all red, too, and blown with red fingers pressed against them. And I stood by a bathhouse under construction, four years old, wearing a little sailor suit, watching as the bricks were lowered on the clay, seeing how the stove builder melodically knocked on them with the handle of his trowel and joked with me as I laughed. For me, that knocking was the very essence, the indisputable height, of stove work, something not at all simple. I asked the stove builder for the trowel and knocked for myself, not as ably and not as melodically, but some sort of sound did come out. My sleeves were covered in Devonian clay, too.

The house is over the Oredezh. The river winds below and we are above. We swing in a hammock tied to two pine trees. More precisely, the little neighbor girl is swinging the hammock; she's sitting on the very edge of the netting and I'm lying next to her, looking at her. I'm now seven, I think, no more than seven, but those rhythmic motions already alarm me. We're a boat on the waves and the river below us now soars up, now disappears, turning into the tops of pine trees. Her loose hair touches me at each rise, gliding along my eyes, cheeks, and lips, but I don't turn, I watch as a damp spot on her dress widens between her shoulder blades. I place my hand on the spot and she doesn't shake it away because she enjoys it, as I do, and when my hand drifts to the left, I sense the beating of her heart. Fast and strong. This is our small damp secret, and my very first love.

SATURDAY

Today they gave me a new liquid medicine that's horribly bitter. I drank it and recalled the first time in my life that I drank vodka. It was on the name day for Yelizaveta, which was being celebrated in a huge apartment on Mokhovaya Street. I remember a parlor flooded with electric light and exotic plants in wooden tubs. I don't remember who Yelizaveta was.

Skvortsov walks over to me. His eyes are sparkling.

'I'm running off to the German front tonight. I propose we guzzle one down.' He lifts the hem of his frock coat and shows the neck of a bottle sticking out of his trouser pocket. 'I have an evil little vial.'

I'd met Skvortsov for the first time right here, at Yelizaveta's, a half-hour before. It's difficult to refuse Skvortsov because if a person is running off to the front, this might be his final request. I agree. At the same time, I waver: I am ashamed to admit I have never yet drunk vodka. Skvortsov leads me to the stairwell and takes out his bottle. He cautiously closes the door. Leaning his back against it, he presses his lips to the bottle for a long time. I don't know exactly how vodka is drunk. I see only that the amount of liquid in the bottle is not diminishing; there are not even little bubbles going in. Instead, I distinctly discern sediment floating in the bottle and it is beginning to seem to me that the drinker's mouth is its source. With a groan of the world-wise, Skvortsov detaches himself from the bottle, which looks suspiciously full to me.

'We are the same age as the century, Innokenty, hence we answer for it.' Skvortsov is standing as if he is already swaying. 'That's why I'm running off to war, understand? Drink, it's your turn.'

'The same age as the century,' that's a *set phrase*, too. One of those repeated many times in a life. Listening to Skvortsov is funny and a little repulsive for me. And drinking after his lips is repulsive but

I cannot refuse: he will think I'm afraid to drink vodka. I take the bottle indecisively.

'It's not for nothing they say "it's as easy as drinking vodka,"' says Skvortsov, encouraging me. 'Bam, half the bottle in one gulp!'

I take one gulp (much less than the recommended) and it burns my throat. I move the bottle aside to catch my breath.

'Don't inhale, drink more!' Skvortsov shouts hysterically.

I take one more gulp and the thought of Skvortsov's spittle rushes through my head. Of the spittle he might have let into the bottle. I feel sick to my stomach.

'Your mistake was that you inhaled,' Skvortsov tells me. 'You shouldn't have inhaled.'

There's a feeling of satisfaction in his voice. He extends his handkerchief to me so I can wipe my mouth but I deflect his hand. I'm again afraid that I'll vomit at the sight of his handkerchief.

I saw Skvortsov a few days later on Nevsky. He waved to me from afar. He hadn't gone anywhere then.

It dawns on me now: if we're *the same age as the century*, then I was born in 1900. An obvious deduction, but for some reason it didn't occur to me immediately.

'Doctor, was I born in 1900?' I ask Geiger.

'Yes,' he answers. 'You're the same age as the century.'

Hm.

MONDAY

Kuokkala. Every day after breakfast, Seva and I tear around the beach. Morning flights have become commonplace for us. I hold the string and steer an airplane kite. Seva holds the string, too, but lower: he's no longer steering anything at all, so it is most correct to say, simply, 'he's holding the string.' That's because each time Seva begins steering the machine, it starts nose-diving right away, and falls feebly to the water's smooth surface. Incidents like this are basically part of the game: catastrophes were a common occurrence at the dawn of aeronautics, too. All that's surprising is that, in our case, they are all firmly linked to my cousin.

Seva is the same age as I am but for some reason he's considered the younger one in our relationship. Of course there are people who aren't offended by a subordinate position: they strive for that and accept it as their natural place in life. Seva isn't like that: he suffers from his subordination but cannot take the other role.

Seva, for example, is cowardly. Well, not cowardly – that isn't nice to say – but timid. He's afraid of strangers, silhouettes in the window, bees, frogs, and grass snakes. I tell him grass snakes aren't poisonous, take a grass snake with my fingers a little below its head and go to hand it to Seva, but my cousin pales immediately, his lips quivering. I begin to feel sorry for Seva. I release the grass snake and it slithers off along the path.

This evening, Geiger sat in my room with me. He has read my conjectures regarding him and Valentina. He assured me that this entry is wonderful in its candor. He, Geiger, is aiming for full openness of my subconscious in every way possible and requests that I not feel shy about expressing my thoughts and feelings. So. As he was leaving, he said:

'My relations with Valentina cannot hinder your relations with her.'

His relations . . .

THURSDAY

I have spent several days lying in bed, without getting up. The weakness was unbelievable. I had no strength to write. A *set phrase* surfaced in my poor brain today, though: 'You have not perfected construction of form, it is not yet time to move on to light and shadow.'

Does that mean I was an artist after all? But if so, is it not only my head that should remember (it obviously does not) but also my hand? And my hand does not remember, either. I attempted to draw something but could not make it work.

The phrase caught on some sort of hook in my consciousness and swung there all day. *You have not perfected construction of form . . .* Apparently I did not perfect it. Meaning I'm not an artist; at best, I'm a chronicler of lives. What did Geiger have in mind by calling me that?

And what did he have in mind by speaking about his relations with Valentina?

FRIDAY

Geiger informed me that the river name 'Oredezh' is now grammatically masculine. And written without a soft sign at the end.

'What happened?' I asked, 'Did the river change its gender?'

'It's not only rivers now: people change their gender, too. But you go ahead and write it as before. I think it's prettier that way.'

Today he showed me a *computer*. Apparently this is an expensive toy. You press one button and a small screen lights up. Press another and photographs are displayed. As if in a 'magic lantern.'

Kamennoostrovsky Prospect by Troitsky Bridge, the 1900s. A tram is running. The colors are indiscernible on the photograph but I see those trams as if they were here now: red and yellow. The horse-drawn streetcar was painted in brownish colors and trams in bright ones. I remember their ring. The conductor on the back platform would ring to the tram driver and that meant they could start. The tram driver had his own bell, too, for carriages and pedestrians. A pedal. He would depress the pedal in order to ring it. How I dreamt of pushing it when I was a child! I would watch the tram driver's stern face and his foot, as if it were separate, someone else's, as if it were temporarily screwed to his motionless body, tirelessly stretching toward the pedal. The foot was shod in ordinary shoes with galoshes that were sometimes holey. It surprised me that this did not impede the interaction of the foot with such a refined object as an electric bell.

The screen fogs and another photograph surfaces. A yardman (1908). Wearing a sheepskin coat and felt boots ... It's probably a junior yardman: they scraped ice and brought firewood to apartments, but there was also a senior yardman that the junior ones were subordinate to. The senior workers practically wore dress suits.

And there's Siverskaya, the road from the flour mill, beginning of the century. Good Lord, we climbed up along this very road each time! Someone is discernible in the photograph: might that be us? On Friday evening we would go to the station to greet my father after the workweek and on Sunday evening we would see him off.

The heads of Petersburg families leaving for the dacha were generally of two types: *dacha husbands* and *champagnolics*. Dacha husbands stopped renting city apartments from May through September (renting was fairly expensive) and went outside the city to their families each evening. Which took loads of time and energy. Champagnolics, on the other hand, permitted themselves to remain in their city apartments, visiting their families on weekends. For some reason it was thought that champagnolics met among themselves during the week, played cards, and drank – naturally – champagne. Based on his prosperity, my father was probably a dacha husband but he behaved as if he were a notorious champagnolic. The whole thing was that he didn't like moving the furniture into storage in May and looking for an apartment in September, then moving the furniture out of storage yet again. Some might object to this and say everyone disliked those things. Probably nobody liked them. But he, in particular, did not.

My mother and I would stand in the station during the evening and wait for my father. Of course we were not alone. Many Siverskaya dacha people waited for their fathers from the city and came to the railroad in the evening. Some would ride there, leaving their carriages on the station square. There weren't many trains, so everyone gathered at the same time, at half past seven, if I'm not confusing things. People would talk with one another on the platform, slapping mosquitoes for one another. Click heels on the wooden planking. Laugh as they anticipated a meeting. My mother would say an evening chill was setting in and take a heavy jacket from her bag and (despite my attempt to evade) put it on me. She would say I simply was not noticing the coolness. I truly was not noticing it.

The train was visible from afar and approached slowly. The greeters would turn to face it as soon as it appeared over the point where the rails met. Once they had noticed it, they didn't let it out of their sight. They were still talking with one another and still enquiring about Siverskaya news, but what genuinely riveted their attention was the larva crawling along the rails and its inexplicable metamorphosis into a steam engine.

I did not know yet which train-car my father was riding in: he would sit in various cars and catching sight of him instantly among the arrivals was a point of honor for me. My father would step on to the platform and kiss us – first me (picking me up), then my mother – and his emergence was indescribable happiness for me. Happiness, happiness, I would say to myself when I caught sight of my father. We would cross the river, climbing that very same road by the mill, our shadows stretching improbably under the endless summer sun. Happiness. We would go inside, have supper, examine gifts (my father always arrived with gifts), read something out loud before bed, fall asleep, and dream.

As an adult, I often dreamt of my father, particularly of my summer father. Aquiline nose, pince-nez, a receding hairline taking shape over his forehead. Wearing a white shirt and light-colored trousers with a wide belt. A watch pocket and silver chain. Maybe intensely waiting for my father on the platform made this guise of his the most distinct portrait in my memory.

I remember his mannerisms. The exaggerated, even somewhat jaunty, pulling at the chain of his pocket watch. A click of the cover, a slight grimace – as if from dissatisfaction with the time, as if it were flying by too quickly. He would look at his watch when he was bored or doubting. He looked when he felt bashful, too. It was a rescuing sort of gesture. Or maybe it wasn't a gesture, maybe it was something greater, connected with the length of time issued to him: a premonition or something? One July evening in 1917 (our last dacha year) we waited at the station for him but he did not come. Drunken sailors killed him that day at Varshavsky Station.

Later, I agonized over the mental picture of my beloved, snow-white father lying on a dirty pavement as gawkers gathered around him and he, who felt bashful, disdained and hated the attention of the street, could not even get away from them. Mama asked at the police station if he had lain there a long time (it turns out it was a long time), asked what he had been killed for (for nothing), as if it would make it easier had it been for something, then she screamed that she'd shoot all those damned servicemen with her own hands; the policemen watched her silently. Because of her grief, she did not understand what catastrophe was occurring and that shooting at sailors is about the same as shooting at waves in the sea or, let's say, lightning. And it turned out what we had experienced was not lightning but heat lightning: the lightning was ahead. We just did not yet know that.

SATURDAY

Because of my father, I thought about the nature of historical calamities – revolutions, wars, and the like. Their primary horror is not in the shooting. And not even in famine. It is that the basest of human fervors are liberated. What is in a person that was previously suppressed by laws comes into the open. Because for many people only external laws exist. And they have no internal laws.

SUNDAY

Robinson Crusoe installed a post at the place of his salvation, marking Sundays on it. Robinson was afraid he would confuse Sundays with weekdays and not celebrate the Resurrection of Christ on the proper day. He made every seventh notch longer, making the notches indicating the first day of each month even longer still. Using a knife, he carved this large inscription into a post: *I come on shore here on the 30th of September, 1659.*' I wonder what year it is now, anyway.

A computer is a hilarious item. It turns out one can type on it as if it were a typewriter. And correct. Correcting is the important thing: it's as if there had not been a mistake, all without nerve-wracking bother, without tedious erasures on five copies. Typists would die of envy. Texts can be saved in the computer and read from the computer. I'm going to learn to type.

At Geiger's suggestion, I read an article entitled 'Cloning,' something in the spirit of Herbert Wells. I did not quite grasp what the article said about 'nuclei' and 'ovule' or what was transplanted where. I liked the part about the sheep supposedly bred from a sheep udder: she was named in honor of the singer Dolly Parton, who loved emphasizing the merits of her bust. Geiger thinks what was described in the article (I have the sheep breeding in mind here) is true. He says he's introducing me to changes that took place in the world while I was unconscious. In order, as it were, to prepare my consciousness.

He also gave me something to read about *cryogenics* – this article is no less exotic. About how bodies are frozen for subsequent resurrection. There is something rather ghastly about the idea itself, independent of the fact of whether or not that sort of freezing exists in reality. If the article is to be believed, there are quite a few frozen people, although there is not yet anyone alive who has been thawed. At the same time, certain experiments can be acknowledged as successful. A chicken embryo was in liquid nitrogen for several months, then thawed, and the embryo's heart began to beat. A rat's heart was frozen to $-196\,°C$ and it began beating after thawing, too. A rabbit's brain had been frozen. After thawing, the rabbit's brain (does a rabbit have a brain?) maintained its biological activity. Finally, an African baboon was cooled to $-2\,°C$. The baboon spent fifty-five minutes in a frozen state and was successfully revived afterward.

MONDAY

Anastasia. It's an astonishing name, simultaneously pleophonic and gentle, with four 'a's and two 's's. She said: 'My name is Anastasia.' She was standing over me like the Snow Queen in new Halifax skates with her hands in a muff, in the middle of Yusupov Garden. What did she utter first? I remember everything: 'Please forgive me.' She uttered: 'Did you hurt yourself?' And I am on all fours. I am looking at her skates, at the flaps of her coat, and at the fur hem from which extend barely, barely – only about a vershok – shins in leggings. I am seeing stars after my fall. Blood is dripping from my nose to the ice and that is the most awful, the most shameful, part.

She bends – no she crouches – and takes a handkerchief from her muff and applies it to my nose: 'I knocked you down, forgive me.' The spot on the ice is spreading and I draw my hand along it in shame, as if I want to erase it, but that doesn't work. The orchestra continues playing, everyone skates past, some stop. The handkerchief smells of perfume and is covered with my blood, but I still cannot stand, I'm at the rink for the first time, and there are tears of shame in my eyes. She gives me her hand – it's warm, from the muff – and I sense it with my entire palm. And then one of my palms is on the ice and the other is in her hand, and there is such contrast in that, such convergence of warm and icy, lively and lifeless, human and . . . Why did I compare her to the Snow Queen? Her beauty is warm.

After all, she had not pushed me; it was I who recoiled from her. She was skating fast, beautifully, sometimes alone, sometimes together with other grammar school girls. It seems she was a grammar school girl, that's how it seemed, what else could she be . . . At times they skated in threes, in fours, crossing arms with one another. Their feet moved so very beautifully – simultaneously and broadly, with a cutting sound. Once I had put on my skates, I stood at the edge of the ice for an entire hour, delighting in the skaters, delighting in her. After the damp chilliness of the changing room and the smell of wooden benches and perspiration, there was the frosty wind on the rink, shouts, laughter, and the main thing, the music. And how she danced when the orchestra stuck up 'Chrysanthemums,' oh my! With some student who, of course, was not even close to her level; I tried not to watch him and saw only her, and my soul was transfixed.

Other falls (pun unintended) in my life were linked with women. I recently described swinging in a hammock. And I retained that because I crashed hard then. The girl rocked the hammock so forcefully that I flew out of it and hit the back of my head on the root of a pine tree. I had a nosebleed then, too, and they stitched up a wound on the back of my head. I had agonizing headaches for a long time after . . .

What comes to mind after all I've said: it was not Anastasia in Yusupov Garden. If I'm not mistaken, she and I met in 1921. And what kind of skating was there in 1921! Why did I decide that had been Anastasia?

TUESDAY

Today I made a chronological discovery: I placed a date on my present day. I placed a date on it and cannot believe it myself.

Valentina usually brings my pills on a tray but today she took them out of a box. She forgot the box on my nightstand. I examined the unusual packaging and read: *Date of manufacture: 14.12.1997.* I initially thought it was a misprint but then I saw, lower: *Expiration date: 14.12.1999.* Not bad.

It works out that it's now either 1998 or 1999 if, of course, they're not using expired medicines. What kind of accident could I have been in that I turned up at the opposite end of the century? What was this: my damaged consciousness playing games? I was certain there was some sort of simple and rational explanation for those figures.

I laboriously rose from my bed and went over to the mirror by the door. Deeply sunken eyes with circles underneath. Gray eyes, circles of dark blue. Lines from my nose to the corners of my lips, but creases, not wrinkles. That's thought to evidence smiles: I have to think I smiled a lot in my previous life. Medium-brown hair, not one strand of gray. Pale. Pale but not old! In 1999, someone the *same age as the century* should have a completely different appearance.

Geiger came in.

'Doctor, is it now 1999? Or 1998?'

'It's 1999,' he answered. 'February 9.'

He was completely calm. A quick glance at the medicine.

'Did you read that on the package? I suggested Valentina leave it here. Hints like that are admissible.'

'Maybe you could hint the rest to me? How I got here in the first place and what happened to me?'

He smiled:

'I'll certainly hint but I won't tell you. I did already explain everything to you. Your consciousness resembles a stomach after a fast: overloading it means killing it. As you see, I'm candid with you to the greatest degree possible.'

'Then tell me what's happening in Russia now. At least in general terms.'

Geiger thought for a minute.

'Dictatorship gave way to chaos. They steal like never before. The person in power abuses alcohol. That's general terms.'

Yes . . . Well, there you have it, Aviator Platonov.

FRIDAY

I haven't felt like writing for two days; I have been thinking about what Geiger said. And about my ninety-ninth year. I haven't come up with anything because I cannot fathom it. It seemed I had grasped it, accepted it, and calmed, but then it was as if I'd come to my senses . . . and my head began spinning again. Geiger is right: if I learn anything else new now, I'll likely go out of my mind. It is better to think about the past.

In Siverskaya, there was a rather long street, Tserkovnaya Street, that ran from the flour mill, past the Peter and Paul Church, to the far bridge that crosses the river. The street rose from the Oredezh and descended to it, too, where the river made a jog. Our squadron was marching along that road. It was not a large squadron but it was fully military and excellently outfitted. In front was a banner with a two-headed eagle, behind that were a bugler and a drummer, and, behind them, the squadron itself. The road was level for most of the way, so one could maintain a measured pace. The banner fluttered, the bugler blared, and the drummer, accordingly, drummed. And so: I was that drummer. Papa bought me the drum for Siverskaya's marches: it was real, stretched with animal skin. Unlike a toy drum, it produced a lingering, resonant, and simultaneously deep sound. And it was such a nice, sweet feeling for me to drum then: *tram-tararam, tram-tararam, tram-tararam-pam, tram-pam-pam.*

Retired generals approached the fences of their dachas when they heard us. They saluted us. For the occasion, the generals wore faded service caps with cockades, to which they placed a hand. Everything below – quilted robes, knitted vests, and other nonmilitary effects – was hidden behind the fence. The generals' eyes followed us for a long time because their youth was passing by before them. There were tears in their eyes.

Where were we going and why? I cannot answer that at all

intelligibly now, just as I apparently could not have answered then. Most likely, this was the happiness of simultaneous motion, a sort of triumph of rhythm. Not the trumpet, not the banner, but the drum made our small flock into a squadron. And it lent our procession something that pulled the walkers from the earth. The drum resounded in one's chest, seemingly at the very heart, and its power bewitched. It entered our ears, nostrils, and pores along with the warm July wind and the sound of pines. When I had occasion to be in Siverskaya years later (in late autumn, completely by chance), I discerned distant drumming in the rain.

SATURDAY

Yes, Anastasia and I met in 1921. And of course it was not at the rink. It was in a building at the corner of Bolshoy Prospect and Zverinskaya Street, where the Petrograd City Soviet settled my mother and me. They gave us a room in an apartment that was subject to *densification*. They were densifying the living space of Sergei Nikiforovich Voronin, a professor at the Theological Academy, and his daughter Anastasia. Accordingly, she was Anastasia Sergeyevna. Simply Anastasia, never Nastya. I don't know why I always called her Anastasia, since she was, after all, six years younger than I. Maybe I especially liked her full name, which I pronounced with delight each time: Anastasia.

Geiger admitted to me that he had no idea how memory was returning in my case. Repeating the flow of events in life itself? Or, most likely, all mixed up, without any order at all? Or perhaps based on whether the events experienced were joyous or sorrowful? It's characteristic for the consciousness to move the very worst aside, into the far corners of the memory, so when memory collapses, the bad is probably the first to perish. And the joyous remains. And so I remembered Anastasia from the very minute I came to. I could not yet say who she was or what she had been in my life, but I did remember. And simply pronouncing her name made me feel light.

All they left in the apartment for the Voronins was the parlor. The doors to the two adjoining rooms – to the right and the left – were boarded up in our presence. With brownish, unplaned boards over elegant 'moderne' doors. A yardman boarded them up as the Voronins, father and daughter, silently watched. My mother and I also stood and watched. The sound of the yardman's hammer was sometimes deep and harmonious, sometimes surprisingly high-pitched. The yardman was drunk. He was not hitting the nails on the heads and when the nails bent, he would bitterly slam them into the wood as they lay there. Afterward, my bed stood by a boarded-up door and I would examine the embedded nails in the evenings. They irritated me very much. I wanted to exchange those boards for others but I could not come to the decision to tear them down. It was frightening to see the mutilated door under them.

They settled Nikolai Ivanovich Zaretsky, a sausage-factory worker, in the room to the right of the parlor. He was a quiet man but not particularly pleasant. He rarely washed and a persistent stale air emanated from him. In order that his socks not wear out, he didn't launder them more than necessary, either, though he darned them fairly often, going to the kitchen for that. And so Nikolai Ivanovich primarily darned socks and conversed in the kitchen, eating exclusively in his own room: sausage that he brought from the factory.

They settled my mother and me in the room to the left. Part of Bolshoy Prospect and part of Zverinskaya, the street leading to Peter the Great's menagerie, were visible out our windows. On the first evening, my mother and I stood by the large windows, gazing at the junction of the two streets. This was like the junction of two rivers, with pedestrians drifting past along the sidewalk and with the unhurried gliding of carriages and autos. The spectacle was entrancing; it was impossible to tear oneself away. A strong October wind was blowing and the window panes tensed under its pressure: the strain was visible. It truly seemed to me that if the wind were to press a bit stronger, the glass would not hold and would spatter an unrefreshing rain on the windowsill, floor, and pedestrians' heads.

Darkness came gradually and we continued standing and watching as headlights were switched on in the roadway, transforming riders in cars to a stream of fireflies. I thought about how we now had a new view in our windows, that we now had neighbors. A female neighbor ... What I had formerly feared (I had never lived with neighbors, after all) had turned into an unexpected joy, though I still had not admitted to myself that it was a joy. Put simply, the thought that Anastasia – whom I had seen – would always be near me now had spread through my body with a palpable physical warmth. On the first floor of the building across the way there shone the shop window of the bookstore 'Life.'

SUNDAY

The church is standing but there is no service. And bells melted by fire are lying there: they fell from burned beams. In the middle is a large bell with a deep crack. The clapper of a small bell is fused to it, though the smallest bell is not there. You might wonder if it ran away. Seeing a shapeless ingot next to it, though, you realize: there it is, the small bell. And you think: today, then, is Sunday, and it's too bad there's no service, so you silently recite the Lord's Prayer. There are traces of the fire on the church walls. It didn't burn recently, though the smell of burning remains. There is a pile of scorched books by the stairway leading into the church: the smell most likely comes from them.

You furtively approach the pile: some of the books are almost untouched by fire, and everything is legible: *Grant repose with the saints, O Christ, for Your servant's soul, that there be no illness nor grief nor sighing* . . . And what should be done for the living, for whom things are sometimes worse than for the departed? Who have sickness and sorrow? And sighing? You look: the altar book of the Gospels. Half-burned. You run your fingers through the ashes and then touch your lips to the book, unnoticed, as if kissing it.

'Platonov, why are your lips black?'

Who's asking? And why should he care about my lips?

'No reason, they turned black from something. Maybe from life.'

I look around – there is such God-given beauty. Sea, setting sun. And if you climb the mountain, it is evident that this is an island. A piece of dry land surrounded by sky. No waves, the surface doesn't stir, it's as if it's polished. This is what watery calm is. And the sun's path on the water: angels flying. It's frightening because as soon as the path disappears, everything will submerge into darkness and it is unknown to anyone *what* will commence in place of that beauty. And it is also unknown who will fly there instead of angels. That must be why daytime was not so bad for Robinson, but sunset was genuinely frightening. The very thought of descending into darkness is what clenches the heart like a vise – it is frightening and you restrain yourself with all your might so as not to scream.

Nurse Valentina ran into my room when she heard my scream. She embraced me and kissed my forehead. She took a handkerchief from her pocket and wiped my tears. She pressed another handkerchief to my nose.

'Blow your nose, sir!'

'But we agreed to speak informally . . .'

'Then just blow your nose!'

I blew my nose. After all, it's impossible to blow your nose into the hand of someone speaking to you in formal terms.

'Did you have a bad dream?' Valentina is looking at me, not blinking. 'Did you have a dream? Tell me.'

'I had a dream. Or maybe something was recalled.'

'Something was recalled? Well, that's important.'

'An island. A weighty sensation.'

'What island? Do you remember the name?'

'Uninhabited. Don't torment me. Lie down with me.'

Valentina lies down with me and strokes my hair.

'Maybe you dreamt you're Robinson Crusoe? Cases like this are not so unusual. When a person has few of his own life impressions.'

'Maybe that's what I dreamt. Be silent . . . Pray for me and be silent.'

MONDAY

In the evenings, Zaretsky quietly drank vodka and snacked on sausage. The sound of a hook-and-eye latch closing, the rustle of a newspaper spread out, the gurgle of fire water. A drunk Zaretsky once told me he carried sausage out through the guardhouse in his drawers. He girded himself with a string under his shirt. He tied the sausage, which was on a thread, to the string in the front and stuck it into his drawers.

'If they feel it,' Zaretsky giggled, 'I'll tell them it's my peepee.

After all, I only take out a little at a time, just to eat in the evening.'

That's exactly what he said, peepee . . . Did Zaretsky himself have one? There are people that details like that just do not square with.

After learning his method for carrying out sausage, I was afraid he would invite me to dinner. Pour some vodka and offer sausage to chase it with, and I'd vomit right there . . . There was no reason to fear: these Belshazzarian feasts were solitary. Zaretsky never ever invited anyone. And though his voice invariably warmed in conversations with women (I heard this more than once), he never even invited them into his room. For the most part, Zaretsky had no need for the organ he successfully imitated at the guardhouse.

I remember Zaretsky's sorrowful figure in the kitchen, at the primus stove, with a smell characteristic only of him: a blend of vodka, kerosene, sausage, and an unbathed body. In the barely glimmering light of an electric bulb. I thought the bulb was simply incapable of shining any brighter in Zaretsky's presence but it shone the same way even without him. Sometimes it died out completely after blinking many times, leaving only the flame of the burner in the kitchen, which illuminated nothing. When the bulb would begin shining again a while later, Zaretsky turned up by the primus once more. His hand on the valve.

He would open the valve a tiny bit, meaning that everything over the flame came to a boil very slowly. He attempted to economize on kerosene that way. Or maybe he simply sought reasons to linger a bit more in the kitchen. No, he didn't become friends with anyone, but even he apparently required some sort of interaction. One might have said Zaretsky was lonely if that word conveyed what went on with our neighbor. Is a worm lonely in a tree trunk? There was, after all, something of a worm about him. Flexibility. Softness. The ability to take on the temperature of his surroundings.

MONDAY

Today Geiger told me:

'The Great Patriotic War, which is also known as World War Two, took place from 1941 to 1945.'

'In my day,' I answered, 'the war called Great began in 1914.'

'There you go,' nodded Geiger. 'It's now called World War One.'

He talked to me for a long time about the Great Patriotic War. I can't believe it . . . I can't believe it. Although, really, why not?

TUESDAY

The scent of flowers in Siverskaya. People grew them at many dachas. When renting a dacha, city people would specially stipulate the presence of flowerbeds, and the flowers were delightfully fragrant. When the slightest wafting of the wind subsided in the evenings, the air turned to nectar. One could drink it in, something we did sitting on the open veranda, admiring a striking sunset (with a candle toward the end of summer, in half-darkness).

Dacha folk loved chrysanthemums, especially after Anastasia Vyaltseva sang her sentimental song about them. She sang it right here, in Siverskaya, at Baron Frederiks's country estate, and I stood on the other bank of the Oredezh, listening to her voice. That voice floated freely along the water, accompanied by lights from the estate, and I caught each note on my bank of the river. I fell into despair when a swooping breeze rustled with the sound of foliage, and I trembled from the cold of the night and new feelings that filled me to overflowing.

We bought a gramophone that year and listened to Vyaltseva from morning until night; almost all the dacha folk listened. And Vyaltseva, a Siverskaya dacha woman, would stroll past other people's dachas, listening to herself. Sometimes singing along. The chrysanthemums truly had faded and fading could be heard in the singer's surname, too: somehow everything came together in her singing, so it was rare that someone didn't cry. Her singing was striking.

About fading. Papa brought an Astrakhan watermelon from the city. We washed it; it was striped and gleaming, with a little tail. We flicked our fingers along the surface – *dong! dong!* – and there was a rich sound, resilient. Genuine. There were no watermelon specialists among us but it was obvious that a bad watermelon could not sound like this. Papa cut it into two parts and yes, indeed: red, flowing with juice, and smelling of summer's end. From each half he then cut off semicircles that sparkled in the sun.

After we had eaten up the watermelon, there remained even, green rinds that were very pretty. I would not allow them to be thrown away and placed them under the front steps so they could be admired afterward. They lost their sheen the next day and shriveled a couple of days later. Even so, I remembered their beauty and would not allow them to be tossed in the bucket; they lay under the front steps some time longer. Flies clinging to them. I realized then that beauty fades very quickly.

I remember how I ate watermelon on Bolshoy Prospect with Anastasia, her father, and my mother. This was in the strange oval room that remained with the Voronins after the 'densification' of their apartment. That watermelon, from the city, remained a puzzle: there was no bread in Petrograd at the time, but here, suddenly, was a watermelon . . . Some person in a uniform overcoat (a lot of people wore overcoats like that at the time) stuck it in Voronin's hands right on the street. He winked, as if to say eat up, and then blended in with the crowd. Voronin smiled bashfully but couldn't explain anything to us.

That watermelon didn't gleam like the one in Siverskaya but that was a different time for us, too. Mama watched as Voronin cut the watermelon. He didn't do it as deftly as our father: the knife kept cutting unevenly. I was watching Mama and she knew I was because we were remembering the exact same thing. I was also watching Anastasia, thinking that she, too, would fade some day, that her fresh, shining face would shrivel like a watermelon rind. Could something like that happen? And I answered: it cannot.

WEDNESDAY

They took my temperature today: it was 36.6. For the first time during the entire measurement period. Geiger said a positive dynamic was in evidence. True, this was the morning temperature and things worsened a little toward evening, to 37.1. The mercury did creep over the red line, only by one mark, but it crept over. I often had a fever on the island, especially at the infirmary.

The infirmary is on a mountain. We lie on wooden bunks pushed close together. There are no bed linens; the planks are bare. And we're bare: nobody has body linens, either. It's useless anyway: many have typhus diarrhea, all the bunks are soiled with it. If you want to turn, you'll certainly get your hand in shit, dried or fresh. Your own or someone else's. The hand will slip along the board. Not everybody has the strength to get up to do their business, so they do it under themselves. And what can you say? There's not even strength to curse.

The whole island is visible if you look down from the mountain; the sea is further out, as far as the eye can see, frozen because it's the month of February. They herd us naked, to go down from the mountain to the bathhouse; it is about two versts. And then back, after the bath, after steaming. With freezing temperatures, twenty below, a snowstorm. True, we walk in the forest so there's no wind. Bare feet slipping on packed snow so someone or other would fall, not so much from the slippery snow as from loss of strength. With a high temperature or a fever, those first seconds are nice but then you freeze immediately, enough that you can't move. Some wouldn't get up again after falling so they were dragged by an arm or a leg. And they would shout. That was the only way to understand they were alive. When they went silent, the snow crunched audibly under our feet.

Of course many of us died after that: a person has his limits. The fact that nobody was clinging to life any longer played a role, too: survival is difficult because once a person is seized by indifference, it is as if he is dying. He'd be lying alongside you, raving or saying something rational, and then he'd suddenly go silent. You'd turn, see his fallen jaw, and understand he died. And he could lie like that for a long time because nobody comes in here and if someone does, they won't rush to drag him out. He lay there and you'd even calm: he wasn't crying out or flailing his arms.

I called for Nurse Valentina in a seemingly calm voice and gestured for her to sit by my bed, asking how things were. But then I couldn't hold back and burst into tears. I'm turning into a run-of-the-mill hysteric.

THURSDAY

There was a place in Siverskaya called the 'Sweltering Countries'.

A beach on the Oredezh under a steep, red clay riverbank. Everything was red in those places and the red horse in Petrov-Vodkin's painting, by the way, is from this very place. Any other horse would have been simply impossible here. This was the color of sweltering countries: I think everything was like that for Robinson. Well, maybe there was also green and light blue, but those colors were in Siverskaya, too, when you really think about it. I thought about the uninhabited island while I sunned in the 'Sweltering Countries'. I sensed the hot sand with my cheek. Robinson wore clothing made of goat skin to protect himself from the sun's rays. Nobody would have been surprised if he had worn that clothing around Siverskaya: the dacha folk there dressed even stranger.

One time when I was lying in the 'Sweltering Countries', I raised my head and did not see anyone. Nobody at all, either on the banks of the Oredezh or in the river itself. Someone else had always been around when I was there. I stood, took my bag, and started out along the shore. I crossed a small bridge over the river – it was empty there, too. At first I imagined that people were simply hiding or had temporarily gone about their business, but there truly was nobody. I walked and was more convinced with each passing minute that something had happened to liberate the earth of people. At least the Siverskaya earth.

This was not simply a sense: it was a certainty. Too much pointed at complete unpeopledness. The wind in the pines rustled in a way that it had never allowed itself to rustle before. The Oredezh glimmered with an unprecedented sparkle. In all of that, one could feel a liberation completely impossible in the presence of people. Everything that had previously been suppressed by human existence now aspired toward the confines of its possibilities: trees in their greenness, sky in its blueness. In how the river meandered, its primordialness showing through; even the very name Oredezh was primordial. Names like that are not given by people, they are created by nature itself, like bent dead branches near the water, like crags worn away by wind. The Oredezh flowed here before there were people, and now it was flowing after them.

The river tossed out bend after bend to meet me and just would not end, the red cliffs rising above it, ever higher. I walked, overwhelmed by the feeling of possessing that splendid earth. The Oredezh's unpredictability, the freshness of its breeze, the swaying of the grasses by the water: all this belonged to me alone. I made the rounds of my holdings, which (a woodpecker drums on a pine) knew splendidly that nobody possessed them any longer, that my power was highly conditional. I was the only one on the entire river and in the entire wood, and nothing from me could threaten them. I was making an inspection of them and passing by them as a commander passes by a parade, head unnaturally twisted, stopping at times and saluting. Something responded to me, waving branches, whistling, and cawing, but there was something that also did not respond, even remaining unnoticed by me. Each of my observations, though, had a paramount meaning because I was now the only one who possessed the fullness of that knowledge.

The road rose along with the shore. Somehow, without my having noticed, the river was running along the bottom of a ravine, outside the confines of visibility. Treetops that barely rose above the precipice spoke of how there was not only water but also earth below. I could have touched those treetops if I had approached the edge of the precipice. But I did not approach.

Houses still stood over the river, only now they were hopelessly empty. These houses were already wound in vines, sprouting with grasses and trees, becoming part of nature. Their roofs were weakening right before the eyes, sagging and ready to collapse at any moment. Their unclosed doors kept squeaking in the wind. Drafts rustled half-rotted curtains in the windows.

I felt horror beginning to grow within me: this was the horror of solitude. The shore began descending again. I noticed a small bridge below, across the river, and dashed toward it. Boards began knocking resonantly under my feet. They swayed and hit against one another, reverberating in an echo. Their noise continued even when I was already on the shore, as if nature's unseen army was pursuing me as the last creature that did not belong to it. I began running (not from fear but from moroseness) and rushed through the woods toward home. It was unbearable to imagine that nobody was expecting me at home, either. The great world could come to an end but this would not yet be a full ending. Even so, I had not lost hope that my little family world was holding out. I ran and cried, feeling tears roll down my cheeks and how the crying impeded my breathing.

It was beginning to darken when I neared the house. I saw my father in a window that shone with electric light. He was sitting in his favorite pose, legs crossed, hands clasped at the back of his head. He was massaging his neck with his thumbs. My mother was pouring hot water from the samovar. All this seemed unreal under a huge yellow lampshade. It seemed like an old photograph, perhaps because it was happening soundlessly. But my father's fingers were moving, completely unmistakably, along his neck, and hot water was flowing from the samovar, steam rising from it. Only the spoken word was missing.

My mother lifted her head. She uttered:

'So you've come back, my chum.'

My father caught my hand and shook it lightly.

What happiness that was. I don't remember any further happiness like that.

FRIDAY

Anastasia was fifteen when we moved to the Voronins' apartment. We handed in information about everyone in the apartment, for ration cards, so I learned her age. On nearly the first day we moved in. A six-year difference, I thought, surprising myself at my own thinking. That thinking compared me with Anastasia, meaning it connected us. Was it by chance that I thought of her in this particular way? I did not compare my age with Zaretsky's.

Almost immediately, I began recognizing Anastasia by her steps. She walked softly, treading from heel to toe. Voronin walked with a shuffle. Zaretsky as if he were on stilts. From my room, I learned about Anastasia's motion based on the barely audible creak of the floorboards. Based on the length of her journey and the clicking of the electric light switch, I guessed where she was going: to the bathroom, the toilet, or the kitchen. The bathroom and the toilet were closer and the light switches there turned with an easy click. The journey to the kitchen was the longest but the kitchen light switch was louder than the others. When someone began turning it on, it rang out with the plaintive sound of a spring; at the end, there was a muffled shot. I felt like going out to the kitchen each time I heard the sound of that shot.

Sometimes I did go out there. Most often at night, when the entire apartment was already sleeping. I would find Anastasia, who had risen for a drink of water, in her nightshirt. In communal apartments, everybody eats and drinks in their own rooms, but the Voronins continued, by force of habit, to do so in the kitchen. The nightshirt was an old habit, too: in communal life, people usually toss a robe over it.

When we happened upon one another the first time, Anastasia begged my pardon for her appearance: she thought everyone was asleep. I answered that she needn't worry – somehow I answered excessively ardently and she cast me a surprised glance. When we happened upon each other after that, Anastasia would be in her nightshirt then, too, but not beg my pardon again. She probably already understood that we were not happening upon one another by chance. And also understood that the nightshirt became her very nicely: it was silky, flowing from her angular shoulders.

She would stand with her back to the kitchen cupboard, pressing her palms into the counter. Her fingers stroked the brown wood (long fingers). This is how our nighttime conversations began; there had never been quieter conversations in my life. We spoke in whispers in order not to wake anyone. Whispering – to say nothing of nighttime whispering – is a special kind of communication. Even if you're speaking of usual things in that manner, they begin to look utterly different. And we were speaking of unusual things.

Gazing at Anastasia's smooth skin, I remembered the watermelon rinds again. Surprising myself, I asked her:

'Do you not fear growing old?'

She was not surprised. She shrugged.

'It's not old age I fear . . . It's death. It's scary to not be.'

'So would you be prepared to not die but instead keep aging and aging?'

'I don't know.' Anastasia smiled. 'But why must one keep aging in order not to die?'

'Well, everything has its cost.'

'Not everything. A gift has none. If I were given the gift of not dying, without any conditions at all . . .'

'Then what?'

'Then I'd live!' She said this with a laugh, almost shouting, then was scared and pressed a finger to her mouth. 'Everybody will come running now . . .'

Nobody came running.

SATURDAY

My normal temperature has held these last three days, so Geiger decided to arrange an outing for me in the hospital courtyard. They dressed me for a long time, painstakingly. The main thing is that they dressed me unusually. In a jacket of incomprehensible material; Geiger called it a puffer jacket. It looks a little bit like what people going to one of the poles wear. Boots with a zipper fastener. That fastener resonated within my memory but not being sewn on boots. I tried fastening and unfastening it several times – it's splendid. Geiger is very afraid of exposing me to coldness or disease. According to him, this is one of the reasons my contact with the outside world is so extremely limited. On the other hand, if everything goes smoothly, daily outings are to be expected.

I panted from the sharpness of the air when I went out into the courtyard. Tears came. I saw several pairs of eyes at the hospital windows, looking at me. They hid when I raised my head. That means there are people here after all.

The snow crunched. I could see my breath. I took off my gloves and rubbed my face with snow (Geiger had requested I wear gloves). I swung a maple branch, creating snowfall. We stood – Geiger, Valentina, and I – covered in snow. Laughing.

And I don't even like snow. On the island, the snow would often stay for as long as half the year. You'd walk around in it wearing cloth shoes tied up with twine (what kind of boots with zippers could we have had there?) and nobody was particularly interested in whether or not you came down with a cold. And there was snow to the waist if you were the first in your brigade to walk along an untrodden path. Even if people walked there yesterday, drifts formed again during the night. You strode as broadly as possible in order to conquer as much distance as possible in one stride. Pitch black, advancing by feel, always knocking a foot into stumps that have drowned in the snow. And there was a two-handled saw in your hands. If you caught a foot on a stump, you and the saw would fall, and you'd think: if snow could somehow dust the top of me, so they don't find me until spring. And I could not be held accountable: what would be left of me in the spring?

I had seen the corpses they found in the spring – they were called snowdrops – their eyes pecked out and their ears gnawed off. In order, one might think, that even the dead would no longer see the group being escorted, no longer hear the foul language. One time or other, I had to drag a frozen person to the trench containing the corpses. I held him under the arms (by then I was not squeamish) but his feet bounced on the hummocks. I dragged and was a bit envious of him: this life no longer concerned him but it still concerned me.

There were times when people froze in the forest. Not through some decision that had matured, but from exhaustion. They'd walked off to the side a little, sat on the ground with no strength left, and freezing was probably easier for them than standing and continuing to work. The sleep-deprived sat for a quick rest . . . and fell asleep. And froze, since sleep is no hindrance for death. Snow drifted over them quickly: just try and find them later. They generally didn't search much for people like that, understanding they had frozen rather than run away; there was nowhere to run to on the island. They knew they'd find them in spring.

Geiger said that if the outing went well, I'd go out every day. As I looked at him, I thought about how he probably lies with Valentina the same way I do. Meaning not exactly the same – oh, no, not exactly the same, I can guess how . . . A hospital is good for romances because it has many beds.

SUNDAY

Today they installed a *television* in my room. Geiger explained for a long time about how it's constructed and how to handle it. I learned fairly quickly. I think Geiger was slightly disappointed when he watched how confidently I pressed the *remote*. He had counted on my surprise being great. Yes, it is essentially great. But moving pictures had surprised me more back in the day, not to mention that the screen was immeasurably larger then. Though it had no sound.

'The word is cumbersome,' I told Geiger about the television.

'Call it *TV*,' he said.

There's something *veal*-like about that, so I'll think a little more about whether it's worth saying or not. Geiger and I watched a story about the news. I hardly understood anything, largely because I was thinking about the sounds the television made: words, music, the wail of sirens. Yes, it's a completely different matter with sound . . .

'What's a default?' I asked.

'Money was devalued last summer.'

'And what can be done now?'

'Probably steal less. But that's impossible in Russia.'

This is already the second time I'm hearing from him about stealing. People have always stolen, though: in 1999, in 1899, and in all the other years, too. Why does that offend him so much? Because he's German? Germans, I think, don't undertake that on such a scale, so they're surprised it's possible to steal so wholeheartedly. That's surprising for us, too, but we steal.

There are buildings on the television screen. There's none of the past monumentality about them, they're somehow light; it's surprising they're even standing. There's a lot of glass and metal. Sometimes one cannot understand the architectural way of thinking – it's something glassed-in. I feel Geiger's gaze.

'Do you like it?' He's asking about the buildings.

'I'm used to masonry buildings,' I answer. 'I'm used to a sloping roof.'

'Well, this is Moscow they're showing. Everything's the way you like it in Petersburg. You'll see for yourself when you start going outside.'

When will I begin going out? I wanted to ask.

I did not ask. I pretended to be fascinated by the television.

There are hilarious cars driving around. Not at all resembling the ones in my time . . . But this time is mine now, too, after all, and Geiger wants me to feel at home in it. He's following my reaction.

'What does it feel like,' he asks, 'to end up in what's essentially another country?'

'It feels as if there are new complications.'

I smile. Geiger smiles, too, with a dose of surprise: he had expected something else.

'Any time has its complications. They need to be overcome.'

'Or escaped.'

He looks at me carefully. In an undertone, he utters:

'You didn't manage . . .'

Didn't manage. Geiger, I think, is a community-minded person. But I am not. A country is not my measure and neither, even, is a people. What I wanted to say is this: a person now, that's a measure, but that sounds like a *set phrase*. Although . . . Can set phrases really be untrue, especially if they're the result of life experience? Of course they can. I'll write that down, let Geiger read it.

Incidentally, Geiger thinks I do not write as people usually do. He does not clarify very plainly what he has in mind. As if you have a light accent, one that's not contemporary, he says, though it would seem unnoticeable to someone who did not know my history. Well, splendid. I, to the contrary, hear that he and Valentina do not speak as people spoke previously. A greater uninhibitedness has come about and also, perhaps, a halting intonation. Completely, by the way, delightful. I am attempting to imitate all that – I have a good ear.

MONDAY

Today I watched television all day. I changed the *channels*. They're singing on one, dancing on another, and talking on a third. They talk animatedly, people were not able to do this before: the main thing is that they'd never developed such speed. Especially the *host*: he pronounces things in a singsong manner, dividing his speech into breaths rather than phrases. He can do anything . . . except that he cannot help but inhale, otherwise he would be speaking without pauses. A virtuoso. A person who's a tongue.

Valentina comes in with my lunch.

'That's how people dance now?' I'm pointing at the screen.

'Well, yes,' she smiles, 'something like that. You don't like it?'

'Why not, sure. It's energetic . . .'

The funniest thing is that's how they portrayed possessed people in the amateur theater in Siverskaya. They were being healed but they danced. Rather, their dancing pointed to their need for treatment. I was acquainted with one of the actors; he sometimes came over to drink coffee. He was imposing and even frightening in the crimson accent-lighting on the stage, but he seemed frail at the table on our veranda. He dabbed his napkin at perspiration that broke out on his forehead. From time to time, he would kill a mosquito on himself and neatly place it on that same napkin. When he left, he would present the trophies to my mother. In his non-theater life, he served as a bookkeeper and his surname was Pechenkin.

'You probably won't like contemporary songs, either,' says Valentina, pouring tea for me.

I already don't like them. I keep quiet; I don't want to be an enemy of everything new.

'Previous songs were melodic,' she continues, 'but rhythm's the main thing in them now. But there's something to that, too, right?'

In recent days, I have noticed that she no longer looks like a medical nurse. She's wearing her hair down now, which becomes her very much. Then again, Valentina's initial appearance became her, too. When I stated that to her, she answered that it was Geiger who had asked her to *act like* a medical nurse. In the first days, they were very afraid the new reality would break me. It turns out that Geiger sought out the pince-nez, old thermometer, and all that. And then they eased up: I, according to Valentina, was hanging in there well and didn't need any kind of operetta. In actuality, Valentina is a graduate student in psychology, writing her dissertation.

I can guess her material.

TUESDAY

On one Saturday celebrating the memory of departed parents, I happened upon Anastasia at Smolensky Cemetery. I was calling on my grandmother and father, and she was calling on her mother. She was leaving and I had just arrived. How had it worked out that we ended up there without loved ones (families usually visit the cemetery together on those days, after all)? I don't remember. I remember only how glad I was when I saw Anastasia. At first we stood for a bit, then we began walking down a tree-lined alley.

'How did your mother die?' I asked.

'From consumption. She had a drawn-out death. And Papa and I kept hoping she would live.'

I took her hand and firmly squeezed it – her fingers were cold. I felt a squeeze in response. We walked together to my father and grandmother's grave. We cleared away dry fallen twigs and wiped the cast-iron fencing with a rag. They died back when it was still possible to order fencing. I could not even buy seedlings now, though: they had always been sold by the cemetery entrance. At first I decided not to weed out the grass (at least let something grow) but Anastasia insisted on it. She said grass means the memory of the person is overgrown and that the person is still present on earth in some way as long as there is someone to cope with that grass. I don't know. I didn't think so. Of course we weeded out the grass.

Then we strolled around the cemetery. Fallen leaves had not yet been cleared from the distant walkways and we inhaled their fusty smell. If your foot scooped up something bright yellow, it would be brown on the other side. The air was bitingly fresh in the nose. And, yes, I had a small drop hanging on my nose then – and so Anastasia brushed it off! She pulled a hand out of her muff and unceremoniously brushed it off. She began laughing. It was horribly awkward but at the same time . . . nice. It was almost . . . Anyway.

Yes, I almost forgot: we ran into Zaretsky then, too. When he saw us, he said:

'And I'm here to commemorate my mother.'

He was holding a pink paper flower in his hand. The neck of a bottle was sticking out of the pocket of his threadbare coat. The entire bottle fit there, but the pocket bulged and the bottle was visible. I'm sure there was sausage in the other. I remember that it genuinely surprised me that Zaretsky had a mother at one time. She must have led him by the hand when he was small. And even earlier, carried him in her womb. How about that! It was easier for me to imagine that he had come about through budding.

And so I'm thinking: if it truly was autumn, then why did I want to buy seedlings? When are Saturdays in memory of departed parents? Three times during Great Lent, at Day of Rejoicing, and at Trinity Sunday. There's Demetrius Saturday in November. Does this mean we were there on the November Saturday? Or did this all take place in the spring – now I had begun to doubt. There was sharp air, there was the muff, but why does it seem to me that it was autumn?

I am no longer certain we were stepping on leaves; it was more likely snow. Brown spring snow, mangy and shaggy. That lets out a wet squishing sound. We heard burbling as we walked past the Smolensky church: water was flowing from the roof into barrels. And steam came from our mouths with our words.

'Imagine, our children and grandchildren will call on us here, too,' said Anastasia. 'They'll walk around on the surface and talk. About, by the way, all sorts of nonsense. And we'll be lying there, below. Silent.'

It sounded as if that would be our children and grandchildren, hers and mine. And that we would lie there together, silent. I walked along, thinking about her words, and imagined myself lying under the earth. And then someone who has already begun missing me and yearning is calling on me. That person will dream of returning to the city of the living from the city of the dead and anticipate living joys for the evening. I was imagining that then, too: how Anastasia and I would leave for home (on foot, along the Smolenka River) and drink hot tea in the kitchen, and I was seized by happiness. And the silence of my grandmother and father, lying here, did not stop me – they were always glad about my gladness. Though it was true, too, that for them – lovers of tea – there was no place at our table.

I've weighed all this again now: well, yes, of course it was autumn. And I did not plan to buy seedlings: this happened in autumn so they were not for sale. The month we met was October. And the meeting at the cemetery took place in November: I remember that we hardly knew each other then. On the way back, we met either a pauper or a holy fool at the cemetery gates. He presented a yellow leaf to each of us and called us a bride and groom. Anastasia blushed. I gave him about ten thousand. Or a hundred, I don't remember: money cost nothing then. I kept my leaf for a long time.

WEDNESDAY

'What do you think, why did the October Coup happen?' Geiger asked me. 'After all, you saw everything.'

That was unexpected. You never know, later it could emerge that Geiger writes historical novels.

'A lot of malice had accumulated in people . . .' I was choosing the words for my answer. 'An outlet needed be found for that.'

'How very curious. Curious . . . So then you're not connecting the coup to the social situation, with the historical preconditions and other matters?'

'But is widespread befuddlement really not a historical precondition?'

Geiger placed a chair in front of my bed and sat, straddling it.

'But it's thought that the disarray of 1917 had its own reasons: you know, a war, impoverishment of the people, I don't know what else . . .'

'There were times far worse, and with no disarray, nothing.'

Geiger put his arms on the back of the chair and his chin on his arms. His chin was covered in wrinkles and shrank in size.

'Your reasoning is interesting. Somehow even unhistorical . . .'

Geiger looked at me, without embarrassment, as someone looks when contemplating. He pulled a little at his ear lobe. He has big ears but that isn't noticeable until he pulls at them: there are many redundant gestures in the world.

After he left, I watched television, what they call, using English, a *talk show*. Everybody interrupts each other. Their intonations are scrappy and rather unrefined; it's unbearably vulgar. Are these really my new contemporaries?

THURSDAY

My nighttime conversations with Anastasia continued. We would sit on stools, sometimes opposite one another but most often side by side, leaning against the wall or cabinet. When we were sitting next to one another, our arms came in contact and I sensed her warmth. Something more than warmth: electricity. We both felt it. I was afraid that sparks would begin to jump between us.

Below, outside, there were sounds of late carriages; their quiet motion was calming. I had learned to distinguish those proceeding straight along the avenue from those passing through and turning on Zverinskaya. From time to time, the rattle of automobiles burst into the night's calm and we feared it would awaken sleepers in the apartment. And it did. The sleepers would shuffle, making their way to the toilet. After flushing the water with a rumble, they would stop in the kitchen doorway and scrutinize us, their sight dim. They said nothing.

One time Anastasia stayed at home by herself when she had

influenza. Everybody went out about their business, everybody but me because there was no business more important to me than being with Anastasia. I stood by her door and could hear my heart beating. I knocked and entered. Anastasia was lying in bed. When I approached, I saw that her nose and eyelids were puffy and red. As if she had been crying.

'Don't come closer,' she said, sounding congested. 'It's contagious.'

I came closer. I cautiously sat on the edge of the bed.

'And that's wonderful. It's always nicer to be sick with someone.'

'There's nothing nice about it,' she said and nodded at a book lying on top of the blanket. 'I can't even read.'

She wanted to sit up but I restrained her: I placed my hand on her shoulder. Four fingers settled on her nightshirt and the fifth, the deftest, ended up beyond the border of her collar. The pinkie. It was touching her skin. All my sensory organs shifted into it, and I became one continuous pinkie.

'You rest . . .' I found the strength within to pull my hand away. 'Would you like me to read to you? They always read to me when I was little and took ill.'

Anastasia looked at me with curiosity. She was breathing through her mouth. She set her book aside.

'Then read to me what they read to you.'

I went to my room and brought what they read to me. As I read, I felt Anastasia's fingers on the blanket. I did not take my eyes off the book. I asked:

'May I hold your hand? I will pull your illness out through it.'

I felt a light squeeze in response. I began reading again. As I read through phrase after phrase, it struck me that I had never read aloud to anyone. At the description of Robinson's fear of becoming ill, I glanced at Anastasia. She was lying, eyes closed, and it was unclear if she was still listening to me or sleeping.

She was listening. She stroked my hand and said:

'It's uncomfortable to sit: the back weakens. Lie down next to me on top of the blanket.'

And after a silence:

'Please . . .'

That *please* nearly crushed me. A lump formed in my throat and I lost my voice. The bed began squeaking when I threw off my slippers and lay down – my stiffened joints might have squeaked the same way. And then my voice returned and I began reading again. After moving a little closer, Anastasia laid her hand on my chest. I felt her feverish breathing on my neck. I looked at her after her breathing became rhythmic: she was asleep. Now I felt joyful and calm. I lay alongside her for a long time and rose only when I heard the turn of a key in the door. I kissed Anastasia on her feverish forehead and left.

I took ill a couple of days later, too. I felt happiness as I sensed the inflammation creeping along my throat with every passing hour. Anastasia and I had one illness for two people. Now Anastasia came to my room and read aloud to me, lying next to me. We understood that what was happening between us went slightly beyond the bounds of taking care of the ill, but we never spoke of that and made no attempt to call it anything. If you call it something, you will frighten it off. If you define it, you ruin it. And we wanted to preserve it.

FRIDAY

One autumn, about two years before graduating from grammar school, Seva came to see me in the Petersburg (which was then already Petrograd) Side. His face was enigmatic. The thing is, he was born with a very expressive face. It was rapt, crafty, understanding, or sad at various times, but this time it was not even a face, it was a mystery. Seva went into my room right away, without saying a word. After asking if there was anyone else in the apartment (there was not), he locked the door behind him with a key anyway. That key had been sticking out of the lock for many years and nobody ever used it. I would not have been surprised if it hadn't turned, thanks to its inherent pointlessness (it had grown into the door, crumbled) or simply because that bungler Seva was turning it. But the key turned.

Seva tilted his head and leaned theatrically against the wall. The sides of the small traveling bag he was pressing to his stomach moved in time with his quickened breath. After restoring his breathing, Seva opened the bag and took out a sheaf of papers.

'Here . . .'

He gave me the entire sheaf, though the contents of all the sheets were identical. They turned out to be news-sheets. The news-sheets called for an immediate change in political power.

'Where did you get these?'

'A man approached me when I was on my way to the grammar school. A stranger. He asked me to distribute them to students.'

'And what did you say?'

'I said I'd distribute them. This concerns saving the Fatherland, you do understand. And in circumstances like that, of course, I . . .'

A bottle of wine turned up in the bag, too, along with the news-sheets. Seva placed it on the table with a confident thud.

'Did he give you the bottle, too?'

'No, I filched the bottle at home. To mark the beginning of the revolutionary struggle. Bring some glasses.'

He had not commanded like that in a long time. I brought glasses. Seva was simply glowing from the realization of his involvement in a mystery. After we drank down one glass each, I asked him if he had read the novel *The Possessed*. For some reason Seva began to speak to me condescendingly and nasally:

'You know, there's no need to bring novels into it, all right? That's all in the past, a hundred years ago. There's an objective necessity now for taking power into one's . . .'

'Fine, no novels. *Coup d'état* attempt. Five years of hard labor, if not ten. Farewell, grammar school; farewell, Petersburg. Are you prepared for that?'

It became clear right then that my cousin was not prepared for that. It was only because I had begun to pity him that I did not laugh out loud. Seva was rosy-cheeked after the wine but paled noticeably and his lips, as it happens, began quivering:

'It just seemed to me . . .'

I could say that the hair on Seva's head stood on end because of a breeze from the window. Perhaps I will say that: what that expression covers does correspond to his condition. Seva was still speaking muddled-headedly and I was looking at him without listening. Why, I thought to myself, had I scared him so much? Why did I interrupt his flight – when, in all seriousness, who would touch him, a grammar-school student? Well, in the worst case, they'd flog him, but even that was unlikely.

Seva was so upset that he did not even drink all the wine. He left the news-sheets and the bottle with me and requested that I destroy them. Of course I destroyed them because neither alcohol nor coups attracted me. I took the bottle with the unfinished wine out to the rubbish bin – it turned out Seva had *filched* it for naught. I threw the news-sheets in the stove and those nuggets of revolutionary thought burned without a trace. Their contents completely escaped my memory.

What remained was a warm September day that strode into my room through an open window. An open window in autumn is such a rarity. The quivering of a palm on a carved (roses and lilies) stand.

A slanted ray of sun that alit on the desk. In focus: a stack of books. A light, thin coating of dust unnoticeable without the sun. A ladybug on a history book.

SATURDAY

Lera Amfiteatrova asked:

'So do you want me?'

I was seeing Lera for the first time but answered in the affirmative, for how else could I answer at the age of fifteen? It was the *so* that struck me more than anything: it aspired to be the result of some sort of communication but, as it happened, there had been no such communication. There had been several glances – mine – at a young woman standing at the other end of a parlor. She caught them. There was more provocation in how she did that than in the glances themselves. Did I want her? I don't know. Maybe I did want her. But I looked at her because she was unusual. I knew from the courageous cut of her dress that she was an *emancipated woman.*

In our class, people didn't hold back when talking about emancipated women, describing, in detail, their outward appearance and moral laxity (Lera presented all that immediately), so I identified her without difficulty. She behaved in full accordance with the commonplace description, with the exception, perhaps, of not having short hair; she fulfilled her part, as they say, 'to a T.' What was surprising was that I, someone not at all remarkable, became the object of her attention. Or maybe that's not surprising. Why display your progressiveness to someone who is already fairly progressive?

She took me decisively by the hand and led me toward the exit as music played in the parlor. It seemed that we were moving in time with that music and that our rhythmic movement was paralyzing what remained of my will. I am now attempting, unsuccessfully, to recall what parlor this was, what music it was. That doesn't matter anyway; it all disappeared immediately. I remember Lera's sweaty palm, despite the fresh breeze outside. Wandering through dark, walled-in courtyards in search of the apartment her girlfriend had lent to her (she said *us*). Lera held the apartment key at the ready in her free hand, and that hand reached in the direction we were moving. Both the key, taken out in advance, and the reaching hand gave our motion a striving as well as an even greater degree of theatricality.

We soared to the top floor on pocked steps. Here, Lera finally used her key and we entered a small room. The only furniture was a bed, table, and chair. Behind the chair was the white flash of a small door that apparently led to a kitchen. Lera walked right up to me. She was slightly taller than I and my nose drew in her moist breath. She tilted her head. Touched her lips to mine. Ran her tongue along my lips. Slowly turned her back to me.

'Now unlace my dress . . .'

Ash-brown ringlets quivered on her neck. I began unlacing.

'Are you unlacing a dress for the first time or what? And is *all this* also for the first time?'

'*All this* for the first time . . .'

Lera sighed deeply. The dress was unlaced and removed. After the dress there followed a light blouse and a petticoat with flounces. Pantaloons and a chemise. A corset that I also needed to unlace (once again to Lera's sighs). I fiddled for a long time with garter fasteners: in the end, Lera undid them when she took off the corset. She sat on the chair. I crouched and removed the stockings from her legs. My hands with the black stockings descended along Lera's white skin. Surprisingly white. Women did not sun themselves then.

Needless to say, the number of Lera's complaints and sighs increased when we lay down in bed. Lera was not shy in directing my motions and she promised someone unknown that she was teaching a boy for the last time. After a while, it seemed that Lera's sighs lost a shade of indignation, but I am not fully certain of that. How old was she? I think she was eighteen, no more. She seemed utterly adult to me then.

Then she smoked, sitting on the chair. Legs crossed, still undressed. Her thumb and index finger held a silver holder with a cigarette and she carefully released smoke from her mouth. I silently watched her after settling myself on the bed, cross-legged. I was seeing a naked woman's body for the first time. After pointing at my cross, Lera asked:

'Do you believe in God?'

'Yes.'

'It's shameful to be a religious believer in an epoch of aeroplanes. I'm a priest's daughter and I don't believe.' She inhaled smoke. 'Why do you keep silent?'

'Did aeroplanes really abolish death?'

Lera began laughing:

'Of course!'

MONDAY

I recalled. I recalled everything about the aviator. I was about ten or twelve years old when my father took me to the Commandant's Aerodrome to watch aeroplane flights. No Commandant's Aerodrome had existed even a couple of years before: there was only the

Commandant's Hippodrome where air demonstrations took place. Once they built the aerodrome next door, the demonstrations have been taking place there ... I know from Geiger that in today's life this is called an *air show* but I like *demonstrations* much better. I think there are too many shows in life these days. I'm speaking as a person who has watched *TV* all week.

July, sun. A warm wind blowing at the lace on parasols. Many people wearing straw hats; a few wearing triangular hats made of newspaper. We'd arrived first thing in the morning, so were standing in the front spectator row. We could examine not only the aeroplanes but also the aviators. I firmly resolved to become an aviator the very first instant I glimpsed those people. Not a fire captain and not a conductor, but an aviator.

I wanted to stand the same way, surrounded by assistants and slowly bring a cigarette to my lips while gazing into the distance. To adjust slightly the protruding ends of a mustache that same way. To fasten the helmet strap under my chin with one hand before starting off toward the aeroplane. Unhurriedly don aviation goggles resembling canning jars. But that was not even where the most important delight lay. The very word mesmerized me: aviator. Its sound united within itself the beauty of flight and the roar of a motor: freedom and might. It was a wonderful word. Later another word – which a poet apparently thought up – came into being, 'flyingman.' It's a decent word, but somehow it comes up short: there is something sparrow-like to it. But an aviator is a large, beautiful bird. I wanted to be a bird like that, too.

Aviator Platonov. That did not exactly become a nickname but people called me that every now and then. And I liked it.

TUESDAY

And I truly am thinking unhistorically here after all: Geiger is probably correct about this. A historical view makes everyone into hostages of great societal events. I see things differently, though: exactly the opposite. Great events grow in each separate individual. Great upheavals in particular.

It is all very simple. There is crap in every person. When your crap comes into resonance with others' crap, revolutions, wars, fascism, and communism start ... And that resonance is not tied to a standard of living or form of rule. Or rather it may be tied to it, but not directly. What is notable: the good in others' souls does not respond at the same speed as the crap.

WEDNESDAY

I hadn't written for an entire week. I felt ill. Valentina thinks I was too cold during an outing; she advises me to dress warmer. Geiger disagrees with her. In his opinion, I described Anastasia's and my illness so diligently that I myself took ill. Geiger is not far from the truth.

It was not exactly that I could not write: I didn't want to, I wasn't in the mood. No mood for it at all. Geiger said that's natural. That I had held on those first weeks, through tension with shock-induced composure, and then fell apart when life began settling into a routine. Yes, I agree, I fell apart. As it happens, though, I don't like my routine. Somehow it's uneven and intermittent – where did it meander all those years? And, most important, where does it lead now? To that strange life I see on television? That life does not yet captivate me. Or Geiger either, it turns out.

Regarding the journal, though, he said I need not worry: after all, nobody is forcing me to write in it every day. Nobody is forcing me; well, thank you for that. So I won't. Actually, I like Geiger more and more. He's sparing with his emotions, even a bit cold, but there's a sense of genuine goodwill that comes through all that coldness.

The opposite is worse, when there is something rat-like hiding behind outward cheerfulness. I had an acquaintance, Alexei Konstantinovich Averyanov. Small and balding, with a large head, a complete toadstool. And he apparently reproduced through spores because how could anyone imagine someone like him with a woman? Although, no, he did have some women, apparently just as small as he himself. Should you converse with him for an hour or two, he's all heart: mild, obliging, and well-wishing without excesses. He laughs with abandon, with a loud, distinct ha-ha-ha, head tilted to the side. And then one fine day it emerges that he is not mild and is not well-wishing but a pathological envier who says these things behind your back . . .

Who was he, that Averyanov? What did he do, how did I know him? I don't remember anything. Though his mushroom-like quality, that worm-eatenness, remained in my memory. Yes, the bulging lenses in his glasses, which made his eyes seem to bulge, too, stayed with me. How did this conversation suddenly shift to him? Oh, yes, Geiger: he's not like that.

'A certain Averyanov just came back to me,' I told him, 'his character and height, even his glasses. But try as I might, I cannot remember what he meant in my life. Why are recollections constructed that way? And what is a recollection from a scientific standpoint?'

'A recollection is a certain combination of neurons, of brain cells. When neurons come in contact with each other, another recollection presents itself to you.'

'In other words I do not have enough neurons to imagine Averyanov in full? Somehow that's very mechanistic.'

'Well, don't you worry, maybe Averyanov will still come to you in all his splendor. Maybe you won't even be glad. Anyway,' Geiger buttoned the upper button on my robe, 'it would be boring if recollections reflected life like a mirror. They only do that selectively, which brings them closer to art.'

Strictly speaking, I don't need Averyanov anyway. What I recalled about him is more than plenty.

THURSDAY

Here is what astounds me about people on television: they're always playing something there. Guessing words and tunes, and also, I read, planning to send someone away to survive on an uninhabited island. They're all cheerful, resourceful, and fairly, I would say, wretched. It works out that they didn't have any islands in their life where they were forced to survive. Is this what their lives are lacking or something?

SATURDAY

I keep thinking about the nature of recollections. Can it really be that what my memory stores is only a combination of neurons in my head? The smell of a Christmas tree, the glassy ringing of garlands in a draft of air, is that neurons? Paper strips crackling on a window frame when it is opened in April and the apartment fills with spring air. Fills with subdued conversation from the street. The evening clicking of heels along the sidewalk, the drone of nocturnal insects in the dome of a lamp. And Anastasia's and my timid feelings, which I remember gratefully and will remember until the end of my life – are those neurons, too? Her whisper, which slips into speaking out loud thanks to her laughter; the aroma of her hair when she's lying alongside me.

After those days of illness, we would often lie alongside one another. Usually during the afternoon, when nobody was in the apartment. We would lie there, embracing. Sometimes not touching one another. Talking. Silent. In one of those minutes, I whispered right into her ear:

'I want you to become my wife.'

Anastasia always laughed easily and I was afraid she would burst out laughing. But she did not. She answered briefly:

'I want that, too.'

Also in my ear. I felt her warm lips.

She and I had not begun speaking with the informal 'you.' It seemed to me that the chastity of our relations should not be subject to any ordeals, even such trifles as the familiar form of 'you.' There was less than a year before Anastasia would come of age, and I had vowed to myself to wait for her coming of age.

'It must be difficult for you . . .' Anastasia once said. 'Without a woman.'

'I have a woman. You.'

She blushed.

'Then I shall be a woman . . . in all ways.'

I kissed her on the forehead.

'I don't want to do that before we are wed.'

The most acute feeling is one left unfulfilled and I experienced that completely. Never before had my formal 'you' been so sensual. I still sense its heat on my lips. A most genuine heat. It is difficult to believe that this is achieved through a combination of neurons.

MONDAY

A person is not a cat and cannot land on four paws wherever thrown. A person is placed in a certain historical time for some reason. What happens when someone loses that?

TUESDAY

Today was an unusual day: I found myself in the city for the first time. After my morning procedures, Geiger asked:

'Do you want to go for a car ride?'

Did I want to? After sitting in my room for so many weeks? I broke into a foolish smile. The last time I had smiled at a proposal like that was as a child, when every trip seemed like a holiday. Even now, though, a trip was no common matter. What lay ahead for me was not a ride in an automobile familiar from my youth but in one of the streamlined apparatuses I had thus far seen only on television. The important thing was that my forced seclusion was ending and I was dipping into a new life.

Dipping is the exact word here. Just take a dip, my parents would tell me at the beach, fearing a cold. But don't swim. I won't, fine, I won't, taking a dip is something fun, too. Fearful that my weakened body would yield to its very first infection, Geiger did not let me out of the automobile. He stopped from time to time and allowed me to lower the window. I would press the button on the door, the window would slide down with a barely audible drone. You can get lost in that . . .

And so we sat for a while in front of the Hermitage, the Bronze Horseman, and St Isaac's Cathedral. I detected no substantial changes in comparison with my time. Well, perhaps asphalt instead of paving stones. Electric poles were made of something different, not wood. We went to Vasilevsky Island; things were generally in order there, too. We set off for the Petrograd Side.

We stopped at the corner of Bolshoy Prospect and Zverinskaya Street (we *parked*, barked Geiger). We got out of the automobile. There is now something unbookish in what was formerly the 'Life' bookstore. Something more likely gastronomical. And the building on the opposite side of Bolshoy Prospect had been two stories smaller. I remember this well because I often looked out the window at it: that building's entire life had seemed to be in plain sight. And they had built it higher.

We headed toward that building. Geiger pressed three fingers on the buttons by the handle and the door opened. We began walking upstairs, not hurrying. The staircase was covered in gobs of spit and cigarette ends: the gobs were the usual but I had never seen cigarette ends like this. They had a very unusual look. Geiger jingled keys by one of the doors.

'This is my friends' apartment,' he said, whispering for some reason. 'There's an excellent view of your house from here.'

We entered. Everything was unusual: floors, furniture, and lamps. That is to say everything was recognizable and it was clear what each item was intended for, but it was surprising at the same time.

The windows faced in two directions: Bolshoy Prospect and the courtyard. Geiger led me to the window that looked out on Bolshoy Prospect. I kept my surprise to myself: it was winter in the city but there were no double windows, these were a special kind, thin. And it was warm in the apartment.

Looking at the windows of my former building, I remembered how Anastasia and I had winterized them. Using a knife edge, we pushed cotton wool into the crevices in the frames and glued strips of paper over it. We boiled paste. Later, my mood always improved at the smell of paste. I recalled the feeling of autumn coziness. It was windy and cold outside but it would be warm at our house. When I took a smeared strip from Anastasia, I felt a curl of her hair on my cheek. I kissed her fingers – she pulled back her hand. You're crazy, they're covered in paste. She licked the paste from my lips.

Geiger pulled binoculars from his briefcase and gave them to me. Aha, exactly, there I am standing with her, it is all visible now. She smears and hands the strips to me, I glue them on. I carefully smooth each strip along the frame. The paper is wet and slippery, and there are lumps under it. Sometimes the paper tears noiselessly and I neatly connect the torn ends. I press them, not smoothing. It is intricate work. This is what should have saved us in the winter but did not save us. The warmth left the apartment anyway.

THURSDAY

My formal *you* and *Anastasia* now seem somehow excessive, comical even, to me. At the time, though, they were nearly a pledge of her – Anastasia's – inviolability. They were to some degree a symbol of my askesis, something akin to a cassock in which a monk would probably find it easier to resist temptations. Or, to the contrary, more complex.

The sensual basis of our relations was certainly present but this was a particular kind of sensuality. It went no further than a glance, an intonation, or a chance touch, and that lent it an incredible acuteness. Lying in bed at night, I would recall our afternoon discussions. Her words and mine. Gestures. I interpreted and reinterpreted them.

Even in the dark, the bent nails gleamed on the boarded-up door by which my bed stood. I would run a finger along them. I thought about how her bed was on the other side of the door. Sometimes I heard a muffled squeak. It was as if we were sleeping in the same bed, divided by a partition. Divided for now, it seemed.

What we were hiding so painstakingly from everybody was, of course, no secret to anyone in the apartment. There are things that are impossible to hide when living under the same roof. Even the professorially absent-minded Voronin doubtless had a hunch about something. He had begun looking at me, one might say, with new attention, and that attention was benevolent. The professor would either slap me on the back encouragingly or smile for no reason. One time he came up to Anastasia and me and embraced us. That embrace was equivalent to a blessing.

Friendship with Anastasia and her father brightened the following months for me. We gathered in their room and drank tea nearly every evening. Properly speaking, this was not tea (one could not obtain tea then) but dried herbs and berries that preserved the aroma of summer. Anastasia had gathered them. Every now and then – after insistent persuasion – my mother would come. She was shy. She considered it very important to maintain a distance when sharing a common area. Her consideration seemed correct to me.

Sometimes, yes, Averyanov, the same one I recalled recently, would sit with us, too, his head inclined on his shoulder, the lenses of his glasses thick. When he came, he would sit in an armchair and sink into it. He spoke little. He smiled but he laughed more frequently. He laughed loudly, as if from excess sincerity. He was Voronin's fellow employee at the Theological Academy, also a professor. Just now I saw him in the chair (a cricket from a coloring book) and recalled everything about him. As Geiger would say, neural contact was restored. When Voronin was arrested that winter, Averyanov provided the primary evidence – of counterrevolutionary activity – against him. They arrested Voronin based on Zaretsky's denunciation but built the case on Averyanov's evidence. Zaretsky could not have articulated the word *counterrevolutionary*.

SATURDAY

Yesterday we went to Siverskaya. I wanted to go by train but Geiger objected. He said there are viruses on trains and my body's resistance is weakened. I think he was exaggerating. My body resisted so much back in its day that a train trip would be a mere trifle for it. But Geiger makes the decisions, not I.

We went by car. As before, Geiger was at the wheel and I was in the seat next to him. Strapped in by a seatbelt. A contemporary automobile (better to say *car*, Geiger advised me) gathers unbelievable speed. That's not so noticeable on city streets but it takes your breath away when you leave the city. When we began passing other cars, I felt my hands grasping at the armrests on the seat. Geiger noticed that, too, and reduced the speed. And what Russian is there (he smiled) who doesn't love fast driving... I smiled, too. I thought about how if we crashed into something at that speed, my body would be smashed to pieces, regardless of resistance. And Geiger's body, too.

The cars ahead of us raised wind-blown snow and spattered us with clumps of mud that kept fogging the windshield. It now let in neither wind nor light. The ingenious Geiger sprayed water on it and cleaned it with *windshield wipers*. After having learned to lower the windows, I began pressing the button, but such a whirlwind burst into the car that I closed the window right away. Yes, that's better, nodded Geiger. That's better.

We *parked* by a railroad station that I did not recognize. Rather, I seemed to recognize one of the station's buildings that has now become a store. So that's how you are now, Siverskaya ... When we got out of the car, Geiger asked me to wear a gauze mask. I shrugged and put it on. In the end, he's the important person here, and I am accustomed to complying. But the Siverskaya air, which is like nothing else, made itself felt even through the gauze. We set off in the direction of the dam, along a street with wretched five-story buildings.

It became obvious in Siverskaya that winter was ending. There's a particular smell of spring, after all, that comes about when there is still snow lying everywhere. Not a smell – perhaps it's more a sort of softness in the air.

'And where is Baron Frederiks's dacha?' My voice sounded muffled, even somehow accusatory, because of the mask.

'It hasn't remained intact.'

The snow was already crumbly; it didn't squeak.

'Why hasn't it remained intact?'

There was Geiger's vague gesture signalling no further 'whys.' We walked down toward the dam. Ruins standing by the water were chock-full of rubbish. We delighted in how frothy streams of water rushed out from somewhere underneath us. I had never been here in the winter, after all, and that made me feel a little better. The town's winter condition could, if desired, explain the fact that Siverskaya bore little resemblance to itself. Everything could come back in the summer, though. Absolutely everything, including Frederik's dacha.

And there it was, the road: it was along this road that we ascended back then, crossing the dam. Red cliffs. My father was alive then, and my grandmother, too. And my mother. I kept thinking about my mother and I didn't want to ask Geiger how she was doing there. *There.* It was obvious, after all, that she died long ago but, well, I was afraid to hear it.

We began walking along Tserkovnaya Street, though the signs say *Red*. If they have in mind the Devonian clay, then that's entirely appropriate. I soon glimpsed our house. The roof and color had changed and it had become boxy or something, but was instantly recognizable. Geiger lagged tactfully behind. I took hold of the gate and carefully examined the house. This was it. I turned to Geiger and he nodded. Even the light in the window was yellowish, as before.

An elderly person came out of the house and headed toward the gate. He slowed his stride when he saw me. He stopped.

'We used to rent this dacha,' I said. 'A very long time ago.'

The man shook his head:

'I inherited this house from my father. Neither he nor my grandfather ever rented it.'

'Maybe your great-grandfather?'

After looking at my mask, he politely asked:

'Are you here for treatment?'

'In a certain sense, yes.'

He nodded. He came out to the street, pushed his hand through the slats of the gate, and closed the inner latch. He walked off toward the dam, unhurried.

The light inside the house did not go off when he left; someone must have stayed there. Perhaps my family. All I would have to do is go inside to see all my dear ones (*so you've come back, my chum*) and grasp that everything but their out-of-time sitting at the table was a dream and delusion, and I would burst into tears from a flood of happiness, just as then, the day of my solitary wanderings. But I did not go in.

SUNDAY

A little bird hops happily
Along disaster's fences,
As it does, it can't foresee
Any consequences.

This ancient stanza came back to me but it's unclear what it has to do with anything.

Perhaps this is about me?

MONDAY

In the winter we rose at six o'clock and day broke toward noon. Morning seemed like the scariest part of the day to me. Even if by evening I felt like I was dying of pain, exhaustion, and the cold, at least in the evening there was hope of nighttime rest. In the morning, though, I would open my eyes with the thought that everything would start all over again today. Often I could not wake up. I would open my eyes and stand (they beat you with a stick for a one-minute delay) but not wake up. I slept in formation as they led us to our workplace: it is possible to sleep while walking, too. We did not wash up, there was no time; sometimes we could wipe our faces with snow or damp moss when we were already at work. All we managed to do was eat a piece of bread and drink it down with water. They brought boiling water to the brigade but it turned almost cold when they poured it. Not that it mattered: there was nothing to brew in it anyway. And there was nothing to drink down with it. I dreamt of only two things on earth: eating my fill and a good night's sleep.

TUESDAY

They came for Professor Voronin in the evening. They were sullen and focused, as befits those representing tremendous force. Who had not come on their own behalf. They were unhurried while searching the room. Fingers unaccustomed to turning pages examined book after book. After they tired of paging, they took the books by the binding and shook them energetically. Bookmarks and postcards fell out; a prerevolutionary ten-ruble note even flew out at one point, whirling. They looked at linens just as thoroughly. Standing in the hallway, I saw their fingers groping the sheets on which Anastasia slept.

Anastasia. She sank into the armchair when the GPU's secret policemen presented their paperwork. The professor was still clarifying something with them but she was already sitting, motionless and silent. I had never seen her so pale. Voronin had a fright, too, from looking at her. He crouched in front of the chair, took her by the chin, and said that everything would turn out fine. They led him to the other end of the room. One of the GPU men brought Anastasia some water; there was a glimmer of something human in that.

Zaretsky did not hide that all this was happening because of his denunciation. Wary of them missing something in the search, he even led the visitors to the Voronins' cabinet in the kitchen. They found a colander, a grater, and several empty jars. It was unclear to everybody – likely even to the searchers themselves – what they were searching for.

'You are responsible for her now,' Voronin whispered to me in the hallway.

We embraced. Then he embraced his daughter. The employee who had brought Anastasia the water forced apart her hands that had joined on her father's neck. Both these actions were probably customary for him. Anastasia did not cry in her father's presence; she was afraid he would not withstand that. She only began crying after he left. When she spoke, the words came out of her with sobs, one after another, like waves of vomiting. It was horrible for her that he left in the evening – rather than in the afternoon or at night, when the order of things seems settled – since evening is a shaky, transitional time.

I went to Zaretsky's door and tugged at the doorknob. It turned out to be locked from the inside with a hook. I pulled it with both hands and the hook flew off. Zaretsky was sitting with his hands clasped on the table. The table was clean; there was not even any sausage on it.

'I'll kill you, you louse,' I said quietly.

'You'll stand trial if you kill a proletarian,' Zaretsky responded just as quietly.

There was no challenge in his words, more likely sorrow. He was sitting motionless; only a bump twitched on his cheekbone. Amphibian. Sorrowful reptile. I walked right up to him.

'I'll kill you so nobody will ever find out.'

I spent that whole night in the Voronins' room. Anastasia was sitting in the armchair and I was on the floor alongside her. She fell asleep toward morning and I carried her to bed. When I placed her on the bed, she opened her eyes and said:

'Don't kill him. Do you hear me, don't kill him.'

She said that as if she were sleeping.

I kept silent because I did not know how, exactly, to respond: fine, I won't? I'll try not to kill? I thought: what will life be like after her father's arrest? I looked at Anastasia; she was sleeping again. I'm going to sleep now, too. The pen fell from my fingers once and woke me up. I'll continue tomorrow.

WEDNESDAY

Continuing. Oddly enough, after the professor's arrest, life went on almost as before. My mother, Anastasia, and I ran into Zaretsky – in the kitchen, in the hallway, and by the toilet – and, surprisingly, we greeted him. My mother was the first to greet him (she was afraid Zaretsky would continue denouncing and hoped this would buy his silence), then I, and then Anastasia, too. My mother greeted him aloud but we only nodded. We were not thinking about future denunciations: put simply, it is difficult to pretend a person does not exist if you are living under the same roof. It is difficult to live in constant hatred, even if it is justified.

One time Zaretsky was walking drunk through the hallway and said to me:

'I myself don't know why I denounced the professor. I went there, so for some reason I denounced.' After taking a few steps toward the toilet, he turned: 'But I won't denounce you, you can rest easy.'

Afterwards, I thought more than once about why he actually did denounce. An insult? But nobody insulted Zaretsky, people simply paid him no attention. Hm . . . Perhaps for him that was the worst insult?

From time to time, Anastasia and I would go to Gorokhovaya Street in hope of being granted a meeting with the professor, but we received no meeting. They also accepted no packages. No matter how Anastasia attempted to speak with the oprichniks there – she smiled at them, adding tinny notes into her voice, and ingratiating herself – nothing helped. Their backwards physiognomies remained impenetrable. I looked at them and imagined grabbing them by the hair and pounding them against the wall full force. I'm pounding with full force, I pound with enjoyment, and their dirty-brown blood is spewing on the government-owned chairs, floor, and ceiling. That's how I imagined each of our trips there. I think they could not help but know that. We went the last time on March 26, and those people told us Professor Voronin had been shot, executed.

FRIDAY

Today Nurse Angela showed up instead of Nurse Valentina. She's young but lacks Valentina's charms. Her appearance is fairly vulgar, not to mention her name. Geiger said Valentina is ill; I did not like his tone very much. I don't know why.

All day I attempted to type on the computer. I felt as if I were a printing pioneer.

SATURDAY

A few days ago, Geiger brought me a book by an American about freezing the dead for subsequent resurrection. He had already offered me something similar. It's fascinating reading, especially as hospital reading goes. The author lists questions that the trailblazers of freezing will be forced to contend with: they are not at all easy. Will widows or widowers be allowed to enter into marriage after the deceased is frozen? What is someone who has been thawed and brought back to life to do when encountering spouses of former spouses? Is there a lawful right to freeze a relative or (I will add for myself) a flatmate? Could someone who was officially declared a corpse and then frozen have lawful rights and responsibilities? Could that person vote after being thawed? That final question genuinely moved me.

In the American's opinion, however, the primary complication lies less in voting than in the freezing and thawing process. Upon cooling, liquid is released from cellular solutions and turns into crystals of ice. As we know, water expands during freezing and this process is capable of damaging the cell. Moreover, what does not turn to ice becomes an extraordinarily caustic saline solution that is destructive for the cell. For all that, if freezing is very fast – there are seemingly grounds for optimism here – the size of the crystals and the concentration of the saline solution end up being reduced.

Glycerin is used to ward off damage during freezing: it neutralizes the saline solution. This way, removing the glycerin from the body becomes the first task during thawing. All other actions are pointless if that is not resolved: glycerin instead of blood does the body no favors. True, there are other questions here, too: why is Geiger bringing me things of this sort and why am I reading it all?

'So it works out,' I ask him on one of those days, 'that it isn't so much a matter of freezing as of proper thawing?'

'That's right.'

'If I understand correctly, nobody has ever been revived during thawing, despite all the success of science?'

'They have,' he answers.

'Who might that be? I wonder. A baboon?'

Geiger looks at me sympathetically and even somehow warily:

'You.'

THURSDAY

I've been thinking all these days about what I heard. At first I seemed to take it all calmly but then a second wave somehow caught me. They'd managed to thaw me: from there, it logically follows that I had been frozen. What can I say . . .

That thought veered off, meandering. It strove not to return to its initial point. I recalled logs that froze into the Neva. Bottles, washtubs, dead dogs, and pigeons: everything that agonizingly melted from the ice in spring. How did I look in icy captivity – like a pigeon? Perhaps like a sleeping princess? Did my bloodless face show through the ice? Were my eyes closed? Or was there no ice at all? Most likely there was not: I read that they use nitrogen for freezing.

Some days on the island, I myself wanted to freeze. To sit under a tree and drift off. I recalled Lermontov then – *I'd like to forget and fall asleep* – and I imagined very well just how that happens. When it is no longer cold, when one wants to do nothing, not even to live. It's not frightening when you aren't thinking about life and aren't thinking about death. You hope: maybe it will all work out somehow, so something will happen that won't allow you to definitively perish.

But that didn't happen. In the spring, under the pine trees, they found people you simply did not even want to describe. Though I remember I did already describe that; they did not withstand overwintering well. So did I freeze there or something? It doesn't seem that way: it is known that good freezing requires glycerin. I look at myself in the mirror without false modesty and think that, in essence, I am pretty well preserved.

Geiger stopped by a few times and slapped me on the shoulder. He would slap and leave without saying a word. What, really, could someone say here?

'And so,' I ask, 'how did you manage to thaw me? And the big thing: how did you remove the glycerin from my body?'

'A specialist . . .' There is respect in Geiger's gaze. 'And there was no glycerin.'

'What do you mean?' I'm surprised.

'There just wasn't any, that's all. And therein lies the mystery.'

FRIDAY

The end of March. Zaretsky died at the end of March. He was found on the bank of the Zhdanovka River with a fractured skull, not far from the sausage factory where he worked. Detective Treshnikov from criminal investigations – a sturdily built forty-year-old with a walrus mustache – came to see us. Treshnikov was ascertaining who had a stake in Zaretsky's death. He inquired as to whether Zaretsky had any enemies or any relatives that might inherit his room. Enemies or relatives (they do know how to formulate things in investigations) . . . we didn't know about either. He asked where we had all been the night before, but we were all at home.

Treshnikov told us that Zaretsky's trousers had been unfastened and that there was a string around his waist. The end descended into his drawers.

'Do you know what the string was for?' he asked.

We knew very well that it was for sausage but for some reason we said:

'We don't know.'

Treshnikov suspected that Zaretsky was a maniacal criminal and had attempted to rape someone. And gotten it for that. We objected, saying we had not observed women coming to see him at all. The latter seemed suspicious to Treshnikov.

'That,' he sighed, 'is a bad sign, when women don't come to see them.'

Later, as a representative of our apartment, I went to the morgue to identify him. I did this without difficulty. It truly was Zaretsky lying on the marble table: small, completely naked, lividity on his face. What he had termed his *peepee* turned out to be surprisingly small. Looking at it was enough to throw off any thoughts of rape.

I noticed no visible injuries to Zaretsky's head: his skull had been struck from behind. Since the murder weapon had not been found, Treshnikov surmised that Zaretsky had been pushed and hit his head on a rock: there were many sharp rocks on the shore. Treshnikov also allowed that it could have been a strike from behind. In that case, it was unlikely that Zaretsky had attacked someone; in fact, the opposite was likely. If not for the deceased's unfastened trousers, Treshnikov would possibly have leaned toward that scenario.

Of course I could have told the investigator that the deceased brought sausage out of the factory in his drawers. After exiting the guardhouse – he himself described this when he was drunk – he would walk down to the steep riverbank, which was deserted. He would unfasten his trousers, untie his sausage, and carry it the rest of the way in his hands. This is all very understandable: it is uncomfortable to walk around with a sausage in your trousers. If I had told him that, Treshnikov would have come to the simple conclusion that Zaretsky had ended up not being the only sausage lover in that deserted place. That a sausage-factory worker had fallen prey to someone's love for that product in our hungry time. After all, the fact that the sausage was not found on the waist string spoke to it having been taken away.

However, I did not even consider telling Treshnikov that, deciding: let him think of Zaretsky as he wishes. Was that my revenge on the deceased? I don't know. I cannot say I especially pitied him. In parting, for some reason Treshnikov asked if Zaretsky had snitched to the GPU. My sixth sense determined that it was better not to lie, so I said he snitched. What did that question mean? Was it a hint that we, too, had motives for murder and that he knew that? The criminal case was closed soon after.

They buried Zaretsky next to his mother, at Smolensky Cemetery, where we ran into him once with the bottle of vodka in his pocket. The sausage factory arranged a funeral at its own expense: it was without particular luxury but, more important, it was said to lack people. It's possible the factory's chiefs decided not to interrupt the sausage-making process and didn't excuse anyone from work. Or maybe there was not a single person among the factory employees who was at all close to Zaretsky. Of course the latter is likeliest. Anastasia and I did not go to the funeral, either. That is obvious.

SATURDAY

Here is something that surfaced from the depths of my consciousness: academic drawing presumes a foundation based on a knowledge and understanding of form, and so drawing based on an impression are alien to academic drawing. Also: form must be introduced into the dimensions so that form does not float and so that drab places do not arise on the periphery of the drawing.

Here is what's interesting: do things like this only turn up in artists' heads? Or everybody's? Geiger's, for example?

MONDAY

Today Geiger showed up accompanied by a boy who was around seven years old. Rather, Geiger stopped by for some of Valentina's papers (they were lying on the windowsill) and the boy looked through the crack in the door: I saw him. When I asked Geiger what happened to Valentina, the door opened all the way.

'She has morning sickness,' said the boy. 'Papa and I came for her things.'

A dark-skinned character with short hair and a bag in his hands came into sight behind him – Valentina's husband, one might presume. Shorter than her. He moved the boy away from the door and slammed it shut. Geiger tossed up his hands.

'Valentina's pregnant again and I – can you believe – am not involved.'

Judging by the slamming door, Valentina's husband was not so sure about that.

'And I'm not involved, either,' I joked.

'Does that upset you?' Geiger asked this seriously.

I went quiet. Geiger's lack of involvement gladdened me.

As a chronicler of lives, I am inclined to believe him.

TUESDAY

Geiger told me it will not be long until I go out into society. I asked what that means, though I understand everything perfectly well. After all, I do watch television and read newspapers. Once Geiger had sat down in his preferred position – backwards on the chair – he explained that I will enter the *public eye* in the near future. In the capacity of, if I may be so bold, a *newsmaker* (this word exists in the world, too). This was bound to happen sooner or later.

'An experiment,' said Geiger, 'requires money, and public interest is money.'

I was silent, pondering this pretty phrase. Its author was silent, too. The sun was shining outside and melted drops were knocking, staccato, on the windowsill. The snow's thawing was taking place under Geiger's engaged observation but without his participation. Approximately the same as my thawing. Geiger admitted in recent days that he still has not grasped exactly what sort of solution had been injected into my blood vessels. An ordinary saline fluid that does not ensure preservation of cells during freezing was found in them. Undoubtedly there was some other sort of chemical additive that simply evaporated during the years of my icy sleep. One must presume that I would not have thawed out so easily if not for that.

After discovering the saline fluid in my vessels, Geiger replaced it during thawing with my blood type; according to him, that process was not particularly complex. The composition of the initial solution was the brilliant discovery of whomever froze me, but for various reasons the formula for that discovery was not preserved. I did not even begin to question Geiger about the reasons, since that was not especially interesting. Knowing the peculiarities of our country, it is simpler to be surprised that anything is preserved at all.

What consoles me and Geiger in this story is that *I* was preserved. We consider that an indisputable achievement.

WEDNESDAY

I recalled something it is impossible not to blush about. But it is also impossible not to begin laughing. How Seva and I went to a prostitute – that could be the title for this story. Both that we went – since that's how things concluded – and that it was one prostitute, since there was one for the two of us.

It was Seva's idea. Not even his idea but his dream. He had told me more than once that if we saved up money we could, for example, go to a brothel. The little phrase *for example* remained, inalterably, in those pronouncements and that made me laugh. One could, *for example*, go to the circus or the movie house, but in my view, going, *for example*, to see prostitutes was somehow strange. More than likely, Seva thought that little phrase defused the situation. Made the proposal less, perhaps, unusual. Judging by how often he returned to this, the topic agitated him considerably.

Seva said that in essence not very much was needed, though we wouldn't collect a sum like that in pocket money very quickly.

According to his calculations, it also worked out that getting one prostitute for the two of us was far cheaper than getting two; we simply needed to arrange things properly. Based on our young age (Seva laughed a little), the girl would think we weren't worth much in terms of bed matters, although we would (Seva made an indecent motion with his hips) simply tire her out.

The occasion presented itself at the end of yet another school year. We were celebrating at our place on Bolshoy Prospect and each of us had received money from our parents as a reward.

'We'll go to the prostitutes today,' Seva whispered in my ear. 'Be ready.'

I didn't answer. I did not even clarify what he had in mind about readiness.

'They get *picked up* nearby, on Bolshaya Pushkarskaya Street.'

I wavered, then nodded. In the end, there had been so many conversations about this that leaving Seva on his own now would have been a betrayal. And, to be perfectly honest, I, too, was experiencing, well, a certain curiosity, let us say.

And so we went. Along the way, Seva told me what exactly to do with a lady and how.

'It might not work out today for one of us,' Seva said, as if by the by. 'That happens when you're nervous.'

His critical gaze at me made it clear whom this might not work out for. He did not permit himself to gaze at me like that very often at all.

The girls were standing in the place Seva had predicted, and that raised my degree of trust in him. When Seva headed toward one of them (the largest of them, it seemed to me), I preferred keeping a distance. He tossed me an absent-minded glance but did not change his direction. After approaching the one he chose, Seva struck up an extensive conversation with her. He pointed at me from time to time and the girl shrugged her shoulders. She didn't even glance at me in earnest because by all appearances the question hinged not on me but on money. In the end, Seva managed to come to an agreement with her and she invited us both to follow her.

'We have two hours with her,' Seva whispered to me along the way. 'Meaning an hour each.'

The girl Seva intended to tire out was named Katya. Of course she was not a girl, either by age or line of work. I scrutinized Katya furtively as I walked to one side of her: she was at least thirty years old. We did not walk long at all. Katya turned into the courtyard of a wooden house and went up to the second floor.

There was nothing in Katya's lodging that I had imagined, neither scarlet drapes nor a huge canopy bed. It was a poor lodging, somewhere Katya simply lived after she was free of clients. And Katya herself resembled a priestess of love least of all. Leaning her elbows on the kitchen table, there stood before us a tired woman not in the prime of youth.

It goes without saying that Seva was the first to enter the room with her. I stayed in the kitchen, prepared to plug my ears at the first moans. But no moans followed. Seva came out of the room a half-hour later, hands in his trouser pockets. As red as a crayfish (had he been steamed?) and already dressed. Katya came into sight in the doorway behind him, also without any particular disorder to her clothing. Her tiredness (he'd worn her out after all, the heel!) had obviously increased. She gestured, inviting me into the room. She smoothed her light-brown and, I think, not very clean hair.

'And so. I said it might not work out for one of us today ...' Seva blurted out.

The cheerfulness of his tone left no doubt that this was a reference to me.

'For whom, I wonder?' I asked him, not without a challenge.

'For me ...'

A forced smile appeared on Seva's face. That smile – along with his inexpressibly sad eyes! – made hearty laughter begin to rise from deep inside me. It came out convulsively when it reached its upper limit, and then I could not stop. I was surprised when Katya burst out laughing, too. She laughed coarsely and meanly, her entire large body shaking, and there was no longer a speck of tiredness in her. Even Seva laughed, squealing a little – there was nothing else left for him to do.

It stands to reason that I did not go with Katya. We paid her for one person. She continued laughing as she received the money. When we went outside, we looked at her windows for a long time. It was a sunny June day. A light breeze carried the smells of warmed wood and of the horse manure that lay here and there on the cobblestone roadway. It stirred the curtains in Katya's window, behind which (I saw) Katya was standing and watching us. I did not retain her face in my memory but the smells and the swaying of the curtains in the window stayed with me. And the dull glistening of the cobblestones in the sun and the wooden houses. Later I learned that women similar to Katya resided in those houses. Geiger and I recently strolled along Pushkarskaya Street – those houses are no longer there, and neither are the women. Their bodies decayed long ago, after absorbing so much sweat and sperm.

THURSDAY

Geiger said that my biological age is around thirty. I barely aged in the liquid nitrogen.

SATURDAY

They came to search our apartment a week after closing the criminal case regarding Zaretsky. Now, though, it was the GPU, not the criminal investigators. By this time, I'd seen both types and could compare. For the most part, criminal detectives were recruited back before the revolution. They were comprehensible people for me, even likeable in a way, with a distinctive sense of humor. Those who worked for the GPU seemed their exact opposite: their gloomy focus did not dispose them to joking. I shared this observation with Detective Treshnikov when they summoned me to identify Zaretsky. He laughed and said the main difference between criminal and political investigation consisted of criminal investigators seeking out a person because of a case and political investigators seeking out a case for a person. Treshnikov showed little respect when speaking about the professional qualities of GPU employees.

They were the ones searching my room, though. I had already seen a search in the Voronins' room and the one taking place now was much the same. The only difference was that many of the objects that the GPU searchers touched had their own histories and my mother and father's contact had lent them a special spirit, my father's in particular since he was no longer with us. It was difficult to see one of the visitors weigh my father's silver watch in his hand and hold it to his ear. He opened it – though not with the touching jaunty gesture my father made – somehow clumsily, like a monkey, as if he were revealing a nut he had found.

It was distressing to observe them rummaging in the linens. I knew my mother's squeamishness and well imagined her feelings when someone else's hands were groping at sheets and nightgowns. I'll launder everything, she was thinking, I'll launder everything thoroughly so not even a trace of those hands remains. Or maybe she wasn't thinking that. She sat in a stupor, afraid to move at all.

She was imagining that my fate now lay on frightening fluctuating scales and she was afraid of tipping the pan toward my destruction.

Of course I'm confusing things: the scales are what occupied *my* thoughts. And my mother was not sitting: Anastasia was the one sitting and I was afraid she would lose consciousness. But my mother was grasping the visitors by the hand and saying I was not guilty of anything. They responded that revolutionary justice would sort things out and she continued speaking, quickly and incoherently, as if she wanted to say an incantation over my unfortunate fate . . .

I looked at the cabinet where Themis stood, understanding that now nobody would sort anything out, that any outcome to the matter was unjust because there was no longer an instrument for weighing. The most frightening thing for me that evening was the sight of the bronze statuette with the broken-off pans: it was even more frightening than those creatures digging in my linens, perhaps more frightening than what threatened me later. The sight of that statuette left not the slightest hope. I suddenly realized in all clarity that the conception of right and not right had disappeared over several years or so. And of up and down, light and dark, human and beastly. Who would do the weighing, what would they weigh, and who needed that now, anyway? Only a sword remained with my Themis.

As they were leading me out, my mother stopped one of the GPU men and whispered a few words to him. This was the one who had been interested in my father's watch. She took his hand and placed something in it. The watch – what else could she have placed there? The watch-lover smirked and did not answer. The hand with the watch slid into the pocket of his breeches. My mother pressed herself against his shoulder, still not understanding that was useless. She spent her final embrace not on me but on him, hoping to at least buy me some lenience. Anastasia was next to me and I did manage to press my cheek to her but when my mother rushed to me, the escort guards were already standing between us.

I turned on the landing and cast a glance at the lighted rectangle of the door. Behind the escort guards' backs I saw my loved ones for what turned out to be the last time. Even now I see them with photographic precision. I know they saw me the same way when I turned. They photographed me for a lifetime: the flash of their grief illuminated me. The two photographs will merge into one after my death.

Outside, I was shoved into a closed van. When the GPU men climbed in after me, the door clanked as it slammed; I had never heard a more hopeless sound. Just under the ceiling was a window covered by a grate: thanks to that, I could differentiate my traveling companions' somber faces. I saw the roofs and upper floors of buildings, too. I recognized several of them and from that understood where we were. I remember that it was not yet dark. Despite the evening hour, the sky was spilled with light: the white nights were approaching. I was parting with the city and felt I would never return to it. That is how things worked out. I have returned now to a completely different city. That one no longer exists.

MONDAY

As a child, I loved monitoring the work of pavers. How they laid wooden hexagons in wood-block paving. How they poured tar on the cracks and spread sand. Wheels rode softly and noiselessly along pavement like this – softness is characteristic of wood; it is alive. Sometimes in the mornings, before leaving for school, I would hear them repairing the pavement, changing blocks that had come out of place. They brought hexagonal pieces on a cart or chopped them there, from stockpiles, so they were the size of the pothole, then drove them in with massive tampers that produced muffled wooden sounds. I heard those sounds in my sleep and they didn't bother me: to the contrary, they made the minutes before getting up even sweeter because the people working had risen long ago. They were suffering from the cold, bent in the damp wind, but I was lying in my warm bed, still lying there, my minutes seeming like an eternity to me. I felt the same thing when yardmen began clearing snow with shovels while it was still dark. They scraped it. Chipped ice. Had quiet quarrels. Unlike me, they were not glad for the snow. They were not waiting for it by mid autumn as I was when, each morning, I opened my eyes, raised them, and went still, looking to see if the ceiling was lit by the reflection of a street that had whitened during the night.

I do not like snow now, either.

Andrew of Crete's 'Canon of Repentance' was being read last week and Passion Week began today. I would ask Geiger to bring me the 'Canon of Repentance' but it is very doubtful he has it.

I miss Valentina. Will she be back?

WEDNESDAY

Geiger told me the idea of freezing people came into the authorities' heads after Lenin's death. The authorities were uneasy, convinced by the Lenin example that a head of state undergoes the same changes after death as a rank-and-file citizen. Preserving bodies in a frozen condition until such time as science would be capable of prolonging biological life seemed to them like a way out. Their natural concern about posthumous existence served, according to Geiger, as a stimulus for research in the field of freezing. They did not even attempt to freeze the leader of the world proletariat himself: in fact they only began embalming him after decomposition was already well underway.

Geiger mentioned Academician Muromtsev's working group, which was instructed to study issues related to freezing after Lenin's death.

'Is that name familiar to you?'

'It is familiar,' I answered uncertainly. 'Yes, it seems familiar . . .'

It turns out that a lot of what I had read about in the American's book was done back in the 1920s by Muromtsev. Rats and rabbits, they all froze and thawed beautifully in his laboratories: everything except monkeys, which were simply impossible to obtain in Leningrad at the time. The laboratory worked very successfully from 1924 to 1926, when Muromtsev was arrested.

As Geiger explained to me, in 1926 the academician flatly refused to freeze Felix Dzerzhinsky, who had a stroke after speaking for two hours during a Central Committee plenary session. The scholar explained his unwillingness to freeze Dzerzhinsky by saying that science was not yet ready for such complex experiments. He attempted in all sorts of ways to prove that the transition from rats to Dzerzhinsky was impossible without experimenting on intermediary forms. But they didn't listen to him.

Muromtsev was accused of sabotage. According to his accusers' account, he had not frozen Dzerzhinsky because he did not wish for Iron Felix to be defrosted at some future time. After several weeks of interrogations, the accused agreed with that account. He admitted that he felt sorry for those people who would live later and need to be involved with Dzerzhinsky, and said he had, well, on the whole, sabotaged the entrance of the Land of the Soviets' leadership into immortality.

THURSDAY

I was not beaten at my first interrogation. Babushkin, who conducted the interrogation, only noted down data for the record. He also asked if I admitted my participation in the plot Voronin organized. He said an honest confession would safeguard me from many woes. I denied all the accusations and Babushkin heard me out pensively. He had a tired appearance that day. It even occurred to me then that he somehow looked grandmotherly, befitting his surname.

After the interrogation, they led me to a dark, vile-smelling cell. I lingered slightly in front of the open door (the sight was awful) and they pushed me, forcibly, over the threshold. I stumbled on something and fell to the floor. I lay, face down, for some time. My eyes were closed but my nose inhaled the stench of the place and my hands groped at a soft, almost rotten, wooden floor. It had been wooden at some time but dampness and sewage had changed its nature. I lay, not stirring, as if I still hoped what was happening was a dream, that I needed to not exhale, not move, and (the main thing) not wake up at this point in the dream, in order that it not become reality.

My hopes were not justified. In the end, I somehow stood. First on all fours, then at full height. I glimpsed the silhouettes of my cellmates – I could not discern more. One of them indifferently showed me my place on the bunks. Nobody asked me about anything and I said nothing. I lay down and truly did fall asleep that time, sleeping soundly, not dreaming. I awoke in the middle of the night from someone's moan, then fell back to sleep. At morning wake-up, I could not understand where I was.

Babushkin beat me at my second interrogation. In reality, he probably had not been in the best condition the night before and had decided not to begin the case half-heartedly. It could also be that he had some sort of errands after work that evening. This time,

Babushkin was fresh and in no hurry. He sat me on a chair, tied my hands and feet, and then, after rolling up his shirtsleeves, hit me in the face with a swinging blow. I felt blood flow from my nose along my lips and chin. When I fell along with the chair, Babushkin tore off my shoes and used a wooden truncheon to beat my heels with all his might. It was unbearably painful but did not lead to serious injury. Serious injury was probably not encouraged, even in his department.

I was not afraid when Babushkin was tying me or when he was rolling up his sleeves. He thought he was scaring me that way. But he did not scare me: he beat me, even taking a certain pleasure in it. Silently. I was silent, too. I saw many beatings later in my life that were accompanied by shouting and cursing, but this was the most unusual because of its wordlessness. After asking a question once, Babushkin decided to beat me until I answered. I did not remain silent out of heroism. It was as if I had fallen into unconsciousness and only feebly understood what was happening.

After not receiving an answer to his question, he asked me another anyway.

'How did you,' he said as he was beating me, and, oddly enough, Babushkin continued using the formal 'you' with me, 'how did you kill your neighbor Zaretsky? Zaretsky wrote to us that you threatened to kill him, but we ascribed no significance to that.' He waved Zaretsky's letter in front of me. 'But we should have.'

Two guards dragged me by the arms to my third interrogation. My feet had swollen so much after the beatings that I could not walk on my own. My shoes would not go on and my bare feet trailed along the corridor's stone floor. At that interrogation, Babushkin read me Averyanov's testimony, which described, in detail, my role in Voronin's counterrevolutionary plot. At that interrogation, I admitted my participation in the plot and confessed to killing Zaretsky.

FRIDAY

Geiger brought me the 'Canon of Repentance' and I read it all day. Slowly, stopping.

Whence shall I begin to weep over the deeds of my cursed life?
What beginning shall I make, O Christ, to my present grieving?

SUNDAY

Today is Easter. During the night, Geiger and I went to St Prince Vladimir Cathedral, where I used to go in years past. Geiger initially did not want to bring me there, fearing I would catch some sort of virus in such a crowd, but I insisted. The whole street was packed with cars and we left ours a block from the church. There truly were many people.

Outside, the police were attempting to handle the crush; we could barely enter. Inside was crowded, too. Stifling. Nothing had changed there, though the icons had completely darkened. Geiger bought two candles and we began making our way forward. This turned out not to be so simple. We joined a narrow flow that was moving in fits and starts. Only after standing for a few minutes did we realize that this was a *trickle*, that's how slowly it was moving. Wax from my candle dripped on my fingers without burning. I sniffed: it was paraffin, not wax.

Another Easter came back to me, too: without candles and not even in a church, but under an open sky. It was not simply open, it was cloudless and bottomless, with flashes of northern lights playing on it. It was the only occasion in my memory when we, the prisoners, were let out of our barracks at night and we gathered by the cemetery church. I had never seen an Easter like that before and probably never will again. Primarily bishops filled the church, so almost no space was left for priests and laymen.

We stood among the graves in melting snow drifts, catching words from the service, which carried out the open doors. It already smelled of spring, too: the breeze was warm, and under our feet there lay *those in the tombs*. For the first time in many months of life on the island, I felt a sense of relief. We knew that a day of excruciating labor awaited us after the sleepless night but nobody returned to the barracks because the feeling of happiness that enveloped us was dearer. Even those who were at the beginning of a long sentence at the camp believed in their impending release. They saw it clearly in the sky's night radiance.

TUESDAY

The long-awaited press conference took place yesterday. True, I was not the one who had been waiting for it and was not hastening it. I was just worried; how would I be received? I didn't sleep the night before or the night after. I was only able to fall asleep this afternoon. I woke up just now, and it's evening, dark outside, and uninviting. I feel the previous worry approaching and will not sleep again tonight: how will I live now? My own obscurity had screened me, as if it were snow, but what now? Now everyone knows my face, I'm a celebrity, but I did not need that at all. If I were a contemporary of modern-day people, my celebrity would gladden me: I think I would bask in it. Only I am not one of them so why should I establish myself among them? They looked at me as if I was a fish in an aquarium, and curiosity was the only thing in their eyes. I felt as if I didn't know who I was. Exactly as in childhood, when they pushed me to the middle of the parlor and said: 'Go intrepidly.'

But I felt trepidation. I peer through a crack in the door before entering the conference room: oceans of people, television cameras. They tell me that many others could not make their way in here. And I suddenly recognize this room. I was in it when I studied at the university. Maybe this is the university? Does remembering the room mean I studied here? A good student question. I have enough sense not to ask anyone . . . It turns out not to be the university. Without my asking, they inform me we are in a building of the Academy of Sciences. There's a mosaic by Lomonosov – 'Poltava' – over the grand staircase (they show it). Was I an academician in my past life?

Everyone applauds when I enter the room with Geiger, and a vice president of the Academy of Sciences. The vice president says that, to his mind, the applause is for the Russian Academy's scientific might and for my human courage. I lower my eyes at his words about courage since all my memories of the freezing are hazy. It is the same with courage.

Some of those circumstances become clear when Geiger takes the floor. He announces to attendees that the freezing was conducted at the Solovetsky Special Purpose Camp by Academician Muromtsev's group, all of whose members ended up there. I shift my gaze to Geiger and he nods to me in the affirmative without interrupting his speech. He had not alluded to the Solovetsky Islands in our conversation about Muromtsev. In essence, I could have guessed about the islands.

Geiger speaks for a long time yet, lingering on the specifics of preserving my body and the medical details of thawing, but I am no longer listening. A lot begins to fall into place in my memory: island, torture, cold. Especially the cold, which was cosmic and insurmountable, and which kept deepening and ended, it turns out, with this.

Afraid of damaging my recovery, Geiger forbids journalists from asking me questions about the past. They ask about the present. I answer the first questions in a somewhat cold-ridden voice, clearing my throat from time to time. My temperature, I say, is normal. My blood pressure is within the norm. I keep sensing the rough surface of the microphone with my lips and hear myself as if from a distance. The pauses in my speech are filled by the clicking of cameras. I utter brief sentences and am ashamed of myself: this is how a thawed baboon might answer, not a person of the Silver Age.

'It's known that in the first weeks after thawing you experienced certain complications with your health. Do you feel better now?'

'Better,' I attempt to loosen up. 'At least better than in liquid nitrogen.'

Applause: what a fellow, he's warmed up and he's joking. I sense that I'm blushing.

'And you spoke with Blok?' shouts someone from the back rows.

Geiger stands and shakes his head reproachfully.

'I did ask –'

'I saw him at a poetry soirée,' I answer, 'but did not speak with him. I did speak with Remizov, in a queue. He lived on 14th Line . . .'

'What did you speak about?'

Geiger knocks threateningly on the microphone with a pencil.

'I don't remember.' Laughter smothers me but I try to restrain myself. '*I* went to 8th Line for provisions and *he* went there, too. And I did not know he was Remizov; only later did I realize that, from a photograph.'

My lips stretch into a smile and everyone in the hall begins smiling. I roar with laughter and everyone roars with laughter. I begin sobbing and there is silence in the hall. Geiger rushes to me (his chair overturns with a crash), takes me by the shoulders, and leads me out to the courtyard through the back door. A car is waiting for us there. A fevered chill hits me: this is how I was frozen through for all those years. And now I will never warm up again.

WEDNESDAY

And I did very much want to speak with Blok. I, someone who knows so little by heart, had memorized his poem 'The Aviator.' Here is its beginning:

> Having swung his twin fan blades,
> A flier released into freedom,
> – Like a sea monster into water –
> Slipped into aerial streams.

Someone even found Blok's telephone number for me, but I never did call. I repeated that number to myself day and night. I can say it even now: 6-12-00.

THURSDAY

They brought us from Kem on a barge, the *Clara Zetkin*. In a hold that was tightly battened down, devoid of light and air. I was one of the last in our batch of prisoners to board the barge and so ended up on the stairway right beside the exit. There were fewer people there, and sea air seeped in through crevices in the deck hatch. That saved my life. Many of those who were pushed into the hold first were crushed or suffocated.

A storm came up about an hour after we set sail from Kem. The waves in the White Sea are smaller than in the ocean but harder to bear: perhaps this is precisely because of their low height. The very weakest began vomiting as the rocking began. People were packed into the hold like sardines, and they puked on themselves and those around them. Because of this, even those who did not usually fear the pitching began feeling ill, too.

But the worst was ahead. Heart-rending screams rang out when the ship began rolling from side to side. This was people dying; they were standing at the sides. A thousand-pood human mass was pressing them against the rusty iron side of the barge, flattening them into pancakes. When their mutilated bodies were dragged along the dock later, a trail of bloody diarrhea stretched after them.

I vomited, too: I was simply turned inside out. The fear of drowning that had seized me in the initial minutes of the rocking passed quickly. The indifference that arose painted me a picture of cold, transparent depths where I no longer vomited or heard the screams of the dying. Where there were no escort guards. In those frightening hours, for some reason I did not think about how – even on the seabed – none of us would break out of this darkness and stench, and that even at that final depth, the rusty hatch of the *Clara Zetkin* would remain battened down and that what lay ahead for us was eternal swimming in our own feces and puke.

They kicked us, driving us out on the dock in the Bay of Prosperity. They ordered those who were in no condition to move to be dragged by other prisoners. Those who were walking and those who could not walk all felt roughly the same. We were happy to remain alive because none of us had seen anything in our life scarier than the belly of the

Clara Zetkin. At the time, we thought we would not see anything worse.

On shore, they formed us into columns and began teaching us how to answer the authorities' greetings. We shouted 'Good aftern—' to the division commander, the commander of the brigade, and the camp's chief, Nogtev, who swayed drunkenly in front of the columns and expressed his dissatisfaction with the greeting because our shouting was disunified. After everything we had lived through at sea, we had no strength left. We wanted so much to sleep. So as not to fall asleep, I deeply inhaled the sea air, which was part of the previous free world. This means, I thought, that a part of that world will still remain in our life.

We repeated our greeting countless times but the wind carried it over the entire island; that made it no better. Nogtev considered our *good aftern—* insufficiently cheerful, and one has to think that was the case. We simply lacked the strength for a cheerful *good aftern—*. Career criminals and academicians, bishops and the tsar's generals all shouted, but their voices did not merge into one. I was standing in the first row, next to General Miller. This was a military general who had gone through the Great War and was still fairly young. Seagulls flew around us and I listened: they, too, shouted *good aftern—* and, apparently, better than we because Nogtev had no grievances with them. I probably fell asleep for an instant after all . . .

When I opened my eyes, Nogtev was already headed toward us. I was certain it was because of me. That my unmilitary appearance had provoked the rage of the head of the camp and now he was walking over to do me in. But no: he was not walking toward me but to Miller, a model of order and bearing. Nogtev's trained eye immediately noticed the person he himself could never become. He was approaching, in his leather jacket, his gait springy, clearly a ruffian. He reached for his Nagan along the way.

'How do you stand before the chief?' Nogtev began yelling. 'You have to keep your eyes peeled, son of a bitch!'

Miller looked calmly at Nogtev. He straightened the rucksack on his shoulder and there was neither fuss nor fear in that motion. His leather jacket crackling, Nogtev placed the Nagan to the general's forehead and lingered for several instants. In those seconds I decided that now he wouldn't shoot. Eyes set narrowly. An overlooked hair on shaved Mongol cheekbones. Lingering in these situations amounts to cancellation.

Nogtev shot.

Two guards dragged the killed man to the guard booth by his feet. They grabbed the rucksack as they went. The body remained, lying in a strange pose: on its side, an arm uncomfortably twisted underneath. Eyes open. With his previous calm, the general continued observing what happened on the shore.

Later they trained us how to turn. We turned to the right, to the left, and around, and a warm summer wind fanned us because it can be warm in the summer even on the Solovetsky Islands. The smell of pine sap and taiga berries blended with the sea's freshness in that wind. The White Sea did not smell like southern seas but its freshness penetrated every cell in the body. A northern sun that did not set glimmered on the crests of the waves. We stood with our backs to the bay, but that glimmering was visible when we turned around, and it genuinely cheered me. It reminded me of the sea in the areas near Alushta, where I vacationed with my parents in 1911.

FRIDAY

Yes, Alushta. We stayed in Professor's Corner at Attorney Giatsintov's dacha; he was my father's master's-degree advisor at one time. When it turned out the Giatsintov family would be spending the summer of 1911 (?) in Nice, the old man offered his Crimean dacha to a former student as a place to stay. That's how we ended up in Alushta, yes, exactly, it was 1911.

Professor's Corner was located a half-hour's walk from the post station. You could ride there in a droshky but we almost never used droshkies. We walked to the station: this was our evening stroll. We walked past cypresses, olives, and juniper bushes, inhaling the damp, strongly scented air. Petersburg air is damp, too, but its dampness is cold and unpleasant; I would say it is unfriendly. I could not express then what I am writing about now, though I felt it very well.

The beach. I loved the beach beyond belief. The sound of the surf, festive and thick, like basses in an orchestra pit. Rolling wet on the sand in order to go into the water again later. And then falling on the sand for good, ears full of water. Near me: hitting at a ball and shouting. The sounds make waves in the water inside my ears but don't pierce through it and I hear all that as if at a distance. If you roll on your side, the watery cork comes out in an invisible stream that flows through the ear. The sharpness of sounds returns. The sun is in the middle of the sky. You look at it through loosely joined fingers and there it is, looking like it will burn through them now. Incidentally, the edges of your fingers are already pink.

Castle construction. Wet sand slides off the middle finger and freezes in the shape of a tower. Walls facing the sea are reinforced by pebbles. Waves – their edge, their froth – roll up lazily. The walls do not withstand the waves for long before needing to be fortified, and made the moat in front of them deeper. Basically, owning a castle is exacting work.

There are two owners: Mitya Dorn, who's the son of a famous Moscow surgeon, and me. We reinforced the castle against possible barbarian invasion, something that is expected (naturally) to come by sea. The barbarians are fierce and their speech is guttural and unalluring. They are cannibals. They arrive in canoes, eating everyone in their path. But Mitya and I are doing well and are safe on our little green island. Cypress branches are growing from the tops of the watchtowers; they rustle beautifully in the wind.

A strong wave rolls up from time to time. As it makes its way along our reinforcements, it does not so much ruin as erode, smoothing contours. It makes the castle several hundred years older, akin to the Alushta Fortress, which is hidden in the greenery not far from here. I pronounce the word 'Alushta' to myself and discover its completely new qualities. What a wet and shiny word, like a watermelon in the sun. Alushta ... Mitya Dorn observes as my lips move but does not ask a thing.

And so we walk from the beach in shirts and short pants, with bucket hats on our heads. We're ashamed to be wearing children's hats but Mitya's father explains that ... But I don't hear the doctor's words: there's a beachy fog and tiredness in my head. I observe the movements of his hairy arms with bulging little bones at the wrists. Long fingers, almost made for a scalpel – he cuts with them, cuts, cuts human flesh. The hair on the phalanges of his fingers is faded, it's only visible when wet.

The sea salt is beginning to make itself felt under our clothes, tightening the skin. The sun falls on my neck when I bend it. Its heat is pleasant after swimming and I walk with my head lowered. Under my feet are cypress twigs, gravel, and, every now and then, beetles and caterpillars. I take them in my palm and they pretend they're dying. I know they're being sneaky but, for my part, I pretend to believe them: I carefully place them in the grass. How many times later did I feel like playing dead so I could be placed on the grass just like that and no longer be touched? They did not believe it and waited for their actual death.

SATURDAY

I've been watching television for several weeks now, how the Americans are bombing the Serbs. Why? For what? I decided to ask Geiger when he came but then forgot because Geiger told me that Valentina has quit her job for good. Her husband wants her to concentrate on their future child. And not on Geiger, I add for my part.

'But what about her dissertation?' I ask. 'And why did she never tell me about her family?'

'Are you jealous?'

No, I'm not jealous. It pains me when people leave my life. All my contemporaries left and now Valentina, too.

Oh, and Geiger also announced that he's gathering documents for my rehabilitation. I apparently reacted a bit listlessly because he launched into detailed explanations. Rehabilitation is required, so he says, for expunging a conviction, though he, Geiger, understands that I personally have no need for rehabilitation. In reality, though, do I need it?

MONDAY

Today they took me to the television station. It's located on the Petrograd Side, not far from Kamennoostrovsky Prospect: it turns out that's where that magical emanation comes from. It's so strange that an enigma has a city address ... As we were driving along Kamennoostrovsky, I recognized several buildings from the beginning of the century. I stopped by one of them not long before my arrest; I needed to return books that Professor Voronin had borrowed to read. It's so strange: the person is already gone but, yes, a book continues to live.

At the television station, they first put makeup on me, powdering my face and applying hairspray from a metal can. In my time this was called an atomizer, but now it's called spray. 'Spray,' of course, is shorter. There are many little words like this in English that are small and resonant, like a ping-pong ball: they're basically convenient and economical. The thing is that people did not economize on speech before.

They fitted me with a microphone at the studio. They said the conversation would be aired as a recording, rather than live (I utter those terms without faltering!), so I won't be nervous. But I was not, as a matter of fact, nervous: if it's recorded, fine, it's recorded. You get nervous when there are a lot of people around looking at you, or encouraging you, or, let's say, interrupting – but what was there here? Quiet. Complete calm. The host was cordial; she sat, legs crossed. I've seen her on the screen many times and she always sits like that. The ballpoint pen in her hand seemed to spin on its own axis. It gleamed under the floodlights. Her fingers were long, with rings. It's obvious that twirling a pen in fingers like that is a winning pursuit.

'Do you recall something new every day?'

'Yes, I do.'

'What did you recall today?'

Her skirt was short, her knees visible. I try not to look below the waist as I answer.

'A building on Kamennoostrovsky. We were driving and I recognized it. You know, the railings there are interesting . . . Curlicued. And its wrought-iron lilies have an unearthly beauty. Not long before my arrest, I walked up those stairs and touched the wood with my hand. That smoothness stayed with me for some reason: my fingers still feel it. I was going to one of the apartments, to deliver books.

And so I rang the bell. The lock clanked. It didn't scrape or squeak but clanked: those were the sounds of solid locks that covered half the door. You enter and there's a distinct smell of an apartment where there are many books. A limping girl opened the door; somehow I grasped immediately that she was limping . . . Or maybe I knew that? Her face was narrow, with deeply set eyes – there's a Petersburg type like that. A shawl on her shoulders. She went ahead of me, not shy about her limp. And there truly were books everywhere and I had brought another four or five. Thank you, I say. Here, I say, they asked me to give you these. I'm probably telling too much . . .'

'No, what do you mean, this is all terribly interesting . . .' The pen twirled even faster in her fingers. 'What impressions of the October Coup have stayed you?'

'You know, none of it stayed with me. It was only later, when I realized what that day was, that I brought back the memory. There was, if I'm not confusing things, sleet falling. More precisely, first there was rain and it changed to wet snow. I went out somewhere, forgot my scarf at home, and the snowflakes were melting on my neck; I felt their melting on my hot skin. There was wind, early darkness, you know that's the nastiest time for Petersburg . . .'

I said something else, too, but at some point a slight motion began to my left: Geiger was signaling to the host to end. She asked one more question to finish up and stopped the recording, not without disappointment I thought, perhaps because Geiger had cut her off early, perhaps because of my answers. Most likely because of my answers: I don't think she heard what she wanted.

After filming, they asked me if I could find the apartment I had gone to. I thought that I could: if I recognized the building, then why not . . . Geiger asked what they needed that for. They answered that they would like to film the moment of my encounter with the past. That's what they wanted to call this show: *An Encounter with the Past*. Geiger said he could not let me be on a show with such a trite title. They offered to give it any other title but Geiger continued to waver. He was not sure a meeting like that would be to my benefit. He thought it should be prepared in advance instead. But the people from the television station persuaded him.

I did not recognize the front entrance when we approached. Instead of the carved oak door there hung something covered with wooden strips. It was swinging in the breeze, creaking. One of the two cameramen flicked at the strips with his fingers. 'Veneer,' he said. He disappeared into the darkness inside. The second cameraman proposed filming as I approached the door. They led me to the corner of the building and asked me to walk over again and go inside. I walked over and began opening the door but suddenly noticed there was a long screw sticking out of it instead of a handle. I hesitated: the encounter with the past had lost its refinement from the very start. I pulled at the screw with my thumb and index finger but the door did not open on the first try. I looked at my fingers: marks from the screw's threads were distinctly imprinted on them. I took hold of the screw again and applied force. The door opened.

The first thing that greeted me inside was the acrid smell of urine. There was no light other than the beam coming from the television camera. It beat right in my eyes so I couldn't see anything. I guessed as I placed my feet on the stairs. I walked up and the beam walked up, too, to my side. I stumbled and the beam stumbled: we had stepped on the same worn stair. I took hold of the railing to be on the safe side. This was an effective gesture in and of itself, completely in correspondence with an encounter with the past, but my hand didn't slide up nicely: instead of carved smoothness – I repeat that my hand remembered that – I sensed a bare metal railing that no longer had wood on it. And though almost nothing was visible, my feet carried me on their own to the door I sought.

Geiger rang and – at first barely audibly, then louder and louder – there was a shuffling noise. The door swung open when the sound reached its upper limit (they knew how to shuffle in that apartment). A person in a holey undershirt appeared on the threshold. He was bald and seemed unsober. When the camera's beam hit him, he squinted and asked the purpose of the filming. They explained to him that I had come to this apartment in 1923 and now wanted to go inside again. The man in the undershirt was not surprised but said he could not let me in today. He had guests today. He invited us to come back tomorrow.

What he did was right in its own way. One day holds no importance for someone who has been waiting nearly eighty years. For some reason I imagined his guests: they were most likely sitting there in undershirts, too, and had been sitting there a long time. And would sit in the future. I knew I would not come back here: otherwise they would remain with me instead of those who lived here before. They would occupy the place of those previous people in my memory, just as they had occupied their apartment. And I recalled the surname of the people who lived in the apartment before: the Meshcheryakovs.

Geiger was the first to walk out the front door of the building. He held the door by the screw, letting the rest of us out. He began telling how he'd been in various countries and how everywhere – despite wars and revolutions – old handles remained on entrance doors. Petersburg seemed to hold on for a fairly long time. Things did not come down to door handles until relatively recently, when people began unscrewing them for scrap metal. According to Geiger, the disappearance of door handles marked the conspicuous end of normal life. And the beginning of a gradual but steady decline into barbarity.

That Geiger certainly does place a lot of importance on door handles.

TUESDAY

Professor Giatsintov's dacha. It maintained its coolness even in the Crimean heat. As I walked from the beach, I anticipated plunging into the dacha's half-darkness – it would chill my overheated body. The coolness in this house was not linked to freshness. It was most likely linked to an intoxicating mustiness that blended the aroma of old books with numerous ocean trophies that had come (who knew how?) to this attorney and professor. Lying on shelves and dispersing a salty smell were dried starfish, pearlescent shells, a giant turtle shell (it was fastened to a sideways stand), a swordfish's sword, a needlefish's needle, a colonial cork helmet, and carved native masks. Speaking of natives, I hadn't even the slightest notion of these items' homelands. It is possible they were somehow linked to Robinson: I counted on that very much at the time.

Carefully moving aside the gifts from the sea, I took the professor's books from the shelf. These were volumes by Mayne Reid and Jules Verne, stories of sea voyages and descriptions of exotic countries: things infinitely distant from jurisprudence. Professor Giatsintov collected at his Crimean dacha what children dreamt about but did not come true, that which his way of life did not encompass and which was not housed within the Digest of Laws of the Russian Empire. I suspect there were no laws at all in the countries dear to his heart.

I sat cross-legged in a boxwood chair (the aroma of boxwood added to the house's smells!) and read Giatsintov's books. I leafed through the pages with my right hand while my left clenched a piece of bread with butter and sugar. I bit off a piece and read. And the sugar crunched on my teeth. From time to time, I would raise my eyes from the book and think about how people become attorneys. Do they dream about that when they are children? Doubtful. I dreamt about being a fire captain and a conductor, but never an attorney.

I also imagined staying in that cool room forever: that I live in it as if in a capsule, that there are coups and earthquakes outside, that there is no more sugar or butter or even the Russian Empire outside, but I keep sitting and reading, reading . . . Subsequent years showed that I guessed right about the sugar and butter but, unfortunately, sitting and reading did not work out. The new life did not lend itself to reading.

Yes, this is important: on one of the cabinets there stood Themis, exactly the same as ours, except for the scales, because apparently nobody in the Giatsintov household had dared break them off. It seems to me now that it was Giatsintov who gave the statuette to my father. It is obviously an item to his taste.

SATURDAY

Today I asked Geiger:

'Did my mother die?'

'She died,' he responded. 'In 1940.'

SUNDAY

Today Geiger and I went to Smolensky Cemetery. We began the morning with a service in the Church of the Smolensk Icon of the Mother of God (I began that way and Geiger sat outside), then we went to the chapel of Blessed Xenia. It turns out Xenia was recently canonized. I remember that my mother and I stopped in at the chapel at one time and people were already revering Xenia then: those who came left little notes. My mother said: 'You write, too.' And I wrote. What did I ask for then?

I can still see my mother on that spring day, in a headscarf tied so tightly it seemed to be squeezing her facial features, lending her a severe and somewhat distressed appearance. At first it was overcast and the wind was blowing, but then blueness took shape on the very edge of the sky. We were sitting by my father's grave and the blueness broadened until it came to our sorrowful place, where it stopped. And so my mother and I sat on the border of blue and gray, and nothing more changed in the sky. I poured vodka into shot glasses; she cut thin slices of bread. Threads of veins ran through the back of her hand; it seemed as if I had not seen the veins before. It's possible they popped up from the cold. Or perhaps it was the beginning of her old age.

'What did she die of?'

I purposely asked this along the way so as not to have to clarify anything at my mother's grave. At one time, my mother had forbidden me to speak of those present in the third person; and she was, despite everything, present here. There would have been a sort of awkwardness to my questions.

'Of pneumonia.' Geiger blew his nose into a paper handkerchief. 'They said she caught cold here.'

We had no trouble finding the grave; it was not far from the walkway. Nothing had changed on the surface since my mother entered. She had entered in the literal sense: the fence was designed for two plots and, as Geiger told me, my mother was buried over my grandmother. The same granite cross was there, the one my father installed back in his day, after my grandmother's death. His name had been carved on the cross after his death, too. When my mother was buried here, nobody carved anything, simply because there was nobody to do so. Despite the absence of a name and a mound, of course my mother was present here. That was perceptible.

Geiger took a flask and a set of silver shot glasses in a leather case out of his side pocket. There was cognac in the flask.

'In 1940, they sent her a notification of your death,' said Geiger, filling the shot glasses. 'What's interesting is that pneumonia was given as the cause of death. After freezing you, the Chekists displayed a sense of humor – even the secret police have one. Pneumonia. Caught a cold in liquid nitrogen.'

We drank without clinking our glasses.

My mother had no remaining loved ones after this notification, and she had nowhere to go but the cemetery. She would sit there for hours at a time, conversing with the departed. She died of the same illness they attributed to me in the notification. Was that by chance? I will not find out until I see her. When thinking about my mother, I had supposed that she might have died during the blockade – perhaps this was because I had been reading about the blockade in recent few days.

'There are graves of other people I know at this cemetery,' I told Geiger.

He nodded but did not answer, likely expecting further questions from me. But I didn't ask. About anything. As we walked out the cemetery gates, I thought: It is good that my mother did not live to see the blockade.

Did Anastasia live to see it?

TUESDAY

My father, who has a cold, is gargling in the bathroom and I am getting on a stool next to him. I want to observe with my own eyes the mysteriousness that gives birth to guttural gurgling sounds, those strange modulations – from rumbling to groans – that you do not hear from your father at any other time. This is how a naturalist climbs to the edge of a crater, striving to reach boiling lava before eruption. At my request, my mother gives me a candle. The flame only slightly illuminates the roiling in my father's throat and the main attraction lies in that concealment. Later, after I had grown a bit and was already gargling masterfully myself, I discovered that it works even without a voice. It works, though poorly, for the voice prolongs the exhale and makes it more powerful. Voiceless murmuring is powerless and pitiful.

WEDNESDAY

Logs. Large logs were called *balany* on the island. At the end of a shift, each of us had to turn in thirteen of these logs per assignment to the Chekist. We worked in pairs, meaning twenty-six in all. The assignment was unachievable, at least for those who had never done this type of work before.

The tree had to be felled and stripped of branches and sticks, but first you had to get to the base of the trunk, which got lost in the deep snow. We dug it out with our bare hands: there were no shovels; they did not even issue mittens. We let our hands warm up by raking snow away with our feet, which might as well have been bare because our footwear was bast shoes worn over footwraps of burlap. After stripping the base of the trunk, we took a two-handled saw to it and began sawing. Initially the teeth would slip from the frozen trunk but the work became easier when the saw's blade entered the pine's flesh. Time seemed to disappear with the identical rhythmic motions; you yourself would fall into another reality. Crouched or kneeling, we would saw until our hands froze on the saw handles. Then we would stand and switch places, while switching hands. We needed to stand in order to warm our frozen feet at least a little bit, too.

Feet quite often became frostbitten and had to be amputated. This did not mean the number of one-footed people on Solovki increased dramatically: those people did not usually survive. They died in the infirmary from general exhaustion or from a stump being wrapped in poorly laundered rags following amputation.

That's how Vasya Korobkov, my work partner, died. He had been saying since noon that he did not feel his feet, but none of the Chekists listened to him. I knew that Vasya could no longer saw: he could not even stand and was sitting in the snow by a tree trunk. I attempted to saw by myself and he just hung on his end of the saw, not moving his arm. Toward the end of the shift, we produced only ten logs, less than half the quota. They left us in the woods until morning to complete the assignment, the usual penalty. Vasya cried, beseeching the Chekists to allow us to return to the barracks. They didn't allow it and began beating him with the butts of their rifles; I was on the receiving end, too. Their cursing drowned in the snowstorm and even their blows could barely be felt in all those white particles.

We spent the entire night in the woods but did not make one more log. At first Vasya lay on the snow, then I laid him on a log, took off his bast shoes and rubbed his feet with snow: they were like ice, cold and hard. Half the night was dark and then the snowstorm suddenly stopped and I saw Vasya's face in the moonlight. Tears were running down it but there was no longer anything pitiful or whiny in that: Vasya's features had become motionless from the cold. His face had lost its ability to cry or laugh, and a significance – even a solemnity or something – had appeared on it.

From time to time, I would run back and forth to warm up, but you cannot run particularly fast when you have no strength. Everything began again in the morning for me, with no sleep or food. They gave me a new partner and forced me to work. Two prisoners dragged Vasya to the infirmary, where both his feet were amputated. He died a day later from blood poisoning.

When I told Geiger one time that we worked in temperatures of forty below, without warm clothes, without footwear, and without food, he told me he did not understand how anyone could remain alive under those conditions.

Well, they didn't.

THURSDAY

I left the hospital. That had to happen sooner or later: Geiger thought further life in the hospital's hothouse conditions would not be helpful. We worked on my move all this week so there was no opportunity at all to write. Speaking of opportunity, it isn't so much the spare time I have in mind as something else.

What this all means is that the actual place I moved into is my old apartment! I am now living there again, on the corner of Bolshoy and Zverinskaya. It turns out that – at the doctors' insistence (read: Geiger's) – the city's powers-that-be bought up my former communal apartment, renovated it, and lodged me there. They allotted the room where my mother and I lived at one time to the medical staff attending to me (Angela, for the most part), settled me in the parlor, and left Zaretsky's room for Geiger, in case he visits. All this was done so that I could accustom myself to my new environment as quickly as possible.

I spent my first day in the new apartment alone. As I understand it, this was how they showed tact regarding my recollections, and I was grateful for that. I walked from room to room. Everything was completely different: floors, doors, and windows. Even the old furniture was different, specially purchased prior to my move. I opened the kitchen tap and the water sounded completely different. In the 1920s it drummed sonorously on the tin sink but now it no longer drummed. And the sink was not tin. Only the size of the rooms remained the same, though I'm not even sure about that. As they told me, neighboring apartments changed their living space so many times during the years gone by and were subjected to so many new floor plans that it was simply pointless to seek out a resemblance with the past.

But it was there anyway. That resemblance manifested itself in its own way in the freshly renovated apartment with new old furniture. In how, for example, I knew for certain the number of paces from the window to the door. In how I could imagine, eyes closed, *what* was visible from each window. But here is the main thing: each time I closed my eyes, I seemed to hear the voices of those who had lived here at some point. For the first time, I grasped in all clarity that I had lost them – the living – forever.

I lay on the bed and closed my eyes. I felt like disappearing, not being, and freezing again without ever thawing. I fell into a dream that was murky and swampy. The dream pulled me ever deeper and more hopelessly, and I no longer understood if I was dreaming of shadows in the apartment or if they were wandering all around while I was awake. I knew that in cases like this one needs the will to awaken, the effort, but it was exactly this that I could not resolve to accomplish because I no longer knew *which* was scarier: dreaming or being awake. I experienced this feeling at one time on the island.

The doorbell woke me up. It was Geiger: how glad I was to see him! If not for him, I would never have woken up. He came to check in on me and brought a bottle of cognac. The cognac and Geiger's quiet voice calmed me. I no longer felt like sleeping: I felt like sitting and talking.

Among other things, I asked Geiger if I could go out to walk around on my own. He responded that indeed this was necessary. He took a wallet from his pocket and gave it to me. He explained for a long time about the value of the banknotes, how to pay for what, and so on. I retained very little. We talked until about two in the morning and then Geiger called home and said he was spending the night at my place. I thought about how I know nothing about him, either his family or what he does outside work. What was this sitting here with me today? Part of his work or outside it?

Geiger has gone to bed in Zaretsky's room, which was prepared for him, but I still don't want to sleep: I slept plenty in the afternoon. I'm sitting and writing. From time to time I hear bedsprings squeaking on the other side of the wall. It's good it's Geiger, not Zaretsky.

FRIDAY

Whence shall I begin to weep over the deeds of my cursed life?

SATURDAY

I was standing by the window this evening. I noticed the cognac that Geiger left (open, by the way) on the windowsill. At first I looked down at the moving cars, then at the sky. In the sky were flying machines that looked very little like aeroplanes. I, Aviator Platonov, was drinking Geiger's cognac and recalling Commandant's Aerodrome, which, as it turns out, is now gone. But how can it be gone? How can an entire world – an entire life with its joys, tragedies, discoveries, waiting at some times, tedium at some times, the pounding of rain on empty benches, or swirls of dust on an abandoned airfield – leave the face of the earth?

Where, one might ask, is that world? Where are the women in the smart dresses who give bouquets to aviators? Where are the men in service caps that slide down to their noses? With canes and with cigarettes in their teeth – where are those men? Where are all of us who'd been standing at the edge of the field? And what sort of Atlantis were we taking to the ocean floor? Where, finally, is the giant inscription, 'Russian Society of Aeronautics,' that decorated the hangar from which the aeroplanes rolled?

I knew all those machines like my own five fingers. I could distinguish them with my eyes closed from the sound of the motors. A Bleriot monoplane from, say, a Voisin or Farman biplane. I knew the aviators' faces: Pégoud, Poiré, Garros, Nesterov, and Matseevich. It's not that I had seen them all personally, it's just that their portraits hung at home. Where are those portraits?

They are gone now, which is why, really, I was drinking the cognac. And why I am finishing it right now as I scribble out these lines. In recent days I was asked, 'What made you want, so wholeheartedly, to become an aviator? Was it dreaming of the sky?' Oh my, oh why! This was not just because of the sky but from all the wonderful accoutrements too: helmet and goggles and mustache.

And, once again, expensive cigarettes. Leather jacket and trousers, with fur lining. You have to understand that aviators were genuine idols, the elite.

Those idols had their weak points, too, though. For example, aviators smelled of castor oil that was used to lubricate the motor. Especially those who flew in fur coats. And many did fly that way: it is very cold there, up high. They still needed to get up there, however. I saw how one aviator drove down the field but could not take off. He drove down the field again with the same result. Everyone laughing, champagne spraying. After the fourth attempt, they waved the flag and sent him to the hangar.

And so: a dream. Well, of course, there was also a dream of the sky. By comparison with that (sky), all of us at the aerodrome were so small:

> But here in the sultry wavering,
> As mist wafts over the turf,
> Hangars, people, worldly cares
> Seem pressed down to the earth . . .

All of us here seem pressed down, that's the thing. But in the sky . . . everything there is different.

SUNDAY

Today I went outside on my own for the first time. I set off along Bolshoy Prospect in the direction of Tuchkov Bridge. I crossed Alexandrovsky Prospect (formerly Alexandrovsky, now Dobrolyubov) using an underground crosswalk. Dobrolyubov, by the way, began as a decent person, studying ancient Russian literature ... It was windy on the bridge and my raincoat (given to me by Geiger) began fluttering. I stopped in the middle of the bridge and walked up to the parapet. The water was black and churned around the bridge support, just as it did more than seven decades ago. I came to look at this water then, after the death of Chebotarevskaya, Sologub's wife; it was terrifying. Many came.

On Vasilievsky Island, I turned on to Maly Prospect and walked, crossing Line after Line on the city's grid of streets. Some things, of course, had changed, but everything is recognizable. I turned right on 17th Line and walked a block to Smolensky Cemetery. Here it was, the cemetery dear to me; my memory had not led me astray. My heart began thumping as I entered the cemetery gates, even stopping for a minute. I started off along the central tree-lined alley, passing the church, and stopped again.

I remembered. Straight: to my mother. My mother. But which way to her, Anastasia's mother? After all, we had come here together more than once. I thought it was to the left. I stepped off the path and began squeezing my way between graves, crunching on fallen branches. I read names. Sologub, Chebotarevskaya ... How about that? I was just thinking about Chebotarevskaya and, there you go, we met here and I was not surprised.

Voronina ... I felt frightened, oh so frightened. I looked away and then looked again, as if I were running. Voronina Antonina. Mikhailovna. That initial A in her name took my breath away. I could not even finish reading. I took a deep breath and tried again: Antonina, not Anastasia. Thus, Anastasia is not denoted here. And what follows from that? Nothing, I fear. It was simply joyful for me to find out that Anastasia was not in this grave.

As I was leaving, I came across a pauper by the cemetery gates. He had no yellow leaves in his hands this time: this was seemingly already some other pauper. And now it's May, so how could there be yellow leaves here? Even so: it occurred to me that if I turned my head, she'd be behind me . . . Fainthearted, I did not turn. When I gave money to the pauper, I asked him to pray for Anastasia and Innokenty.

'For health, for repose?' he asked.

It began to drizzle.

'I don't know . . . I cannot be sure in either case.'

All the same, it is too bad I did not turn around. This was a moment when anything might have happened.

MONDAY

On a May day in 1921, Ostapchuk and I were knocking together wooden display boards. They asked him:

'What is your name?'

And he said:

'Ostapchuk. Ivan Mikhailovich.'

After the clerk wet her pencil with saliva, that's what she wrote down, right there, on one of the boards, on its fluttering sheet. She had a copying pencil; her lips and tongue were violet. Her hair was tied with a scarf, golden under red. The sun had been shining all morning. Completely insignificant events take place for some reason and this is how they are recalled.

The display boards were for agitational purposes and thus intended for use with posters. We were making them on the Zhdanovka embankment in the yard at a carpenter's workshop, to fulfill our labor service. We did not even know *what* would hang on them, what sort of agitation. We simply took old boards from a huge pile, sawed them up into pieces of the correct size, and placed them neatly on the ground. We tossed two boards on top, width-wise, and fastened them to the boards lying on the ground. Then we turned them over and nailed frames made from wooden strips along the edges. The result was a display board.

Ostapchuk took off his high-collared jacket and shirt. I told him: 'You'll catch cold. It's cool, you know.'

'No,' said Ostapchuk, 'I won't catch a cold in the sun. My body should feel the sun for once.'

Ostapchuk's body truly was defiantly white, unpleasantly white, like some night creature's.

'And I want to spare the jacket and shirt, too,' he added a few minutes later. 'I wouldn't want to ruin them working.'

I did not understand Ostapchuk's apprehension: his clothes were blatantly shabby. But I kept silent. I did not take my things off. Anticipating a later camp habit, I already felt then that the more a person was wearing, the better.

During the break, they brought us each a hunk of bread, lump of sugar, and mug of carrot tea from the workshop. Ostapchuk poured out his tea and offered to do the same for me. I wavered at first but he insisted. Ostapchuk carried himself like a person who firmly knows what he is doing. I poured out the contents of my mug, too. And then Ostapchuk took from his rucksack, lying on the boards, a bottle containing a cloudy liquid. From his sly squint, I understood I should express approval. And indifference about the poured-out tea, even if it was carrot. I expressed both things, though drinking homebrew with Ostapchuk was no great joy.

'My wife's relatives from the village sent it,' said my drinking-mate. 'Do you have relatives in a village?'

No, I did not have any relatives like that. I did not even have a wife.

Ostapchuk poured homebrew into the mugs with a gurgle. He

shifted the bottle from mug to mug without raising the neck but not spilling a drop. The smell of impure alcohol made itself sharply felt in the air.

'To the success of our agitation,' said Ostapchuk.

Judging from the grimace he fabricated, he did not believe in that success. We clinked with a tinny sound. I sipped from the mug and, between swallows, ate up my bread and then the sugar, too. Ostapchuk limited himself to the bread, neatly placing his sugar in his rucksack after licking it a few times.

He and I lay on the boards for the remainder of the break. Ostapchuk told of his life and I watched clouds float across the sky. They floated very quickly, changing form and even color as they went. They appeared from behind the workshop's wall and soon hid behind the roof of the next house. Each was the embodiment of fluidity and changeability, unlike Ostapchuk, who had served as a watchman at the Pulkovo Observatory his whole life. The observatory was not in operation so there was nothing for him to watch over for the time being.

I experienced a feeling close to happiness from the smell of the boards, from that May day, and even from Ostapchuk's stories. Everything that I saw and felt on that day distinctly spoke to how life was only beginning. And if life's simplest events are so fresh and joyful, then what can be expected from outstanding events that still lie ahead? That is how things seemed to me then.

TUESDAY

Seva says to me:

'Join the party of the Bolsheviks!'

It is already June. Sun. The sun is breaking its way through oak foliage in Petrovsky Park. We are walking along a path, stepping on last year's acorns.

'Why join?'

'To organize the revolution. According to Marx, revolutions are the locomotives of history.'

It turns out Seva is now a Marxist.

'What if,' I am asking, 'the locomotive heads the wrong way? After all, you're not the one steering.'

Seva does not allow that possibility. He looks at me with anger; this gaze of his appeared some time ago.

'The party,' he says, 'is strength. There are so many of us! Everyone cannot be mistaken.'

In the first place, they can.

In the second place, it is enough for the engineer to be mistaken.

In the third place, this can be a matter of intentional action. Bad-intentioned.

I don't say any of this to Seva because I don't want to anger him more. In another situation, I might have said something, but I don't want to now. This summer day is dear to me, as are the whistles of steamboats on the Neva, and our walking along the path. 'The party is strength.' And Seva, I think as I walk alongside him, is weak. And is raging at me out of his own weakness because I know him through and through. He attaches himself to people who seem strong to him and hopes they will give him part of their strength. They will not give him anything. For a moment, it occurs to me that if Seva were to become a tyrant, I would be the first person he would destroy.

Seva, where are you now? In which grave?

WEDNESDAY

As I was carrying out the rubbish this morning, I noticed a person rummaging around in the *container*. Despite the wonderful name, a rubbish bin remains a rubbish bin and people are not shy about rummaging around in it, as before. This person was not shy, either. He set all the things that caught his eye on the cover of the container and examined them in more detail. He asked me to show him my rubbish. After looking over everything I had brought, he unexpectedly asked:

'So, is it true they thawed you?'

I told Geiger about that.

'That's fame,' he told me. 'And recognition.'

FRIDAY

Geiger brought me eyeglasses today. The frames are massive and the lenses are plain glass: they're so nobody recognizes me. He said he could have just bought dark glasses but, in the first place, they're impractical to wear, and in the second, they attract attention in and of themselves. After the press conference, people truly have begun to recognize me on the street.

'Keep that image in reserve,' said Geiger. 'Never be filmed in the glasses.'

I won't. I removed the glasses when a television crew came to film me later that day. It took them a long time to set up the camera and lights, and powder my face. The interview itself went on for about an hour and a half, too. And I sat that whole time without glasses.

'What are the main differences between that time and this one?'

The journalist's face was indistinguishable because of the bright light. It is hard to speak when you cannot see your conversation partner's face.

'You have to understand that even sounds were different then, ordinary street sounds. The clopping of horses completely disappeared from life and if you take motors, those sounded different, too. Back then there were single shots from exhaust fumes, now there is a general rumbling. Klaxons are different, too. Oh, and I forgot something important: nobody shouts now. Before, though, junk dealers shouted, and the tinsmiths and the women selling milk, too. Sounds have changed a lot . . .'

'Sounds, though, that's only half of it. I think words changed, that's what's important. They changed, didn't they?'

'I suppose,' I answered. 'I suppose some changed. It's just that it's easier to get used to new words than to new sounds or, let's say, smells.'

'I keep trying to draw you out on historical topics,' he laughed, 'and you keep talking about sounds and about smells.'

Blood rushed to my head. Oh, how it rushed.

'Do you really not understand that this is the only thing worth mentioning? You can read about words in a history textbook but you cannot read about sounds. Do you know what it means to be deprived of those sounds in one instant?'

I took a deep breath. I am calm when I'm alone or with Geiger. He understands I have been deprived of my own time and so does not say too much. Forgives me my hysterics. Now he gently but firmly saw the television crew out. Their bewildered mumble-mumble-mumble was audible from the hallway.

When everybody had gone, I put on the glasses and looked at myself in the mirror for a long time.

SATURDAY

I don't know how it happens that exact opposite things can be denoted by the same name. There was one Chekist on the island, a scoundrel the likes of which the world had never known, and, well, his surname was Voronin. How can that be? Why? Or is there no logical consistency in the use of a name? I dreamt of retribution against him, inventing it during work, and that gave me strength when it seemed I already had none remaining. For a while, I wanted to ask God to enter him on those lists where nothing is ever crossed off, where there is no forgiveness if you end up on them, but I feared his name would cast a shadow on Anastasia's father. I recalled Zaretsky and how I wished him ill, and then how Zaretsky died; I was unbearably ashamed because, essentially, Zaretsky possessed human traits, but Voronin did not. I will not describe what Voronin did.

People ask me again and again how I survived in the camp. They mean not only the physical side of life but also the side that makes a person a person. It is a legitimate question because camp is hell, not so much for the bodily torture as for the dehumanization of many who land there. In order to prevent the remnants of what is human in oneself being destroyed, one must leave that hell for at least a time, if only mentally. To think about Paradise.

SUNDAY

Oftentimes, you'll wake up early in the morning at the dacha and everyone is still asleep. You tiptoe out to the veranda so as not to wake anyone. You step carefully but the floorboards creak anyway.

That creak is soft and does not disturb the sleepers. You try to open a window noiselessly but the sash does not yield, the glass rattles, and you already regret you started doing all this. But you are happy when you open the window wide. The curtains don't flutter, there's not the slightest breeze. You're surprised at how thick and pine-scented the air can be. A spider crawls along the sash. You place your elbows on the windowsill (the old paint is peeling and sticks to your skin) and look outside. The grass is sparkling with drops and the shadows on it are sharp, because it is morning. It is as quiet as in Paradise. For some reason I think it should be quiet in Paradise.

This is essentially it, Paradise. My mother, father, and grandmother are sleeping in the house. We love each other: being together is soothing and good for us. All that we need is for time to stop moving, so as not to disturb the tranquility of that moment. I want no new events: let what already exists be, is that really not enough? Because if everything continues on, those dear to me will die. Those sleeping peacefully in the house will die. Without knowing what a terrifying precipice our happiness hangs over. They will wake up, live out the events destined for them, and then the end will come. It is obvious, after all, where the course lies. It awaits me, too. But most likely it awaits my grandmother before the others; I still see no alarm in her eyes. Surely she has a hunch that our well-being is illusory, that it is only for the moment.

Paradise is the absence of time. If time stops, there will be no more events. Nonevents will remain. The pine trees will remain, brown and gnarled below, smooth and amber at the top. The gooseberries by the fence will not go anywhere, either. The squeak of the gate, a child's muffled crying at the next dacha, the first pounding of rain on the veranda roof . . . all the things that changes in government and the falls of empires do not wipe out. Whatever happens outside history is timeless, liberated.

MONDAY

Geiger was here. Before he left, he said, all of a sudden, that Anastasia is alive.

Anastasia is alive.

May 24, 1999. Anastasia is alive.

TUESDAY

A sleepless night. I call Geiger early in the morning so we can go see her together. He clears his throat for a moment and answers in a rusty voice:

'She's in the hospital.'

'What do you mean she's in the hospital?'

'Hospital Number 87. That's unimportant. It's too early now anyway; they only take calls in about two hours.'

I look at the clock: it's six in the morning, which is why his voice sounds like that.

He calls me himself at 8.30.

'We have to postpone the trip. Anastasia Sergeyevna isn't ready yet.'

I'm silent. Because I do not even know what to ask. She's in Hospital Number 87 and does not want to see me.

'She said she's not ready,' Geiger mutters. 'You know, it's understandable in the circumstances. A woman . . .'

But I do not understand. I'm not judging, I'm not angry, I simply do not understand. I call Geiger again in the afternoon.

'Maybe she didn't register that "I" as *this* I; something like that is possible at the age of ninety-three, is it not?'

'Her memory really does seem on and off ...' Geiger begins muttering again. 'But I think she registered everything about you.'

Then I especially do not understand. What is this? Shyness? But one can be shy after twenty years or, well, after thirty, though not after sixty or more. A meeting like this is almost posthumous and how you look makes no difference here. And even then, it basically seems to me that at that age it makes little difference if you're a woman or a man. But what do you know: it doesn't seem that way to Anastasia.

WEDNESDAY

I know she's somewhere nearby but I cannot see her. How am I supposed to live with that? How long must I wait? I cannot even do something to distract myself from thoughts about her. I used to read a lot and watch television, studying, as they say, the new reality. But now I think only about Anastasia; moreover, I am not just recalling her, I am attempting to imagine what she's like now. I am attempting and I am afraid. It's not me I am scared for, it's Anastasia. I am afraid of her fear of startling me.

I remember how she said she never wanted to die – and she has not died yet. She did not want to age, either, so maybe she has also not aged? Doubtful ... I am purposely not asking Geiger anything about her appearance. What is she like now? Bald? Toothless? Bald is not certain but toothless probably is.

Her hair was soft, like ... silk. I did not want to describe it that way since it has somehow become a common expression; everybody uses it. But truly, like silk. Like her silk nightgown that I sometimes touched during our late conversations. Silk has the attribute of draping. Maybe even cascading. My hair is coarser: it can curl, gather in locks, stand on end, but not cascade – it cannot. Because it is not silk. I would bury my face in Anastasia's hair and ask in a whisper, how is it like this? What is the nature of this wheaten flow that is quiet, fresh, and spill on her shoulders? I would ask: does this belong to me, is it now my attribute, too? Of course, she answered, how could it not since the attributes of each of us are becoming common attributes, ours. I placed my hand under that flow and drew it to my hair. And might one think, I would ask, that this is my hair? That, she answered, is the only possible way to think.

She is at Hospital Number 87. Where, I wonder, is that hospital?

THURSDAY

Today Geiger told me how her life turned out. I had not asked him about that: I knew the information was not likely to gladden me, but I did not think of interrupting him.

Anastasia waited for me a fairly long time, until 1932, then she married Pozdeev, the chief design engineer at the Baltic Factory. In 1933, their son Innokenty (Geiger give me a significant look) was born, which makes it clear she was thinking about me even then. But was no longer waiting for me.

In 1938, Pozdeev was accused of collaborating with foreign spies and sentenced to the firing squad. Innokenty died during the first winter of the blockade. As Anastasia said later, her two main losses were associated with that name. After Innokenty's death, she had no desire to even live, let alone fight, and she lay down alongside the little boy, to die. They found her in an empty apartment, brought her to the hospital, and then evacuated her to Kazan.

After the war, Anastasia married a professor and entomologist, Osipov. Despite the birth of their son Sergei (it was her father's name this time) in 1946, the marriage did not end up lasting. Anastasia stated, with disappointment, that Osipov (in accordance with the object of his studies) turned out to be a small person. In the end, Anastasia left him, taking her son with her.

By all appearances, the abyss stretching between the former spouses was so vast that the boy even received his mother's surname, Voronin. Or maybe this was not related so much to the abyss as to Anastasia's selfless love for her father. Sergei Voronin saw his father two or three times when he was a child and remembered that vaguely. And when the boy grew up, his father was no longer alive: Osipov died unexpectedly on one of his Central Asian expeditions.

To a certain extent, Sergei Voronin's fate repeated the fate of a father unknown to him. Oddly enough (or perhaps not, given the odds?) he also became an entomologist. Late marriage and early divorce awaited him, too. There were some differences, however, compared to his father's life. The first was that Sergei Voronin had a daughter (1980) whom he named, obviously, Anastasia. The second and most substantial difference was that this researcher did not die in Central Asia: due to the type of insects he studied, he did not even go there.

During perestroika, he went off to a university in the United States of America and remained there. His former wife continued living in Petersburg but her daughter preferred not to remain with her. At the age of fourteen (after yet another argument with her mother) she moved in with her grandmother, and the two Anastasias began living together. Three weeks ago, the elder Anastasia ended up in the hospital.

The elder Anastasia. She was seventeen and I was twenty-three when we parted. She is now ninety-three and I am around thirty; that is my biological age, if Geiger is to be believed. I was lying in liquid nitrogen and she was maturing, blossoming, fading, and growing decrepit. Apparently her character changed for the worse: she quarreled with colleagues at work (what was her profession? I wonder) and called her husband an insect. She probably did call him that, her entomologist husband. How could she not?

Somehow, it is a relief for me that she remained Voronina.

Do I want to see her?

FRIDAY

Very much.

I very much want to see her.

SATURDAY

I rose early in the morning, had some coffee. I found the number for City Hospital Number 87 in the telephone directory. I called. As I had expected, the hospital is far away, on the outskirts – I cannot reach it on my own. I ordered a taxi. I sensed that I would go to see her today but told Geiger nothing. I needed to go there alone.

I got in the car and we headed south. It was nice to ride through the old part of the city, but my soul began pining when we reached

Kupchino. It is not a Petersburg-like district. We stopped at the hospital: it is squalid, befitting the district. Dilapidated. Cracks in the windows are stuck together with strips of paper; there is plywood in some places instead of glass. Old buildings are not as dispiriting as this, even in the same condition: even those not cared for have a dignity. The new ones are flimsy and inauthentic; it is immediately visible that they are shams.

Two people in white lab coats were smoking under the canopy, spitting thickly on the ground. Two camels. I walked past them to the information window. There was an old woman there with her glasses on a cord.

'What room is Anastasia Sergeyevna Voronina in?'

She put on her glasses. Wetting her finger with saliva, she paged through something. I had forgotten to ask on the telephone when visiting hours are here. And about indoor shoes and about a gown.

'Fourth floor, room 407.'

'When are visiting hours?'

'Visit when you like,' she said, not looking up.

She didn't open her lips.

'So how does she look now?'

'Who?'

'Voronina.'

She didn't answer. It would have been better for me to ask about a gown. Or about the shoes.

'By the way, there are two camels standing out there.' I pointed at the entrance. 'You should look at the entrance, not at me.'

I walked up the stairs (the elevator wasn't working) and only every other light was lit. I nearly fell into artificial plants in the half-darkness. I had run into these mass-produced objects several times already in my new life, primarily in government-run institutions. Their beauty is dubious for my taste, though they don't require light. They most likely require the opposite: the less light, the better they look. It is strange that I was capable of thinking about them in this condition. It was from excitement.

Everything I am writing now is from excitement. From my flickering consciousness that seems not yet fully thawed. I don't know why I wrote all this: after all, I did not go anywhere today. I found the telephone number, address, and even a photograph of the hospital in the directory but I did not go. I only called and found out the room number: 407. I did not have enough resolve to go.

SUNDAY

The day began the same as yesterday. I rose early in the morning, had some coffee. I ordered a taxi and consequently went after all. Hospital, windows stuck together, two smokers by the entrance – everything was just like the photograph. And the witch at Information, her glasses on a cord.

Here it is, fourth floor. I walk along the corridor, reading rhombuses with the room numbers: sometimes they're in place, sometimes they're broken off. The numeral 407 is penciled on a door. I knock. My heart is knocking, too. From inside (not immediately) someone suggests entering – the voice is female, coarse, and almost male. I press on the door: it's jammed. The same voice suggests pressing harder. The door opens, shaking spasmodically. And this all shakes me a little even now, as I write.

I enter and the sharp smell of urine hits my nose. Eight beds in two rows. Eight old women: seven are lying, one is half-sitting, the one by the window. She's apparently the one who answered. I attempt to guess which of them is Anastasia.

'Who are you here to see?' asks the sitting woman.

Yes, she had answered: a rare voice. I can only imagine having a voice like that nearby for an entire life . . .

'Anastasia Sergeyevna.'

'Voronina? And who are you to her, her grandson? Or just a relative?'

A good question; the main thing is that there is a choice. I look at the questioner. Her face is not visible against the light, there is only a voice.

'Just a relative.'

The old women begin moving around in their beds; some of them lift themselves on their elbows a little. A tin mug falls from one of the bedside tables; I pick it up. On the rim of the mug, where lips touched it, is dried-up chewed bread.

'Well, if you're a relative, then take care of her,' advises the voice. 'The old woman's been lying in shit for two days and nobody will come.' And she unexpectedly reduces her volume: 'Nobody wants to wash old women.'

Nobody does. My eyes are becoming accustomed to the lighting and I am beginning to distinguish the speaker's facial features. There is no fierceness in them. A rural snub nose with tiers of wrinkles extending from it. Gray hair coming out from under a headscarf.

'Katya, don't you cause a fuss,' sounds from one of the beds. 'A person has come here for the first time, and you're attacking him.'

'And where was he before?' wonders Katya.

'Wherever he was, he's not there now, [This, I notice, is exactly right.]' Did her granddaughter come yesterday? She did. And washing? A nurse could do that, by the way.'

Katya chews at her lips, as if she's weighing that possibility, too.

'You can wait until kingdom come for our nurse here.' Her voice sounds almost conciliatory. 'She won't lift a finger without a hundred note. Probably boozing it up in the staff room.'

And I still have no idea which one here is Anastasia. They are not pointing her out to me because they think I know her. Finally, the woman who has been talking with Katya waves a hand in the direction of one of the beds.

'Don't listen to all of us. Go to your grandmother.'

I understand where I need to go, and I take the first step. Essentially, I knew this from the first second but was afraid of confirmation. Now that the confirmation has been received, I go. I examine the bedside table without looking up at Anastasia. Bottle of mineral water, tube of lotion, glass with dentures. These are Anastasia's dentures.

Anastasia. She is lying with her eyes closed. Mouth half-open. Breathing heavily. Sometimes bubbles form when she breathes and burst right away. Her left hand is on the blanket, clenched in a fist, as if threatening someone. Whom? The Bolsheviks who killed her father and sank me into liquid nitrogen? Life in general? I take that hand by the wrist and bring it to my lips. I did that so many times, barely touching, nearly imperceptibly. Studying every line at the bend of the hand, sensing the invisible hairs. And now the hand is different, completely different. Wet from my tears. The fist unclenches slowly: it is too late to threaten. And there is nobody to threaten.

'Maybe you could . . . wash her after all.'

That's Katya.

'I'm ready. I just don't know how it's done . . .'

'None of them know at first. We'll give you hints.'

She would make it even on the Solovetsky Islands.

They order me to pull an oilcloth out from under the mattress and unfold it. After taking Anastasia by the shoulder, I shift her on her side (her flesh is light) and put the oilcloth underneath. Anastasia is in a disposable diaper (I think that's what it's called?), the same kind I've seen babies wearing on television.

'Don't be afraid,' Katya commands. 'Everything becomes habit.'

I am not afraid. I recall how I dreamt of seeing Anastasia's nakedness. I cast a glance at her face. Anastasia's eyes open slightly but there is no awareness in them. That is even better.

'Take it off. It's good her granddaughter started buying those things: at first we got by with cloth diapers.'

I unfasten the diaper. I separate it from her flesh with a peeling sound. Smell. To be blunt, it is a strong stench. Well, and so what if there's a stench? I inhaled and touched just about everything on Solovki. The only person close to me is lying in front of me and if that person's condition is like this, it must be taken for what it is. It is happiness that the person is here and held on until my return to life. I ball up the diaper and place it neatly on the floor.

'Now take the bedpan out from under the bed and put it on the oilcloth. Lift the old woman by her lower back and put her rear end on the bedpan.' Katya stands and shuffles as she fumbles for her slippers. 'Her granddaughter deals with it on her own. You'll learn, too.'

Katya leaves the room for a minute and returns with a sponge and pitcher. The water in the pitcher is warm and – judging from the color – has manganese crystals in it. Oddly enough, Katya's officer-like tone helps me: it does not allow me to ease up. I pour a little water with my left hand and wash Anastasia's groin with my right. I cautiously guide the sponge.

'Spread her legs wider, otherwise it won't all get washed!'

Do not be silent, Katya, do not be silent: this would be impossible to do in quiet. A piece of feces floats into the bedpan under the flow of the water.

I wipe Anastasia with a towel. I wipe the oilcloth. I take out a disposable diaper and wash the bedpan. I am ordered to rub everything with lotion so there is no irritation. I press lotion out of the tube on my fingers and touch her groin. I feel my hand shaking. I so desired this flower at one time.

MONDAY

It is the last day of May; tomorrow will be summer. I am writing just after midnight: strictly speaking, it is already summer. I remembered something summery when I was going to see Anastasia in the afternoon.

I run into her by chance on the corner of Kamennoostrovsky and Bolshoy. Where are you going? Home. So am I. She and I walk along Bolshoy Prospect, the sun in our eyes. The clattering wooden soles of her shoes echoing. She is trying to step carefully: they clatter no matter what, they are those kind of shoes. At the corner of Ordinarnaya Street a droshky comes out of nowhere. At the last instant, I extend my arm and hold Anastasia back. Her bosom touches my arm. Something within me explodes: from the contact but even more from fear that she could fall under the droshky. On a sunny day. In a warm Baltic breeze. She would be lying on the pavement and the wind would rustle her dress. Legs awkwardly twisted, the worn wood of her soles visible. I had always been afraid for her: what if something suddenly happened to her, she being so ethereal and fragile? She turned out to be more unbreakable than I thought. Life had made her that way.

I ran into her granddaughter as I approached the door to the hospital room. I had noticed her on the stairs and realized who she was. I walked two paces behind her, my heart pounding like yesterday. Before I had got a good look at her I already knew there was a resemblance: the hair, the gait, it was all like Anastasia's. I probably expected that, perhaps even hoped for it, it is just that she truly did resemble her when she turned around. By the door. After noticing me.

'Are you Innokenty?'

I nodded. I was afraid my voice would fail me.

'And I'm Anastasia, too, but I go by Nastya.' She offered her hand to me. 'As soon as I saw you on television, I knew right away that you'd come.'

She smiled. I realised I was still holding her hand. A cool hand. Thin, each bone making itself felt.

'My doctor told me about Anastasia . . .'

'I know. I'm the one who told your doctor.' Her hand slipped out of mine. 'I thought it would be important for you.'

Important . . . Her smile is like Anastasia's. They say children become like their grandmothers and grandfathers, not their parents.

The stench in the room no longer hit the nose like yesterday. It had not lessened, it simply stopped making itself felt. As before, Anastasia was unconscious but even so, it seemed to me that she was better today than yesterday. Her eyes were open. There was no focus in her gaze – it moved aimlessly around the room – but it moved.

Nastya and I washed Anastasia's hair. To begin, we took away the pillows and wrapped a towel around her neck so the water wouldn't trickle. Then I brought a basin with warm water. We carefully placed it where the pillows had been and began washing. I held Anastasia's head and Nastya squeezed shampoo on her hand and lathered the hair with massaging motions. Anastasia's hair was short, almost like a buzz cut. This, along with the unblinking gaze, lent her a look of complete madness. When I poured water from the pitcher to wash off the rest of the shampoo, Anastasia blinked a few times but nothing in her gaze changed.

'I remember her hair long,' I said to Nastya for some reason.

'They cut it at the hospital so it would be easier to wash.'

Then we washed her body with a sponge, placing the oilcloth and towels under her. Nastya cut her nails. Anastasia neither resisted nor participated.

'My grandmother was basically fine just a few days ago,' said Nastya. 'Even here at the hospital. She managed to refuse to see you. But now, you can see yourself how . . .'

Nastya and I ran across some journalists as we left the room. I squinted from the many camera flashes.

'What did you feel when you saw your sweetheart after so many decades?'

I squeezed my eyelids even tighter and did not unsqueeze them. That's what I sometimes did as a child; that saved me from a lot. That is how I saw myself on the evening news.

TUESDAY

It rained this morning. The rain pelted against the panes, as if someone were pounding them with a directed stream. My apartment is on the corner and the wind came from one side, then the other. Lying in bed, I watched as the water flowed along the glass in thin, translucent waves. I rose out of curiosity when the waves began blinking in many colors. Down below were a police car and an accident. Right then I recalled another accident: two truck drivers, on this very spot, also in the rain. And I was standing by the window just like this – what year was that? Everything on this earth has already happened . . . I pressed my forehead to the glass. Two cars had bumped into each other. Not exactly hard: only the headlights were knocked out. And there were two people standing in the rain: wearing suits and neckties, all in one piece after the accident, cursing away to one another. Like the truck drivers, incidentally.

Geiger stopped by briefly, brought money. This was not the first time he brought me money and I keep not asking where it comes from. I would like to hope it is from the government, by way of compensation, or from the Duma there, from the president. I wonder, do they have a budget for thawing out the population? And the banknotes are just hilarious, small by comparison with before. Of course I will need to ask where they are from.

Nurse Angela came over: she washed the floors and gave me an injection. At my request, she no longer comes over every day, so it was good timing with the floors. The injection, though (so it seems to me), was made from pure meanness, because what is the sense of injections that are not made regularly? She simply jabbed me in the rear so I won't get too arrogant. In the beginning, after all, I preferred that she not spend the nights here and then I asked that she come by less often: needless to say, she is offended. In what capacity did Geiger bring her to me? I wonder. She irritates me tremendously.

At one in the afternoon I called for a taxi. Nastya and I had agreed to meet at the hospital entrance today. At two, right after her classes end at the university. Nastya is a student in the economics department. In my view, that's an unusual choice for a young woman, but life has changed, completely changed. How much do I know about this life to speak of what is unusual?

I was at the hospital at 1.30. I walked around the building, attempting to guess which windows are Anastasia's. I remember that the glass in her room had cracks stuck together with strips of paper. But the hospital windows abounded with those strips, they were all over the place – how could you guess? Of course Andersen's story and the chalk crosses surfaced in my memory. My grandmother read it to me before bed. The reading lost its intonation and then its sound, too, as she read further into the story. Of the two of us, my grandmother would fall asleep first.

Nastya came at exactly two: now that's precision. She was fragrant with some unfamiliar aromas, delicate and almost imperceptible. Women smelled different in previous times: how could I not recall Anastasia's hair here? Maybe I'm old-fashioned but that wave of freshness that . . . I seem to be confused.

What I mean is this. When we sat down on the bench to put on our shoe covers, Nastya leaned back slightly and my face ended up at the back of her head as she was straightening that strange footwear over her sandals: the smell of Anastasia's hair had broken through Nastya's delicate perfume! I involuntarily moved closer to her and she turned around right then, as if she sensed everything with the back of her head and caught me in my motion. I blushed: she had sensed and caught me. And might be interpreting everything incorrectly.

A surprise awaited Nastya and me: Anastasia had been transferred to a private room. The hospital's chief physician came down to greet us in the lobby in order to take us there. He's a large figure, thickset, with a big head. He is not bowlegged, however, I noted. A white lab coat was thrown over his three-piece suit. There was a stethoscope on his neck: who does he listen to in his office? I wonder.

'I'm the chief physician of this hospital,' he said and touched a badge on his lab coat: 'Chief Physician.'

He smelled of coffee so it was obvious what he had been torn away from. He smelled of a cigarette, too. I had to think he had hurriedly stubbed it out in an ashtray when they'd called him from downstairs. And why, one might ask, did they call? Why did they transfer her to a private room? Had they interpreted my closed eyes as an expression of horror, as my full lack of acceptance of living conditions at the hospital?

'Even under our complex conditions, we decided to provide Voronina with her own room. The decision was natural, if you consider ...'

He was primarily addressing me and only rarely Nastya. I nodded but was not listening, entranced by the rhythm of all the doors flying past us. One of the doors opened and we saw Anastasia. On some sort of technically advanced bed, not even a bed but a vehicle with numerous handles, buttons, and wheels. In snow-white linens. In the center of the room.

It was a strange sight. Anastasia was a part of ordinary life when she was lying in the overcrowded stinking room. She was floating, as it were, in the stream of a daily routine that was doleful but natural. Now she was no longer part of something larger. She was juxtaposed against something larger, like any object pulled from life. The monument in the center of a public square, the coffin in the middle of a church. And Anastasia was also already apart from the realm of bodily discharges. When Nastya took out fresh towels, they told her she need not wash her grandmother any longer; they said they would wash her themselves.

Grandmother.

WEDNESDAY

It was sunny when I woke up. I opened the window: warm weather. Nastya called at around eleven and proposed we meet at metro stop Sportivnaya in an hour. It turns out that metro stop is right near my building, by St Prince Vladimir's Cathedral. Nastya was already standing there when I came out. With a gray canvas bag and a sweater tossed over the bag. Her shoulders uncovered. Her hair was down, as Anastasia's was when she would go out to the kitchen in the middle of the night nearly a century ago. I (a gentleman) took Nastya's bag; a pink streak remained on her shoulder. There were barely discernible freckles around the stripe. Maybe Anastasia had those, too; I had not seen her shoulders. Although no, I had seen them, the day before yesterday.

We went into the metro and Nastya bought tokens.

'I've never ridden on the metro before.'

'You haven't missed much.'

We rode down a moving staircase, boarded an underground train, exited it, boarded another train, and this was all for the first time. It seems that I truly hadn't missed much. It particularly annoys me that there are speakers on all around, for advertising. You can turn away from posters but how can you get away from the sound? I pressed my ears; Nastya laughed.

After leaving the metro, we ended up on a walkway made of concrete squares. I was walking this leg of the journey for the first time. To the left there stretched a row of unpainted garages, to the right a wasteland with stunted birch trees planted in a line. In the midst of dried-out mud with tire tracks, these birches were not nice to look at. Their life was torture. Their squalid flirtatiousness was bleaker than the garages' rust, which at least had no pretenses. We were walking through a Petersburg that I did not yet know. The hospital arose in front of us about twenty minutes later.

Anastasia was nicely dressed but unresponsive, as before. Sometimes she opened her eyes and it seemed she would begin speaking at any moment. But she did not speak. Only labored breathing escaped from her sunken lips. A nurse was keeping house in the room for the first several minutes (the glassy-metallic clinking of a tray), but then she went out. We sat on chairs to Anastasia's left. I took her by the hand and pressed lightly. Anastasia opened her eyes. And closed them. Her hand remained in mine. My fingers cautiously drew her fingers apart – we had loved doing that at one time.

When I was convinced that everyone had left the apartment in the mornings, I would go to her room and sit next to the bed. Of course she heard me coming in and taking the chair – I did see her eyelids quivering. We both knew she was not sleeping but that moment when her blue eyes opened was dear to us. We both wanted me to be the first person she saw. I would bend and kiss her eyes, feeling her lashes with my lips. Anastasia would take a hand out from under the blanket and slowly, as if only half-awake, move it toward me. The hand was thin, with dark blue veins, like a special bed snake. Our fingers would join and press against each other, sometimes until it was painful, until something cracked, and only my thumb would remain free and with that – in spite of the pain, or maybe even because of it – I would stroke Anastasia's hand.

'My grandmother once said the reason for the catastrophe was some Zaretsky,' Nastya quietly uttered. 'That all the troubles began with his denunciation.'

'One could put it that way . . .'

I felt her gaze.

'Or could it be otherwise?'

'I cannot rule out that everything began even earlier. It's just unclear exactly when.'

Nastya took me by the arm on the way to the metro. And that was nice.

THURSDAY

Nastya and I met at Sportivnaya again and went to the hospital. I forgot to put on my glasses and people recognized me in the metro. They asked for my autograph, even several at once. We got out at the next station and I rooted around in my bag for a long time: the glasses were found after all. There were television crews at the hospital when we arrived; Nastya noticed them from a distance. I took off my glasses so as not to reveal my alternate image. We walked through a formation of journalists and I didn't utter a single word. Once we had entered the hospital, a dark-haired young woman with a microphone moved to greet me. I could have walked past her, too, but I stopped. Something about her face won me over.

'Do you love her like before?' she asked.

Yes, a nice face. Only someone with a face like that can ask questions of that sort. Those who had been standing on the street came into the admissions area, too, and surrounded us.

'I love her.'

Like before?

FRIDAY

Even as I was waking up, I realized I was taking ill. Nagging pain in my joints, aching cheekbones. Watery eyes. I called Geiger and said I seemed to have influenza. The flu, agreed Geiger. He ordered me not to leave the house. He came over about forty minutes later, bringing medicines.

'It was obvious,' he said, 'that riding the metro would end up this way because you don't have immunity to today's infections. But this is something you have to go through, too. It's just important not to go to the hospital for now: it's dangerous for both you and Anastasia. It's probably even more dangerous for her.'

I don't have immunity yet; however, she apparently does. After Geiger left, I attempted to call Nastya but didn't catch her at home. At the appointed time, I went out to the chapel by the metro. Nastya was standing there and I approached her uncertainly, even somehow sideways, covering my mouth with my hand. She noticed me walking from afar and followed my approach with slight surprise. She moved a lock of hair behind her ear with her thumb (a gesture of uncertainty). Remaining two or three steps away, I explained to her what happened. She understood everything and we agreed to call each other.

Solitariness awaited me at home. Geiger's morning visit didn't count: it is his doctorly duty to care for me. Yes, he fulfills his duty responsibly to the highest degree, even in a friendly manner, but that just doesn't compare with how I once sat by Anastasia's bed when she was ill. Even lay there. Read *Robinson Crusoe* to her while she held my hand. And now, after meeting an eternity later, our hands had touched again. As then, Anastasia was lying in bed and was again sick. It is true the illness (illness?) is different now, but Anastasia is different, too. She has changed a lot.

Nevertheless, the fact that she is here makes everything easier. Her existence on earth is evidence that my previous life was not just a dream. After lying down in bed, I can close my eyes and think that Anastasia will walk over to me now, take me by the hand, and share her coolness. This can still be imagined, too: she will rise from her hospital bed, come here, and take me by the hand. Nothing is impossible during a person's life: impossibility sets in only with death. And even that is not necessarily the case.

SUNDAY

I spent all day yesterday in a drowse. Geiger is uneasy: he had not expected that the flu would be so severe.

'You're paying for not being sick all those decades,' he told me. 'It's an adaptation process.'

Nicely stated . . .

A nurse comes to see me three times a day. Not Angela but a dull middle-aged woman, a sick man's dream. Takes my temperature, gives me pills. Sometimes gives injections. She calls Geiger each time (I hear his distressed, mosquito-like voice on the other end of the line). He comes to visit every evening now.

The last time I took ill was on the island: of course, care was different there. Different. In the evening the medical attendant took my temperature: it was 39.5.

'Excuse me from work tomorrow,' I requested.

'I can't,' he said. 'The quota for being excused has already been used up. Just go for light work. It's 39.5, so I'll intercede.'

I barely rose in the morning. The weak barracks light bulb blurring in my eyes. Darkness, November, five hours left until sunrise – and what was the sun there? Worse than the light bulb. I could not believe my ears at the job assignment: ditch-digging. And I had no strength to walk. Not even strength to object. It was very bad, though perhaps a little easier than typhus.

I was standing in water up to my knees. I had bast shoes for footwear but it was even more difficult in bast shoes so people took them off before working in a ditch. I felt an icy cold with my feet; the rest of my body felt fever. Such a fever that the water would start boiling near my feet any minute now. The soles of my feet slipped along the swampy, peaty earth. I pulled earth out of the water, shovel after shovel. It came up to the surface with a squishing sound. As if it is parting from its environment. Bleeding black ooze, shovel after shovel. I could not go on. I lay on the edge of the ditch.

Voronin. I saw Voronin walking with his revolver, but I had no strength to even stir. Yes, it appeared he'd shoot me now, too. And everything would end for me: ditch, wake-up, thin gruel. Zaretsky did well: he had none of this. They whacked him with a heavy object; he didn't even suffer. But I was beaten at interrogations and smothered in the hold of the *Clara Zetkin* so they could finish me off, weakened, on the edge of a ditch. One shot and I'd be gone. No more being read to by my grandmother when I was ill, no dacha in Siverskaya, no Anastasia. That was how much I, alone, would drag off behind me. Or maybe that would all remain somewhere, in some part of the universe, not necessarily in my head after all: it would find itself a tranquil harbor and exist there.

Voronin kicked me and, to my surprise, it didn't hurt. Maybe because I no longer correlated myself with my body. Well, he kicked ... Someone told Voronin I was ill and he kicked me again. I should have shut my eyes, as if I had lost consciousness – why did I not close them? Or lose consciousness for real because assimilating what happens is so difficult when fully conscious.

Voronin acted as he always acted. After beating one of us zeks, he forced him to urinate in a mug. He brought the mug to my face and ordered me to either drink it or go to work. He cocked the gun and counted to three ...

They say that what was done in concentration camps has no statute of limitations. I will send that description to the office of the public prosecutor, police – or what is it – the supreme court: let them hear about Voronin. I feel my temperature rising as I write. There is noise in my head. I will make it to the Day of Judgment, charging Voronin not so much with torment and murder as appropriating the surname dearest to me. Do they attach significance to surnames *there*?

Then I truly lost consciousness. That saved me from being shot and I ended up in the infirmary. Upon recovery, I was sent to an isolation cell on Sekirnaya Mountain, for refusing to work.

MONDAY

Today Geiger announced that nurse Angela will no longer be coming to see me. Well, that's reasonable. I understand why they sent her to me but I don't consider it correct. I don't need such a vulgar nurse.

TUESDAY

One of the television channels showed a film about me today. It was compiled from extracts of interviews that I gave recently. The extracts are interspersed with Solovetsky newsreels, set to sad music. The music takes the place of all the sounds and words from that time, which were, of course, not musical. Especially the words.

They say that a half-truth is a lie. The falsity of that newsreel is not even that it's straightforward flimflam filmed at the order of the GPU. I never saw anyone in the infirmary in clean linens, nobody read the newspaper or played chess in the common room, etc. I repeat: that is not what's at issue. It's simply that, in some strange way, the black-and-white figures darting around the screen stopped corresponding to reality: they are only its faded signs. Just as petro-glyphic drawings in caves – animals and little figures of people – are hilarious and remind one of real people and animals but say nothing about life back then. You look at them but the only thing that is clear is that bison were four-legged and people two-legged, essentially the same as now.

There were Solovetsky sounds, though: a head striking the bunks when a guard came in, took a zek by the hair, and beat, beat him against the bunk's support post until he was tired; or the snap of nits pressed by a fingernail. There were smells, too. Of squashed bedbugs. Of unwashed bodies: after all, we worked every day until we were worn out but we hardly washed. And that all wove together into the overall smell of despair, the color and sound of despair, because it only seems that they are concealed within the soul and out of reach for the sensory organs.

Of course the sound of the forest and the swaying of ferns and the smell of pine cones and the sky also existed on the island. If you placed your hands to your eyes in the fashion of binoculars, closing out the surroundings, then you could imagine that this was not the sky over Solovki but somewhere over Paris or, at the very least, over Petersburg. Things of this sort gave birth not so much to hope as to a change of fate (it was not foreseen), and they seemed to attest that elements of the rational still exist on earth, in nature if not in people. Here there is also the creak of a door in the wind (a listless sort of creak but then a sudden energetic slamming) and the smell of the fire at the logging site. You look at the fire for a minute, toss in a piece of kindling or two, and that seems to ease things. It burns as it should. Human laws can be revoked but it turns out the physical ones cannot.

I took in the newsreel footage (they showed it with stylized crackling) and recognized a lot. I recognized the Holy Gate: oh, how my heart missed a beat when I entered it for the first time. After all, by stepping from the boat to the dock, I was already in the camp, but I only acknowledged my imprisonment after entering the gate. By mistake I wrote impoverishment, which is not so bad, either. I recognized the chief, that scoundrel Nogtev. Regarding scoundrels, by the way: it seemed to me that Voronin flashed somewhere there, too. Was it him or not?

Take Voronin: who is he now? A heap of bones if, of course, he was not cremated. He instilled such fear in all of us at the time, but now he is dust, a small gray figure in the footage. And I called him a scoundrel; I continue to hate him. It's just that if this is happening now, it works out that I hate the present-day him and it's already obvious who that is. Who, then, do I hate? If I feel all that for the him that was then, does that mean he is not dust? Perhaps Voronin became a part of me by remaining in my memory and I hate him within myself?

WEDNESDAY

Nastya called and asked after my health. It's nice that she's concerned. I catch myself thinking I miss her. I asked after Anastasia's health. I cannot bring myself to say 'your grandmother's,' though that is what Nastya always calls her. Everything is fine, she said, meaning, as usual.

So Nastya said all our troubles began with Zaretsky. Unlike with Voronin, though, I feel no hatred toward Zaretsky. I feel pity – mixed, perhaps, with disdain – but it is pity. How he choked down his sausage after locking himself in: you could only pity him, after all. I don't even know what short-circuited in his weak brain and why he informed on the professor . . . In the end, something else is important: he was not a cannibal by vocation. Like, for example, Voronin. It is terrible that he was killed.

Since the film, people have been calling with interview requests; I refuse. I agreed for the first weeks after I was 'discovered' (as they say), but quickly realized I was repeating myself. I began attempting to say the same thing differently, but it came out worse and worse each time. I shared that with Geiger. He answered that there is no disgrace in repetition; he said all famous people do it, so I can boldly continue. According to him, the present-day press is constructed on an advertising principle: the more repetition, the better. He elaborated on an entire theory according to which a person's striving for something new yields to an attachment to the old. This is especially vividly pronounced in children, who always reread more willingly than they read. Maybe that's how things are: I always preferred *Robinson Crusoe* to all the new books . . . But I began refusing interviews.

Of all the callers, I only decided to help out one young miss: her voice was trembling. That is what trembling voices do to men. True, I agreed to answer only by telephone and just one question. She asked it for a torturously long time.

'What's the main discovery you made in the camp?'

That's essentially a banal question, like everything that contains the words 'main,' 'most,' etc. It's strange that she had to bleat on so long to ask that. The more banal the question, though, the more complicated it is to answer.

'I discovered that a person transforms into swine unbelievably fast.'

THURSDAY

Today they called me from the 'Frozen Foods' company. They offered me an advertising contract. I hung up.

I typed on the computer yet again today: I typed up several pages from *Robinson Crusoe*. I write by hand much faster, though.

FRIDAY

As of today, I have been ill for a week. It seems, though, that I'm on the mend. My temperature is not high – around 37 – but I am mighty weak. Geiger stopped by early in the morning; he insists on bed rest. I am lying here even without his insistence, however: I have no strength. He laughed when I told him about the frozen food. He said this current era is a pragmatic one, that I should have thought hard before declining. As he left, he advised regarding advertising proposals more attentively, but I could not understand from his face if he was joking or not.

Nastya called, which made me feel even more lonely. She spoke sympathetically with me but I think she called out of politeness. That can be sensed from someone's tone, after all. And what else could I count on? No, I have no pretentions regarding special relations with her; that is not what I have in mind. I simply feel that I am a stranger to everyone here. They have their life, their ways of speaking, moving, and thinking. They value other things. And it is not that their things are better or worse than mine: they are simply different. To those alive now, I came here like a person from another continent, perhaps even from another planet. They are interested in me and scrutinize me like a museum exhibit but they do not consider me one of their own.

Solitude is not always bad, though. When I was on the island, I dreamt only of solitude. I went to sleep very quickly after lights out – simply fell on the bunk – but several minutes would pass on the borderline before I collapsed into sleep for good, and that was a time for my reveries.

I imagined Robinson Crusoe trudging along the surf at the water's edge: I was transferred to his island from mine and even if I had not changed places with him (why would he need my island?), for several instants I took his place in that blessed, uninhabited land.

My bare feet sensed a carpet of leaves in a tropical forest where it was fresh even in the heat and green in winter because there was no winter there. The carpet crunched lushly underfoot. I turned huge leaves that resembled ladles toward myself and from them drank with delight the liquid that had collected after a night rain. It spilled unevenly, falling into my nose and eyes, twisting in the air into a tight, glimmering braid.

I never conversed with anyone other than parrots and they told me only what I wanted to hear from them. There was no compulsory work here, no escort guard, not even my prisoner comrades, humiliated and enraged: there was no longer anything that did not correspond to a human way of life or that I did not want to see. Those who created the Solovetsky hell had deprived people of what was human, but Robinson, after all, did the opposite: he humanized all the nature surrounding him, making it a continuation of himself. They destroyed every memory of civilization but he created civilization from nothing. From memory.

MONDAY

I read somewhere that Themis was depicted by Greeks without a blindfold over her eyes. Without scales, without a sword. The figure we know now is the Roman Justitia, who succeeded Themis. Well. The Romans, fine; Justitia, fine. I liked her that way. The raised hand with the scales (without scales at my house, of course), a sword in the other hand and even the blindfold over the eyes. A long dress dropping into folds, the left breast uncovered. That excited me as an adolescent.

Sometimes I would take the statuette from the shelf and place it on my desk. My finger would slide along her smooth polished surface. I would take her in my hand, surprised at how precisely she settled there: my fingers easily went into the folds of the dress and her raised arm became a rest for my hand. I admired the tactile perfection of the form. This is most likely what made me an artist . . .

An artist! I had been coming to this for a long time: simultaneously recalling and not recalling. Sometimes you recall something in a dream and do not believe it is the truth. But now I suddenly believed: I was an artist . . . Fine, I was not, I just wanted to become one, but: an artist. The answer to the question of who I was, after all, has come now, when I was thinking about Themis. It manifested itself in my consciousness in all its preciseness. Themis. Form. Perfection. And I: an artist, a student of the Academy of Arts. Sphinxes on the embankment. Vase, horse, Apollo. Pencils scratching on paper. Why had I not remembered that?

Just now I found a pencil and decided to draw something. Vase, horse . . . But it didn't come out. Apparently I'm too excited. Despite the late hour, I called Geiger and asked him about my discovery.

'Yes,' he said, 'you studied at the Academy of Arts, and very successfully, too. In light of certain circumstances, you didn't graduate.'

As I listened to his weakening voice, I realized I had woken him and that realization was not without malicious pleasure. In recalling who I had been, I experienced not only joy but annoyance, too. It seemed to me that Geiger should have hinted to me about this long ago. I even told him as much. He (pause) answered that he himself had doubts on this score but in the end chose to stick to his decision. The fact that I had now filled that hole in my memory confirmed the correctness of that course: he said I should recall the most important things in my life on my own.

Well. And what if I had not recalled?

TUESDAY

Geiger came over this morning with a set of watercolor paints, paper, and sable paint brushes. My call seemingly made an impression on him. He examined me carefully and gave me permission to leave the house. I called Nastya right away. We met at Sportivnaya and rode to the hospital. Anastasia's condition remained almost unchanged. I say 'almost' because just before we left, she raised herself on her elbow and called Nastya by name. Her eyes were looking at the ceiling as she did. It is unclear if they saw Nastya.

On the way back, I proposed going somewhere for lunch. We came out of the metro at Ekaterininsky Canal, which has now been renamed. The little restaurant that Nastya brought me to looked out on Kazan Cathedral. The canal's granite separated us from the cathedral and its unseen waters flowed somewhere below.

'Order for both of us,' I requested. 'It's been about a hundred years since I was last in a restaurant.'

'Eighty-something,' Nastya corrected me.

'I was being coy.'

We were sitting opposite one another by a window and the huge cathedral took up the entire window. It looked at us with obvious reproach because it had seen me out for walks so many times with Anastasia. Sitting with her on granite steps that were cold even on summer evenings. The final picture that remains in my mind is from autumn: a newspaper tossing about hysterically between the columns. In the dusk, it resembles a medium-sized ghost and Anastasia and I look at it silently. Both we and the cathedral were eighty years younger then.

Now it has seen me with Nastya. This is not what you think, I could have told it. But I did not. My mouth was busy with the beefsteak Nastya ordered but this was not even about the beefsteak: I myself did not understand what was happening to me. Do I like

Nastya? Of course I like her. Being with her is easy and nice. I had not experienced those two feelings in either my camp years or (even more so) in the decades that followed. Do I consider that I am somehow being unfaithful to Anastasia like this? No, I do not. When that question came into my head there, by the window, I got worked up, but I've calmed down now at home. I've realized how absurd the question is.

My gaze fell on Geiger's paints: when had he managed to buy all that today? Or maybe he didn't buy them today? Maybe everything was purchased for the future and had been awaiting its time?

WEDNESDAY

Picture windows curtained in canvas. Plaster copies of ancient statues. Michelangelo's slave, the Discobolus. Apoxyomenos, head doubly tilted – forward and to the side, a difficult perspective. Proto-forms: sphere, cube, cylinder, pyramid, cone, six-sided prism, triangular prism. Parts of David's face: nose, eyes, lips.

For half of last night I attempted to draw with paints. Nothing came out.

THURSDAY

Some popular magazine or other has commissioned me to write an article about 1919 in Petersburg. This is very opportune for me right now. For whatever reason, the drawing just is not coming along but maybe writing will work out? The pay isn't bad, either; I had not expected it would be so much. I warned the editors right away that I will not be writing about events or even people: they knew all that without my telling them. What interests me is the most minor of everydayness, things that seem unworthy of attention and are taken for granted by one's contemporaries. This everydayness goes along with all events and then disappears, undescribed by anyone, as if it had taken place in a vacuum.

They nod to me: write, they say, no need to ask, but then I can't stop. So, I say, shells remain within layers of rock: billions of shells that lived on the ocean's floor. We understand what they looked like but we do not understand their natural life outside the layers of rock: life in the water, among rippling seaweed, illuminated by a prehistoric sun. That water is not in historical compositions. You, they laugh in the editorial office, are a poet. No, I object, summoning the spirit of Geiger: I am a chronicler of lives.

FRIDAY

I climbed Sekirnaya Mountain with two escort guards and felt my stomach cramping from fear. I was ashamed of my fear because I had never before been so afraid, even when I was on the way to Solovki. The escort guards were calm or – more likely – indifferent people, which in camp terms is the best thing possible. They did not urge me on and they barely cursed, but they also displayed no particular interest in my fate. They did not even speak about anything amongst themselves. It was obvious they had tired of camp life and were now simply conserving their strength. It was not just prisoners that the camp wore out.

As we were climbing the mountain, an inconceivably beautiful expanse opened up before us. Yellow forests. Dark blue lakes. A leaden sea somewhere at the very horizon. I recall: the forests were not completely yellow. Green spots of spruces were visible, as if someone had poured one paint into another but had not stirred. I began feeling uneasy. I took that beauty as a sign of my rapid demise. I thought that something like this could only manifest itself before death, as the best thing that one is granted to see during life. The escort guards could have seen it, too, but they were looking in the wrong direction.

They led me to an isolation cell located in the church and knocked with their rifle butts. A lock clanged on the other side of the door, like a wolf's teeth in a fairy tale. As if it were swallowing me. I was ordered to enter; the escort guards remained outside. I cast a parting glance at them after stepping over the threshold. It was rough for me, very lonely, that they were leaving. As if a child had been surrendered to a shelter by his relatives. Even those people seemed like relatives to me before the face of the death awaiting me.

I was led to the upper chapel and ordered to take off my shoes and strip to my underwear. Seeing that the floor was cement, I asked permission not to remove my socks. They struck me in the face. I entered my new cell barefoot, in my drawers, and my face bloodied. It was actually good that they struck me. It was easier for me that way.

SATURDAY

Today I came to the metro a half-hour early to meet Nastya. That did not happen by chance, however: as I was leaving the house, I realized it was still early. I sat on the parapet near our meeting place and thought: What, I cannot wait to see her? I even shrugged my shoulders. No, I decided, I simply do not feel like sitting at home. It's dreary at my place, there are only ghosts there.

I watched workers lay asphalt on the roadway. Unwashed, unsober workers wearing dirty (once orange) vests tossed hot asphalt by the shovelful and a roller flattened it. Their faces were awful, too. There were not even faces like this when they laid the wood-block paving. It began raining, first finely, then harder. The water collected in bulging puddles on the oily, smoking asphalt. Smoke mixed with steam: hellish work. Does asphalt last long when it is laid in the rain? And by faces like those, too.

I saw Nastya from afar: fragile, with an umbrella. Resembling a statuette, something I (as an artist) value very much in women. When she noticed me, she picked up her pace and almost began running. Because I'm getting wet. I froze for so many years and now I'm getting wet. She ran up and sheltered me from the bad weather. She took a tissue from her pocket and wiped off my face – very nice! The rain stopped right then. Nastya clicked her umbrella and it collapsed. After grasping it as if it were a wet bird, she neatly folded its winged pleats.

We descended into the Metro. Thanks to Nastya, I already knew how to stand on the escalator during the descent: one step lower than a female companion, face turned toward her. Drops glistened on my female companion's hair. A damp imprint from the umbrella smudged on her bag.

'You know, Nastya, I remembered who I was.' I paused a bit. 'An artist. A beginning artist.'

She looked at me with mild curiosity. She doesn't know how long it took to recall that.

'Were they able to find your work from back then?'

I shook my head in the negative. Nastya turned me in the direction we were moving and we disembarked from the escalator.

'That's fine, you'll draw new ones. You will draw?'

She smiled.

'I don't remember how it's done. Nastya, can you imagine, I don't remember . . .'

SUNDAY

All day yesterday I compiled, in my head, a plan for the article. It came easily, with no effort at all. I am an artist, after all, an artist, not a historian. A sequence of events is not important to me: all that concerns me is the fact of their existence. I wrote down the points of my plan as I recalled them, without any logic at all.

There were no new things: everyone wore old clothes. There was even a sort of chic to that: *a difficult time*, a beloved *phrase* then. Know how to survive a difficult time: wear out existing items and do not don the new ones, even if you have them. We wore out items with enthusiasm.

Newspapers were not sold but pasted to the corners of buildings. Groups of laborers read them. It brought people together.

Secret trade of provisions. Open trading was forbidden.

Water did not go all the way to upper stories. Water was stored there in bathtubs. People filled bathtubs to the brim with water but washed themselves in basins.

Also about clothes: everyone went around wrinkled because when it was cold we slept without undressing.

More often than not, lamps did not burn; the electricity operated for a couple of hours each day. People made kerosene lamps.

Waste pipes froze in the winter. We did not use the toilet but went to privies in the courtyards, more often than not with chamber pots, to empty them. But there were not privies in every courtyard.

Trams were a rarity; one had to walk. And if trams did show up, they were crammed full.

An unusual sight: no smoke from chimneys in the winter. There was nothing to heat with. People took apart wooden structures for firewood. Doors between rooms were sawed up. One time Anastasia was sick and I borrowed fifty logs from the yardman, then racked my brains for a month about how to repay it. In compensation for the firewood, I had to give him a silver saltcellar that had belonged to my grandmother. It was a pity.

Ration cards. For sugar, bread. I acquired galoshes for myself with my labor card.

Long hours waiting in line for kerosene at Petrocommune.

Flatbreads made of potato peelings. Carrot or birch tea. Also about food: a fallen horse lay for a long time at the corner of Bolshaya Morskaya Street and Nevsky Prospect; a piece of meat had been cut from its croup.

The most popular gifts in 1919: sealing wax, paper, nibs, and pencils. I gave Anastasia a jar of molasses.

I am attempting to reconstruct that world, which is gone forever, but I end up with only meager shards. And also a feeling – I don't know how to express it correctly – that we differed from one another in the world back then, were alien to one another and often enemies; but when you look now, in some sense it works out that we belonged to one another. We had our time in common and that turns out to be quite a lot. It connected us to one another. I'm frightened that now everyone is alien to me. Everybody except Anastasia and Geiger. I have only two people who belong to me, but back then it was the whole world.

MONDAY

Today I asked Geiger why it took me so long to recall that I had been an artist. And to explain (my voice suddenly gave me away here) how it is that I cannot manage to draw anything now.

'It's something to do with the brain cells that are responsible for that realm,' said Geiger. 'By all appearances, they weren't restored after thawing.'

'But that was my primary activity . . .'

'Maybe that's exactly why those cells didn't restore themselves.' After a silence, he added: 'On the other hand, you write very well. Your creativity, as they say now, lost one channel but gained another. Are your literary descriptions really not a form of drawing?'

A graceful answer.

TUESDAY

I was thinking about Sekirnaya Mountain again today. Painting and literary descriptions are all powerless here. Well, what kind of description can convey round-the-clock coldness? Or hunger? Any story implies a completed event but there is a dreadful eternity here. You cannot warm up for an hour, or two or three or ten. And it is impossible, after all, to accustom oneself to either hunger or cold. The residents of the second floor of the isolation cell are barefoot, wearing only their drawers, and sitting on beams. The room is unheated. It is forbidden to speak, forbidden to move. The beams are high and feet do not reach the floor. After several hours the feet swell so much that it is impossible to stand on them. The torture lasts and lasts, and that lasting kills. How can you describe that torture? You would need to write for as long as it drags on. Hours, days, months.

It is rare for someone to endure for months – people lose their minds but more often die. You sit from early morning, you feel your dangling soles and a draft wafting along the cement floor. The boards dig into your thighs. Then, when your feet already seem to feel nothing, there comes a full-body agony and the impossibility of sitting. You imperceptibly place your hands under your legs and attempt to push back from the beam the slightest little bit so there will at least be some sort of motion.

The guard's eyes are in the door window. They watch for your hands to tense, for your bent-at-the-knee legs to raise slightly higher than your comrades' feet. The guard enters; he has a stick. He beats you – on the head, on the shoulders. You slip from the shelf and hit your head on the floor, shrieking wildly. And you seem detached from your tormented body. From your own beastly shriek. Is that you shrieking? Are the guards who ran in kicking you? Tying you up? He twists your arms and ties them behind your back, to your feet. You are no longer a person, you are a wheel, why do they not roll you?

They drag you up steps and haul you into the 'lantern.' The 'lantern' is the upper part of the church, which formerly served as a lighthouse. There is neither light nor glass now. Only wind, the strongest wind on the top of a hill. You resist it for a time but then your resistance vanishes. And time – that continuousness that is impossible to describe – vanishes. You give yourself over to the will of that wind: it will heal your wounds, it will carry you off in the right direction. And you fly.

THURSDAY

Today when we were at the hospital, Anastasia uttered, 'Innokenty.' Without regaining consciousness, just like when she mentioned Nastya's name before. And so her consciousness is glimmering, some sort of events are taking place there, someone is present in it. Nastya and I, for example.

FRIDAY

Anastasia called me by name again.

I bent over her and said:

'I'm here, Anastasia.'

I repeated that several times, slowly and distinctly.

I asked:

'What did you want to tell me?

She was lying with her eyes closed. Breathing heavily.

Did she hear me?

SATURDAY

He resembles Karl Marx, but wearing glasses. His right hand rests on a cane, the left draws on a board with a long metal pointer that has chalk at the tip. How the eye is constructed. The eyeball, covered by eyelids from above and below. All the invisible lines are being drawn as if they were visible; the form is depicted as transparent.

It suddenly occurred to me that it probably would have been better if Marx and his numerous followers had drawn. They could have copied Michelangelo's David, rubbed away the extra pencil lead with stale bread, and gone to Plyos to make sketches. I think there would have been less grief in the world. A drawing person is somehow loftier, gentler than a non-drawing person. Values the world in all its manifestations. Takes care of it.

I shared these notions with Geiger. He pursed his lips and went silent. He answered my direct question about my theory by saying he could not corroborate it. He does know one universal villain who was an artist in his youth. What can you say about that? The influence of art has its own limitations.

MONDAY

Today I went alone to see Anastasia: Nastya was studying for her last exam of the term. I telephoned for a taxi and went. It has become impossible to ride the metro: the glasses don't rescue me because people recognize me perfectly well in glasses, too. The taxi driver also recognized me. He looked at me for a long time in the rear-view mirror and then asked:

'Forgive me, but did you feel anything there, in the ice? Were there any, you know, desires?'

'There was the desire to be thawed.'

A pause.

'That's very understandable.'

Anastasia greeted me with silence and said nothing that day. Her arm (yellow spots on skin) hung off the bed. I sat on a chair by the bed and took her hand in mine. It seemed that her hand responded, squeezing slightly. Maybe this is how any hand responds when you take it. A simple contraction of muscles.

I bent toward Anastasia's ear and asked if she remembered our hands touching? In that previous life – did she remember? Her eyelids quivered but did not open. I began telling her about how we decorated a Christmas tree. How I took the ornaments from the box and unwrapped them, the paper they were wrapped in rustling. After finding and straightening each thread, I gave the ornaments to Anastasia. I touched her fingers with my fingers, in everyone's sight, by the way. Anastasia's and my work offered that opportunity.

That was in the evening. But the tree turned out to be completely different when I went into the Voronins' room in the morning. The tree (tinsel, ornaments) sparkled in the dim December sun. The vent window was open and the garlands were clinking, barely audibly. There do exist, I whispered as I held Anastasia's hand, sounds that are rare and resemble nothing else. The sound of garlands in a draft, for example: it is all so glassy, so inexpressibly fragile, does Anastasia remember it? I love that sound very much and recall it often.

I reminded Anastasia in a whisper about other dear things, too. About how, for example, she once took my hand, saying she wanted to see my fate. She drew her fingertip along the tangle of lines and said something; it gave me chills. I did not hear her words because my ears were not working. Of all my body parts, there existed only the palm along which Anastasia's finger was gliding. It investigated every mount, every line. The longest turned out to be the life line. I wonder if it took the frozen time into account in my case?

THURSDAY

I came to at the infirmary. Not in the same rotten barrack where I had ended up before but in a clean, lighted room. Everything – floor, ceiling, table, chairs, bed – was white and so somehow I calmly thought I had gone straight to Paradise after being beaten on Sekirka.

This was not Paradise, though: there were not things like these there. There was a bentwood chair painted with generous white strokes and the paint had frozen in rivulets on the iron bed knobs; they would not have painted like that in Paradise. The room was white but earthly. Leaning out of bed, I finally spotted non-white objects, too: a light-blue pail with a reddish rag. On the pail, dripping red letters read 'LAZARUS.'

All the rest was essentially non-white, too. The floor, for example. Indeed, it turned out to be light brown. I lay there and was surprised that the floor could have seemed different to me a minute ago. Not only colors were returning but smells, too. The room smelled pronouncedly of medicines, and bleach wafted from the pail with the mysterious inscription. I do not think there's any need for either of those things in Paradise.

A medical nurse entered the room and I squeezed my eyes shut. This is a camp habit: pretending you are not there. Go still if you hear someone moving. Merge with the darkness. See nothing and be unseen.

After wiping the floor, the nurse took the pail with the rag and left. Male footsteps sounded. Through my eyelashes, I saw shoes crossing a floor that was still wet. I could not remember when I had last seen shoes at the camp. Folds of trouser legs rested on the shoes. The whiteness of a lab coat replaced the trousers' stern blackness. The man who had entered leaned over the bed and called my name.

His arrival reminded me of Geiger's first appearance, though it could be that everything was reversed and it was Geiger who later reminded me of the man who had entered. As is known, one can pass through time in both directions. What is important: I opened my eyes. The stranger looked at me, silent. A professorial little beard, glasses. I was silent, too, because it was he who should speak. And he began speaking:

'Your first task, Innokenty Petrovich, is to recover.'

That seemingly assumed a question about a second task, but I did not ask it. Remembering the pail, I asked:

'Is LAZARUS a nickname for the infirmary?'

'It's a special nickname, shortened.' He smiled. 'Laboratory for Absolute Zero and Regeneration in the USSR, only it's doubtful you have heard of it.'

Heard? Well, yes and no. There existed several laboratories on Solovki about which nothing was precisely known: neither their type of activity nor even their names. But people from one of them – from this one, as I was beginning to understand – were called *Lazaruses* at the camp. One time I even asked someone why they were called Lazaruses but received no answer.

I had seen the Lazaruses several times at the dock. They were disembarking from a boat and made the impression of people who were doing well by camp standards: well-fed, dressed properly, and (I had learned to determine this flawlessly) not beaten. Unlike my conversation partner, the Lazaruses did not wear shoes, but even their boots were a sign of prosperity. I also recalled that the Lazaruses on Big Solovetsky Island arrived from the island of Anzer. And departed for it.

'Are we on Anzer now?' I asked.

His gaze was surprised.

'Yes, we are on Anzer.'

SATURDAY

The day began with an early call from Nastya. Very early: six in the morning. They had just reported to her from the hospital (my heart fell for an instant) that Anastasia had come to. Nastya intended to stop by for me in a taxi and asked me to be waiting for her at the front door in twenty minutes. I went down ten minutes later. There were almost no pedestrians on Bolshoy Prospect yet. Cars seldom drove by, either. The sun rising behind Peter and Paul Fortress reflected yellow off the upper stories. Of course I had already seen that.

Early one summer morning, in around 1911, we are waiting for a carriage to the train station. There are upper stories and sun and a cool morning breeze. I am wearing short pants (straps crossed); there are goose bumps on my knees. I'm jumping to warm up, though, to tell the truth, I'm not really very cold. More likely: anxious. I am worried the carriage won't show up . . . and we won't go to Alushta. My sandals slap resonantly on the paving stones. That sound is gradually drowned out by the clip-clopping of hoofs. I whisper: Happiness, happiness! The carriage has arrived.

The taxi has arrived. I sit with Nastya in the back seat. Birzhevoy and Dvortsovy Bridges, then Senatskaya Square, Moskovsky Prospect. Our travel may not be to Alushta but it seems southerly overall: it is becoming warmer in the car. I roll down the glass and place my elbow on the window. My arm lacks will and my fingers move like underwater plants – listlessly and melancholically – from the wind's power. What will I tell Anastasia? What will she tell me?

A nurse stopped us right by the room. When she regained consciousness, Anastasia requested that a priest be called, and he was now taking her confession. The priest came out around ten minutes later, carrying the Holy Gifts on extended hands. Then the nurse was in the room for a short while. When she came out, she said we had only five minutes: Anastasia lacked the strength for more. I looked at Nastya and she nodded. She felt my fear. Lightly, she pushed me forward right by the door. I opened it.

Anastasia's gaze greeted me. I took small steps toward it, as if to a streetlight in the dark. I felt Nastya's hand on my shoulder, but that didn't help me. I would even say it hindered me. I probably should have gone in to her alone. My voice froze in my throat and I did not utter a word as I approached the bed. I sank to my knees and pressed my forehead to Anastasia's hand. I sensed her other hand – almost weightless – on the back of my head. The hand moved. It was stroking my hair, as it had stroked it in another time. There we were in our apartment on Bolshoy Prospect and everyone was still alive: my mother, Professor Voronin, and even Zaretsky. He was alive, too. They had all gone out about their business, and Anastasia and I remained. She was ailing and so I went in to see her. And I placed my forehead on her hand and she stroked the back of my head. I had been seeing all this, awake, and it turned out I was speaking, speaking out loud. They were silently listening to me: Anastasia, Nastya, and the nurse. Suddenly Anastasia broke the silence. She said:

'Zaretsky.'

It sounded like a gate squeaking. Or a nail on glass. It was not her appearance that was furthest from how she was then, it was her voice. I raised my head. Anastasia was looking at the nurse.

'Zaretsky, after all, is *my* sin.'

The nurse nodded, obviously out of politeness. It's doubtful she knew anything about Zaretsky.

'What do you mean, Granny?' asked Nastya, her tone assuming no answer.

'I . . . What do they call it now? Put out a contract on him . . . Exactly that, a contract! And that's it, the trouble.'

'Granny!'

'That's your grandmother for you. Trouble . . .'

Anastasia inhaled sharply and had an uncontrollable coughing fit. The nurse pounded on her back and raised her on the pillows. Without showing Anastasia, she signaled to us to leave. Her precautions were unnecessary: Anastasia could not see anything anyway. She was half-lying, breathing heavily, and her eyes were closed. We went out.

Several minutes later, they wheeled Anastasia out of the room on a stretcher. The stretcher was racing at a speed unusual for a hospital but we didn't lag. Those coming in the other direction jumped toward the walls of the corridor. The stretcher flew off into the wide-open doors of intensive care at full speed. Those doors closed in front of us.

An hour later, an intensive-care doctor came out and told us Anastasia was in a coma. We stayed, to stand by the intensive-care doors. They brought us chairs a while later and we sat on them until evening. At around ten, they requested that we go home, citing hospital regulations. I did not even know it was already ten: after all, it's light outside. Nastya and I understood this wasn't about the regulations: they felt sorry for us. We left.

SUNDAY

We went to the hospital in the morning. No change.

Geiger called in the evening. It turns out that yesterday marked a half-year since the day my consciousness returned.

Will Anastasia's consciousness return?

MONDAY

Everything is as before. Under these circumstances, that can be considered a piece of good news.

WEDNESDAY

We were at the hospital today and yesterday. We sat on chairs in the corridor. They asked us what the point was in our sitting if we would not be let into the intensive-care unit anyway. The point, we say, is that we are nearby.

The chief physician invited us to his office yesterday and announced that his staff were doing everything possible. He served us cognac. His face was rosy after the cognac and he grew rather uninhibited. He said there was basically no hope whatsoever. He gave Nastya and me business cards, for the second time, I think. As he saw us out, he straightened the lab coat tossed on his shoulders. According to Nastya, the suit under his lab coat was expensive. And would have completely lost its effect if the lab coat were all buttoned up. The suit under the lab coat reminded me of Academician Muromtsev. There was nothing else of the academician whatsoever in the chief physician.

Muromtsev. His suit, shoes, and, most important, his manner of speaking, were all very atypical of Solovki. He examined me once a day, sometimes with the attending physician, sometimes separately. Little by little, I began to understand that his interest was separate, too, and only partially coincided with the doctor's interest. I did not, however, need very long to surmise about that interest. One time,

Muromtsev asked the nurse to leave us by ourselves and then, as they say, he filled me in.

After the academician's refusal to freeze Felix Dzerzhinsky's corpse (1926), the Laboratory for Absolute Zero and Regeneration in the USSR was arrested en masse and sent from Leningrad to Solovki. Attempts to justify themselves through the absence of experience in freezing people were unsuccessful. Muromtsev's letter to the Central Committee of the Communist Party – in which he stated in detail the results of freezing rats and explained his refusal to freeze Dzerzhinsky – did not help, either. According to the investigator who interrogated Muromtsev, a resolution written in Joseph Stalin's own hand was on the letter and it deemed the academician's decision a mistake. It was indicated in the resolution that when working with Dzerzhinsky's body, it was necessary to employ the very same scientific methods as before, regarding the deceased as a large rat.

At the same time, the letter about freezing obviously made an impression on Stalin. From Muromtsev's point of view, that explains the happy fate of the LAZARUS employees. They not only avoided the firing squad, they were also accommodated in humane, by camp standards, conditions. After ending up on Solovki, the laboratory workers found out the author of the resolution was feeling a personal interest in the experiments they had conducted. He had not yet crushed all his enemies but he knew he would certainly deal with them and then the time would come to think about immortality.

That interest manifested itself to its full extent when Stalin telephoned Academician Muromtsev one day. He asked if the rats used in the experiment remained alive. After receiving an affirmative answer, Stalin proposed continuing the experiment on live people. The academician had not expected scientific guidance from the political leader but nonetheless ventured to object along the lines that upon filling blood vessels with a solution, it is not so particularly important whether the organism is dead or alive, that it might as well be dead upon freezing in any case, and, finally, where would he find live people for goals like those, anyway?

Stalin went silent. He sincerely did not understand the problem since there were still so many live people at the camp. The political leader asked the academician to pass the phone to the camp chief and ordered him to find live people. Assuming he was being blamed for the conditions in which he held prisoners, the chief promised, in a weak voice, to find live people. He was, of course, not being blamed for anything, though.

Live people were found in the isolation cell at Sekirka. From the camp chief's perspective, these were people ready to do anything. They had no exaggerated expectations about how long they would remain alive. Their advantage over other live people lay in the fact that they would choose freezing voluntarily. These people did not need to be subjected to beating that would ruin human material and, thus, the experiment's purity. People from Sekirka were delivered to Anzer, fed well for several months, and then used for the experiment.

Muromtsev told me about much more (he later invited me for walks more than once) but each day I listened to him less attentively. I walked along the shore with him, nodded to him when his speech broke off, and laughed when he laughed, though I was thinking about my own matters. Sometimes I was not even thinking, I was simply watching as muddy shreds of foam floated along the shore. As sharp Anzer rocks tore open an ebbing wave. Muromtsev and I had a warm relationship: in some sense we had a common cause. But one circumstance existed that gradually distanced me from him: Muromtsev remained alive. And I was preparing to die.

FRIDAY

Today after the hospital, Nastya invited me to her place. Rather, to Anastasia's place, to an old, roomy apartment not far from where Znamenskaya Church had stood. Which, to my surprise, no longer exists. The metro is there: the underground world triumphed over the celestial world.

It turned out that Nastya had prepared lunch for my visit. First borsch, then pork braised in wine, unbelievably tasty. I, of course, have eaten well all these months – on Geiger's orders, meals were brought to me in a dinner pail – but a meal in a dinner pail is one thing and a meal from Nastya's warm hands is another. One is government-funded, the other is homey . . . I even feel awkward for writing so specifically about food.

'You didn't really cook this all specially for me?' I asked.

How silly my formal 'you' sounded. She smiled: that's exactly how she cooked it. Specially. Her leg touched my thigh as she was clearing dishes from the table. There was not the same intensity in our formal 'you' that there had once been with Anastasia. Times had probably changed: what was cherished then now seems ceremonious and absurd. Nastya and I needed to somehow begin speaking on informal terms. But how?

While looking at books on the shelves, I saw . . . Themis. The statuette of my childhood with the broken-off scales. The shelf with Themis cast off from the remaining shelves and began sailing around the room. I had just been eating Nastya's borsch, spoon by spoon, and it turns out Themis was standing behind my back. I extended a hand to her and then withdrew it right away. Nastya noticed the gesture.

'My grandmother's statuette. One of the few things remaining from the old time. And do you recognize this?'

My photograph stood alongside Themis. Anastasia must have ended up being my mother's heir. Who else could my mother have left all that to? My father took the photograph not long before his death.

Siverskaya, 1917, I am standing, leaning against the railing of the small bridge. Arms crossed on chest, gazing (at my father's request) into the distance. The rapid flow of the Oredezh under me, underwater plants coiling in its current. If you watch them for a long time, they seem to be river snakes (is there such a thing?) swimming upstream. The smell of water and pine trees, a muted cuckoo's call from the forest's depths.

'Why look into the distance?' I say to my father. 'It's so unnatural, it's as if I'm not noticing you with the camera.'

'No,' answers my father, vanishing behind the tripod, 'it's a gaze into eternity because a photographic portrait includes your present and past and maybe the future, too. Irony, of course, is therapeutic, but sometimes –' and here he straightens up and looks at me pensively '– there is no need to be ashamed of pathos because laughter has its own confines and is incapable of reflecting the sublime.'

My father then adjusts the camera so I can snap him and he stands on the bridge the same way and looks into the distance. There is undoubtedly more eternity in his gaze than in mine. Several weeks remain until my father crosses into eternity. Overall, everything is already prepared at Varshavsky Station.

SATURDAY

My crossing into eternity was supposed to be implemented on Solovki. From my conversations with Muromtsev, I understood that I had no chance of surviving after freezing. He was unfailingly good-natured during our walks, though it is unlikely he was experiencing a personal interest in me: more likely he wanted to form a general sense for himself about who would be frozen this time.

After finding out I was a religious believer, the academician told me that my agreeing to be frozen was not suicide on my part. He thought a decision to return to Sekirka would have been suicide to a far greater degree.

'You have only two paths,' Muromtsev uttered in a monotone, 'and both appear to lead to death.'

At least he was honest. I shrugged my shoulders:

'All paths lead to death.'

'If you decide to become a Lazarus, you'll live two or three months in complete comfort. To my taste, it's better to die sated and doing well. In any case, the choice is yours.'

And I made it. I became a Lazarus.

SUNDAY

Anastasia died. I am leaving for the hospital, where Nastya will wait for me.

Anastasia died.

MONDAY

Today we worked on funeral preparations and that distracted us from her death. Anastasia was not exactly alive but was not quite dead as Nastya and I were ordering things and making arrangements. She was a silent participant in the discussions, if only because they revolved around her.

Yesterday another event took place that is inextricably connected with Anastasia. After leaving the hospital (we did not arrive in time to see Anastasia's body in the room), we went to my place. Nastya had offered to see me home because my condition worried her. I truly could not handle myself. Anastasia's death, which was natural and expected, evoked a lucid sadness in Nastya but affected me completely differently.

It shook me. I was speaking loudly and incoherently; my voice was not minding me, and every now and then it cracked. I seemed to calm down after we left the hospital grounds but I fell apart again in the taxi and shouted at the driver. Most surprising is that I remember everything down to the most minor details: even that when I was quarrelling with the driver, I was thinking that I would be ashamed of myself for that later.

At home, I sat in an armchair and began to weep. The last thread that linked me with my time had broken with Anastasia. Nastya sat down on the armrest. I felt her hand on my head. I took her hand in mine and kissed it. I kissed it several times. Nastya cautiously retracted her hand:

'Don't do that. It's really just her you need, isn't it?'

I was gripped with fear that I would lose Nastya too.

'I want for you to be her.'

That was our first night. As I entered Nastya, I knew that she would certainly conceive today. This knowledge of mine uncovered feelings and made them unbearably acute: it pierced me, cut me to pieces, spilled into her, and I called out. At that moment, I truly no longer understood if this was Nastya or Anastasia. And she and I never again used the formal 'you.'

Part Two

FRIDAY [GEIGER]

Innokenty announced to me the other day that he hasn't been keeping his journal for a couple weeks now. He just kind of announced that, by the by.

I did already know he's not keeping it. Only it hasn't been a couple of weeks, but almost a month, although (as the saying goes) who's counting?

I didn't hold back and clarified anyway about it being a month. He responded by calling me a German, ha. Then he smiled and said that, for him, that's praise. And I smiled, as if, abgemacht.[2] I responded that it's praise for me, too.

And the important thing: I took advantage of that conversation and convinced him to continue the journal. True, to do that I had to promise Nastya would do the same. And even I. Otherwise, according to Innokenty, he'll feel like a *lab rat*. So there you go . . .

So we'll all write, each at our own computers. Then we'll merge everything.

I have observed that, for some reason, writing is pleasurable for Innokenty. A sort of replacement for drawing, which somehow went wrong for him. He's not writing these days because life is now more important to him than creating something.

2 Agreed (Germ.).

207

I'm a different case. I speak poorly. I write poorly. There's neither life nor creating, just science. Everything that I need to write about Innokenty would basically fit in a logbook.

Or maybe not everything?

FRIDAY [NASTYA]

Everybody has to write! That idea seemed a little weird to me at first but then I thought, well, why not? Some kind of three-way journal's pretty interesting.

The first thing, which I have to start with – because no other news is more important – is that I'm pregnant! I think it happened on my first night with Platonov. His behavior then kind of scared me. It seemed like he lost consciousness once or twice, for a second. That's understandable: he loves me double, for my grandmother and for me. That doesn't bother me, though. I actually like it.

What bothered and worried me is the thought that I'm not a virgin. That's just a detail for a contemporary person but my beloved is unusual. He only started using the informal 'you' with me on our first night, something he never did with my grandmother. Geiger quoted Bunin with regard to Platonov: 'A person of a bygone age.' They regarded virginity very strictly in that bygone age: do not dare lose it! But my kind friend did not so much as ask a question on that score. Although I think he noticed everything. Felt it keenly, you might say.

We moved to his place on Bolshoy and I've heard nothing from him but words of love ever since. Of course I'd guessed before about *how* he regarded me but, after all, he couldn't say anything to me then.

Meaning he's talking now. And I'm talking because I really love him. Platosha's smart and affectionate. He's also, by the way, very good in bed: you wouldn't say this is a guy who's just been thawed out. He's good and I tell him that all the time. He smiles back. Now that's somebody with a nice smile.

Smile, sweetie!

SATURDAY [INNOKENTY]

And so, a continuation of the notes. If I am to be exact, these are no longer notes. Based on the fact that it has now been suggested that I use a computer, I thought up the word *printings*. I informed Geiger and Nastya about that and they nodded listlessly. They do not like it, oh, they do not like it. And it's not pretty enough for them. Truth be told, it's not for me, either, but I don't let on. I am testing how far my friends' tolerance will go.

So far, they are tolerating. Geiger is basically happy that – to express it in a preindustrial way – I'm again putting pen to paper, since it turns out I wrote nothing for about a month. I somehow wearied of my previous scribblings and thought I had stopped, but here I am starting again, induced by Geiger. I'll put it bluntly: not without hesitation.

Geiger put pressure on me in the sense that the journal is an ancient genre and is thus natural for me. I, after all, stated in Bunin's way, am 'a person of a bygone age.' And I kept a journal wonderfully for half a year so why not keep it further? He already spoke to me about the 'not-bygone age' at some point. It is a vivid phrase, I remembered it. True, I have only read early Bunin and don't remember reading that there, but I understand Geiger's motivation. It is important for him to document what happens in my brain. But why do I need that? As Geiger himself said, I wrote for an entire half-year; is that really not enough?

I told him that these notes make me into someone unusual, the subject of an experiment. Rather like some sort of rat, at a time I should be blending in with this new way of life and, well, basically (I giggle, forcedly), I have a young wife and I am not in the mood for notes in the evenings. Geiger objected: rats don't keep journals and nobody is impeding me (a glance at Nastya) from blending in with a new way of life. He was, put bluntly, insistent.

Geiger convinced me that the course of my rehabilitation should remain for science. Reacting to the rat, he suggested putting everyone in equal positions: me, Nastya, and him. In his opinion, events will be presented from three angles so there will be multiple dimensions of views about what happens. It's supposed to comfort me that everyone in our troika will write, since I will no longer be in a special position. Anyway, Geiger convinced me.

The most important thing is last: Nastya is pregnant.

MONDAY [GEIGER]

I wonder: how does Innokenty perceive Nastya? She came into his life without my involvement. Very felicitously, in my view. Something that's genuinely good can't be arranged. It happens on its own.

Take Nastya. More than anything, she loves him. Beyond that, she loves him and all the fullness of his life. With his feelings for Anastasia, with his camp experience, with his current fame.

His fame, it seems to me, is an object of particular attention for Nastya. She simply basks in it. That's excusable: Nastya is essentially still very young.

She's pretty smart. That's important for a person like Innokenty. She's emotional. Maybe overly emotional, which can be annoying sometimes. In our case, however, that quality of Nastya's is most likely a plus. Innokenty is growing accustomed to his new time thanks to her active help.

Basically, Russian women are surprisingly lively. I, a German, like that about them.

Nastya's also practical. Not tight-fisted, not sparsam,[3] but practical. Since Germans have already come up, that quality is, of course, German. It manifests itself in her with certain details and phrases.

For example, we run across a watermelon stand on the street. Sure enough, Innokenty wants to buy a watermelon right then and there. Nastya announces that the watermelons are better in the nearby supermarket. And cheaper. But the thing is that he wants to buy the watermelon here and now. He likes that life itself is revealing its riches to him. And a supermarket is, well, excuse me, another matter. Here it's a find, there it's procurement.

There's nothing bad in her practicality. It's simply a little unexpected for her age and mentality. How does that go along with her emotionality?

Or maybe that's the style of this era? A generation of lawyers and economists.

Only where, one might ask, is the dream?

Where is the flight?

---

3 Economizing (Germ.).

TUESDAY [INNOKENTY]

After Anastasia died, I asked myself if my relationship with Nastya is not infidelity. Not in the sense of man/woman but in the most absolutely human dimension possible. If I am to be entirely frank, that question came about even before Anastasia's death and before my relationship with Nastya, but I was afraid to ask it. Even of myself. Because I could guess where this course was heading. Then, after asking that question, I was afraid of answering it in the first weeks after Anastasia's death, though it was already impossible to set aside.

What is difficult to do under ordinary conditions sometimes works out easier on paper. Or on the computer, in my case. I answer the question about whether my life with Nastya amounts to being unfaithful to Anastasia with a firm 'No.'

The main proof is Nastya's pregnancy. Anastasia and I *should* have had a child but we no longer *could* have a child. Nastya is carrying Anastasia's flesh within herself, which means that the child she and I will have is partially Anastasia's child. If Russian history were not so pitch black, then Nastya would have been Anastasia's and my granddaughter. Is this just a matter of history, though? And is it worth piling all the blame on history?

Just recently, I have noticed that in Russia people have come to like a phrase about how history has no subjunctive mood. *Phrases* come up now, too, as in my time, and people repeat them whether or not they have relevance. History, you see, does not have ... Maybe it does not, it's just that there are cases when it grants something like a second attempt. This is repetition and simultaneously non-repetition of what already was.

Otherwise, how can you explain that I was granted one more chance for life? That I – if we are to call things by their real names – have risen? That Anastasia lived long enough to see me in that late meeting? That I met Nastya, whom I love and who loves me? Could all that simply be separate cases or, even, chance? Of course not. Nastya and I (and Anastasia!) are dealing with pieces of the same mosaic because when many chance things come together in one common picture, that amounts to a consistent pattern.

I cannot force myself to go to Anastasia's grave. I am afraid of believing she has died.

WEDNESDAY [INNOKENTY]

Now, as life is settling into a routine little by little, happiness shows through everything, through the most common everydayness, no matter what I do. Everydayness is essentially happiness: to go where you want, read what you want . . . And, finally, to simply live. But my main happiness is in Nastya and in expecting the child. In the evenings, when I sit with Nastya on the sofa, I caress her belly. Where the changes are still almost unnoticeable. But what is supposedly noticeable – or so Nastya says – is only the fruit of my imagination. Well, fine, she knows better: no matter how you look at it, she knows her belly better.

I think about the little one constantly. I wrote 'the little one' just now and it almost seemed as if I was identifying the baby with the male gender. That is not actually how I see things. It even seems that I might want a girl more. She would continue that series: Anastasia, Nastya . . . It is unclear, however, how she should be named. It's inconvenient when an entire family carries the same given name.

WEDNESDAY [NASTYA]

Platosha's favorite topic is the child. That's a bit unexpected . . . Where did a man get so much motherliness? It would be more correct to say fatherliness but somehow that doesn't sound as good. He started caressing my belly in the evenings and it's ticklish. He asks why I tense up when he touches me. I shrug but I do know why: so I don't laugh from the ticklishness; the laughter would probably offend him. I'm also afraid of farting. Gas has been bugging me during my pregnancy, especially after supper. I think the gas makes my belly larger and my Platonov takes that as the baby's growth.

We kept thinking about which apartment it would be better for us to live in now, mine or Platonov's. We decided on Platonov's. We – that's Geiger and I – decided and Platonov didn't interfere, the sweetheart. Geiger said it's best for a thawed person to live in familiar surroundings. He's a real pro so it's best not to argue with him about the life of the thawed. There's no need to argue anyway: the apartment on Bolshoy Prospect is better and more comfortable. We can rent out my apartment; why let it sit empty? Although Geiger did wheedle support for Platosha out of the government, it's already clear now that we can't get by on that alone. Because our government's support is pretty listless.

Platonov will have lots of new expenses now he's a celebrity here. He'll be quite the awesome partier: just about everybody wants to meet him now. I want for him to be the best. A real social lion, not a Kunstkamera exhibit. The baby and I will just be here for him; we don't need more than that.

THURSDAY [GEIGER]

I just read that calendar dates reside in linear time but the days of the week are in cyclical time.

Linear time is historical but cyclical time is a closed system. Not even time at all.

Eternity, one might say.

It works out that the history set forth by the three of us isn't aspiring to go anywhere. It's the most reliable history.

Maybe it's not even history.

FRIDAY [INNOKENTY]

Marx. He taught drawing. He was imposing and, yes, there was a striking resemblance to the author of *Capital*. As a professor of art, he could not help but understand that. Did he hope that the new authorities would not touch a person with an appearance like that or something? Did he joke? Protest? I cannot recall his first name so why not simply call him Marx?

He walks past the easels, swaying. Squeaking the parquet floor. His fat finger scratches a little at his beard. He says:

'Form floats on the sheet. It is essential to take charge of that format in its entirety and construct a world in it.'

Construct a world. A voice that is muffled, from deep within. As if there is someone else there inside that person, sitting and giving orders.

SATURDAY [GEIGER]

I was at the Platonovs' today. I'm going to call them both that, even though their marriage is unofficial for now. It's a good name. Everything that the name Plato comprises carries within itself a shading of wisdom.

Does this couple carry that shading within, too? To some degree, yes. Innokenty by virtue of the circumstances of his life. By the number of things he's lived through. Nastya by virtue of innate qualities.

I don't mean to say that Nastya's wise: it would be silly to say that about a girl. What I have in mind is that she's arranging their life together rationally. A feminine wisdom or something.

Basically, wisdom is experience more than anything. Experience that's processed, of course. If there's no processing, then all the bruises you get are useless.

When I spoke about that out loud, Innokenty objected, saying that processing can happen without bruises, too. That sounds authoritative from the mouth of a person with such baggage in his life. If there aren't any bruises, though, it's unclear what to process. Innokenty didn't really clarify this, and I didn't even begin to ask.

Then there was a wonderfully tasty supper. Candlelit, by the way. Nastya secured the candles in two holders she'd brought from home. She explained that they were her grandmother's and asked if Innokenty recognized them. He made an indefinite gesture. Nastya, I think, wanted very much for him to recognize the candleholders.

Of course, he could have recognized them. At least as gratitude for the supper.

After supper they sat on the sofa. I was in a chair. Innokenty didn't take his hand off Nastya's belly. I inferred from that that Nastya's pregnant. I asked about it, as if I were joking. They answered completely seriously: yes, she's pregnant.

That makes me happy. Very happy. I congratulated them.

At Innokenty's suggestion, we played lotto. People played that in his day. People don't play it now but does that really matter? Particularly since it's so nice to play. So cozy.

As I played, I thought about how Innokenty had earned this coziness like nobody else.

I was also thinking that if I were president, I would make the population of the Russian Federation play lotto in the evenings. Of everything that the authorities could undertake right now, that seems like the best thing.

SUNDAY [INNOKENTY]

We had a nice evening with Geiger yesterday. He became very animated when he learned of Nastya's pregnancy. Well, yes, it is always pleasant for a natural scientist when someone in his care reproduces: that speaks to good vitality. I am joking. Our relationship with Geiger is human first, then doctorly and all the rest. That has become even more obvious since I left the hospital. He might look a bit aloof but I do know him. He's a very heartfelt person in his own way.

Geiger's characteristic love for truisms is another matter. This is, rather, his love for a formula, perhaps even for a *phrase*. Well, things such as the blood pressure increasing after coffee or, let's say, punishment following crime. And I read the other day that it turns out that coffee does not always raise blood pressure, far from it. I won't even speak of crime and punishment.

Geiger recently said of Nastya that she is surprisingly pragmatic for her age, that young people grow up fast. Someone on the outside might think that's praise but I have already studied Geiger pretty well. He regards this quality of Nastya's as paradoxical and he does not like paradoxes. He is no friend of paradoxes. I even imagine, roughly, what kind of phrase *phrase* he's using as a starting point here: *romance is characteristic of youth* or something of that sort. The thought that romance can combine with a businesslike attitude irritates him to the depths of his soul.

Geiger is a person of rules. He likes a phrase because it formulates a rule. His strength (he is absolutely reliable) is in rules, but there is a weakness there, too: he fears exceptions. I am sure that Geiger understands that life is more complicated than any diagrams, but at the same time, he values them. For him, this is a question of the world's orderliness. In Russian life, though, the exception is the rule, it's just that Geiger doesn't understand that. Or rather he does not accept it.

One topic yesterday was bumps and bruises that allegedly automatically engender experience. Bruises subjected to processing are what experience is: that is exactly what was said. But that isn't how it seems to me. Meaning it's possible that bruises can engender experience. But they might not. My main impressions, for example, are not connected with bruises, though I had oh so many bruises. In the literal sense, at that.

MONDAY [NASTYA]

Today I managed to reach an agreement for renting out my grand-mother's apartment. It all came together quickly, what can I say. I told Platosha that I hadn't run up the price and was rewarded for moderation. He kissed me on the nose. His gaze was absent; details like that don't interest him. I rubbed my nose on his chin.

'Do you understand, you bonehead, that it'll be easier for us to live now?

'The main thing,' he answered, 'is to live, the rest will somehow follow.'

'Effort, by the way, is needed for it to follow.'

It works out that I'm earning the riches for the two of us. Does that make me bitter? Not at all. It would be a catastrophe if Platosha began earning the riches, too. He and I are both strong in that we're different and complement one another. That's called an ideal marriage. I envelop his life in comfort and he makes up for everything he missed out on when he was frozen.

He reads a lot. There are two stacks of books by our bed: the one on his side is large and, well, mine is small. I flipped through Platonov's collection yesterday: history, philosophy, literature. Nothing to sneeze at. And what's in my pile . . . it's mortifying to even talk about that. Detective and romance novels. Items predominantly for us ladies. *Written in Russia.*

My books can always be set aside, even thrown away, but Platosha's, well, no can do. Ugh . . . This is something that makes me jealous. I crawl under his hand and whisper:

'Are you very busy, Innokenty Petrovich?'

He laughs. Asks forgiveness. He asks this very zealously and I resist feebly. It turns out that I'm more interesting than the book that's flying to the floor. It lies there, flattened, its cover facing up, observing our finale and apotheosis. I look at it from time to time. And so, on a nice high note, my eyes meet with Arnold Toynbee, for example. This disheartens me a little. The most touching thing is that a minute later my Platonov reaches over me for the book and gets down to reading again. Right now, as I write, he's reading a book about how the USSR conquered the cosmos. Somehow unexpected.

Is it very awful that I, a pregnant woman, am doing gymnastics like this? I'll need to ask the doctor.

TUESDAY [INNOKENTY]

Today I read a book about Solovki: it describes the Kem transit camp. That, as it happens, is the place I last saw my cousin Seva. Somehow, I do not want to write about that.

WEDNESDAY [GEIGER]

Innokenty told me that 'a certain Belkov' from the government called him. He spoke with him for a fairly long time.

Of course he meant Zheltkov. A person who's well known to everyone but Innokenty. Zheltkov offered all kinds of support. He left his phone number so Innokenty can call him if need be. He promised to 'stop by for tea' if he's in Petersburg.

Sehr demokratisch.[4]

WEDNESDAY [NASTYA]

Zheltkov from the government called Platosha. Zheltkov *himself*. He offered 'all kinds of support.' True, as someone noted, it's worth doubting when they offer all kinds of support: a proposal like that carries no obligation. But I think Zheltkov's beside the

---

4 Very democratic (Germ.).

point here: what can he offer if Platosha doesn't need anything?

And Platonov's quite something himself: he talked without any particular emotion, quite impassively, one might say. Without exaggerated (ah!) joy, even without any agitation that's difficult to suppress, meaning v. calmly. I waved a hand in front of him, to say: Come back to life a little. Inside, I was proud of my Platonov: the country's leadership is calling him and he's talking like that, no fuss. Like a man.

THURSDAY [INNOKENTY]

Of course Geiger isn't as straightforward as I described him in recent days. I'm striking back at him about Nastya's pragmatism. He already understands that words like that wound me and now he's keeping quiet. It is best to be quiet, Geiger ... And so: though I exaggerated something in my notes, in the main, I do not think I was mistaken. Geiger is a smart and shrewd person who believes in social ideals that are reflected in his various types of statements, not infrequently in fairly pompous pronouncements. As I have noted, Geiger knows a lot of them. Outwardly, he utters them offhandedly, but in his soul he values them very highly.

What he seems not to understand is that reality tires of pronouncements and then tends to evaporate from them. Only *phrases* remain and they are not used at all as one might expect. Let us suppose that in my time we liked the phrase about peace to the people and land to the peasants. And what happened? Instead of peace, they received civil war and instead of land, there was requisitioning of farm produce followed by collective farming. Nobody could have even contemplated that, even Geiger if he had lived then. How would he have adapted his slogans to reality?

Or those discussions of his about experience: I keep thinking about those. Maybe bruises do engender some sort of experience but I continue to think that kind of experience is not the most important thing. Let's say that in childhood I often saw the deceased in church: that's a *bruise*, too, if you will. But as I remember now, those deceased did not engender a fear of death in me. I examined them carefully and was not even afraid of stretching to touch them. One time I stroked an old man on the forehead: his forehead was cold and rough. My mother was scared and dashed over to pull me away, but I didn't really understand why.

Only years later, when I was maturing, did I discover death and feel horrified about it, but that was not a result of my meetings with the deceased. The discovery was predicated on the logic of my inner development.

SATURDAY [GEIGER]

The topic of experience touched our Innokenty very seriously. We had yet another conversation on that score. Innokenty said it wasn't the beatings in the camp that formed him. It was other things entirely. A grasshopper's chirping in Siverskaya, for example. The smell of a samovar that's boiled.

I attempted to explain to him that this is taken into consideration, too. In the end, any action takes place set against some sort of backdrop. He just waved me off, though. The grasshopper, he says, is the main action. And the samovar, too.

'Good.' I asked, 'Do you acknowledge history as a chain of events?'

'I acknowledge that,' answered Innokenty. 'There's just the question of what to consider an event.'

For Innokenty, history is not just outside time. Its particularity also lies in that it consists not of events but of phenomena.

Or there's this: a historical event is anything that can exist in the whole wide world. Including, it stands to reason, a grasshopper and a samovar. Why? Well, because, as it turns out, both those things disseminate calmness and peace. And in that, he said, lies their historical role.

MONDAY [NASTYA]

The day started with disappointment. Our intended tenants called to turn down the apartment. When I asked why, they answered that it was something personal. I informed Platonov of what happened and he took it calmly. I'm sorry, though. I spent a lot of time and energy on the search, found a married couple without children, and now this. I'll have to start all over again. There's no such thing as luck, it occurred to me. And then I recalled a little story from Platosha's youth, about an Australian resident who goes to the bottom of the sea in search of human happiness. That's who we need.

Interestingly, this evening we were at a reception at the Australian consulate. This was basically the first time I'd been to a foreign reception; it was hilarious. The consul appeared in the beginning and welcomed everybody on behalf of the citizens of Australia. Among other things, a non-Australian spoke: he started explaining why Serbia needed to be bombed; nobody was expecting to hear about that. The funniest thing is that he was bug-eyed, like the 'Australian Resident' toy, and his speech turned out to be a retelling of Platonov's story.

There was a buffet after that. People kept coming up to my Platonov and expressing gratitude for his courage. He would set aside yet another tartlet and politely thank them. He said he'd simply had no choice. I admired my gallant companion. We never did figure out why they'd invited him to the consulate. Maybe they were gathering courageous people there that day.

TUESDAY [GEIGER]

Innokenty has changed. The fear of what didn't exist in his time is no longer conspicuous. The current time really is *his* now, too. He's settled in pretty well.

He's hanging in there calmly, if not exactly confidently. And it seems like he's growing accustomed to his role as a celebrity.

People invite him everywhere, they're glad to see him everywhere. I heard him on the telephone answering, 'Thank you . . .' and 'I'll have to take a peek at my calendar . . .'

Innokenty truly does already have a calendar. It's Nastya.

Of course she likes this life more than anyone. Nastya's in seventh heaven and doesn't hide her feelings. It's rather amusing. At times she takes on a weary look when recollecting her pregnancy. Even then, though, she sparkles with happiness.

And I'm glad of it. You'd have to look really hard for a source of positivity like that. It's very important for my patient.

THURSDAY [INNOKENTY]

Of all my Solovetsky years, Anzer was probably the only human time. I cannot call that time 'happy,' only because each day of my physical recovery drew me closer to the day of my departure. To the day, I whispered to myself, of my *death*, because neither I nor the other Lazaruses nurtured any sorts of illusions about the results of the freezing. Muromtsev did everything to extend the time we spent at Anzer but what did the gift of a few weeks mean by comparison with a life taken away?

We felt like animals being fed for slaughter who – unlike ordinary animals – know that. In fact there was something animal-like in our life: there was some sort of stupefaction that did not allow one to fall into despair. It was as if they were holding your head under water and then suddenly let go, allowing you to inhale, so you gasp for air with your mouth, not thinking much about what awaits you afterwards. You are simply glad that you can breathe.

Muromtsev petitioned for the Lazaruses to have complete freedom of movement. They were granted passes allowing unlimited movement around the island. After breakfast (which was, by the way, very filling), I would head out for a walk. I wore a short sheepskin coat and a hat of wolf's fur with soft officer boots on my feet. Along the way I would run into half-undressed prisoners with wheelbarrows: they were exactly the same as I had been, not long ago at all. Their eyes silently followed me: it was strictly forbidden to talk with Lazaruses. I would go down to the water and stroll along the shore.

Although snow had already accumulated in the middle of the island, especially in the wooded parts, it barely lingered on the open shore. Only in certain places, catching on the bushes, did it unobtrusively make its presence known and even in those spots it blended with the sand, becoming unnoticeable. There were astonishing sandy beaches on Anzer. Stepping along the sand, I felt its softness even through the boots and imagined I was in the south: summer, the damp brim of a bucket hat, and grains of sand between sweaty toes.

The water was not summery, so I tried not to look at it. The sea had no azure skies above, so there was nowhere for it to take on the corresponding color. But the sand had a completely summery look. True, it was cold, but, well, I wasn't touching it anyway.

I am now reading about outer space. It's interesting that the first to make it there were dogs.

FRIDAY [GEIGER]

Today Innokenty signed a contract to advertise frozen foods. That resulted from the callers reaching Nastya.

Innokenty told me at one point that they'd called him. He hung up. I probably would have hung up, too.

But Nastya didn't hang up. She spoke with them in a businesslike way, learned the size of the fee, and was impressed.

She's right about something. The money that the authorities allocated to support Innokenty comes up categorically short. And it doesn't arrive regularly, either. I've had to hold paid consultations at the clinic and that's not fully legal. But the proceeds went toward our patient.

It's interesting that it was Nastya who told me about the signed contract. With a certain pride. Innokenty hasn't commented on it at all. Is he feeling awkward about it?

If the connections with frozen foods continue, I'll be able to turn down the consultations.

FRIDAY [INNOKENTY]

Nastya has changed somehow. If compared with who she was before Anastasia's death, she's slightly different. I discover a new Nastya each day, and that's a great pleasure.

To what degree does she resemble Anastasia?

SATURDAY [NASTYA]

There's a big press conference planned for next week at a news agency. At first I thought it was the agency's initiative, but they let slip that the event is paid for by a vegetable company. By an improbable (oy!) coincidence, it's the company Platosha advertises. How curious: the vegetable merchants don't just advertise their own cabbage but also the person who advertises the cabbage. They've thought everything through.

Incidentally, my Platonov signed a contract for a series of advertising spots. Right after signing, they brought him to a studio to film the first spot. He refused weakly, said he wasn't dressed for filming and all that, but they said the opposite was the case: he'd need to undress. I whispered to him that there was no reason to be especially nervous: he had clean underwear. That was no reassurance, though.

We came to the studio. There's a container made of some sort of special material standing there: it's silvery with a hundred polished rivets. There's cotton wool soaked with glue along the edges of the container, as if it's icy, and there's gas coming out of it, imitating liquid nitrogen's coldness. The gas spreads along the floor around the container in fluffy layers. They undress Platosha to his underwear and plant him in the barrel. Actually, he's barely visible in that container – just his head and shoulders. Off-camera, they ask Platosha:

'What helped you endure here for so many decades?'

He takes a package of frozen vegetables and raises it over his head: 'This did!'

The whole studio rolls with laughter.

And I suddenly feel sorry for him.

SUNDAY [GEIGER]

Innokenty and Nastya described filming the advertising spot.

On the one hand, it's comical. On the other, though, it degrades the tragic element of Innokenty's life. In his own eyes, first and foremost.

It imagines that he spent all those decades lying in a barrel. He didn't give a damn, just sustained himself on frozen vegetables.

What tackiness that is, anyway. Schrecklich.[5]

MONDAY [INNOKENTY]

A couple of days ago, I was filmed for an advertising spot: Nastya made an agreement with an agency for a whole series of them. It's

5 Awful (Germ.).

unbelievable stupidity and it's embarrassing to even talk about, but they pay an insane fee. I never would have thought it would bring in so much money.

I'm reading now about what happened in the country after my arrest. The authors keep expressing the thought that the entire country became a prison camp. Of course, even back then I heard bits of news from the newly arrested and knew some things thanks to Muromtsev, whose connections to the country's capitals had not been cut off. But still, I had not imagined the true scope of the Terror.

Muromtsev. He was a sincere person, carefree, too, in a way. I think the fact that he was already residing on Solovki is what saved him from worse troubles. He was located in the center of the vortex, where, as we know, it is calmest of all. If he had not already been imprisoned, Muromtsev would have been shot thirty times for what he told me during our walks. As for me, I no longer hid my judgments from anyone – not just Muromtsev – when I was preparing to be immersed into liquid nitrogen. My words most likely made it to the camp's authorities, but were regarded with total calm. Knowing that all my judgments would be frozen along with me. And would never thaw.

It surprised me greatly that other Lazaruses were cautious, as was the way at the camp. Maybe they truly believed that they would be thawed someday and were afraid of possible accusations in the future? Their fear acted upon me, oppressively. Could it really be, I wondered, that even the distant future would not lead us out of this Bolshevik hell?

Muromtsev sometimes invited me to his apartment (he had a separate apartment!) and treated me to coffee with cognac. When his lips touched the coffee cup, his mustache sank unexpectedly low, its spiky ends sticking out. It was obvious that the academician's mustache was treated to special care. A small beard embellished his face, too, and his delicate round glasses shone splendidly, but the very finest thing about Muromtsev was his mustache. That mustache, along with the coffee and cognac, instilled hope. So long as people who looked like that existed, normal life did not seem irretrievable.

During one of our conversations, Muromtsev said to me:

'The real terror will begin soon.'

'What?' I inquired. 'So this is unreal?'

'There's no reason to be ironic. Two things are needed for real terror: society's readiness and someone who will take charge. Society's readiness is already there. There's just one small thing missing.'

'And so who will take charge?'

Muromtsev was silent.

'The strongest one. He once telephoned me, as you know. Well, then: his strength can be felt even over the telephone. It's animal-like somehow, not human.'

I believed Muromtsev: he worked with rats.

TUESDAY [NASTYA]

Zheltkov called this morning – I answered. Rather, his aide called and when I responded that Platonov wasn't at home, Zheltkov himself intervened in the conversation, and said that's even better.

'You and I are going to hatch a little plot: we're plotting a tea party so your husband doesn't know. We'll invite him when it's a done deal, so to speak.'

'Are you in Petersburg?' I asked.

'What about you?'

Loud laughter in the phone. I laughed, too, but mostly to be polite. We said goodbye until evening. Zheltkov's a great guy. Humorous, easy to talk with. True, according to Zheltkov, Innokenty Petrovich had apparently been dreaming about a tea party like this for ages, practically requested it, and now it is finally happening. But that's just how he is: it doesn't ruin anything, it even enhances Zheltkov in some sense, as if, you know, we're all human beings here, we can make something up if need be. When somebody's totally lacking weaknesses, somehow that's not human ...

Platosha and I bought some pies and various kinds of Middle Eastern sweets at the bakery. The doorbell rang at six that evening. We opened the door. Two guards (with wires in their ears) came in first, followed by uniformed people from the 'Nord' bakery, and only then Mister Zheltkov. About a dozen photographers and TV correspondents were behind Zheltkov. Two more guards completed the delegation. Feeling lost, we backed into the large room and the guests (this was reminiscent of a military offensive) advanced toward us.

We drank tea for about ten minutes, just long enough to fulfill the requirement of setting up the shot and carrying out the filming. Put bluntly, I wouldn't say any soul-searching conversation came out of it. And how could it have been soul-searching when only Platonov, Zheltkov, and I were sitting at the table, despite inviting everybody to sit with us? The rest of the delegation stood by the wall, clicking camera shutters and chatting on their walkie-talkies. We took a sip each and the whole group of them departed, noisy and stamping. We were left with a large teapot inscribed 'From the Government of the Russian Federation' plus three cakes from Nord, and we've only managed to open one of them.

I wonder if that's how he always drinks tea?

TUESDAY [GEIGER]

Nastya called. She told me how Zheltkov came by unexpectedly this evening.

I already knew. I saw it on TV: they showed everything. Innokenty Platonov and Zheltkov, patron of the thawed.

The issue wasn't really about Zheltkov. Nastya called because of the pies and cakes: they're delicious but there's nobody to eat them. She invited me to stop by tomorrow for tea.

Of course I'll stop by.

WEDNESDAY [GEIGER]

We drank tea. I'm not Zheltkov, I can't be so quick. I stayed very late, until 1.30, and took a taxi home.

I wasn't expecting Innokenty to start discussing dictatorship and the Terror. About what a misfortune it was for the people. (Nastya silently drew my attention to the pies.)

And then he spoke his mind, saying dictatorship is, in the final reckoning, society's decision, that Stalin was expressing a societal will.

'There's no societal will to die,' I objected.

'There is. It's called collective suicide. Why do pods of whales beach themselves, have you thought about that?'

I had not thought about that.

'Are you saying,' I said, 'that Stalin was only an instrument of that suicide?'

'Well, yes. Like rope or a razor.'

'A view like that frees the villain from responsibility: you can't hold the rope accountable.'

Innokenty shook his head.

'No, the responsibility remains with the villain. You simply need to understand that the villainy could not help but be accomplished. People were waiting for it.'

Waiting for it?

FRIDAY [NASTYA]

This morning I woke up before Mister Platonov. I sat cross-legged on the bed, examining my sleeping husband. There was no serenity on his face – there was suffering. His lips trembled sometimes, his eyelids, too. From what, one might ask? After all the blows of fate and losses, there's such a happy ending. He found it all: widespread attention (come on, this is even full-fledged fame!) and money; he even found his lost Anastasia in my person.

I really wanted to wake him up but didn't dare. I would have had to explain that, well, when he was sleeping . . . An explanation like that might traumatize him. Geiger's already warning me all the time that I need to be careful with him. And so I didn't wake him up, I just kept watching him. Hand on the blanket, threads of veins running just under the skin: there's something childlike in how they show through. Just think: the hand of a hundred-year-old person! The hand that touches me.

In an interview for one of the women's magazines, they asked me (in an interview! with me!) if I give Innokenty Petrovich high ratings as a man. An obnoxious question, of course. And I answered that the question is obnoxious but couldn't help myself and said that as a man Innokenty Petrovich is, well, whoa!

I sat and sat and then crawled under the covers again. I started thinking about all kinds of stuff. Yesterday, for example, yet another advertising agent – representing some kind of furniture company – contacted me. He asked Platosha to bring it to the attention of the public that furniture prices are rising rapidly everywhere but at their company, he says, where they've been frozen for three years now. The client's thought is that TV viewers will perk right up and start buying their furniture. For this low-key statement, they're offering Platosha a figure fifty per cent higher than what he gets for the vegetables . . . so that's something to think about. And furniture, yes, would be a little more respectable than vegetables.

SATURDAY [INNOKENTY]

Marx says to me, tapping with his cane:

'Construction lines are the foundation of the work. You haven't perfected construction of form, it's too early to move on to the light-and-shadow model.'

But I apparently moved on. Why, one might ask?

SATURDAY [GEIGER]

A proposal came to Nastya: they invited Innokenty to host a corporate event. At a cooling-unit factory, by the way. It was Nastya herself who told me. She was asking for advice.

I took her by the shoulders and advised her to slow down.

Nastya wasn't against that. According to her, the reason she'd approached me was that the proposal seemed questionable to her.

Well, wonderful that it seemed that way. Because I'm already feeling alarmed about Nastya's proactiveness. Innokenty senses that.

'You probably see Nastya as very pragmatic,' he said to me the other day. 'In Russian terms, self-interested.'

'No, I don't see her that way. I think it's still childishness speaking in her. It's simply speaking in a contemporary way.'

Innokenty looked at me with a lingering gaze.

'You know, I think the same thing.'

We both started laughing.

I can tell you when I didn't feel like laughing. When I saw the television advertisement with Innokenty. I don't watch television, I just turn it on for a short while during supper. For the evening news. And then right after the news, there's Innokenty in a barrel. And liquid nitrogen and vegetables. And that strange text . . .

At first I wanted to have a serious talk with Nastya. Then I thought, well, maybe she's right in a way. Money's definitely necessary. Money. Geld.[6]

6 Money (Germ.).

MONDAY [INNOKENTY]

I see that all Nastya's activeness irritates Geiger. In a conversation with me, though, he himself defined it as childishness. That's very correct: it truly is childishness. That sort of perception of the matter helps me, too, reconciling me with what it is about Nastya's behavior that's disagreeable to me. No matter how it manifests itself, though, Nastya's childishness moves me, sometimes almost to tears. At times it scares me because it belongs to another world and it's so incongruous with me and my experience.

I fear that we will never completely bond because my experience – I have already spoken of this – did not form me. It killed me. I'm reading a lot now about the Soviet time and, well, it seems I stumbled on the thought in Shalamov's writings that one should not tell of the horrendous events in the camp after living through them: they are beyond the bounds of human experience and it may be better not to live at all after them.

I have seen things that burned me up from within: they do not fit into words. Shipments of female prisoners were delivered to the concentration camp and raped by guards immediately. When signs of pregnancy appeared for the unfortunate women, they were sent to Zayatsky Island – *the island for Juliets*. This was the place they punished *sexual debauchery*, which is severely penalized in the camp. The conditions were terrible on this absolutely bare island, where the wind blew eternally, and many did not survive. I write that and now shadows that were once people wander along what I wrote. The words crumble to dust: they do not come together into people at all.

If power is to return to words, the indescribable must be described. Thin faces of women from the Smolny Institute under the slobbering lips of GPU men. Under their unwashed hands. These bastards reeked of sweat and stale alcohol, and when they called for the most beautiful women to 'wash the floor,' the women could not disobey.

The wail of a woman whose husband was shot, five children were taken away, and who was, herself, sent to Solovki. There they raped her and infected her with a social disease. A doctor informed her about the disease. She rolled along the frozen ground by the front steps of the infirmary. At first they did not beat her, ordering her to stand. Then they began kicking her with their boots, ever harder and more frequently, beginning to enjoy themselves, becoming animals. She shouted loudly, her voice high, briefly going quiet after blows to the gut. The most terrifying thing about her wail was not its strength but the unfeminine bass note that concluded each of her high-pitched screams.

I saw that. And I have been unsuccessfully driving it from my memory ever since. That's what I live with, what so separates me from Nastya and makes us people from different planets. How can we live together if we are so endlessly different? She has a spring garden and I have that abyss. I know how terrifying life is. But she does not know.

TUESDAY [NASTYA]

Today was Platosha's press conference. My husband looked far more confident at this one than the previous one. That occurred to me during the press conference and was confirmed for me after watching it in the evening rerun. There's no point in describing it: it's all published in *The Evening Paper.*

TUESDAY [GEIGER]

I watched Innokenty's big press conference this evening.

He was sitting in front of an advertising display screen. That lent the proceedings an extraordinarily commercial look.

Innokenty has become more self-confident. He answered calmly.

He twirled a pencil in his fingers. Nastya told me later that the vegetable PR agency brought the pencil (it's a good thing it wasn't a frozen carrot). To create an image of confidence. I don't think Nastya needs that sort of thing.

There was no getting around some of the lovable ad-libbing that life abounds with. When Innokenty was answering a question about the level of government support (a disappointed hum in the hall), the TV camera cut to *Motherland LLC* on the advertising screen.

It wasn't just the cameraman who noticed the patriotic firm. A reporter from one of the newspapers pointed at the advertising screen and asked Innokenty if it didn't seem to him that the Motherland truly was an LLC with regard to him. The joke went flat, though. Innokenty didn't know what the abbreviation meant.

He still didn't laugh when they explained all that to him. He began discussing, in all seriousness, how there's nothing bad in the Motherland having limited liability. Everyone, he said, should be liable for his actions. Only personal liability can be unlimited.

And then he said it's pointless to blame the government for one's troubles. And it's pointless to blame history, too. One can only blame oneself.

The correspondents then grew gloomy. One asked:

'And you really don't blame the government for the fact that you landed in a camp? That they turned you into a block of ice? That your life became utter punishment, for unknown reasons?'

'Punishment for unknown reasons does not exist,' answered

Innokenty. 'One need only think about it and an answer will certainly be found.'

Interesting logic. In a strange way, it coincides with the GPU's logic. They always helped find answers at the GPU.

TUESDAY [INNOKENTY]

I keep asking myself if Nastya resembles Anastasia. Just after we met, it seemed to me that she resembles her. But now, apparently, no. I cannot identify the changes that have taken place in Nastya. Has she become more uninhibited? More self-confident? They say you can only get to know a woman through marriage. Perhaps that is yet another *phrase*, a cliché, but does that mean it's incorrect?

Yes, Nastya was a little different during the time we were not living together. But it would be strange to maintain the style of our previous relationship when the circumstances of our interaction have changed. For example, we now see each other naked – does that mean we should use words from another time? It's simply that Anastasia and I did not have this phase of life together, otherwise I think she, too, would have changed. And it's already high time I stopped comparing Nastya with Anastasia. Nastya is her own person, she is not that sheep Dolly and not a copy of her grandmother. She's a completely separate person. Why am I measuring her using someone else's scale?

WEDNESDAY [NASTYA]

I was awoken during the night by something like quiet whimpering. When I turned on the nightlight, I saw it was Platosha. He was crying in his sleep and his face was wet from tears. He was trying to say something but wasn't opening his mouth, and his voice was thin, somehow almost like a child's. That's why it seemed like he was whimpering. A face with closed eyes isn't usually expressive but there was so much grief on his . . . Not a face but a tragic mask, reflecting what he'd suffered there, in his previous life. Wake him up? Or don't wake him up? I wanted to cut that troubling dream short right away but was afraid that would only be worse. I touched my lips to Platosha's eyes and sensed the salt. He opened his eyes but didn't wake up. He closed them again and went on sleeping, without groaning.

Then I couldn't go back to sleep. All kinds of daytime stuff started getting in my head. I remembered that today I'd made a final agreement about renting out my apartment and even accepted a deposit. I started deciding what to leave in the apartment: the furniture, of course, dishes, and some other stuff. Take: favorite books, all sorts of intimate little things, my grandmother's things. In these cases, you usually put together a list but I didn't want to get up, didn't want to wake up Platosha.

THURSDAY [INNOKENTY]

Several GPU men raped a young woman in the medical department. I was lying on the other side of a wooden wall and heard everything. I couldn't stand. I shouted to the doctor but there was no doctor. I began pounding on the wall but nobody paid me any attention. I continued pounding. One of the rapists came in, dragged me to the floor, and kicked me several times with his boot. I lost consciousness.

When I came to, I heard crying on the other side of the wall. The doctor's voice was audible, too, and the jingling of medical instruments. Then the doctor came to see me.

'I can point out one of the employees who was there,' I said. 'He came in to beat me and I remember him.'

The doctor carefully helped me lie on the bed.

'Do you really remember?' He turned at the threshold. 'If I were you, I'd forget as soon as possible.'

It's surprising, but I knew who was lying on the other side of the wall. This was the same unearthly creature I had seen once in an apartment on the Petrograd Side. A railing with wrought-iron lilies on the stairway, the smell of books in the apartment. She walked ahead of me. Limping. I moved slowly behind her along bookshelves. She limped, yes. Hair gathered at the back, shawl on her shoulders, and if you looked, she was exactly like a librarian, especially with all those books around. I had brought her several more books: some of the ones Professor Voronin borrowed from this family. The Meshcheryakovs: the surname blended with the address and was thus preserved. The Meshcheryakov family. What kind of family was it? I never did find out.

I never even learned her name. Did I not want to? Did I think a mystery could not have a name?

We went to their library (really, all the rooms there were a library). Two armchairs on opposite sides of a round table. She turned around, stood behind the chair further away, and placed her hands on its back. I was regarding her for the first time: no, she was not a librarian. Not at all.

'Here.' I held the books out to her. 'They asked me to give these back to you.'

She remained silent so I said:

'Thank you.'

She smiled. Her face was astonishing: gothic with sunken eyes. And a vein twisting around her thin neck. And that limp ... She answered:

'You're welcome.'

She did not offer me tea because tea was simply not compatible with her – what, would she boil water on a kerosene stove? But she did not even offer me a seat. A queen. I stood and looked at her. I imagined the happiness of pairing with her. Not happiness: it was something else. There cannot be happiness with a woman like this, there could only really be the sweetness of pain. She was particular and that particularity attracted. Everyone. There is a reason that even the animal-like GPU men hunted for her in the medical department. The soloist women from folk-dance ensembles no longer got them worked up. They, the bastards, wanted the ethereal.

She came to me that night at the camp after everyone left. She hobbled in. Crawled in. She remembered me from Petersburg back then, too, and had recognized me here. She sat on my bed and then lay down, because she could not sit. I caressed her hands. I caressed her hair: it was wiry, stiff with clotted blood. Silently. I already knew that I needed to be silent with her. But our touches were deeper than words. Toward morning, she pressed her lips to my ear:

'Thank you.'

I wanted to answer her but she covered my mouth with her hand.

'I would no longer exist otherwise.'

Her hand smelled of medicines.

Lying alongside me, she was Anastasia. When she left, I knew I would kill the GPU man. I felt at ease and fell asleep.

FRIDAY [GEIGER]

Yesterday they contacted me from the Smolny building. They said the governor is inviting me and Innokenty to meet with him. Since the question of Innokenty's apartment had been decided at the gubernatorial level, I replied that I would ask Innokenty to come.

I called him. He had nothing against it. Basically, he regarded it very calmly.

We arrived there just before twelve today. We had to wait a little; the governor was meeting with someone. There were already journalists in the meeting room when they invited us in. They sat the conversation's participants in armchairs by a round table.

The governor read a few phrases from a piece of paper. I can't remember a single one of them now other than the final phrase. It said that Innokenty, like no one else, should understand the difference between democracy and dictatorship.

Innokenty thanked him. As I understand things, nothing more was required, but Innokenty decided to respond. Essentially, why not?

Innokenty said that the proportional level of evil is approximately identical in all epochs. Evil simply takes on various forms. Sometimes it presents itself through anarchy and crime, sometimes through the authorities. He, someone who has lived so long, has seen both.

The governor thought for a moment and asked how Innokenty feels.

The answer wasn't formal here, either. The guest told the governor about changes in temperature and blood pressure. Of course that was unexpected. Aber schön.[7]

---

7 But lovely (Germ.).

SATURDAY [INNOKENTY]

Yesterday they telephoned me from some political party and proposed that I join. I played at wavering. They explained to me that this was the governing party and that if I wanted to achieve anything . . . But I have Nastya, what else can I achieve? I thanked them and hung up. Then Geiger called with an invitation from the governor. And I agreed right away to go with him and for some reason didn't even think about mentioning the party's call. Because maybe it coincided with the invitation? What do they want from me? Advertising? Did they like my ads with the vegetables?

When the governor hosted us today, I had the opportunity to scrutinize him up close, imagine to myself what political authority looks like. And it looks, put bluntly, ordinary, nothing outrageous: large bald spots, a groomed and somehow simultaneously wrinkled face, spots on the skin. I looked at the governor and thought about how being near him caused me no agitation, the same as if his presence were televised. Yes, that's the exact comparison: the object of observation is nearby and fully visible but there's no contact with him: he's on the other side of a screen.

And my life is on this side.

SUNDAY [INNOKENTY]

No, I will write about my cousin Seva after all. About Seva at the Kem transit point. About Seva in a leather jacket, wearing a service cap with a red star.

We zeks had already been standing in formation for more than two hours, waiting for the chief who would decide our fate. Rather, our *fates*, because even here, each person had his own. The chief appeared and he was Seva. He walked in the company of several Chekists. I cannot say I was very surprised when I saw him, at least after the first second. In essence, one might have expected something of the sort from him. He had found that big strength he was seeking and was now acting in its name.

He did not notice me right away. First he sat down at a table and poured himself some water from a pitcher. Drank it. And then raised his eyes and noticed. He appeared to be smiling but it only appeared that way. It was a spasm, not a smile. He immediately lowered his eyes to the paper on the table. After scratching his nose, he began reading it: surname and place for assignment. His voice shook, despite the forced severity. It began breaking as the letter 'P' approached.

'Platonov!'

There was fear and entreaty in Seva's gaze. He was undoubtedly thinking that his kinship to me would compromise him. That the Chekists would inform on him to the proper place right away.

'Here!' I answered.

Seva and I, two aviators. At the sea, an even more northern one now than before. Only this time he was the leader, all the strings were in his hands. Where were we flying?

'Remain on Popovsky Island until my special instruction.' His voice has become a wheeze.

'Yes, sir, remain!'

I looked at the floor. The paint on the boards was peeling. A camel had formed there; it was just lying there on the floor. They do well, those camels, in warm regions. They can spit on everything. I sensed Seva's relief even without seeing him: I did not let on that I knew him. I had enough sense to understand that a transit point was not the best place to recognize someone.

From that moment on, the hope arose in me that he would pull me out of the camp. Or, say, leave me here with light work. I expected that today or tomorrow he would somehow find me or simply summon me. To cheer me, for starters, and then – who knows? – to ease my lot.

None of that happened. Seva was not interested in either meeting with me or – even less so – in my staying constantly alongside him. With his mistrustfulness, I think he considered that too dangerous for himself.

Seva's special instruction appeared twelve hours later. They sent me to the 13th Brigade of the Solovetsky Special Purpose Camp. That was one of the harshest places on Solovki. Had Seva set my destruction as his goal? I don't know. I am certain only that he suffered in signing his instruction. Maybe he was remembering our argument over the locomotives of history.

TUESDAY [GEIGER]

They didn't invite Nastya to see the governor. Innokenty stated this complaint to me after the fact.

Originally, he said nothing of the sort. From this it follows that the complaint originated with the uninvited herself. Innokenty requested that in cases like this I mention Nastya separately.

She's been walking around looking pale. It's obvious that the pregnancy is not progressing very easily. The nerves are from that.

About the outing to the governor, by the way. While we were waiting, Innokenty told me that the other day he finished reading a book about heroes of outer space. Oddly enough, of the multitude of heroes, it was the dogs, Belka and Strelka, that made the greatest impression on him. He spoke anxiously about them.

TUESDAY [NASTYA]

Platosha and Geiger went to see the governor but nobody invited me. It's not that I especially wanted to see that governor guy – in theory I couldn't care less about him – it's just that, according to etiquette, the invited's wife should be with him. The thought likely didn't occur to Geiger but Innokenty Petrovich could have considered it. At first, I didn't tell him what I thought on that score but then I said it when we were making love. He: oh, that is pretty embarrassing, I didn't figure things out right away, it didn't even cross my mind.

It's too bad it didn't. That's all, I don't feel like writing more today.

THURSDAY [INNOKENTY]

I studied the GPU rapist's routes. I didn't so much study them – because how could I follow someone who moved about the camp freely? – I simply worked at the repair workshop, not far from where those routes ran. The GPU man's surname (I found this out fairly quickly) was uncomplicated: Panov. As for his routes, they weren't elaborate, either: they led to the command-staff bathhouse that stood behind the workshop.

Panov usually appeared on Saturdays with his entire GPU shift; sometimes he came in the middle of the week. At first I thought this character was meeting with ladies there, but it became clear that he preferred arranging those meetings for home. Panov went to the bathhouse so often solely because he loved steaming a while. He valued bodily enjoyment in the broader sense, but steaming was the most important thing to him. It seemed to me that the way our paths crossed in that huge place (it happened on its own!) was not accidental. It definitely convinced me that I would finish off Panov after all, as I had schemed.

There wasn't even any need for me to run after him: he himself walked past me and I saw him through the workshop's dulled window. One time I took a bucket with a rag and washed the window. They all laughed, wondering why. I cannot (I said) stand dirt on window glass. This is still a habit of mine from home. Well, if it's from home (they were laughing anyway) that's another matter. For all that, I could now see Panov well: walking back and forth. He sometimes went back alone, from which I could conclude that on those occasions he was the last one in the steam room.

One time, he moved wearily (head lowered, finger in his nose) past the window, and I slipped out of the workshop through the back door and made my way to the bathhouse without going out to the road. There was no light in the changing-room window. The door to the bathhouse was locked. I soon discovered the key under a wooden grate by the door but left it in place. I had found out the most important thing: Panov stayed in the bathhouse after it was supposed to be closed and staff were to leave, under camp regulations. They left him the key and he closed the bathhouse on his own.

I could have already left but I lifted the wooden grating again. It was knocked together roughly, with large gaps between the slats. I pulled a hacksaw blade out of my trouser leg. One end was sharpened and the other was wrapped in coarse fabric. I placed the blade in the gap between the boards and it settled well. I pressed two fingers on its edge. It sank all the way between the gaps, not counting the small end it could be pulled out with. But it was impossible to notice if you didn't know about it. Only I knew about it. And that secret made my life easier.

FRIDAY [GEIGER]

They called me from the presidential executive office. They announced, in ceremonial terms, that Innokenty and I are invited to Moscow to receive state awards.

I remembered right away: they'd called me a couple months ago. They'd asked who, besides me, was worthy of an award for a brave scientific experiment. I answered that, to begin with, I don't know if I'm worthy of that. They politely interrupted and proposed that I think about it anyway. Wahnsinn . . . [8]

If taking part in the experiment was brave for anyone, it was Innokenty. I named him.

This time, it was my interlocutors who expressed doubt. They were concerned that Innokenty Petrovich was, in some measure . . . *the object* of the experiment.

'No,' I retorted, unexpectedly fervently. 'No, no, and no.'

He was the most genuine subject, if they could appreciate what those words meant. He entered the experiment consciously and was its subject.

And so it turns out that people in the president's executive office are capable of listening. They gave awards to both me and Innokenty.

8 Insanity (Germ.).

Though I'll receive the Order of Honor and he'll receive the Order of Courage. On his side, they valued courage over all else. Which, as I told him when I informed him about the award over the phone, certainly begets honor.

Innokenty regarded that news impassively. He asked only if Nastya was invited to the ceremony. No, she wasn't. And it's doubtful I could change anything here.

FRIDAY [INNOKENTY]

Geiger just telephoned me and told me something strange about awards. It's not so much that I don't believe it (oh, the things I've had to believe after being thawed!) but that it's a poor fit. What is more, Geiger found out that invitations to the Kremlin don't include relatives. Nastya will be offended again. Or maybe it was just a prank, I mean about the awards? I have read about cases like this.

FRIDAY [NASTYA]

The tenants are moving into my apartment tomorrow. Today I went there to sort out a few final things and took the honorable award-winners with me. Thus, we went by taxi: Honor to the right on the back seat, Courage to the left, and I in the middle, as who knows who.

Well, let's suppose Motherhood: could I become a Mother Heroine? Yes, no problem.

They're bashful because I wasn't invited to the ceremony but I console them as much as I can. With all my heart, I do not want to go to Moscville. It's one thing to go for a ride to the Smolny with a baby in your belly but another to be caught in traffic in a foreign land. It's gratifying, though, that they both remembered me this time. I do love them both, even that dorky Geiger!

We put the apartment in relative order, gathered up four bags of things that I'm hesitant to leave among people I don't know, and brought them to Bolshoy Prospect. The statuette of Themis seemed like a particularly valuable object to me, left to my grandmother by Platosha's mother. Themis's scales were broken off: at my husband's hand, according to lore. I purposely took Themis down in his presence – ceremonially and unhurriedly – but he didn't react. He nodded listlessly when I placed her on the cabinet in the dining room.

'What can be higher than justice!' I shouted, to wake this person up.

He thought for a minute and said:

'Probably only charity.'

After Geiger left, he admitted to me that he had a headache. So of course he's not up for thinking about justice.

SATURDAY [NASTYA]

Platosha truly didn't feel very good yesterday. I put him to bed and he went right to sleep. I called Geiger a while later to report to him about Platosha's overall state. I also told him that his favorite childhood toy no longer makes him happy.

'He wrote,' Geiger reminded me, 'that the statuette was somehow linked to his first steps in art. Practically even inspired him to take it up. And now he's in a sort of stupor with that. His difficulties with Themis are apparently on those grounds.'

'So what should I do with her?'

'Nothing, let her stay there. Maybe she'll help him with a breakthrough.'

There you go. Well, she'll stay.

MONDAY [INNOKENTY]

I keep thinking: why, after all, did I decide to finish off Panov back then? Impulses like that vanish quickly in the camp. It's not so much that you lack strength (of course there isn't any), it's just that you see no point in a vendetta. The feelings evaporate. Next to nothing remains of them and they are directed at self-preservation. Later, when I was waiting on Anzer to be frozen, I no longer had any sufferings and hurts. They were gone after all the beatings, abuses, and tortures. There was exhaustion.

But I sighed with relief on that quiet evening after hiding the shiv in the grating by the front steps to the bathhouse. Carrying something like that on me wasn't safe. It was unnecessary, too. I needed it to be in this exact place; now all that was left was to wait for a convenient moment.

That moment came but I never did kill Panov.

On another evening that was just about as quiet, I realized he was in the bathhouse alone. Yes, everything connected with Panov happened on quiet evenings. I slipped out of the workshop and approached the bathhouse. I saw the electric light in the dressing room from a distance and recalled the night the limping young woman was raped. I attempted to enter that state when the hand delivers a blow on its own. Not even a blow but a jab, a cut. Some sort of subtle and elegant motion leading the narrow hacksaw between Panov's ribs. I did not want him to suffer, I wanted that he not live, that his stinking existence simply cease.

I soundlessly raised the grate and pulled out my shiv. In the last rays of sun, I admired the sharpened part and the shine: how many times had I run files of various sizes along it, applying the last touches with the finest file? I hid it all, hid it from those who were in the workshop. Platonov, they say . . . I draw them away, take them under my elbow, and lead them toward the wall. Platonov, who are you crafting that shiv for? Nobody asked, nobody caught on. And on that very same evening, I admired the shiv, not very worried that, say, Panov would notice me. I was so on edge that he would not have escaped me anyway.

I walked up to the changing-room window before opening the door. A motionless Panov was lying on a wooden bench. He was lying on his back, arms stretched along his body, which itself was corpse-white and displayed no signs of life. I began watching his stomach, striving to detect even the slightest breathing motion, but there was no movement.

I realized what this picture in the window reminded me of: it repeated the sight of Zaretsky's body, which I saw at the morgue and identified. I looked at what Zaretsky had been and thought that justice had triumphed. And realized I was not glad about that triumph. And wanted very much for Zaretsky to be alive.

Panov's hand twitched and scratched his chest. I inhaled deeply. I did not know myself what I experienced at that moment – gladness or disappointment. I knew one thing: I would not kill Panov.

TUESDAY [INNOKENTY]

This afternoon, we flew to Moscow by airplane. Geiger is teaching me: the words 'by airplane' can be skipped; he says it's obvious how you're flying. Just as certainly, he says, as you no longer need to say 'call *on the telephone*': it's enough simply to 'call' ... We had supper just now in the hotel restaurant and are sitting in our own rooms.

Unlike Dr Geiger, Aviator Platonov rose into the sky for the first time today: that is the peculiar sort of aviator he is. Not one to indulge in superfluous flights. And this lone flight of mine today did not work out well. As the airplane gathered speed on the runway, I began to feel rather unwell, stifled, and nauseous. Geiger (he said I went very pale) switched on the ventilation over my seat and I felt a bit better. It finally eased for good after the plane gained altitude.

A picture of my last visit to the Commandant's Aerodrome with my father surfaced in my head. The end of August. An air demonstration, rain, umbrellas over the crowd. Aviator Frolov's aeroplane was closest to us in the line of aeroplanes. People awaited his flight with particular excitement: it had been announced that today he would demonstrate aerobatic maneuvers never seen before.

Frolov is standing under the wing of his aeroplane, an unlighted cigarette in his mouth. He slaps himself on the many pockets of his overalls in search of matches. He finds them. Strikes one. The matches are damp in the rain. And here I am, thinking the following: if Aviator Frolov suddenly crashes today (this is aerobatics, after all), it will turn out that his wish – which was, in essence, simple – was not fulfilled before death itself.

I feel sorry for the aviator. I ask my father for matches and run across the field to Frolov. That isn't allowed and the master of ceremonies whistles at me, but I'm running to deliver the matches to the aviator. He somehow understood everything so is already walking to meet me. Smiling. I keep running, holding the matchbox in my extended hand. We meet. The aviator takes the matches and lights his cigarette. He takes the first drag; his face is surrounded by puffs of smoke. He shakes my hand firmly when we part. I nearly cry out from the strength of his grip but manage to hold back. So that's an aviator's handshake. As I return to the crowd of spectators, I again cross part of the airfield, but the master of ceremonies isn't whistling this time. He's standing, turned away.

And there I am alongside my father, looking at the airfield. Aviator Frolov's turn comes. He finished smoking his cigarette long ago and is sitting in the seat of the aeroplane. The propeller is working. The aeroplane jerks and shudders, held back by eight aerodrome workers. At the aviator's signal, the workers let the wings go and fall down. Finally. The machine frees itself from the last thing that held it down. Jumping with one wheel then the other, it runs along for a brief distance and soars into the air. It gains altitude abruptly, somehow almost too abruptly.

Flight. The aeroplane floats in the air like a large bird. It is not entirely clear what holds it there. It might be clear when people explain about the laws of physics and the construction of an aeroplane. But it is not clear when you look at its solitary soaring in the sky. And it is astonishing. And very frightening to think of the person sitting in it.

There is a reason I had been afraid ... A reason. It all happened after the complex maneuvers had already been demonstrated. Frolov's aeroplane was flying in for a landing from the distant heavens. His circular and smooth descent was interrupted all at once. Even now it seems to me that the only possible comparison (which later made it into all the newspapers) is to a bird that was shot. Despite its explicit romanticism, that corresponded to what I saw: the right wing broke like a bird's and the machine lunged downward, turning on its own axis.

They later wrote that a cable connecting the biplane's wings snapped and the construction lost its rigidity, but the only thing clear in those moments was: trouble is nearing. Of course it might still have been possible to hope the aviator was executing an aerobatic maneuver and would now come out of his nosedive – but there was the broken wing, which had almost separated from the machine and was shuddering in the wind, leaving no hope.

The crowd at the aerodrome went silent all at once. Everyone already knew the aviator was flying to his own death. He was somehow flying for an unbelievably long time and the aeroplane's spinning looked comical, thus especially frightening. Each time the machine turned its upper part toward us, Frolov was visible, sitting in his pilot's seat, and his hands were arranged differently each time: he was likely pulling desperately at various levers, attempting to draw the machine out of its tailspin. The moments of his flight kept lasting and lasting, and I had time to think that this was extending his life and that I was seeing him alive now and an instant later he would be dead and everybody knew it: both he, tearing at the machine's levers, and we, frozen in speechlessness . . . I prepared to catch that dreadful moment of the transition from life to death but, of course, caught nothing.

When the aeroplane's nose plunged into the ground (the wooden crack of its structure), the silence exploded into the crowd's thousand-voiced scream. The human mass rushed toward the aeroplane from all sides, instantaneously flooding the airfield with itself – just as spilt coffee spreads over a tablecloth. People were already prepared to run, too, and the aeroplane's strike into the earth served as their starter. I rushed along with them, foretelling the aviator's condition based on the machine's broken wings. I ran and shouted but slowed my run without realizing it myself, falling further back from the first row, and deserting those who needed to be the first to approach the person who had been smashed. And the slower I ran, the louder my scream became, as if I was attempting, with that desperate scream, to make up for my absence in the forward line.

When I finally did see Frolov, his appearance turned out to be less frightening than I had feared. Cleaved forehead, stream of blood from the mouth, hand unnaturally turned. That hand had taken the matches from me. It had shaken my hand, firmly, until it hurt. Now it was not fit for any handshakes, even the weakest. I recalled that hand later, when I read this well-known verse by Blok:

> Too late, now: on the grassy plain
> A crumpled arch of wingspan . . .
> Caught in the engine's tangle of wires
> More dead than a lever: a hand . . .

More dead than a lever: I knew the cost of that detail.

WEDNESDAY [NASTYA]

I watched the report from the Kremlin on TV. My guys were on fire today. Award-winner Platonov found the opportunity to speak about Belka and Strelka during the ceremony – I think it was very appropriate and showed a love for nature. Geiger was pretty good, too: he tossed out a quick 'thank you' and returned to his place. Without glancing at the supreme commander-in-chief. He doesn't like him very much; well, what's to love about him if you come right down to it? Long story short, I was proud of both award-winners.

WEDNESDAY [GEIGER]

Innokenty and I are on the way back from Moscow. We're in a train compartment: we decided to take the train after all.

He doesn't handle flying well. He has memories of some aviator who perished. Perished before his eyes.

I'm writing.

Innokenty is examining our medals. He put the two little cases in front of himself: Honor in one, Courage in the other. Pensively chews at his lips. He has the look of a person stricken by bewilderment. It's amusing to watch him.

This morning they gathered us at the presidential executive offices on Staraya Square. I knew all the future award-winners, or almost all.

Shortly thereafter, they loaded us on a bus and brought us to the Kremlin. We waited for the ceremony in a hall with a low ceiling. We ate pastries and drank juice.

A manager from the protocol service was going around the hall. He offered to take gifts for the president. One is not to present anything to the president oneself.

He approached us, too, but Innokenty and I just threw up our hands. We weren't planning to present anything to anyone. Disappointment flashed over the manager's face.

Innokenty was in the lavatory when the manager invited everyone to go ahead to the ceremony. His disappointment deepened.

Innokenty was called first from our pair. After glancing at a paper, the president praised his courage and compared him with Gagarin.

'I'm afraid I do not deserve the comparison with Gagarin,' Innokenty said dolefully, 'because my courage was forced. It is probably more akin to the courage of Belka and Strelka, who also had no other choice. So it would be better to compare me with them.'

There was applause in the hall and the president smiled

uncertainly. He joined the general applause. He obviously had not expected anything about Belka and Strelka.

Innokenty just put on both medals. I see them on his chest through bottles of mineral water. They suit him.

FRIDAY [INNOKENTY]

Geiger and I returned from Moscow yesterday. An unusual trip. As I walked through the Kremlin, I thought: if I had found myself here in the twenties or thirties, I could have met one of those who . . .

All our hopes and all our hatred rose like steam, to the top of the world, right here. They warmed themselves in that here, inhaled it. And if one truly could have ended up at the Kremlin during those years, then told them to their face about all the thoughts we had about our life . . . Of course it's funny: you can't even manage to open your mouth, nothing, not one word; you do well if you simply manage to cast a glance. Just to catch a passing glimpse of them: that's something in itself already. To die from heartbreak but catch a glimpse.

But I looked at the current one: my heart did not break. It did not even beat faster. And not because he's this way or that way but simply because this is not my time, it isn't native to me: I sense that, so cannot become close to this time. I experience nothing but an abstract interest in what's happening. It's just the same as if I had been presented to the president of, let's say, Zimbabwe: yes, it's the president, yes, it's captivating, but nothing responds inside. And you can tell him everything you want, but . . . that doesn't tempt you. It isn't interesting.

After the ceremony, they invited us for a glass of champagne. I drank the Kremlin champagne and suddenly thought to myself that this is the drink of power. I am always having ideas like that. I imagined power and the ability to conquer being poured down my throat along with the champagne, and, most importantly, with these attributes, a certain special responsibility for the country that transforms a bureaucrat into a ruler so that the country's business becomes his personal business and the country itself becomes a part of his own 'I.'

I shared my reflections about the beverage with Geiger but he didn't approve of my line of thinking:

'Where there's a good bureaucrat, there's no need for a ruler.'

Wonderful. A European view. I lifted my glass to Geiger's glass.

'And where have you seen a good bureaucrat in Russia?'

We clinked and the glass slipped from my hand. I watched as it flew, as if in slow motion, and knew that in an instant it would spray champagne and shards in all directions, and it kept flying and, there, it finally fell and the spray flew all over, just exactly as I imagined it. I had become a witness to some sort of strange time phenomenon: not real time and even more so not the past – maybe the future? After all, I saw that picture for an entire eternity before the glass smashed. Several staff members ran over, suggesting I not worry. Essentially, I wasn't worrying anyway.

SATURDAY [GEIGER]

I keep recalling my trip with Innokenty.

Especially the conversation over champagne, which he likened to a beverage of power. What a strange fantasy! That drink, he says, transforms a bureaucrat into a ruler.

I don't know what the current president drinks (I'm afraid it's something else) but he hasn't worked out to be one or the other ... Innokenty, however, astounds me. A person who lived through the harshest of tyranny and utters the word 'ruler' so lightly! Unglaublich ... [9]

There's a reason the glass fell from his hand.

SUNDAY [INNOKENTY]

There's a word-processing program on the computer that automatically corrects mistakes. I have the strange impression that sometimes the editor in there gets too involved and corrects a great deal more than necessary: adds something or, vice versa, erases something. It is my profound belief that the editor is too intrusive. Thanks to that program, I have the constant feeling of an outside presence ... I reported this to Geiger: he laughed and said he hasn't paid attention to these things for a long time. The usual computer insolence, he says.

MONDAY [NASTYA]

Just the other day, Geiger brought me a packet of papers. Platosha's journal from the first half-year of his new life: the notes from the

9 Unbelievable (Germ.).

notebooks have been entered on the computer and printed out. According to Geiger, he brought them so I can understand my husband better. I do, by the way, understand him pretty well already. But what genuinely struck me in those notes is how minutely he describes all kinds of details, the older they are, the more lovingly! I told him about that and he answered that he's writing a blueprint for the impending universal restoration of the world. My sweetie is joking.

I wonder if in a blueprint like that Platosha's recollections would be of equal value to the recollections of other people's – for example, mine? Although who needs my ancient history? By historical standards, ugh, it's not even the past, it's still the present. What could I describe that's so special?

For example, lining up in the morning at kindergarten, like in prison or the army. Breakfast filled with sorrow. The urge to vomit from lumps in the semolina porridge; a bleach smell from the washroom blowing in when a draft gusts. Sitting over the porridge, I carefully pick out the lumps with a spoon, but sometimes they get missed and I'm forced to push them away with my tongue. And that's when I vomit.

I have no love for those details and who would? But someone must come to love and describe them, too, otherwise the world will remain incomplete. Maybe I should be frozen, too, so I can appreciate them in a hundred years and present them to my descendants?

MONDAY [GEIGER]

The document regarding Innokenty's rehabilitation arrived.

It is stated that rehabilitation is 'due to the absence of elements of crime.' Meaning that he wasn't part of a counterrevolutionary plot and didn't kill Zaretsky. Nobody had any doubts about that as it was.

It's important to have the paper anyway. In a bureaucratic country like Russia, you always have to be ready to prove you're not a camel. In our case, it's all crystal clear: the government is guilty, meaning it should acknowledge that.

Innokenty wasn't even moved by the paper. I even thought I saw displeasure flash in his gaze. Does he really disdain the government so much that he doesn't need rehabilitation? No, I haven't noticed anything like that in him.

Maybe it seems to him that a paper like that is too cheap for all his sufferings?

I asked him:

'Do you recognize the government's right to declare you guiltless? If you don't recognize it, that's understandable, too.'

He shrugged his shoulders.

'Only the Lord God can declare me guiltless. What the government does isn't as important.'

Well, that's one way to look at it.

TUESDAY [INNOKENTY]

There came a moment in the life of each Lazarus when he was injected with a sedative and sent off for freezing. The injection was a final and secret kindness toward the person being experimented on and it was shown by Academician Muromtsev. The high-level authorities believed that people should be frozen not only while they were living but while they were awake. The academician, though – justifiably considering sleep a form of life – deviated from that instruction, and the Lazaruses were grateful to him for it. Without doubt, it is easier to plunge into the kingdom of absolute zero while sleeping. In the time before their injections, the Lazaruses frequently recalled the Russian saying that sleep does not hinder death. These words sounded cynical if applied to Muromtsev's goals, but in a strange way they must have strengthened the academician in his decision to inject the sedative.

I thought about Lazarus as I drifted off. His fate was my only hope. If it was possible to resurrect a man dead for four days who was already giving off a stench, then what could be impossible about resurrecting a person frozen according to all the rules? I understood that finding me alive upon defrosting was out of the question but I did not want to depart with a feeling of desperation. The Lord had resurrected Lazarus four days later. When would they resurrect me? And would they? I wanted to believe that they would.

Thinking now about my thawing, I – in light of the number of years that passed – ask myself: did my thawing become the resurrection of an entire generation? After all, any detail that I can now recall automatically becomes a detail of the time. And perhaps this is not a matter of detail but the whole? Maybe I really was resurrected in order that all of us grasp once again what happened to us in those terrifying years when I lived. I am sharing this with Nastya. And what if, I tell her, everything truly was schemed up for me to attest to? I did, after all, see everything and remember everything. And now I am describing it.

THURSDAY [NASTYA]

My overall state hasn't exactly been luxurious in recent days. I'm nauseous, don't feel like doing anything, and could just lie around without getting up. But no, there's tons of various things to do, the main one being that I have to cook so Platosha can eat. He's not fussy at all, he'd get by with a heel of bread, but this does mobilize me. He tells me:

'I'm already having dreams about frozen vegetables from the ads. Can we really not use that money to hire a housekeeper?'

We can. It's just that I, for example, don't want there to be someone other than us two hanging around the apartment. It's easier for me to make lunch myself. It's more than 'easier,' it's very enjoyable for me to cook for him. And he needs that so much: Platosha isn't just some husband off the street: he's special, the same age as the century. He requires care.

I'm laughing here, but there's some kind of frailty in him. Yesterday he slipped and fell in the bathroom. It's good the bathtub is plastic not iron; he didn't hurt himself badly, just scared me. I flew in, with one leap, and saw him lying in the bathtub. Smiling.

'I lifted one foot,' he said, 'over the side of the bathtub but the other one came out from under me.'

Mamma mia! 'I lifted one foot over the side' really is something an old man might say, not a man in the prime of life! Who is, yes, a full ninety-nine, though that doesn't hinder him, hmm, as a husband, not the teensiest bit. I told Geiger about that fall and he scowled. He asked me to keep a more careful watch on Platosha. How much more careful could I be . . . ?

Oh, and Geiger went through the hassle of getting official rehabilitation for award-winner Platonov; he says that could be important. He's surprised the document arrived so quickly and thinks that is because of Platosha's fame. The hero himself is maintaining his indifference, which is a bit strange. I understand that for the most part he doesn't need anybody's rehabilitation and this scrawling isn't worth a thousandth of his sufferings, but there's nothing offensive about it. He looks at Geiger almost angrily.

FRIDAY [INNOKENTY]

It seems stupid somehow, but I collapsed in the bathroom the other day. With a crash. Nastya came running in, anxious, and I pretended everything was fine, though I actually did hurt myself. I told her my foot went out from under me on a slippery spot, but slippery had nothing to do with it. My leg simply buckled and I fell. The most unpleasant thing is that this was not even the first time. Last week I caught my foot on a curb when I was running across the road and nearly fell. A day later, I went out for milk and did fall then, on the steps to the store.

It's somehow especially shameful when a young person falls, arms flapping, with instant fear in the eyes. That's not such a big thing for an old man, but for someone young – ugh! – despite the fact that I'm already a hundred. And everybody helps you get up, everybody sympathizes: how very revolting to be the center of attention! This aversion of mine apparently comes from my father. And it's very strange: for some reason, I thought of him when I was lying on the steps at the store, thought about *him* lying silently outside Varshavsky Station.

My falls are beginning to worry me, and there was that glass at the Kremlin, too. I don't know if it's worth speaking to Geiger about this; he fusses over me as it is and if I tell him, it's farewell, quiet life, and hello to tests, and things being banned.

Maybe it just seems this way to me, but everything began after the statuette of Themis returned to our apartment. She reminds me about my fiasco with art and the sorrowful events that took place before my arrest. I am not ruling out that this is all a matter of the psyche. As it happens, Geiger did tell me that half of all illnesses originate in the psyche. Just as, by the way, recoveries do. It's important to find the right mindset. I will try to handle that myself.

[NASTYA]

The award-winner has a new fantasy. He wants to fill in the gap in time that came about after he was frozen. He and I are now gathering books and films from the 1930s through to the 1980s. It's really mostly movies: despite the Soviet drivel in them, they show the way of life very precisely. And the fashion: wide trousers and rolled-up shirt sleeves in the 1950s. Cigarette trousers and pointy-toed shoes in the 1960s. Platosha pokes me in the side:

'Just look at their faces: the faces are completely different and half a century hasn't even gone by.'

'Well, yes, well, a little different but not that much . . . So what are faces like now?' I ask him.

'Do you really not see? Nervous in some way, mean, a "Don't touch me!" expression. Not everybody's, of course, but a lot.'

'So you like Soviet good looks more?' I nip cautiously at his ear. He shrugs his shoulders. It appears he doesn't like it.

MONDAY [GEIGER]

Innokenty's watching old films and newsreels now. He says there's a hole in time for him so he's filling it in.

I watched a fifties newsreel with them yesterday. It's remarkable. Like being on another planet.

He stopped the video player when they were showing a Komsomol woman close up. Yes, the face was expressive. I noticed, by the way, that the epoch is reflected more vividly on female faces than male. Maybe because female faces are more animated.

'There were still millions in the camps but there's unfeigned happiness on her face. Unfeigned!' Innokenty walked right up to the screen. 'Why is she so happy, huh? Despite everything.'

Nastya grimaced. Yes, female faces are phenomenally animated.

'And why doesn't a drug addict sense the reek in a drug den?' I said. 'Why do people prefer utopia to reality?'

'I, by the way, did not prefer it.' Innokenty took the remote and switched from the video player to the television. Channels flashed by. 'So now everybody's supposedly free, but what a sour look they have! I was sure joy would come with freedom.'

'It turns out,' Nastya said, 'that it's better to be in utopia and be happy than to be free but sorrowful.'

Innokenty threw up his hands. The remote fell with a crash.

I didn't initially want to write this: Innokenty worries me. Some sort of trouble with his health. Problems with his motor functions. And I can't yet understand what the exact issue is.

Nastya told me about *Platosha's* fall in the bathroom. I myself saw the smashed glass in the Kremlin. Of course it could be accidental to fall and to drop the glass and the remote, but something in all this puts me on my guard.

I've begun keeping a more watchful eye on Innokenty. An

uncertainty has appeared in his gait. It's unnoticeable if you don't look closely, but it wasn't there before.

TUESDAY [NASTYA]

Entrepreneur Tyurin called us yesterday. That's how he introduced himself: Tyurin, entrepreneur. Evidently an oilman. Platosha spoke with him, putting on the speaker phone so I could hear (our Platonov is adapting by the hour, not the day). Tyurin said he's arranging fireworks in the evening on Yelagin Island and wanted very much for us to come. I suddenly remembered: mamma mia, he's in the top ten on the *Forbes* list! A Moscow person – there aren't any like him in Petersburg. Or Siberia, either, where he pumps his oil. If you toss aside local patriotism, then all the money, careers, and everything else, too, it's all in Moscow. That should be recognized as an indisputable fact; it's not even an issue to get distracted by, like I am now.

Anyway, according to Tyurin, entrepreneur, he stopped by Petersburg today and felt like arranging fireworks in the evening, at the last minute, no advance preparations. He asked if we were offended that this essentially unknown person popped up out of nowhere. Unknown, Platosha agreed, but we're not offended. Life, said Tyurin, should be casual: if you feel like fireworks today – and on Yelagin Island in particular – then there will be fireworks. Those words would be music to the ears of the homeless man who rummages around in our bin: he simply doesn't know what life should be, otherwise he'd have arranged for fireworks on Yelagin.

Platosha conversed unenthusiastically with Tyurin but I made an energetic sign to him, to pull himself together. I understand that all that shooting things off on Yelagin is horrifically money-oriented and ostentatious, but even so . . . I really wanted to go. 'I really want to go,' I wrote on a slip of paper and put it in front of Platosha's eyes.

'Fine,' Platosha told him, 'we'll come.'

We didn't have to come: they sent a limousine for us . . . Just now, he, my sovereign master, came up behind me. He read the word 'limousine' and started laughing.

'Stop,' he said, 'stop writing about limousines.'

You're right, sweetie, you're right . . . No, I'll say two other things anyway. After the main fireworks there was a salute, and the volleys were named. The first volley, of course, was dedicated to Tyurin, and the second one was for Platosha. And also – maybe the most surprising thing – I noticed a fantastically beautiful diamond ring on Tyurin's finger. I told him that, in front of everybody, so it would be nice for him. And he took off the ring and held it out to Platosha, as if it would suit him better. And he winked at me. Platosha refused but Tyurin placed the ring in his palm and closed his fingers over it. A very showy gesture, regal, as one of the journalists said (I already saw that shot in several newspapers today). Though Tyurin, I repeat, is probably money-oriented, and not a king. The ring, however, truly is amazing – I examined it all morning. Platosha, the silly man, doesn't want to put it on.

[INNOKENTY]

What an appropriate abbreviation that is anyway, LAZARUS, even if you consider that I didn't lie there for four days. I have seen icons depicting Lazarus's resurrection: he's walking out of a crypt and the people standing nearby are covering their noses. Fine . . . According to Geiger's description, I didn't look so good when they took me out of the nitrogen. I did not, however, smell.

Lazarus's first death was not sudden: he was sick, very sick. My departure for freezing was not unexpected, either. It works out that we both had time to prepare ourselves. And his and my thoughts before departing were possibly the same, too. And then the Lord resurrected him: so how did he live with that? Even I, after all, who was returned to life by the mere mortal Geiger, cannot fully realize the extent of what happened. I arrived at the only thought possible: that the Lord thawed me, employing Geiger's hands.

How did Lazarus's life turn out after his resurrection? Yes, it is allegedly known that he lived another three decades and was a bishop in a Cypriot city, but I don't mean the details that are called biography. What concerns me is what he felt after having already once departed the world of the living.

After all, it is not accidental when a person returns from wherever he was. It is a change to the natural course of events or to a decision that has been made. There should be weighty reasons for any return. A person has special tasks when the return is from the great beyond and not just anywhere. Lazarus of the Four Days attests to the Lord's omnipotence.

What do I attest to? In the final analysis, to the same thing. Beyond that, though, probably also to the time I was initially placed in. Those living in that time of mine did not yet know what to attest to for their descendants, did not know exactly *what* would prove useful decades later. But I know. This helps me to some degree, though of course it is only to some degree because my attestations are futile anyway. For all that, it's good if they serve the resurrection of my previous time, even if a resurrection like that is incomplete.

I think ever more often about resurrection. Nastya's name speaks to that, too. Sometimes it seems to me that Nastya has resurrected

Anastasia, that they are seamless and compose a common life, purposely created for me from two different lives. At times, that thought seems like insanity to me because it denies the uniqueness of any separate life. I can speak with certainty about only one thing, that I love them both.

THURSDAY [NASTYA]

Platosha received a proposal to host a corporate event for a gas company. He turned it down. Put bluntly, I was a little blown away when I heard the amount of the fee. I didn't reproach Platosha, not one word: he's a man, it's his decision. The gasmen, however, didn't back off. They contacted me and explained that they're drilling test holes in the Arctic, meaning that, under the circumstances, they needed Innokenty Petrovich – even if they had to sweat blood. If not in the capacity of leading the corporate event, then at least in the capacity of a guest. And the fee would not even be reduced. All that was required of Innokenty Petrovich would be to show up with the Order of Courage, propose a toast to the company's general director (and his wife), and wish everyone success in extracting gas. That was already a different matter. It's funny, of course, about the toast and the director, but not burdensome or shameful. Platosha agreed.

I asked him to tell Geiger that this decision was made without my knowledge, otherwise our mutual friend would simply devour me. It's interesting that Geiger understands the meaning of banknotes but when talk turns to methods for earning them, that's when the grimaces and all that 'You see, Nastya,' and the like start. I don't want to look more mercantile than everybody else – maybe I dream about being Lady Hamilton, too – but someone has to arrange the means for existence. Really, it's strange the German's not the one doing that.

Be that as it may, we went, the sun scorching us, to that corporate event. The scene for the action was the Yusupov Palace, where – at the entrance and on the staircase (wow!) – there were black servants in livery and cut flowers everywhere. In the foyer were members of the board of directors, Duma deputies, movie actresses, bandits, zombies with a Soviet look, fashion models, correspondents, and professional schmoozers. In short: everybody that loves gas.

Vadim, head of the company's PR department, greeted us. He embraced us both around the shoulders and reported to us in a loud whisper with no introductions whatsoever:

'I'm liking that journalist woman Zhabchenko more than anybody. Her invitation was specifically for one person: her. And you know what she did? Do you know?'

'No, we don't,' we answered in chorus.

'She gave the invitation to her husband and showed up herself a half-hour later and said she was on the list. Showed her passport, too. The guards checked her and the lists, and, naturally, let her in.'

'And is her husband Zhabchenko, too?' asked Platosha.

'Well, there's the whole trick. Who would look at the initials with a surname like that? The little bitch! Forgive me . . .'

Vadim smiled charmingly. A minute later he was already talking with somebody else. They brought us champagne. I jokingly asked Platosha if the champagne would impede his performance. He smiled and slapped himself on his jacket pocket. That's where he had the printout of his toast, provided to us by the very same Vadim. In that toast, the person who had been freed from icy captivity was to raise his glass to the health of the Savchenko couple – Vitaly and Lyudmila – who wage war with ice near the North Pole itself. Everybody knew that the couple waged war with ice without leaving

Nevsky Prospect, but a statement of that sort was considered admissible as poetic license.

Platosha looked rather tired at the palace. Yes, he was smiling — that smile does look good on him! — but it came out kind of forced. Of course he drank quite a bit, too much, I'd say, but his tiredness wasn't because of that. It had engulfed him in the first minutes after we arrived at the banquet.

The serving of the dishes, for example, displeased him: about two dozen waiters carried roast piglet around the hall on a platter and, behind it, also on a platter, sturgeon and lots of things I didn't even know the names of. I asked Platosha if he was sick but he said he was only feeling a light indisposition.

A retired admiral was sitting at the table with us, a kindly fellow who was making sure not one toast went by without drinking a shot. A half-hour later Platosha asked our neighbor if it was true that he had as much free time as a retired admiral. The admiral answered that it was the absolute truth. He smiled, displaying the whiteness of his false teeth. Platosha soon repeated that question again and then again, but the admiral answered just as kindly as the first time.

It's too bad the promised toast wasn't at the beginning of the evening: then the effect would have corresponded better to what the gasmen had planned. But since the toast was conceived as a culmination, it came closer to the end. It didn't evoke much protest from the hall when Platosha proposed drinking to the Zhabchenko couple who wage war with the ice. I'm not even sure everybody heard his toast. It's interesting that the Zhabchenko couple, who were sitting in the far end of the hall and yelling louder than everybody, heard it. After the scene to get into the banquet, it didn't surprise them that a toast was being proposed in their honor. Even their declared war with the ice didn't surprise them. They stood and bowed.

And we received the fee anyway.

[INNOKENTY]

Here in my old apartment, I sometimes feel as if I'm on an island, in the middle of the sea of someone else's life. Poor Robinson Crusoe.

[GEIGER]

Innokenty worries me more now.

His movement is increasingly less confident. Sometimes I see him veering slightly when he walks.

If you don't look closely, you won't notice. But I look closely. I want to figure out the course of this thing, to grasp how it will develop further.

The problems aren't only with motor functions, though. It seems like his working memory is starting to break down. He frequently loses his train of thought if he's suddenly distracted while he's speaking.

I don't want to talk about this yet with either him or Nastya. I don't want to scare them. I keep hoping it's temporary.

And that corporate event with the gasmen. I understand that alcohol was the reason for the mix-up. Even so, I don't like this incident. How can you forget what you studied all evening the night before?

And the corporate event itself, that was Nastya's escapade. No matter how much they both convince me she had nothing to do with it, I can smell it: Nastya came up with it.

I want to let her have it in the head but am refraining. She's amusing.

SUNDAY [INNOKENTY]

Today we went for a walk around the cemetery at Alexander Nevsky Monastery. I really love walking around cemeteries. Nastya does not, though. One time during a walk, she said she's tormented by the thought that our happiness will end someday. I answered that it will indeed end someday, perhaps even soon: after all, anything under the sun can happen. I said that and regretted it: Nastya began crying. Somehow, that was not really like her.

It was very nice, though: diffused September sun, leaves on the ground in individual yellow spots, not yet a complete cover. Nastya walked, holding me by the arm, pressing her cheek to my shoulder, which slowed our motion. We examined inscriptions on gravestones. Old gravestones are very beautiful, more beautiful than even today's expensive ones. And the inscriptions were simply wonderful because their old orthography cannot compare with the new: it has a soul. Our literature's Golden Age is tied to that orthography as well.

Even my childhood and youth are tied to the orthography, too, though I am not part of the Golden Age. Platonov (a gaze over a pince-nez), when is the letter *yat* written in the roots of words? My memory has lost her face, figure, and voice, but that gaze over the pince-nez has remained. Although why, in fact, 'she,' when it could be a man? Yes, it was definitely a man: a ribbon from the pince-nez in the frock-coat pocket. The letter *yat*, I answer, is written in a series of words of age-old Russian origin . . .

Something familiar revealed itself on a granite gravestone that had risen up in front of us, but I still didn't understand what. No, I understood. I understood: the name, of course. Terenty Osipovich Dobrosklonov, 1835–1916. And the phrase, 'Go intrepidly!' Actually, it's not written there, but of course not everything under the sun is written.

Go intrepidly into the Kingdom of Heaven, Terenty Osipovich. The taxidermied bear by the door, my running through the enfilade of rooms, and the triumphal recitation of a verse. Theoretically, this could be another Terenty Osipovich, but I feel in my heart that it's the same one. As it happens, he died a year before everything began. A year before, meaning Terenty Osipovich was lucky. He died peacefully, in full ignorance regarding the imminent changes, and was among – one would like to believe – a circle of people close to him, hoping for their carefree lives.

Eighty-three years have passed since 1916 and one must suppose that little is left of Terenty Osipovich: skeleton, wedding ring, the buttons of his luxurious full dress uniform (and maybe the uniform itself!) and, of course, the two tails of his beard. Yes, a small part of him, next to nothing, but it is part of him, the very same Terenty Osipovich who cheered me at a difficult moment during the sixth year of my life. And there he was, lying under the ground, two meters from me . . .

'If this grave were dug up,' I said to Nastya, 'we could see a person I met for the last time in 1905.'

Nastya's long drawn-out gaze at me. Expressively keeping silent. It seemed she did not want to dig up Terenty Osipovich.

'Simply put, he is one of the witnesses of my childhood,' I explained. 'My father called him by his full name to me and I remembered it. That happens. It was one of the first names that lodged in my memory. And I suddenly stumble on him here, can you imagine?'

'No meeting is more surprising.'

Nastya pressed even harder against my shoulder. She saw that nobody was planning to dig up Terenty Osipovich.

[NASTYA]

A strange stroll: that's what I'd call a story about today. We walked around the Nikolsky Cemetery at Alexander Nevsky Monastery. This was not, by the way, the first time we were taking a stroll at a cemetery: Platonov has – how to put this? – a certain weakness for these strolls. They don't exactly weigh on me but on the other hand, I can't say they improve my mood much; they're not exactly Disneyland. Though I do need to walk, because of the baby.

And so we're strolling and strolling, when suddenly Platosha is standing still by one grave. Terenty Osipovich Dobrosklonov is lying there: it would be a sin not to remember a name like that. Terenty Osipovich coined the phrase 'Go intrepidly,' allegedly uttered to my future husband during his childhood. I can't argue: the phrase is a good one – no worse than Terenty Osipovich's name – but the impression this grave made on Platosha is beyond description.

He told me, in detail, everything connected with that phrase and then even said that if Terenty Osipovich were dug up, there'd be nothing to reveal but a skeleton and a full dress uniform. Well, yes, I agreed, there's no reason to labor under delusions here. And he thought a bit and then said the beard, too, would probably be revealed. Metal items of some sort, as well. And I was suddenly feeling like he was somehow saying that for real, all businesslike. That a little more and he'd dig up that grave and reveal all. We stood by the grave for almost an hour.

The saddest part of our stroll is that Platosha's leg twisted again when we entered the monastery grounds. He said it was because the road by the gate is paved with cobblestones and he's already become used to asphalt. I nodded but – under the pretext of surging emotions – I grasped him firmly by the arm. And I laid my head on his shoulder to totally reduce the distance between us. He wasn't walking very confidently at all. I don't know, should I tell Geiger about that? He's over-cautious and will start dragging his patient in for testing, and hospital things are already getting under Platosha's skin. I'll wait for now.

TUESDAY [INNOKENTY]

Much depended on what seat you took in the lecture hall. It was most interesting to sit at a point with a well-defined line of sight. For example, steeply below and with a three-quarters rotation, which is the most interesting view on Michelangelo's Dying Slave. His head is thrown back a lot already and if you take a seat in the first three rows, the lower part of the chin – which is always unseen – is revealed, along with the nostrils. The eye slips below the nose and the forehead isn't visible at all. Those who had the power to build a complex form according to the laws of perspective, as well as to see and maintain proportions, aspired to sit in those spots.

And, by the way, Marx is Alexander Vasilyevich Pospolitaki. I figured that out through a book about the Academy of Arts. I recognized the professors in a group photograph and found his surname in the caption. He died at the White Sea–Baltic Canal. I think his appearance was too colorful. What fit with the 1910s fell into complete disuse in the 1930s. Alexander Vasilyevich turned out not to be sensitive to the change of styles.

[GEIGER]

I've been reading everything Innokenty wrote all these months, so it's as if I've come to appreciate his view.

Sometimes I see things exactly as he does. As if I'm listening with his ears.

The clanking of instruments tossed on a tray.

The crackle of a bandage torn off.

The smell after washing floors: lemon, sometimes strawberry. It lifts the mood if it's not cloying.

This is the smell of changes. Only sensing that did I grasp how radically life has changed. It used to smell of bleach: I did catch that time.

During my internship, I earned extra money as an orderly and washed the floors with bleachy water. It's supposedly a disgusting smell but it does connect me with my youth. My heart beats faster when I sense it.

It turns out that you can even warm to something disgusting and then sigh about it some time later. And then there is the beautiful.

My time hasn't been interrupted, but here I am, capable of grieving for the past.

And then there's Innokenty: he has two lives that are like two shores of a large river. He's looking from the present shore to the past shore.

He didn't swim across that river: there wasn't even a river. He simply regained consciousness and the water was behind him. What had been his road became the riverbed. And he didn't walk that road.

He once told me he yearns for the years unlived.

THURSDAY [INNOKENTY]

I have been reading Bakhtin. From time to time Geiger brings me books that, according to him, an educated person should know, at least through an initial reading. He brings the best that appeared in various fields during my icy slumber. As I was reading, I thought: Robinson was tossed on an island for his sins and deprived of his native realm. And I was deprived of my native time, and that was for my sins, too. If not for Nastya . . .

By the way, it turns out she's read Bakhtin. She called those deprived of a time and space the *chronotopless*. Geiger laughed hard; he appreciates Nastya despite his difficulty relating to her. But I didn't laugh. I suddenly thought about those deprived both of their time and the space they inhabited: they are, after all, the dead. It works out that Robinson and I are half-dead. And perhaps even dead, at least for those who knew us in a previous time and previously inhabited space.

SATURDAY [GEIGER]

I called Innokenty and Nastya came to the phone. She said *Platosha* had headed for Smolensky Cemetery. That she'd gone with him several times but frequent strolls around cemeteries (breathing loudly in the phone) had become rough for her.

'Strolls around cemeteries?'

'Yes, around cemeteries. It's his new hobby.' Nastya went silent. 'He's searching for previous acquaintances.'

I went to Smolensky Cemetery. I remembered where his mother's grave was and went in that direction. I saw Innokenty a couple of minutes later at the end of a tree-lined walkway. Wearing, at my suggestion, dark glasses so he wouldn't be recognized. People recognize him anyway.

He walked, limping from time to time. He had a newspaper-wrapped bundle in his hands. *The Evening Paper.* The bundle was strange and initially distracted me from the limping.

After greeting him, I asked Innokenty what might be carried to the cemetery in a bundle. Innokenty blushed. He muttered something unintelligible. I wouldn't have asked if I'd known my question would agitate him so much.

'You don't have to tell me . . .' I smiled.

'I have nothing to hide.'

Innokenty unfolded the newspaper. In it lay the statue of Themis. Well, how about that. Why, one might ask, does he need that at the cemetery? What kind of justice was he restoring here?

This began to seem funny but I held back. Why, why . . . He was carrying it, supposedly, to his mother; he didn't go to see Anastasia. There was apparently some story connected with Themis. But there really was nothing to blush about . . .

We slowly moved toward the exit along the tree-lined alley. I walked with my head down. As if I was contemplating something. I was watching his feet.

He truly was limping.

We'll get down to serious testing in the coming days. I didn't say anything to him about that.

[NASTYA]

Plastosha has infected us with plain old bare description. He keeps repeating: describe more! I catch myself thinking over how best to describe this or that. Even Geiger, I heard, is attempting to express something. And really, why not Geiger, too? On what grounds do I deny him artistic capabilities? In German, by the way, 'Geiger' means 'violinist.'

SUNDAY [GEIGER]

So, let's say there's a choir at a morning concert.

We had a choir like that at school. It goes without saying that I didn't sing in it – with my ear! But I listened and was thoroughly absorbed during morning concerts celebrating various holidays.

The happiest morning concert was for the New Year.

The choristers assembled in rows on a wooden structure (light clattering) that I don't know what to call even now. Benches installed in three tiers on a stage.

According to the choir master, this design revealed the singers' vocal possibilities most fully. They were somehow arranged there so the sound floated in a special way: right to the soul. At least to mine.

The girls' voices were wonderful – like sterling silver – and it was they who defined the beauty of the morning concerts. I called their voices 'morning voices' to myself.

I listen to music in the car every day, some of it choral.

How rarely morning voices now sing. One might say they do not sing.

There's competent and professional articulation, but there's no magic. There's no morning.

[NASTYA]

It's 1993; my mother and I are in Tunisia. We're abroad on holiday for the first time (and some of the first to go!). And without my father for the first time. Although it's at his expense: he sends us money from America. Officially, it's like he hasn't left us yet, like he's still there to earn money, but, it's obvious what's going on with him. During one of his visits, I was watching him out the window and saw a young woman waiting for him in our courtyard. It's not that he didn't think he had to hide: he simply hadn't thought about it. It never occurred to him that he might be noticed. They kissed and set off, hooking their pinkie fingers – a variation from abroad that people here weren't using yet. I ran into this little twosome later in the city; my father was embarrassed. She was American; she had come with him and was staying at a hotel. As I understand it, he spent the greater part of the day in her hotel room.

Anyway, what was I talking about? Yes, Tunis. I wanted to describe Tunis, one of my most vivid impressions. Carthage, which should have been destroyed, and that senator (what's his name?), I forget ... The beach. Heat that gives way to coolness in the hotel lobby. African fruit and vegetables as part of an 'all-inclusive' package. On the very first evening, I had the runs, of a very high quality; this also turned out to be included.

Evenings were something special. Surprisingly fresh and pleasant. Not what I expected from Africa at all, who would have thought ... Maybe it was the evenings that made this land so attractive. Accordingly, they attracted aggressors from various tribes, including my very own mother. I got tired returning her abuse and counted the days until leaving because it was impossible to switch my plane ticket. This isn't about my mother so why am I writing all this?

This is about Platosha. I sense there's something happening that's not good, and I'm feeling uneasy. I already spoke with Geiger: he's worried. Very. The conversation with him basically left me reeling. I didn't even understand half of what he told me but what I did understand was enough to put me in a daze.

[GEIGER]

Our computer guy informed me that word processing program doesn't always insert the day of the week in the notes.

I asked if it's possible to restore the lost days. He answered that it's possible: everything's possible, he said, in a virtual world. Everything's a question of time and effort.

I suddenly wondered: but is it necessary?

TUESDAY [INNOKENTY]

I again spent time at Nikolsky Cemetery after Nastya left for classes. It was painful for me to see it: I do remember it unpillaged. There are no longer beautiful marble gravestones here, the ones that stood in my childhood. I asked myself why those gravestones could have been needed: for reuse? For paving the streets? What happens to a people that ravages its own cemeteries? The same thing that happened to us.

On days for prayers in remembrance of the departed, my parents and I would visit some of our relatives here. I loved those outings because they were like trips outside the city, with greenery and a pond: it was like a park, not a cemetery. And just a few steps from Nevsky Prospect. No sorrow could be sensed there at all. Even death was not sensed. Perhaps I did not fear death, either, thanks to that cemetery. I feared it, of course, but somehow without panic.

There was another place I did not fear death: on the island. Unlike Nikolsky Cemetery, it could be felt everywhere there. One cannot say that death *arrived* for its victims at our barracks: death lived in them. Death's presence became so everyday that we no longer paid attention to it. People died without fear.

They buried the dead simply, without coffins. They carried the corpses out of the infirmary and tossed them into crates on a cart. Four corpses fit in a crate; they were covered with a plank lid. If the corpses didn't fit, an orderly would crawl on the lid then stamp on it. They brought the crates to a pit and tossed them below. The pit was filled in when there was no more room. There were many pits of that sort and I had occasion to be near them from time to time. They did not evoke horror in me.

I was horrified only once: when one of the corpses began moving. That's what it was: one of the naked, decomposing corpses. Looking at its slow shambling, I did not even allow the thought that it was alive. Nothing in that person reminded me of the living. Then he suddenly extended a hand in my direction and introduced himself:

'Safyanovsky.'

And his left eye could not open because of his swollen eyelid.

I was now standing over the grave of Terenty Osipovich and remembering how lovely his help was for me that time. What a precise word he had found after all. He was lying two meters from me, essentially a trifling distance. His grave was squeezed between two manmade hills and was reminiscent of a boat between waves.

I suspect that Nastya thought last time that I was planning to dig him out. Am I? Most likely no. Though digging up his grave would not be so terrifying. No more terrifying than seeing slow shambling in the Solovetsky grave. The dead Terenty Osipovich probably differed little from the live: his head looked like a skull even during his life. Yes, I wanted very much to see him. If I could have lowered myself those two meters to him, I would have. If he had said 'Go intrepidly!' to me from there, I would have gone.

[GEIGER]

Innokenty needs to have magnetic resonance imaging of his brain immediately. The machine broke down at our clinic; I had to arrange for it to be done at another.

You can count the machines in the city on one hand. There's a huge wait for each one.

I attempted to explain *who* exactly requires testing. They nodded sympathetically. Explained that there was a six-month waiting list for appointments. Offered a quicker version: four months. And that's for a person who had been frozen. O, mein Gott . . . [10]

I gave them three hundred dollars. They set his appointment for the day after tomorrow.

[INNOKENTY]

Some strange things with my memory. Short-term lapses.

At morning prayers, people ask the Virgin: 'Deliver me of many and anguishing remembrances,' and I ask that, too. My lapses are of a different nature, though: at times I forget what I had been planning to do a minute before.

But the cruel memories remain.

THURSDAY [NASTYA]

Platosha signed up for a reader's card at the Historical Archive.

'What,' I ask, 'are you going to search for there?'

'My contemporaries.'

'I'm your contemporary, too,' I laugh. 'Who else do you need?'

He didn't laugh, though.

---

10 Oh, my God (Germ.).

'Well, various people,' he says, 'who aren't very important compared to you. Minor witnesses to my life.'

I snuggled up against him and he kissed my forehead. I love his kisses on the forehead. I love his other kisses, too, but the ones on the forehead are something special, even friendly, fraternal. That's what's lacking, more often than not, even in the very best lover. I understand now why my grandmother prized him so much. And, when it comes right down to it, she remained faithful to him her whole life. And I love him no less. I didn't used to say things like that, either to myself or to him. Today I said it before going to bed. Standing half-turned toward him. He placed his hands on my shoulders and turned me to face him. We stood like that for a long time. Silent.

They're doing tomography tests tomorrow. This worries me.

FRIDAY [INNOKENTY]

Today was the scan Geiger arranged. What's happening with me does not gladden him (or me, either, to tell the truth) and so there we were at the consultation center. Geiger was somehow unusually solemn. He said we need to clarify my fortune. I noted that I squandered my fortune long ago. The joking looked like pathetic cheering-up. Geiger was not laughing. And nobody assigned to the scanning machine was laughing.

Before getting down to work, they asked me if I suffer from claustrophobia. What can someone who lay so many years in an icy, insulated container say? It's interesting that I began doubting if I did not as soon as they asked me about it. I doubted as I took off my shoes. I had no answer as I lay down on the scan table, either. This was the first time that question had come up for me. And I answered 'no.'

When the cover closed over me, and the table and I began slowly riding into some sort of tube, I thought that I probably should have said 'yes.' This reminded me too much of coffins traveling into a crematorium: they had shown that on a TV show. And the apparatus's cover reminded me very much of a coffin cover. No wonder the doctor asked me to close my eyes. Why did I not close them?

The last thing I saw as I rode into the tube was the doctor hiding behind a metal door. Metal! And I was not to budge in that tube. I imagined what Gogol must have sensed, if it's true what they say about him ... A quiet panic seized me. I closed my eyes right away. Imagined the starry vault of heaven over my head. It eased. Something began buzzing and mechanically creaking, then went quiet. And began buzzing again. That smart machine was imaging my brain. I am certain that the dearheart will see why my legs are buckling and why I have become forgetful. It will report everything, calmly and impartially.

I rode out of the tube. As I laced my shoes, I saw Geiger taking the image from the doctor's hands and looking at it against the light. Based on Geiger's face, it wasn't clear if he was satisfied or not. He said goodbye and left for his clinic. With the image under his arm.

[GEIGER]

A catastrophe.

I don't know how I held myself together in Innokenty's presence. It's a genuine catastrophe – that became clear even from a cursory glance at the image.

I scrutinized everything at the clinic, clutching at my head. The amount of dead cells is beyond description.

The scariest thing is that I don't have the slightest notion of the direct reason for cell death in Innokenty.

Of course it's clear in general terms that it's the freezing, but what's the mechanism? What's the specific mechanism for what is happening? Intervention is impossible without a distinct understanding of that.

And it all began as a 'success story' . . .

Everything was in perfect order after the thawing. They did tomography on Innokenty when he was still unconscious. The tomography machine was in working condition then . . .

An important question: what to say to the Platonovs?

Or not say? And if I say something, should it be to both of them? One of them?

To whom?

[INNOKENTY]

I went to the archive today. They practically greeted me with ceremonial bread and salt. They apparently feel a kinship with me: I myself am nearly an archival phenomenon. They inquired as to what historical period interests me. It's not a historical period that interests me, it's people. Plus the sounds, smells, and manners of expression, gesticulation, and motion. I remember some of those things, but have already forgotten others. Definitely forgotten. When I said that, they coughed a bit and smiled. It's possible they thought I had not yet fully thawed. They asked me to clarify the years. Well, I say, roughly 1905 through 1923. For Petersburg. And 1923 through 1932 on Solovki. They sent a red-headed employee with the surname Yashin into the storeroom for 'cartons.'

A carton is a large box with archival materials. Yashin brought several of them, concerning various periods. In each carton there lay an inventory. I opened the inventory of the first carton and got lost in it. There were listings of institutions and their employees, archives of clerical offices, instructions from the powers that be, and even a selection of newspaper clippings. After delivering all that, Yashin continued to stand some distance away, and I felt his sympathetic gaze on the back of my head.

His sympathy turned out to be enterprising. In the end, Yashin approached me and offered his help. He asked what names interested me most of all.

'For you these names won't –' I began but Yashin interrupted.

'Write a list and the estimated years of activity for those people. How about a list of ten people to start?'

What were Terenty Osipovich's active years? Everything is, however, more or less clear about Terenty Osipovich: his journey ended at the Nikolsky Cemetery. And my strange comrade Skvortsov? Skvortsov who was banished from the line in starving Petrograd. The same age as the century. And Voronin from the Cheka? I felt his activity to the fullest, with every cell in my body. Skvortsov and Voronin, two dissimilar birds who flew through my life ... I wrote down ten names and gave them to Yashin.

TUESDAY [NASTYA]

I keep thinking about Platosha's health. I'm feeling anxious. These fears seem almost funny to me during the day but at night, not so much. What actually causes them? Nothing. Nothing! Geiger has some concerns that I hope will come to nothing. But they've scared me.

This morning I went to 'brush my teeth': I shut myself in the bathroom and sobbed soundlessly. I turned on the water to be sure it couldn't be heard. I even blew my nose without trumpeting sounds – I just quietly wiped off the snot – because people blow their noses when they cry.

Although they also blow their noses for no particular reason.

[INNOKENTY]

Yashin called and said he had found information about Ostapchuk.

'Write this down.'

'I'm writing.'

Ostapchuk, Ivan Mikhailovich. Born 1880. Worked as a watchman at Pulkovo Observatory from 1899 until 1927.

(In 1921, I add for my part, he and I were knocking together display boards at no. 11 Zhdanovskaya Naberezhnaya. While lying on pieces of wood, we drank murky homebrew sent to him from his wife's relatives in the village.)

And so, in 1927, he leaves for that same village: Divenskaya, which, by the way, is located not far from Siverskaya. He is leaving, I think, from pure fear, because he has a presentiment of the Terror. It apparently seems to Ostapchuk that it is easier to survive the Terror in the village. If that is the case, then Ostapchuk was laboring under a misapprehension.

Several months later, they arrest him in the village for anti-Soviet agitation and propaganda. One of the pieces of evidence of that activity was the knocking together of agitational display boards on a sunny May day in 1921. It turns out that materials declared by the investigation to be anti-Soviet had been hung on those boards later. I, too, could have fallen within the investigation's field of vision by taking part in preparing the display boards, but somehow I did not. Was it because I was incarcerated for murder by that time? Doubtful. If I were the investigator, I would have done the opposite, connecting one case with the other since a murderer is without doubt the best candidate for pursuing anti-Soviet agitation.

Now the most interesting part: anti-Soviet agitator Ostapchuk ended up on Solovki in early 1932. Might we have met? Theoretically yes, if Ostapchuk had been sent to the Laboratory for Absolute Zero and Regeneration in the USSR. But they did not send him there and our fates drifted apart again. He returned to Leningrad in 1935 and got work at his good old Pulkovo Observatory, where he worked right up until his death, which followed in 1958.

Yashin learned all that from Ostapchuk's personal dossier, which was preserved in the materials of the Pulkovo Observatory. In those same papers, he found an indication of Ivan Mikhailovich's cemetery plot, too: Serafimov Cemetery. Appreciating the employee's dedication during his life, the observatory did not forsake him after his death, either. According to Yashin, the institution's financial reports preserve not only the bill for constructing a memorial stone, but also bills for wreaths and flowers for the deceased's grave. Receipts every five years for buying 'silver-tone' paint figure into things, too, evidencing regular touchups to the fencing. In the upper right-hand corner of the stone is chiseled an inscription, in Latin unknown to Ostapchuk: *Per aspera ad astra.*[11]

---

11 Through hardships to the stars (Lat.).

[GEIGER]

Today I spoke with Nastya. I explained everything to her. Rather, I explained everything that I could because I myself understand little.

I won't write here about the medical side of things. I've been describing that in the medical records these past few days so repeating it now would be stupid somehow. Especially stupid since my description contains only questions.

Nastya sensed that and panicked. She grabbed my arm right away. She was in hysterics.

It's good it's that way. It would be worse if the emotions were internalized. It's much more difficult to come out of that state.

I'm in a foul mood. A doctor shouldn't become attached to a patient. That's worse for both.

It's just that Innokenty isn't a patient to me. After I successfully pulled him alive out of the liquid nitrogen, he's become something like a son to me. It sounds pompous but that's how it is. Especially since I don't have a son. Or a daughter.

I wonder if Nastya will inform Innokenty about what's happening with his brain. I didn't forbid her anything. Even I don't know whether to inform him or not.

And if he asks? Well, if he asks, then . . . I don't know that, either. I seem to have studied him well, but I can't size up his reaction. If he's to be informed, it would probably be better if Nastya did it.

I'm looking at my arm now: there's a bruise – she grabbed me for real. And she's for real, too. Despite all that silly giddiness in her head.

THURSDAY [NASTYA]

There was a conversation with Geiger. I'd been expecting that. I already knew not to expect good news. It's hard for me to reproduce what Geiger said in detail but the essence of it is devastating. The cells in Platosha's brain have begun a mass 'die off.' In speaking of 'dying off,' Geiger had in mind not their full death but a sharp weakening of function. Beyond that, a lot of cells are dying and only a very small number of them are being regenerated. In his opinion, what speaks to regeneration is the fact that Platosha has stopped limping on his right leg. At the same time, his overall condition is worsening and fairly quickly. Geiger will begin examining Platosha's spinal cord in the coming days: he sees problems there, too.

I'm reporting everything intelligibly *now*, but I was like a crazy woman when I heard what Geiger had to say. Now I'm ashamed. He was already wary of me (could I really not see?) and now he'll completely avoid me. I didn't ask Geiger if it's right to tell Platosha all this but now I realize it's up to me to decide. On the one hand, it's horrific to hang that sort of weight on someone who's ill, but on the other, he'll soon realize people are hiding something from him, and then his situation will be even worse. I thought and thought but didn't come up with any-thing. Then I saw him in the evening, started bawling, and told him everything. Not everything, of course. Only as much as I'd been planning to if I decided to tell him. And it turned out I decided to.

He heard it all out calmly. He said that it could only have been expected. That the decades spent in liquid nitrogen had to manifest themselves somehow.

When we were lying in bed, I said:

'We'll pull through it all. We just can't lose hope.'

He hugged me. Pressed his lips to the bridge of my nose. He whispered:

'Of course. I've been working on that all my life.'

[INNOKENTY]

Nastya told me the results of the MRI. It's better to pronounce all three of those words – magnetic resonance imaging – because the abbreviation sounds a little scary. As, by the way, do the test results.

I went to Serafimov Cemetery today. I knew from the description in the archives that Ostapchuk's grave is right alongside the cemetery church. I found it without difficulty: the inscription *Per aspera ad astra* catches the eye from a distance. It was recently refreshed on the browned stone with the same paint they used on the fence. It's interesting that – in the masses of everything Ostapchuk talked about on that notable day – the conversation, as it happens, did not turn to the stars. The day we met, which became the day we parted.

Even at this time, it did occur to me that I would never see him again. And that turned out to be enough for me to commit the meeting to memory. It's not that my contact with Ostapchuk made a huge impression on me: the thought that we were parting forever was huge. I just could not fathom that, and it was scary because the loss of any person and any thing is a part of death. Which is the loss of everything.

Here at Serafimov Cemetery, I unexpectedly see Ostapchuk in the flesh, pouring homebrew into mugs. Woven of contradictions, his nose puckers from the impure scent, welcoming it joyfully at the same time. Ostapchuk is bare-chested: he has taken off his high-collared jacket because he's being careful with it and doesn't want to wear it out for no reason. He's sitting on the curb of his grave and partakes of the drink, covering his nose with his fingers (this is a strong drink) and lifting his chin. I follow the movement of Ostapchuk's Adam's apple.

Now it's my turn: I take out the vodka I brought with me and pour it into silver shot glasses brought from home – we didn't have luxuries like this in 1921, but all the safer for both of us. We drink because it befits the place (we're not going to knock together display boards here) and, truth be told, I have long felt like having a drink with Ostapchuk. He's two meters away from me now – maybe not alongside me and maybe underground – but he is here. I think this time he's wearing a high-collared jacket or even something solemn if, of course, he did not have last-minute regrets about putting it on because everything could be horribly ruined in the ground.

It isn't so scary to be in Ostapchuk's presence. Unlike him, after all, I – with my ghastly MRI – am alive and will possibly still live for some time. I am capable of moving around and, for example, riding a tram down Savushkin Street to the cemetery gates or buying vodka and odds and ends, but the main thing is that I can leave here, leave this cemetery alive. Unlike our Ostapchuk, who lies under that beautiful inscription day and night. At night he's in the cold light of the stars, to which, if one believes the inscription, he so strove, due to his place of employment.

SATURDAY [NASTYA]

Platosha came home drunk yesterday. I asked:

'Where, if you don't mind my asking, were you drinking?'

'I don't mind, my dear. At Serafimov Cemetery, with Ostapchuk.'

'So who's this Ostapchuk?'

'Ostapchuk, my darling, is deceased.'

He kissed me and then sat for about another hour and a half at the computer.

[GEIGER]

I understand very little of what's happening.

I'm not capable of affecting it.

I'm terrified.

Today I dreamt that an automobile is hurtling along at very high speed. And I'm at the wheel of the automobile. Only there's bad luck: there's basically no steering wheel. Or even brakes. You don't need an interpreter to understand that dream.

Yes, I know that cell die-off is the result of the extended super-cooling. Only that doesn't give much information. I don't have an answer to the question of exactly how it's all happening.

Why did the cell degradation begin only a half-year later? After all, if a cell is damaged, it's logical to suppose it won't 'wake up' in the first place. But it did wake up and stayed wonderfully awake for half a year!

And what if I were to allow that the degradation began right away and acquired its avalanching character only now? But that's not it, no: Innokenty has been under very thorough monitoring.

One might suppose that we'd changed rehabilitation methods and provoked cell death. But the methods haven't changed. They haven't changed!

My brain is in overdrive.

[NASTYA]

Time magazine named Platosha 'Man of the Year.' The name of the magazine is appropriate for him, and it's a nice title, too, but there's obviously little joy. Even a week ago, we would have been happy and arranged a celebration, but ugh . . .

Platosha looks at us from the magazine cover and from all the billboards and advertising kiosks, too: *Time* has great advertising. They found an excellent photo: the subject of the shot obviously doesn't know he's being photographed while he's talking with someone, smiling. Of course the photo is black-and-white and the lighting's amazing, but the nicest thing about it is the wrinkles formed by his smile. Platosha's like a movie actor.

My pace slows involuntarily at every kiosk. Handsome. Oh-so handsome! And I think: nothing can happen to him, to someone like that. There is surely some kind of logic in events! It's one thing for an elderly monk with a drab gaze, someone worn down by life . . . but here's someone who looks like a playboy (nobody knows he's not a playboy, after all), some kind of Brad Pitt – how, you might ask, does this picture fit together with 'cell die-off'?

[INNOKENTY]

First I read *Robinson Crusoe*, then the New Testament, the parable of the prodigal son.

I once told Nastya that mercy is higher than justice. Just now I thought: not mercy but love. Love is higher than justice.

[GEIGER]

After work I stopped by to see Innokenty.

He was at home by himself. I was seeing him for the first time one-on-one since the sad news about his condition.

It was easier in Nastya's presence. She doesn't allow silence to hang, sprachfreudiges Mädchen.[12]

And here we were, silent half the time. Neither he nor I wanted to talk about the test results.

[INNOKENTY]

Nevsky Prospect. Aviator Frolov's funeral. Seva and I have come to see that brave person off on his final journey. My parents are mourning the aviator, too, but at home. They didn't come, so as not to cry in public: they knew they couldn't contain themselves. Seva and I are crying, though, it's fine. I, a twelve-year-old, am not ashamed to sit on his shoulders, so I can at least see something; many people are sitting like that. We agreed that he will sit on my shoulders later, but somehow it didn't work out that way. It was forgotten. My hands are clasped under Seva's chin and I feel Seva's tears falling on them.

Now the funeral procession comes into view and seems to be riding past us yet again. I scrutinize that spectacle so greedily afterwards, replaying it in my memory so often that it remains iterative in my consciousness. The procession hurriedly returns to the top of

12 Talkative girl (Germ.).

Nevsky as if it were being filmed in reverse, then it again begins its majestic motion forward.

Officers with a cross, banners with Christ's face, and wreaths come first. The cross is in the center, the banners are to the sides, and the wreaths are at the back. Behind them march two columns carrying the deceased man's medals and honors. And there, finally, is the hearse with a high canopy rising over the procession. Under the canopy is a closed coffin. In the coffin is the departed, who is dear to all of us. Icarus, as is written on one of the wreaths.

All that drifts slowly toward us. Shouts and conversations go quiet around us. Only the clip-clop of horses harnessed to the hearse is audible. I am grasping at Seva's hair but he doesn't notice. I'm attempting to imagine Frolov in the coffin, his arms crossed on his chest with an icon, a paper band on his forehead. Pale. The smell of tobacco from his lips. The aroma of his final cigarette, smoked thanks to me.

We're standing with our backs to Gostiny Dvor, and the huge crowd is flowing past us, like a sea, in the direction of Alexander Nevsky Monastery. The sea is viscous; it envelops everything that crosses its path: the cars of the horse tram, carriages, streetlights. Everything that falls into this stream is immovable to an equal degree, regardless of its own nature.

Finally, I dismount and we join that crowd because it is only possible to move in one direction: toward Nikolsky Cemetery. We walk along Nevsky, past Yekaterinsky Garden, along Anichkov Bridge, through Znamenskaya Square, and, well, consequently, we walk all the way to the monastery. I do not understand why I have yet to visit Aviator Frolov's grave at Nikolsky Cemetery.

So that's the picture. I do not remember the season. On Nevsky – if, of course, there is no snow – one cannot discern the season anyway. You will hardly find any trees here and people dress somehow incomprehensibly, without concern for the season. When it comes down to it, there just aren't seasons here. There is a wintertime and a nonwintertime, and everything else is lacking in our part of the world.

[NASTYA]

The other day, Platosha said we should get married. I realized what that means. He wants to move our relationship into the realm of eternity. He believes it's no longer possible to trust time. That his days are numbered. He doesn't say that directly, but a sort of mosaic came together from individual phrases he's thrown out on various occasions. I'm the only one who sees it because I interact with him constantly. Well, maybe Geiger, too. Yes, Geiger, too, of course.

Geiger doesn't know about the proposal but he senses Platosha's general condition well. And I sense Geiger's. I think he's suffering no less than us, but he doesn't discuss the illness, either with Platosha or with me. I'd been waiting for comforting words from him but they haven't come. At first that was very hurtful but then I realized what the deal was. Geiger's a rational person and simultaneously honest in the German way. He doesn't know what's going on with Platosha, so he finds no comforting words. I think comfort that's not based on facts would not only seem pointless to him but also immoral. He's strongly mistaken about that, though.

Platosha, by the way, isn't saying anything either, for different reasons. He's a courageous person and prefers to keep everything to himself. He's afraid of traumatizing me. He's not afraid of traumatizing Geiger, but they're concurring here that there's no point in discussing the incomprehensible. So everybody stays silent. When I attempt to bring it up, neither of them keeps the conversation going.

Oh, and Zheltkov called to congratulate Platosha on 'Man of the Year.' I was gesturing to Platosha: invite the guy to tea, he loves it. He didn't invite him.

[INNOKENTY]

Zheltkov called twice this week, once when Nastya was here, once when she wasn't. I didn't tell her anything about the time she wasn't here. He said then that he had an interesting political project for me. That I, as a person who's been around for ages (is he implying the liquid nitrogen means I'm from the Ice Age?) could be useful . . . I didn't let him finish. Above all, I said, I am a nonpolitical person.

'But you,' he objected, 'you didn't even listen to the gist of my project!'

'And it's a good thing I didn't. What if it's a state secret and I have to live with it after turning it down?'

'Well, not that much of a secret,' growled Zheltkov. 'Fine, we'll make do without any projects. It would be better to have tea, right?'

He burst into the same laughter as during the tea party.

Why does Nastya think that laugh is sincere?

[NASTYA]

Today Platosha went to see Geiger at the clinic for yet another blood test, and I went to St Prince Vladimir's Cathedral. I walked through the park that they say used to be the church cemetery. There were maple and poplar leaves on the paths here and there, but not yet a complete covering. I suddenly realized it's already the beginning of autumn. Slight fading but not yet an avalanche.

We'd gone to the cathedral together before this but here I was walking by myself; something sank inside me. Will the day really arrive that I'll come here alone? If those had been only thoughts, I could have somehow driven them away, but then it proved to be autumn, too: a sort of overall departure. As I was walking by the church gates, past the panhandlers, they didn't even pester me, they just followed me with their eyes; that's the sort of look I turn out to have.

The evening service was underway – I don't know what it's properly called. The church was in half-darkness, illuminated only by candles. After entering, I headed for the left side altar where there's an icon of St Panteleimon, the great martyr and healer. A prayer to him hung by the icon and I read it. Then I pressed my forehead to the icon's glass, standing there a very long time. I told Panteleimon about Platosha. About how much he suffered and agonized during his life but the most important thing is that we're now expecting a child. Alongside me, people were kissing the icon and the glass under my forehead was no longer cool, but I kept telling and telling. Soundlessly moving my lips. The warmth of the glass I had heated transformed into Panteleimon's warmth for me. Quiet prayers wafted to me and calmed me.

Then I stood by the Savior, by the icon 'Joy of All Who Sorrow.' Never before have I had a conversation like this, but now it happened. This was a genuine conversation, though only I spoke. The answer to me was hope, which came to replace despair. A special joy of the sorrowful.

I came home after Platosha. When he asked where I'd been, I told him, though I hadn't initially planned to. I was afraid the story about the church would reveal to him how serious his condition seems to me. I was afraid that might finish him off completely. But I couldn't have even guessed that such joy would come to me that I'd be able to share it with him.

He told me:

'You're glowing all over. I'm afraid your glow will turn into its opposite if things don't go well for me.'

To be honest, I hadn't expected that.

'Are you proposing that I plead for you and not believe it can come true? Do you remember – it's somewhere in Chekhov – about the priest who goes to plead for rain and brings an umbrella with him?'

'You don't need the umbrella. Just plead.'

He kissed me on the forehead. He's not right. Not right!

[INNOKENTY]

An ambulance came for Nastya. She had been complaining for several days about a heaviness in her belly but had not allowed me to telephone for a doctor and today it all got worse, so we had to telephone. It's good we begged with the doctors to take her to the Nevsky Maternity Hospital, where she has been receiving care since the beginning of her pregnancy. I don't understand why I, a fool, had not insisted on the hospital earlier . . . Of course I do understand. She was scared to leave me on my own. And I am scared to be left. But what can be expected now? Just the thought of that makes me feel ill. I really should have insisted. Taken her by the hand and brought her to the hospital.

I felt absolutely nauseous when we got to the maternity hospital. I did ask to go to her room and sit alongside her, but no way! Why did you arrive so late, sweetheart, it's almost night! As if we'd chosen when to arrive ... They would not let me past the admissions area. And they took Nastya to a room on a stretcher. What a distressing spectacle when someone close to you is taken away on a stretcher. Ugh.

I sat for about another hour on a couch in the admissions area. People came to look at me: I think the entire hospital staff checked in at my couch. To look: they looked but they did nothing to unite me and Nastya. Not. A. Thing. In the end, they asked me to leave the couch, too: they said they were supposed to close the hospital for the night. I left without uttering a word. Of course I could have told them *how* bad I felt but I could not find the exact word.

I ended up on Nevsky Prospect a few minutes later. I started going into the metro – I even bought a token – but didn't ride.

'Are you going in?' asked the attendant. 'We're closing, by the way.'

Then close. I changed my mind about taking the metro when I pictured being at home without Nastya. After leaving the metro, I headed toward Moscow Station; I decided to sit there a while. People, lots of people, though I had been dreaming of a bright place without people. I didn't feel like talking with them or even just seeing them. I didn't feel like knowing they exist. Because after parting with Nastya, it would be better on the whole if they weren't there. My loneliness was only more pointed because of their presence. I sat in the station for about an hour and a half.

I went out to Znamenskaya Square – I remember when it was still called that, still with the church and the brilliant monument. I imagined the emperor returning to his place, with a stonelike tread.

There were cars with flashing lights in front of him – they stopped traffic for his majesty, they had not been expecting him. His horse stepped slowly: the clatter of hoofs, sparks on the asphalt. I returned, so why can't the emperor return? Both of us are history.

I plodded off toward the Nevsky Monastery. I was tired, my legs were giving way. A kitchen table someone had carried outside stood in front of one building. I sat on it. My feet drummed lightly on it, making a muffled drumming noise. I had never sat like that before on Nevsky. On a kitchen table. I rested a little and walked on.

To my surprise, the entrance to the monastery was open. People were standing by the gate, waiting for something. A minute later, a vehicle with 'MuniWater' written on it, showed up and drove through the gate at low speed. I walked after the car, in no hurry. Nobody stopped me; I obviously resembled a MuniWater employee in some way. Maybe with my pensiveness. People who handle water are often pensive.

I hesitated and then decided to go to Nikolsky Cemetery. It turned out the vehicle was headed there, too. It was still driving just as slowly, as if feeling its way, and its headlights grabbed trees and monuments from the darkness. They became improbably three-dimensional, moving in the electric beams, changing places, losing their own shadows and acquiring others'.

Work was in full swing at Nikolsky Cemetery. Illuminated by powerful floodlights, two roaring earthmovers had extracted soil from the graves (so it seemed to me) and piled it in areas of open ground. No, it was not from the graves. When I walked closer, it was clear the vehicles were working on the small road: they had dug a trench. I could also see that overlooking the trench were not just mounds of black earth but also several coffins that had been raised to the surface. Over the long course of their existence, the rows of graves had ceased being rows and some burial places took up nearly half the little road. Those graves had obviously needed to be dug up.

I remembered that Terenty Osipovich's grave protruded, too, and the thought that it might have to be disturbed in order to extend the mysterious trench – well, yes, that thought flashed. After walking along the trench, which stretched past the second earthmover, I stopped (a pertinent image), as if rooted to the ground: Terenty Osipovich's coffin was already standing on a small hill of fresh earth. Of course I could not be certain it was actually Terenty Osipovich lying in the coffin but the coffin was hanging over his grave: who would be there if not him?

I walked right up to the coffin. One of the boards on its side had fallen off but the illumination from the floodlights did not reach the gap that had been left. Nothing was visible through it. One could not be convinced that this was Terenty Osipovich without opening the lid. But how could you do that?

As I was pondering, a flexible pipe extended from the vehicle that had arrived. It slithered from a giant reel that rotated with an unexpectedly high-pitched sound. Water lines were being laid through the cemetery at night so as not to disconcert anyone. They neatly placed the pipe in the bottom of the trench. Everyone watched as if entranced while city authorities turned to the departed after having provided a water supply to the living. Without the others noticing, I stepped toward the coffin and laid a hand on the lid's half-rotted wood. I groped around the edges. There turned out to be a small gap where the lid came together with the coffin. I dug my fingers into it and pulled the lid upward with force.

The force was unnecessary: the lid lifted easily. I again cast a glance at those around me: they were all observing the laying of the pipe, as before. In one motion, I raised the lid slightly and moved it to the edge of the coffin. A person's remains became visible in the beam beating down from the floodlight. That person was Terenty Osipovoch. I recognized him immediately.

Gray hair was stuck to his skull. Solemn dress uniform, almost untouched by rot. He was, essentially, like this in life. True, he lacked a nose and two black holes gaped instead of eyes but other than that Terenty Osipovich resembled himself. For an instant, I waited for him to appeal to me to go intrepidly but then I noticed that he also had no mouth.

[GEIGER]

Nastya is in the hospital.

They didn't let Innokenty in to see her today; they ordered him to come tomorrow. He called and told me about it. He also asked me to find a description of the aeroplane 'Farman-4.'

I asked:

'Why?'

He said:

'Since we're restoring a general picture of life as it once was, let's have it. Add it to our other texts.'

I'll add it, that's not complicated. Just open the encyclopedia and write.

But. I feel uncomfortable. I don't know if it's worth supporting endeavors like these.

And so, 'Farman-4' is a biplane, with two pairs of wings. Two-seater. Manufactured during 1910–1916. Engine: sixty-five horsepower, propeller diameter 2.5 meters. Weighed 440 kilos, capable of lifting 180 kilos. Fuselage made of pine, wings and wheel covered with creamy-yellow canvas. Sehr raffiniert.[13] Frolov flew in a Farman (that

---

13 Very refined (Germ.).

sounds like a little verse). Unfortunately, he also crashed in one.

I don't know why I'm writing all this. It's not easy to do. Even so, it's easier than writing about the results of Innokenty's tests.

[INNOKENTY]

Last night I wrote until I fell asleep right at the table. I dreamt of Frolov's aeroplane. In my dream, I even remembered what it was called: 'Farman-4.' Now that is memory: it even preserved the '4' – who would have thought? I dreamt that his plane was running along the airfield but just could not take off. The aviator sees that there are all kinds of leaves, grass, and flowers under his shoes, and it all blends into a dark-green mass. Maybe it would be better not to take off ... He could just keep riding and riding – what's wrong with that? He could just bounce on the hummocks, the wings trembling occasionally.

But that's not what we loved him for.

[ ]

I stayed the night at Innokenty's. We talked until around three.

He took out the vodka, first one bottle, then another. I didn't think of objecting: what kind of objections could there be here? We did drink both bottles.

I was basically afraid he would start asking me about his health. He didn't.

Nastya's health worries him far more now. He's very afraid the baby will die.

The conversation somehow slid on to how life is structured these days. Innokenty called it anarchy. I noted that authoritarian rule usually comes after anarchy. Which is essentially very sad.

But Innokenty – Innokenty who did time! – said authoritarianism may be a lesser evil than anarchy.

He compared the populace of a country to deep-sea fishes. They can only live under pressure, he said.

I attribute that statement to the quantity of vodka consumed.

An unpleasant discovery: during the time we sat around, Innokenty choked several times. Some sort of swallowing disorder, and this is not a matter of the throat. It's a problem with the brain.

[INNOKENTY]

I went to see Nastya today. She is ill and looks it: she's pale, even green. I have never seen her like this. I sat with her until late in the evening, until they showed me out. During lunch, I ate nearly her entire portion because she couldn't eat. Her attending physician is of the opinion that this is due to toxicity in her body.

Put bluntly, the food is not from the Metropol. This is what I think: the cooks here aren't especially trying to make lunch not taste good, right? They just don't put in everything that's called for: stated simply, they steal. They're our people. They just cannot help themselves.

But Geiger says you cannot control these people, or anyone else, by coercion. He and I argued half of last night about the advantages of democracy. I see those advantages even without his comments. They might be natural and appropriate in some places, but they just cannot seem to develop in our country. In Geiger's ancestral motherland, for example, they can, but not here.

I think the whole issue is personal responsibility. Per-so-nal. Individual. When that's missing, there needs to be some external corrective action. If, for example, a person has problems with his spine, they put a brace, a fairly severe thing, on him. But it holds up the body when the spine cannot. That is exactly what I'm going to tell Geiger. I cited a marine example but now I'll cite a medical one.

[GEIGER]

I examined Innokenty the other day and noticed that his arms and legs have become slightly thinner. The reason: decrease in muscle mass. This testifies to problems with the spinal cord.

Innokenty had a positron-emission tomography scan today. There is little joy. Why did I regard this as limited to the brain, anyway? It was to be expected that the cooling would affect the entire body. Including the spinal cord. But what, what, exactly, was the effect? If only I could understand that . . .

[ ]

Nastya was discharged today. It turns out they did an ultrasound during the course of her treatment. And they reported the most important news, too, when they discharged her: it's a girl. A daughter. I have been thinking about that all day today. For some reason, I had imagined it would be a boy. That doesn't mean that a girl is worse, there are simply things that seem to go without saying.

On the one hand, I could offer more advice to a boy because I have gone through that rather complex journey. On the other hand, my journey began almost a century ago. It's a big question as to whether that experience has any value now. So then, in terms of experience, it makes little difference if I have a daughter or a son. As a man, it's probably nicer for me to have a daughter. And, when it comes down to it, all the best things in my life are connected with women.

I just reread this: what silliness! It's obvious, after all, that the abstract points here don't apply. People love a specific person, not a boy or a girl. After being born, a person ceases to be an abstraction and then . . . But will I have a *then?*

[ ]

I'm at home again. *We're* at home again! Us and our daughter: I just found out we're having a girl. Why didn't they say right away that I'm having a girl – were they afraid to jinx it? They didn't believe in a happy outcome? Or is it ineradicable Soviet-era spitefulness, plain and simple? It's pointless to guess and, really, not very interesting.

I think our daughter will pull us both – him and me – out of this pit. When we were riding home from the hospital in the taxi, I said:

'Platosha, sweetie, two ladies are totally depending on you. You just can't pack it in now.'

And he even smiled in response, but so very haggardly that I almost burst into tears. I swear, it would've been better if he hadn't smiled. I nestled up to him, put my head on his shoulder and then wrapped him in my arms. The driver looked at us in the mirror and that's how we rode the whole way: hugging.

[INNOKENTY]

Yashin telephoned and said he had something interesting for me. When I arrived, he brought me a file with materials about my cousin Seva. It came after the archive sent an inquiry to the public prosecutor's office: Yashin dug deep . . . He's a professional, I had to admire him. Even the way he pulled out the papers sheet by sheet seemed somehow very adroit. In white gloves; he's a red-head himself. I found myself on the first sheet, in the list of those who had been assigned to the 13th Brigade. With Seva's signature. Opposite two surnames was a notation instructing particular strictness of incarceration. One of those surnames was mine. Did Seva really want so badly to get rid of me?

He and I had flown so much on the aeroplane kite, I in the front seat, he in the back! Seva had not moved into the front seat, not even at the transit point: he did not shoot me, did not deprive me of my life using his own will. He granted that I die my own death – if, of course, death from exhaustion can be considered one's own. We ran and I slowed down because I saw Seva gasping for breath. We slapped our feet along the damp sand, slipping and raising a spray, and the kite flew majestically over the sea – where we could not run to follow it – and it seemed that he and I were flying with it. Our aeroplane dove when we stumbled, but that was almost unnoticeable: it looked as if it had caught another airstream.

How is it that Seva faltered so his aeroplane corkscrewed down? I discovered – from all the documents that Yashin brought – that my cousin was shot in 1937. The documents did not refer directly to torture during the course of the investigation but, based on isolated cries that found their way into the records, one can gather that there was torture. Based on cries and, most important, the particularities of the information that lurched from Seva like uneven waves. Only at the first interrogation was there a conversation that was more or less substantive. The rest – since there was nothing for Seva to tell – read like unsuccessful attempts at guessing the investigators' wishes.

The protocols, which are usually short on words, did not economize on detail this time. They told, at length, what Seva said as he begged for his life, how he sobbed loudly like a woman and fell to kiss the interrogators' feet. In the final interrogations, after obviously losing his mind, he proposed they release him to go conquer desert regions of Uzbekistan. He demanded they come to him ten years hence and eat fruit in the garden he would plant. Seva described to the interrogators all of them drinking tea at an evening hour when there is no longer intense heat and it is easy to breathe. Judging from the detail of the notes, Seva's speeches made a big impression on his listeners. One must suppose that the investigators tired of the interrogations and themselves dreamt of a quiet garden life. In some strange way, I, too, felt a sense of peace after reading this.

[ ]

Today Innokenty and I spoke seriously about his health for the first time. 'More precisely, my ill health,' he corrected. It's good he's joking . . .

I recalled the joke about how a man is brought to the hospital with a knife between his ribs. 'So is it very painful?' the doctor asks him. 'Oh, no,' answers the man, 'only when I laugh.'

I told that joke to Innokenty. He nodded. Muttered something like how that's about him. Then he lifted his face and there were tears in his eyes.

I didn't bring up the topic, Innokenty did. He started talking about the changes he's noticed in himself. If I didn't know for certain that Innokenty doesn't read medical books, otherwise I would have thought he was quoting a description of the symptoms of a brain disorder.

Judging from all that, his working memory has suffered most tangibly. He forgets things that just occurred. Fortunately, not all of them.

Even so, he recalls events from the beginning of the century without particular difficulty.

Hysteria has manifested itself: it was noticeable even today. In the middle of our conversation, Innokenty suddenly announced that he no longer sees any point in keeping his notes.

'What does "no longer" mean?' I asked. 'What's changed in comparison with the previous months?'

'Well, you yourself understand perfectly well where my road now leads.'

'No, I don't understand. Unfortunately, nobody understands that yet.'

He looked right at me. His look was mean.

'I should write, just so you can defend yet another dissertation?

Innokenty had never talked like that with me. I kept silent

because I didn't know what to say. He abruptly walked up to me and embraced me:

'Forgive me, Geiger. I'm monstrously unfair.'

And I've already defended all possible dissertations, by the way.

[ ]

I went to the archive again, to continue familiarizing myself with Seva's dossier. From time to time – when Seva was definitively worn out – idyllic pictures of the garden in the desert yielded to curses aimed at the interrogators as well as Soviet power in its entirety. It is interesting that at one of those moments Seva recalled our conversation about the locomotives of history. He cited those words to his torturers and said:

'I didn't think that locomotive would carry me here. Innokenty did, after all, warn me: go on foot.'

New interrogations involved clarifying Innokenty's fate. The fact that Seva had personally sent me, his own cousin, to a hopeless place was deemed as especially sophisticated craftiness and part of a criminal plot. When they pressured Seva yet again, he produced not one plan but an impressive three, though not one of them corresponded to my situation at the time, something Seva did not know.

After learning they had frozen me, he advanced a fourth version. It consisted of them intending to drag the virus of revisionism – which had eaten away at me – into the communist future by freezing me. No spirit could be sensed now in what Seva uttered: there was only a tormented body. It wanted nothing beyond the cessation of torture. It did not even want life: the self-incrimination reflected in the transcripts boded nothing but the firing squad for Seva.

In revealing ever more new details about himself and me, my unfortunate relative even demanded that I be thawed and interrogated with prejudice. Several pages pasted into the dossier recorded that an attempt of the sort was undertaken. It ended lamentably for the interrogators. After clarifying whose instruction had ordered the freezing experiments, the attempt to defrost me was deemed revisionist and I remained in place. Unlike, by the way, the interrogators, who were handed over to a court.

[ ]

Platosha and I decided to legalize our relationship before God and people. First, before people: marrying requires a stamp in the passport. There's actually a long wait at the registry office but Geiger helped with that. One of the heads of the passport service turned out to be his former patient.

'Was he frozen, too, before he worked at the passport service?' I asked Geiger.

'The opposite,' said Geiger. 'He froze after he got there. But sometimes he thaws out: they'll register you without a wait.'

So even Geiger has a sense of humor. My relationship with him is better than ever.

After that I went to St Prince Vladimir Cathedral and made arrangements for our wedding. They asked: with or without a choir? With a choir, of course. How could it be without a choir? I told Platosha about all that in the evening, including Geiger's help speeding up the process. And he said:

'If Geiger's in such a hurry, that means things aren't good for me. He's the best informed of all of us.'

I started saying Geiger's not at all in a hurry, but then the telephone started ringing. They were asking Platosha about yet another interview. He refused and hung up. He already either couldn't recall our previous conversation or just didn't want to continue it. Never mind, as they say. Sometimes it's rough being with him.

[INNOKENTY]

I am ashamed of myself. I'm feeling afraid and thus tormenting those around me and, really, there are only two of them. Why am I doing that? It doesn't even make things any easier for me. I'm afraid that some sort of latent irritation has appeared in me because I will depart and they will remain. If that is truly how things are, then my behavior is doubly shameful. I need to watch myself carefully.

I told Geiger the other day that I don't intend to write any longer. But now I understand: I do intend to. Because of my daughter. If she is not fated to see me alive, I will appear before her in written form, as they say, and my pages will accompany her throughout her life. There is no point in writing about the major events: she'll find out about those anyway. The descriptions should touch on what occupies no place in history but remains in the heart forever.

An abandoned narrow-gauge railway substation, for example. Everyone forgot the substation and everyone forgot the narrow-gauge railway. I don't remember where it was or where the railway led, if it even did. It stretched, rusty, through grasses; it was already nearly invisible. Some other children and I were playing under the platform and the sun made its way through cracks in the boards. Grasses stirred, grasshoppers chirped, there was a hot spell. And a cool breeze was blowing there, under the rough flooring. The platform was high so we were all able to stand at full height underneath. We were sitting in pairs, though, leaning against one another's backs. Sitting was good, soft: grass grew under the platform, too, though it wasn't thick, and some mosses were also growing. One boy had nobody to lean against. And so, he said:

'There will be a thunderstorm. It will be the end of us.'

We could see nothing to portend a thunderstorm, but that's only how it seemed: an absolutely leaden cloud was approaching from behind the grove we weren't looking at. Unlike the boy who had warned us, we were self-absorbed and had not noticed anything. Later in life, I have observed that solitary people sense more subtly and notice nearing changes before others. And so that cloud rode into the sunny splendor, with a full complement of rain, lightning, thunder, and even hail. Hail the size of pigeon eggs, as is commonly said. Maybe a pigeon egg. I have never seen their eggs but the hailstones truly were large. The way they drummed on the boards made me think the boards would not hold out long.

I'll add that lightning flashed and thunder boomed. It didn't even boom, it cracked, infernally loudly. As if the sky were breaking into two uneven parts (the sun was still shining, far away). I, of course, had lived through thunderstorms more than once even before this, but in all those previous storms, seconds passed between lightning and a clap of thunder. My mother and I sometimes counted them. This time, though, the claps of thunder rang out together with the lightning, and that was scary. We were sitting as before, pressing our backs against one another, but now it was fear rather than a friendly feeling that bonded us. Water poured through the cracks in the boards, flowing behind our shirt collars and streaming, cold, along the body. And the boy who remained unpaired shouted in the intervals between lightning:

'Heavenly electricity!'

I became desperately sorry for him and that sorrow overpowered fear. I moved away from the back I had managed to cling to and gave up my place to the shouter. He did not so much as stir, though. He was enjoying the horror of his solitariness. And the fullness of knowledge.

[ ]

I looked at the menologium in search of a name for our daughter. According to the doctors' calculations, she should be born around April 13. St Anna is celebrated on that day. I told Platosha that and he was glad. He said that name reminds him of mine and my grandmother's. I'm glad, too: Anna's a beautiful name and not everybody can be Anastasia in any case. I decided to look to see who else is celebrated on that day. It turns out there's Prelate Innokenty, educator of Siberia and America. Amazing.

We're continuing to prepare for the wedding, mentally, at least, because we don't want any celebrations at all. Geiger is our only guest. Platosha asked him to keep notes about the wedding. Geiger wavered slightly but didn't dare refuse: Platosha did write for him for more than half a year.

Oh, this is important: we did register (what a Soviet term!). We came to the Petrograd District registry office and registered, wearing sweaters and jeans. Some old bag came out, lips pursed, to welcome us but Platosha stopped her. He calmly said that was unnecessary. She understood and wasn't even offended. She limited her performance to 'Sign the registry here.' We signed.

We had a beer in the nearest pub: I had non-alcoholic, Platosha had German unfiltered. Over all, Platosha's mood has lightened a bit in recent days. No, that's not the word: it's changed. He isn't gladder now, but he's calmer, and that's an improvement of sorts.

[ ]

I forgot to say: the thunderstorm was short and the sun soon peeked out. The streams through the cracks became ever thinner. I glanced stealthily at the boy who had shouted about heavenly electricity. He was sitting, hands folded, with the sorrowful look of a prophet. Something in him was otherworldly. I wonder who he was and what became of him.

We watched the sparkling of the flowing water for a while longer. Now there weren't even thin streams. Water initially covered the cracks as if it were a film but that thin film tore suddenly, turning into uniformly large drops. We went out into the open expanse and saw a rainbow. Our rusted narrow-gauge railway was departing underneath it, as if riding under a bridge.

[ ]

Innokenty and Nastya married today at St Prince Vladimir Cathedral.

Innokenty asked me the day before if I would describe the wedding. I offered to film it for them. He took me by the arm and said:

'No, please describe it in words. In the final reckoning, only the word will remain.'

A debatable statement. I kept silent. But I'm writing: I did promise to write.

The other thing is that I'm not the best describer in this case. I'm a stranger to the Orthodox service. And the Lutheran one, too, when it comes down to it. Though I was christened as a Lutheran.

And so, the wedding. It lasted about forty minutes: that's the only thing I can say with certainty.

The meaning of its parts is beyond me, with a few rare exceptions. For example, when the priest asks each person if they are marrying of their free will. And when they both drink from the same chalice. That goes right to your heart.

When Nastya drank, Innokenty looked at her so marvelously. I can't think of the words. As if inspired, perhaps. Yes, inspired.

It would have made a tremendous photograph. Sharp focus on Innokenty's eyes and Nastya's face slightly fuzzy. And the glimmer of the bronze chalice. Maybe a photo like that will appear. Someone was taking pictures there, some journalists.

Crazy thoughts kept creeping into my head. Things like, there's Innokenty, born in 1900, and Nastya in 1980. That's what you'd call an age difference.

Will Innokenty like my description?

I'm writing and thinking: maybe the wedding will pull him out of his depression?

[ ]

We didn't go to bed the night after our wedding. We sat on the bed, nestled against one another. And didn't utter a word. Not one. We held hands and felt the same thing. We lay down toward morning. Went right to sleep.

This afternoon, Platosha was watching TV and suddenly said:

'How can invaluable words be wasted on TV series, on these wretched shows, on advertising? Words should go toward describing life. Toward expressing what hasn't yet been expressed, do you see?'

'I see,' I answered.

I truly do see.

[ ]

What happiness that I met her.

[ ]

Innokenty and I talked over tea about the role of the individual in history. We had to talk about something other than medicine.

He repeated his favorite thought about political leaders. That the people find exactly who they need at that particular moment.

I cautiously said:

'How do you picture that: everybody in 1917 needed the exact same thing? Old, young, smart, stupid, righteous, guilty? They all needed the exact same thing?'

'And where do you see smart there? And, most important: righteous?'

Harsh. There was a time when the notion of universal guilt irked me in Pushkin. Find out, he says, who is right, who is to blame, then punish them both.

For Innokenty, that frame of mind is connected with his overall condition. Which is worsening.

[ ]

Geiger and I debated. In my opinion, he has a strange notion that someone is tossing the noose down upon us from above again and again. That we're not the ones who braid it. Quite the defender of the Russian people . . . And at one time he was telling me about his hopes: there, he thought, Soviet power will go away and we'll start living! And . . . so? Have we started living now? Soviet power has been gone for how many years now: did we start living?

And its arrival was not accidental: I do remember it well. The Bolsheviks are now called 'a handful of conspirators.' And how was this 'handful of conspirators' able to topple a thousand-year empire? It means Bolshevism is not something external for us.

So Geiger does not believe in a collective impulse for perishing and does not see rational reasons for it. But reasons can be irrational, too. *All, all that threatens to destroy holds for the mortal heart a joy of inexplicable delight* . . . That, of course, is not always how it is, and it's not for all people (here, Geiger is right), though it is for a great number of them! For enough to turn the country into hell. My cousin succumbs to the oprichniks, my neighbor goes to snitch on Professor Voronin. Voronin's colleague Averyanov gives monstrous testimony about him. Why?!

Well, who cares about him – my cousin – he's a weak person, he wanted to establish himself. Averyanov, let's say, was envious: a natural feeling for a colleague. But why did Zaretsky snitch? Out of considerations based on principle? But he had no principles (or considerations, either, I suspect). Money? But nobody was giving him money. He himself told me when he was drunk that he didn't know why he snitched. I know, though: out of an overabundance of shit in his body. It – that shit – grew in him and waited for the social conditions to spill over. And they did.

In that case, though, maybe he is not to blame for snitching on Anastasia's father? Maybe the social conditions are to blame? I think Geiger thinks so. But then it wasn't social conditions that snitched on the professor, it was Zaretsky. That means he committed a crime and his getting bashed on the head turned out to be his punishment. The justified, I emphasize, punishment of a villain, though few knew of that. Everything looks more complex with respect to who bashed him. Is he a villain or an instrument of justice? Or both? How can all that be explained to Anna?

Sitting at the computer, Innokenty asked me:

'Where is the Internet's content located?'

At first I didn't understand the question.

'What do you mean where? It's in the Internet . . .'

'Can you name the specific place where it's stored? Or am I to understand that it's evenly spread around a network?'

'There are computers that store the information. They're housed in data centers –'

He didn't let me finish.

'So there's nothing mystical about it and there are fully dedicated machines that store that content, right?'

Right. I didn't understand what surprised him so much.

[ ]

Geiger explained to me how the Internet functions: its content is distributed in a series of computers. If you think about it, it would be pretty much impossible otherwise, but I had almost come to believe in some kind of special system standing over computers. Almost a special reality arising from the very fact of the connection between computers.

It suddenly occurred to me that this is a sort of model for public life. Which, when it all comes down to it, is not life but a phantom. Plunging into it is not without its hazards: it can sometimes become clear that there is no water in the pool. Life and reality are on the level of the human soul – that is where the roots of everything good and bad are located. Everything is decided by touching the soul. Probably only a priest works on such things. Well, and maybe an artist, too, if they're successful at it. I was not.

[ ]

Platosha says he thinks all the time about Anna: that's what we already call our little girl now. I know it's early and we shouldn't, but what can we do if she's come into our lives? We already sense her character, for example. When she stamps her little foot in my belly, we understand there's a feisty young woman growing. Platosha asks me to call to him when she's kicking like that. One time we both saw my belly swaying from Anya's little foot!

He wants Anya to know everything about him. That's why he's now planning to write much more thoroughly. I said to him:

'Don't make things more complicated for yourself. She'll grow up a little and you'll tell her everything.'

'No,' he answers, 'I'll write: everything's firmer on paper, more reliable. Oral stories, you know, blur in the memory, but what's written doesn't change. And what's important is that it can be reread.'

I do know why he's writing, though! Good Lord, there's no secret there. He thinks he won't live until she's born.

One time in Siverskaya I saw an aeroplane taking off from a poorly mown field. As it sped up along the runway, the aviator drove around potholes, bounced on hillocks, and – oh, joy! – suddenly ended up in the air. Watching that machine move spasmodically around the field, frankly, nobody expected flight. But the aviator took off. There was no more hillocky field for him and no more laughing spectators underneath his wings: there appeared a sky with sprawling clouds and the colorful earth like a patchwork.

For some time, I have seen that picture as a symbol of a fitting course for life. It seems to me that accomplished people have a defining trait: they depend little on those around them. Independence, of course, is not the goal but it helps achieve the goal. There you are running through life with the weak hope of taking off and people are looking at you with pity or, at best, with incomprehension. But you take off and from up high they all seem like dots. That's not because they have instantly diminished but because the view from above (lectures on the basics of drawing) makes them into dots, into a hundred dot-faces oriented toward you. With open mouths, it would appear. And you're flying in the direction you chose and tracing, in the ether, figures that are dear to you. Those standing below delight in them (perhaps envying a little bit) but lack the power to change anything because everything in those spheres depends solely on the flyer's skill. On an aviator splendid in his solitude.

[ ]

Platosha told me about some aviator's flight in Siverskaya. Based on the tone of the story, I understood immediately this was not so much about the aviator as about Platosha: he has differing manners when talking about others and himself. He talked and talked, then suddenly pondered.

'What are you thinking about?' I asked.

'What pothole did I trip in, anyway? Why didn't I take off? What ruined my artistic abilities?'

At first I tried persuading him that his abilities couldn't have just left him, that they'll certainly come back. That's not simply consolation: I myself firmly believe it. The comparison with the aviator is, of course, lovely, but it's lame if applied to Platosha. He hugged me and said he's already lame. Then we sat, silently, for a long time. Rocking slightly.

Innokenty decided to write for his daughter. To describe his life.

He also appealed to Nastya and me with an unusual request: help him write.

'How?' I asked. 'How can someone be helped in describing his own life?'

'Not the life itself but what's on its fringes. I'm simply afraid I won't have time for everything on my own.'

And so Innokenty will tell us what to describe.

This will be about specific things, not general things. About what everybody perceives identically.

Mosquitoes in Siverskaya, for example.

What else did he already allude to? Visiting the barbershop, a bicycle on a wet path . . .

As I understand it, he's painting some sort of big, important canvas. At the same time, he's recruiting helpers to sketch the background. They'll draw the secondary figures along his contours . . .

'I'm not refusing to help,' I said, 'but I'm a poor helper. Writing isn't my calling.'

'To the contrary, Geiger, I value you because you're succinct and write simply.'

'And me,' Nastya said, 'what do you value me for?'

Innokenty thought for a bit.

'For the exact opposite qualities.'

I understand it's impossible to refuse. But I don't understand how to regard this endeavor. As his vital necessity? As an eccentricity? As a progressing illness?

The latter would be the easiest of all, but I'm not in any hurry to see that.

Something strange. Platosha asked Geiger and me to help him with his descriptions. Yes, yes, of course, we answered. To be honest, though, I don't know how to go about this. If you ask, you risk offending. I couldn't stand it and asked the next day. Platosha wasn't the teensiest bit offended.

'Treat it,' he said, 'as a life story.'

'Yours?'

'Mine. And a life story in general.'

*

The request for help with my descriptions surprised them both a lot: is that really so strange? They nodded to me about everything, but their faces, their faces . . . Of course the backdrop for my behavior is unfavorable: possible brain failure and so on and so forth. But is the essence of my idea truly not obvious? Yes, every person has particular recollections but there are things that are lived through and recollected the same way. Yes, politics, history, and literature are all perceived differently. But the sound of rain, the nocturnal rustling of leaves, and a million other things – all that unites us. We're not going to argue about that until we're hoarse or (you never know) smash each other over the head. That's the basis for everything here. That's what needs to be worked with, that's what I'm requesting of the people dear to me. May their voices appear amid what I've described. They won't distort my voice: to the contrary, they'll enrich it.

After all, the only thing I'm working on is finding a road to the past, either through witnesses (there are no more after Anastasia's death) or through recollections, or through the cemetery, where all my life companions have moved. I'm attempting to come closer to the past in various ways, in order to understand what it is. Is it separate from me or am I still living it, even now? I had a past even before my icy slumber, but it never possessed the separateness it does now. Everything that I have recalled about my past has not drawn it closer to me. I think of it as a hand that was chopped off and sewn back on. Perhaps that hand moves somehow, but it is no longer mine.

In essence, the years in liquid nitrogen changed nothing regarding the past. They intensify the problem but do not engender it: the problem existed previously, too. Its essence is that the past is cut off from the present and has no relation to reality. What happens to life when it ceases to be the present? Does it live only in my head? That same head that is now losing tens of thousands of cells a day and raising suspicions even among those close to me? Living people – with my recollections and their own – must be let into my head right away ... After reviving our mutual recollections, perhaps those people will also revive what belongs only to me.

Siverskaya of the 1900s was the dacha capital of Russia. The mosquito capital. Especially in June. I think there are plenty of mosquitoes there now, too – you could even rename it Mosquitskovo in their honor – but now there's sprays, coils, and creams. But back then? Well, maybe creams. Other than that, though, I think it was mostly fires. These were fires that burned old rags, leaves, and other little things that made a lot of smoke. Anyway, the technical side doesn't interest Platosha.

The details are important to him, like the cautious, even somehow helicopter-like landing of an insect on the arm. A mosquito isn't a fly, it doesn't move around on the arm. It works where it lands. It pokes its little proboscis into unprotected skin and starts sucking blood. You swat it on your arm and the blood smears on your skin. When I was a little girl, I heard that if you swat a mosquito at the scene of the crime, the skin won't itch. I think that's an exaggeration, with a moral: punishment should follow crime. In the same place, at the same time. Blood atonement, as they say.

Nocturnal buzzing is the peskiest. It's probably worse than a bite. Comparable to dental drilling: you still don't know if it'll be painful, but the sound of the drill already permeates you. You listlessly defend yourself through your sleep or just duck under the covers. It's stuffy, so you duck back out a minute later. And it's stuffy in the room, too: the windows are closed because of the mosquitoes! It's double suffering, from the mosquitoes and the stuffiness. You finally toss off the covers and give your body over to the mosquitoes. At least it's not hot. What's interesting is that the mosquitoes don't exactly rush to a naked body. Maybe they're stunned by the grandness of the gesture. Or maybe all that nudity shocks them.

Will Platosha like what I wrote?

*

I felt an urge to draw – that hadn't happened in a long while. I set Themis on the dinner table and moved a lamp from the desk to the bookshelf after removing the books. The lighting came out fairly well, with a shadow. I set up the easel, took a sheet of paper and a graphite pencil, and began drawing. Even before much had appeared on the sheet, I felt like the drawing would come out. After all my numerous attempts, today my hand suddenly recalled the motions. It found confidence with each stroke and I was no longer thinking about the rules of drawing: my hand knew everything on its own.

When it was finished, I turned on all the lights and carefully began examining the drawing. There were many shortcomings in it but that wasn't important. I had managed to draw something sound for the first time in the months after thawing. My main complaint was probably about the shadow. I remembered that they had taught me not to blacken it, not to fill the paper's pores with graphite. The paper should shine through slightly, even through the strokes. According to a definition from Marx, from blessed memory, it is better to 'not quite' than to 'overdo.' I could apply that definition to art in general.

I took the sheet from the easel and laid it on the table. I went to the kitchen and opened the breadbox. Next to the fresh bread there lay some stale pieces Nastya had not thrown away, saving them for the pigeons. I was lucky: among dried-out bread as black as tar there was a stale little piece of white bread. I crumbled it finely on the drawing. Using circular motions and pressing lightly, I rolled the crumbs along the surface of the drawing until they absorbed the extra graphite. I carefully brushed the blackened crumbs on the floor with a wide brush. I blew away the finest ones.

All the lines remained but they had become much paler. I took the pencil and went over the drawing again. It was slightly different now: the accents had changed positions. And I liked it better this way. I felt joy. It also occurred to me – no, it did not *occur* to me, it simply jabbed: despite the massive mortality of my poor cells, does this mean that some were restored?

July 1913.

Moderately warm evening rays cut through a barbershop. Dust swirls in the rays.

Barber number one – a bald, middle-aged man – is preparing to cut the hair of someone middle-aged but not bald. Empty snipping of scissors in the air. He shifts into work mode: the full-fledged sound of hair being trimmed.

Barber number two is also aging and bald. He lights the spirit lamp and passes a straight razor over it. He goes over the client's cheeks with a shaving brush.

Keeping in mind possible complexes and envy, can one entrust one's hair to a bald barber? It's a question . . .

Both clients answer in the affirmative. The second client risks less because he is only being shaved. In this case, it's impossible to inflict much damage to the appearance. Only to cut the cheeks.

The barbers converse with one another.

They're having a long discussion – maybe over an entire day – about the prices of provisions. They can't bring clients into the conversation, other than with regard to opinions about individual products. But the clients can't be brought into the fullness of the conversation.

They repeat individual words and even phrases one after the other. Pensively, several times.

The clients can't repeat like that. To do that, they would need to acquire the special rhythm of cutting hair. Its special tranquility. And that is only accessible to professionals.

Yashin from the archive called as I was writing that. He said Voronin turns out to be alive.

I didn't even understand immediately who he was talking about.

When I realized, I didn't believe it. That camp scum Voronin is alive! That uncommon swine is alive!

This was the first time Yashin called me instead of Innokenty. This is a special case, he said, the doctor should decide.

Yes, it's special. And it's not very clear what to decide here.

Geiger examined me yet again. He requested that I close my eyes, extend my arms, and touch the tip of my nose with each hand. I couldn't. Meaning I could but not on the first try; as I understand things, that doesn't count.

'That doesn't count, does it?' I ask.

He smiles listlessly. Put another way, he appreciates that I'm such a cheerful guy. True, he suspects that this cheeriness is from hysteria and he is not so far off the mark.

Whence shall I begin to weep over the deeds of my cursed life? I was reading the 'Great Canon of Repentance' aloud to Nastya. There is an astonishing phrase there: *When God wishes, nature's order is overcome.* We repeated that many times.

Innokenty and I were talking about higher justice. He loves that expression.

So take the way they pinned Zaretsky's murder on him and dragged him off to Solovki. Where, I ask, is the higher justice in that undeserved punishment? And he answers that – from the perspective of higher justice – there's no such thing as undeserved punishment.

That sounds lovely, though not especially convincing. What's called *then punish them both* . . .

And then there's that other matter: that the GPU man Voronin, scum to end all scum, surfaced the other day. There are no evil deeds he hasn't committed.

It's becoming clear he safely reached the age of one hundred. That he retired with the rank of general back in his day and is receiving a special personalized pension. He's living in the Kirov building on Kamennoostrovsky Prospect.

I wonder what Innokenty will say about that when he finds out. What will he say about higher justice? Innokenty who, to the contrary, is catastrophically losing his health.

All that I'm doing now is stating the changes in his body. And unfortunately there are many. Too many.

If everything continues developing at this speed . . .

Yes, I'm giving Innokenty certain medications. Yes, they ease the course of the illness. But they don't affect its causes. As before, those causes remain hidden.

Why are the cells dying? Why is that only happening now? Why is it only certain groups of them? Nobody knows the answers.

Only God, as Innokenty formulates it. And since my relations with the heavenly sphere are pretty troubled, no information is passed on to me.

When God wishes, nature's order is overcome. Platosha read to me out loud from the 'Great Canon of Repentance' and we discovered those amazing words for ourselves. No, not 'amazing,' that's somehow too cheap for them. Words filled with joy and hope. Their meaning has long been obvious to me, but I couldn't express it that well. Of course I'm relying on Geiger, too – he's not exactly the lowliest person in medicine – but I rely far more on Him, in Whose hands there is medicine, and Geiger and Platosha and I.

We can only receive His help through the power of faith in Him, meaning through the power of our plea. Two things have to come together here: faith and the desire to recover. Not only the ill person but also his loved ones should display them both. The loved ones, I think, to an even greater degree because they have more strength (they're the healthy ones) and the ill person is prone to depression.

On another topic. The sudden resurfacing of Voronin, whom Geiger has already contacted. First off, this person I share a surname with is, contrary to expectations, in his right mind. Also contrary to expectations, Voronin isn't against meeting with a former zek: I was sure he wouldn't agree. According to Geiger, he reacted without particular sentimentality, just saying, 'Let him come.' Now Geiger wants to prepare Platosha. To lead up to it cautiously: what if, say, Voronin happens to be alive . . .

I don't know what sort of feelings the news about Voronin will provoke in Platosha. There are lots of scenarios, right up to the desire to kill him. It's frightening to utter 'the natural desire.'

For now, I decided not to show my drawing to anyone after all. I'll practice more and draw something truly worthy of Nastya and Geiger's appreciation. If my skill were to return to its full degree, I would draw Zaretsky. Portrait of a person mournfully bent over sausage. I would draw him compassionately rather than mockingly. If not with love then at least with pity. After all, he had nobody to pity him and not one tear was spilled at his funeral. Not one.

In general, I think that when you describe a person in a genuine way, you cannot help but love him. Even the very worst person becomes your composition: you accept him into yourself and begin feeling responsibility for him and his sins – yes, for his sins in some sense, too. You attempt to understand and justify all of that, so far as it is possible to do so. On the other hand: how can one understand Zaretsky's action if he himself does not?

'Are you an atheist?' Innokenty asked me.

'No, I don't define myself that way. I'm most likely a person who trusts scientific knowledge. If science proves to me that God exists, well then . . .'

'Don't delude yourself. Science hasn't been able to answer the most important questions. And it cannot, not one of them.'

'For example?'

'How did *everything* arise from *nothing*? How does a soul come about and where does it go? There's oceans of questions and they all lie beyond the boundaries of science.'

'Possibly. Even so, it's difficult for me to step across those boundaries.'

Although I sometimes step across them.

I'm stepping across them now, where things relate to Innokenty.

He read me a phrase from a church canticle. Its point is that if God desires it, the natural order of things is overcome.

In Innokenty's and my case, the framework of science is tighter-fitting than ever: it's just poking into my ribs. Squeezing religious thought into me: that only He can help here.

Geiger and I talked about God. He does not deny the possibility of God but first and foremost he believes in facts presented by science. Though there is no need to believe in facts, it's enough to know them. There are many of those facts – hordes and hordes of them – it's just that they all relate only to what is not fundamental. It even sometimes seems to me that those facts distract from what is fundamental. Of all the millions of small explanations, it is the one that is all-embracing that doesn't come together. And won't come together because those things are located in different dimensions. So Geiger is waiting in vain here for a transition from quantity to quality. A explains B, B explains C, and so on until infinity, but where is whatever explains all that infinity in its entirety?

An abundance of discoveries befogged the heads of my former contemporaries who made atheism a fashion, too. Even then, they were reminiscent of a ladybug on the highway who's charmed by her own motion and crawls a dozen meters. The ladybug seems to think she's learned and grasped everything. She will never find out, though, where the highway begins and where it leads. I shared this comparison with Geiger. He narrowed his eyes:

'The ladybug is God's creature, though, despite her arrogance. And God allows varying views.'

A cunning Teuton; you can't get the upper hand.

'Of course the ladybug is God's creature, which is why she was granted wings. An insect needs only to fly up into the sky to see the entire road, don't you see? There was a children's song about that.'

'Why "was"?' he laughs. 'There still is.'

Geiger finally reported to Platosha about Voronin. Gradually, after preparing him, but he told him. Platosha raised his eyes to Geiger and looked at him for a long time. I thought (feared) he'd rush to Voronin's right away but he didn't. He asked calmly when we're going to see him.

From this, one might think at first that Platosha was somehow reacting inappropriately to the news. I think Geiger had that impression. But it seems like Platosha goes through the most significant things in silence. Although ... Geiger offered him his hand as he was leaving. Maybe he expected some sort of inference or something about news that stunned us. But then Platosha suddenly said:

'If it's no trouble, Geiger, describe weapons stopped at the station in Siverskaya. They're being transported on open, flat-bed cars. Autumn 1914. Fog changing to mist.'

Autumn 1914. Fog changing to mist.

The weapons' barrels are raised upward. Dark green, gradually emerging from grayness. Pensively aiming into the sky, the splendor of their matte luster.

Drops flow down them and fall heavily below. The drops flow along the metal platforms, along wheels that shine in the places they touch the rails.

A kingdom of motionless metal; God forbid it budges. It rattles and shakes softly, answering the military trains passing through.

Sooner or later, they'll pull the wheel wedge out from under the foremost car and bring over a steam engine. Everything will start into motion. Sorrowful motion to the west.

All that harsh metal will oppose the softness of the human body. Its – the body's – oneness. It will scatter into small pieces.

The weapons will lose their pensiveness and perhaps even dry off. They will shoot unceasingly, both hitting their targets and missing. Actually, they can shoot when they're wet, too.

After Nastya went to the university, I read. Later I watched the news on TV but quickly shut it off. I took the photograph of Professor Voronin off the chest of drawers and examined it. There's the professor sitting in an armchair, legs crossed. His elbow is leaning into a small table with a pile of books. There's a cane in his hand (he never carried a cane). His hair is combed back; there are symmetrical islands of gray on a beard that is still mostly black. A particular academic chic. I search the professor's eyes for traces of future suffering – that happens in old photographs, it's discovered in hindsight – but no, there seems to be none of that ... Could he really not have foreseen it? Or was he conforming to the photographer's expectations and looking at himself through the photographer's eyes?

The wrenching motionlessness of pre-revolutionary snapshots. Nastya, it occurs to me, never saw her great-grandfather in motion. But I saw. And, incidentally, I see. I freely enter the silver frame and observe the professor setting the cane aside and rising slowly from the chair. It is possible there's even a sigh or, let's say, a crack of the joints, since the person has been sitting motionless in that photograph for nearly a century. His gait is slightly pigeon-toed and I could have showed that to Nastya, but that would not be the same thing. No matter who or what I might show, it would be my portrait.

I take the album about Solovki from the bookshelf. I open it to page seventy-seven (I even remember the page!) and see a photograph of a person with the exact same surname: Voronin. You cannot say his face is ferocious; Nastya confirmed this, too, when I showed him to her. I wanted him to have a sharply sloping forehead and fangs coming out of his mouth. Reflecting his inner substance. But no: he has a high forehead, well-proportioned features, neatly combed hair, and is smoothly shaven. He turned out to be tenacious, like all vampires. With his appearance, he could have worked as an assistant school principal or the director of a club and nobody would have discovered his inclination for bloodsucking. He and I will meet tomorrow. I am astounded at my calm. Perhaps that is because the news about Voronin is too unbelievable.

I have always been surprised that one name is capable of denoting such various entities. It works out that Voronin can be this way and this way. How did he become who he is, anyway? That's a good question.

We headed to Voronin's in the evening: Platosha, Geiger, and me. I just went to be with them since the agreement was only for Geiger and Platosha. Yes, plus some *Chistov From-the-Organs*. Voronin insisted on the presence of this Chistov. But, well, anybody in Voronin's position would have proceeded that way. Only would just *anybody* end up in his position? So this one's actually fearful for his worthless life now. The louse. What was it my grandmother said about Zaretsky? That she *put out a contract* on him? I think, in the Zaretsky case, that was my grandmother's delirium. But on Voronin, I'd put out a contract. I know you can't talk like that, but I'd do it if I knew where and how. All I'd have to do is imagine how he'd tormented Platosha...

And so we – meaning the three of us – went to see Voronin and I was thinking: well, how about that, Voronina going to see Voronin, though we're not exactly birds of a feather! I'd even forgotten I've been Platonova for a little while. I held back a bit, watching them walk. There was wind, almost a hurricane – the right sort of weather when you're going to meet a villain: so here I am! My companions were walking, bent forward, fighting a wind mixed with leaves and large but still sparse raindrops. The collars of their raincoats fluttered in their fingers. That, it occurred to me, is how the arrival of payback might look, although of course there was no talk of payback.

Chistov was already waiting for us by the front door. When we entered the hall, he took a paper out of a binder and asked Platosha to sign it. It was a release form saying Platosha has nothing against Voronin and isn't planning to prosecute him. Chistov pulled an expensive pen out of his pocket, placed it and the paper on the binder, and froze, holding it all in front of Platosha. A pause hung.

'Without this, Innokenty Petrovich,' said Chistov, 'you and I aren't going to see Mr. Voronin.'

Innokenty Petrovich pensively took the pen.

'What's in the pen?'

'Ink, imagine that.'

There wasn't the slightest irritation in Chistov's tone.

Platosha signed the paper and Chistov put it away in the binder. He stuck the pen back in his pocket.

'You know, I understand your emotions,' he said in just as even a tone, 'but I want you to understand me. The law is the law. Everything must take place without any incidents. Do you promise?'

'I promise,' answered Platosha, somehow very seriously.

And he repeated:

'I promise.'

The three of them went up to the apartment and I stayed downstairs, by the elevator. Maybe, it occurred to me, our SS officer will kick the bucket at the sight of Platosha? That sort of incident seemed allowable to me.

*

The meeting with Voronin. It was strange.

I'd foreseen various scenarios, but not this one.

I thought there would be mutual damning. Or reconciliation. But there was neither one nor the other here.

Voronin was sitting in an armchair when we entered. He was holding a cup with both hands. Warm sweater, trousers, slippers. Skull taut with skin, fluff at the sides.

I suspect he thought to have the cup so his hands would be full. In order to have the opportunity not to be the first to offer a hand – he was afraid nobody would respond. I, for example, didn't plan to offer him a hand under any circumstances.

But maybe he wasn't afraid. Maybe I'm attributing too much subtlety to his feelings.

There was someone else with us, wearing civilian clothes; Voronin invited him. After we entered, he half-sat on the windowsill and it was as if he was no longer there. The ideal escort. He was, thus, by the window, and Innokenty and I were at the threshold.

'I know that you were resurrected,' murmurs Voronin. 'I wanted to have a look at you.'

His voice is already almost gone, but his will remains. It's the last thing that will leave him.

He wanted to have a look at zek Platonov: there he is, delivered. Under surveillance, by the way. Delivered and remaining silent.

'So, have I changed?' Voronin asks Innokenty.

'Yes.'

'You, however, have not.'

A woman enters the room and takes the cup from Voronin's hands. She remains, to stand, rocking from heel to toe. Squeaking the parquet.

A fly buzzes by the window pane.

'Catch it, would you, Chistov?' Voronin suggests in a whisper.

Chistov slowly slides his hand along the glass and catches the fly with a brief, precise motion. He explains to us:

'The fly doesn't see when you extend your hand behind it.'

He removes the fly from the room. The woman addresses Voronin:

'Do you need anything else, Dmitry Valentinovich?'

Without answering her, Voronin looks at Innokenty point-blank:

'Don't expect repentance.'

The woman sighs and gazes into the cup.

'Why?' asks Innokenty.

After closing his eyes, Voronin quietly but distinctly utters:

'I'm tired.'

He's tired. Chistov, who returned, points to his watch.

We leave.

Life is constructed so very astonishingly. Voronin turns out to be the only person who has remained to bear witness to my time. I searched for the dead so they could bear witness, if not through words then at least through their presence, but then someone who is alive turned up. Now he is not so much a criminal as a witness. I feel that and he feels that. And there is no hatred between us. Something akin to – yes, yes – solidarity is appearing. Just as you find a common language even with a savage on an uninhabited island. In a sense, Voronin and I are now on an island, the two of us. There are just the two of us from our time. It's another matter that his witnessing differs little from that of the dead. Voronin's appearance is somehow posthumous, too.

He said: don't expect repentance. I ask myself yet again: why? Why was he left alive until the age of a hundred if not for repentance? He is a great criminal and it is possible the Almighty delayed his departure, giving him an opportunity to change his mind. Voronin said he's tired. Everybody decided that was a signal to end the meeting. I think, though, that he was speaking about his condition, when there is no longer either rage or penitence. The soul submerges into slumber.

*

Tea on an open veranda in autumn. Smoldering coals fanned by a boot. A boot as soft as an accordion. And clean: otherwise how would you fan coals with that at the table? Really, they could be fanned in some other place, but the people sitting at the table want to see everything from the very start. The samovar is large and the water in it is slowly coming to a boil. Everybody's waiting for the first little wisps of steam to appear: steam is still only floating from the mouths of the people sitting there. It's very noticeable in the rays of a weakened sun that warms no one. The air is harsh, with smells of pine and the river. A dog barks on the other side of the fence; its chain hits audibly against the doghouse. Supposedly it could relax and not bark much if chained up, but no, that's not happening. It's agitated. Participating in public life.

Everyone, no matter who, is dressed warmly; some are wearing scarves. Hands reach toward the samovar: it's already capable of warming. The discussion is endless '*Titanic*' and 'Ferdinand' and it moves in waves, now quieter, now louder. The conversation turns into muttering (everyone has withered a little) that prefaces the samovar's churning. That's it, it's boiled. The teapot for the tea concentrate appears right away and catches the first stream from the samovar, still gurgling. A time-out for it to steep. One cup follows another. They sit and drink tea; one could say they're reveling in it.

The event is dated 1914. Or 1911, for example. Platosha insistently asks that all descriptions be dated. Why? I ask. That way, he says, it shows that fundamental events (like the tea-drinking on the veranda) are capable of defining completely different times, meaning they're universal. According to him, that line of reasoning in favor of precise dating is equally applicable *against* precise dating, too. It works out, I realized, that the line of reasoning is universal, too.

Let's say it's 1907.

A child has a cold and a severe cough.

They read *Robinson Crusoe* to him.

The cough is so deep that the reading alone isn't enough for recovery. The doctor recommended cupping.

They do this as a family. His grandmother reads, his mother and father set out the jars on the nightstand and prepare the wick.

They grease the child's back with petroleum jelly, using light round motions.

His father will place the jars. He takes the most crucial tasks upon himself.

The patient is seven and he is afraid. This is the first time they have cupped him.

It becomes genuinely scary when they light the wick, wetted with alcohol. That might have suggested thoughts of the inquisition, if the patient had known about that.

An open flame is always scary.

The boy is lying on his stomach and grasping a pillow with his arms. He's burying his face in it. A moment later, he senses the first jar on his back.

It's not as painful as he had imagined. Maybe it's not at all painful.

Carefully, he lifts his head. Watches his father's hands.

His father moves the wick inside the jar a bit, removes it, and lowers the jar on the boy's back. Of course it's a little hot.

He can feel the jars pulling his skin into them. His father winks at him. His mother uses a blanket to cover his back, with the jars on it.

His grandmother continues reading *Robinson Crusoe*. The book is curative in combination with the jars.

A new rush of fear before the jars are removed. The boy seems to think they sank themselves into his back for good. They remind him of mean little fishes. Maybe piranhas.

His father carefully runs his right index finger along the lip of a jar and it comes unstuck with a loud smacking sound. Fifteen first-class smacking sounds.

*

My walking has worsened. I have the sensation of walking on moss. I carefully place my foot, as if I'm afraid it will collapse. Exactly where I'm headed no longer presents a mystery for me: losing thousands of cells a day, it's impossible not to guess how this journey will end. These losses cannot go on forever.

I have made it a rule not to complain, even to Geiger, not to mention Nastya. Since the reasons for what is happening are unclear, complaining brings nothing but distress to anyone. Especially since, hm, this is not my first departure from life. But. Death in the camp seemed like a way out and now it seems like a departure. A departure from those I love. From what I love. From my recollections, which I have already been writing down for so many months.

Today I woke up early in the morning; it was still dark. I lay motionless, so as not to awaken Nastya. I observed, as I am wont to do, wandering automobile headlights on the ceiling. Trolleys, which replaced horse trams, used to run along Bolshoy Prospect. I would watch them for hours, attempting to understand the secret of the trolley's self-propelled movement. For some reason, it excited me more than the movement of automobiles. Maybe that's because of the magnitude, unwieldiness, and loudness of the trolley, something that, at first glance, was not created for moving around within an expanse, let alone transporting city people. But if – it occurred to me – a construction of that sort were enabled to leave its location, it could be destined for defensive and (even better) offensive purposes. I imagined the motion of hundreds of trolleys on the field of battle and it was a majestic spectacle.

From time to time, in testing the soundness of the trolley, I would place a five-kopeck coin on the rails. The experiment seemed so important to me that, in my childish lightheartedness, I reconciled myself in advance to possible losses: rather, I simply did not think about them. My father cautioned against those losses in order to wean me off this dubious amusement. He supposed the trolley could go off the rails and mildly noted to me that I should weigh the possible damages before deciding on this risky experiment.

What could I say here? By that time, I already knew five-kopeck coins were no impediment for the trolley: it simply did not notice them. I watched each time to see if the giant would shake when riding over them: it never once shook. What my father was correct about is that readiness for losses is indeed characteristic of experimenters, even adults. I come to the conclusion that they are large children and that for them the torn-off head of a doll – as the history of our unfortunate Motherland has confirmed – does not differ from a human head.

Returning to those same blessed years, I will say that I accumulated a collection of shiny, flattened little pieces of metal. Touching them with the tip of my index finger, I still sensed the remnants of the embossed image, but that didn't ruin the pleasant impression of smoothness. Yes, smoothness – even the polishedness of those former coins – is a recollection specially preserved for me. In the land of my childhood, where nothing ever went amiss, they became a worthy currency. Their astonishing surface and my index finger were made for one another. In the more than hundred-year history of placing five-kopeck coins under the trolley, my experiment was one of the first. I will note as well that my actions were not the result of blind imitation: I thought this up myself.

I fear all that will sink into oblivion if it is not written down. It would be a noticeable gap in the history of mankind, but the largest loss would be for Anna, whom I think about all the time. Quite a lot of things have already been described for her, but I simply cannot cover everything. Luckily, I am receiving help now and this has begun to go faster.

1910. Early March. A two-story wooden building not far from the railroad. On sunny days, the spring melt begins and is heard by all the building's residents. The drops open a path for themselves in the iced-up snow and all sound different, depending on the size of the hole in the ice. Everything closes up at night and freezes over so the drops nearly have to do their work all over again in the morning. From nearly a clean slate, though of course the snow is no longer very fresh in March. Like a pockmarked face, it is uneven and pitted with tracks from dogs, cats, and crows – everyone who walks near the two-story buildings. That snow is covered with a thin layer of stove soot that invariably shows through even fresh snow. Or maybe it is fresh soot. It deliberately flies in each time there is freshly fallen snow, covering it out of a pure aversion to whiteness.

There are huge puddles – entire ponds – along the railroad embankment. These puddles freeze over at night, too, but they are so deep they do not have time to freeze through to the bottom, and do they even have a bottom? In childhood, you fear they do not. The trees stand in icy bark until midday, but it melts after that. The water in those puddles is cold and black. There is no reason even to think about entering one of them.

Keep thy mind in hell and despair not. I was paging through a book about Mount Athos and my eye fell on those words. I set the book aside and began doing something else but the words surfaced and stung. After all, they are about me. *Keep thy mind in hell* – that is the condition I had already plunged into several weeks ago. *And despair not,* that is what comes to me with greater difficulty. I rushed for the book and could not find that spot immediately but eventually did. It has been said of those words that they are a revelation attributed to Silouan the Athonite. I do not know who Silouan the Athonite is and I am not even sure if I understand those words properly, but they boosted me a little.

My present hell is that death is far scarier here than on the island. Of course I clung to life there, inasmuch as I could, but I did not fear death. When the expanse of my life began shrinking to nothing, death nearly seemed like an exit to me. I felt my worn-out body hungering for it, but my spirit fought that desire. My spirit was awake.

Now I am fearful of death like never before. I have everything: a family, money, and my strange fame, but all indications say they will not be gladdening me much longer. Money and fame mean nothing in the face of death, that is already obvious. Parting with someone close scares me – my funny Nastya, whom it now feels I have known my entire life. And with Anna, who is living in her and is my continuation. Whom I might never even see. Understanding all that keeps the mind in hell. This speaks emphatically about the mind, about understanding using the mind. And using something else, too, so as not to fall into despair.

1916. A bicycle on a dirt road after the rain. It moves along with a quiet hiss.

The wheels raise moisture from the road, throwing it on the bicycle's fenders. The moisture flows off them, to the ground, in large muddy drops.

Sometimes the wheels drive into wide puddles. The sound of water parting. Two waves diverge from the center of the puddle, toward its edges.

The bicycle jolts on tree roots from time to time. A bag with tools jangles. It bounces the cyclist on the seat's springs.

It's growing dusky.

The cyclist presses the small wheel of a hub dynamo to the bicycle wheel. There is light and buzzing. The movement of a small circle of light along the road.

Did bicycle lights exist in 1916? I don't know.

I think they existed.

It doesn't matter.

*

I am remembering ever less of what happened a minute, hour, or day ago. I feel uncomfortable when Nastya sees my obvious memory lapses: they are obvious, although – luckily – they are infrequent for now. In those situations, I remove the conversation far from contemporary life, to somewhere at the beginning of the century. Just as the hard of hearing ask their own questions instead of answering. In changing the topic yesterday, I took it upon myself to tell Nastya about a grammar-school staging of *The Inspector General*, in which, by the way, I participated. Nastya immediately saw through that but did not let on. She said that will be the basis of one of the descriptions she has taken on at my request. Yes, of course, that's wonderful, I responded. I asked myself, though: but can she describe my life without that basis? Using only the feelings that inspire her? If she were to learn to find and describe things that fit with me, my life could continue in my absence.

A grammar-school staging of *The Inspector General*. Marya Antonovna and Anna Andreevna, from the neighboring women's school, are rustling with dresses brought from the theater. The smell of mothballs accompanies the dresses from the wardrobe room to the school: the smell doesn't get aired out as they carry them, it seems to grow even stronger in the fresh air instead. The way a wine's bouquet begins to blossom, become fragrant in all its nuances, and gladden after the cork is removed. One is left thinking the dresses taken from the hangers were granted a similar characteristic: to the extent, of course, that all the nuances of mothballs are capable of gladdening.

There is hardly any scenery: a small marble table from the principal's office, a candle burning on it. A bookcase (carried in from the library) with books; moreover, books a half-century old were chosen. Khlestakov approaches Anna Andreevna. The stage's boards creak under his feet, and that's very audible in the front rows: there's a good reason that art demands distance. Anna Andreevna, says Khlestakov . . .

He touches her with his hand. His hand shakes and his voice shakes. The character, it must be understood, isn't nervous at all, but the boy playing him is nervous, sensing the girl's arm through the dense material of the dress. He has yet to confess his love to anyone and uses this theatrical confession or, actually, finds it in that text ... What, really, does he find in it? In rehearsal he uttered the text pretty sensually. It cannot be ruled out that he's falling in love because of what he utters.

It's stuffy in the school auditorium despite open windows; June has turned out to be hot this year. Outside, the tops of the poplars are covered in fluff and windlessly still, as if they were sketched. Anna Andreevna has beads of sweat on her forehead, as does Khlestakov, and everybody in the auditorium understands *what* is happening between them and they're elbowing each other, waiting for how this thing will end. This tenderness was not envisaged by the play, but it's so obvious. Everything's noticeable for the spectators, you can't hide anything from them. They're attentive. They clap their inky hands at the end of the scene. My Platosha shows through in Khlestakov, but the 1914 model for Anna Andreevna was, I suspect, reduced to dust long ago.

I did not sleep last night: I was recalling Pushkin's 'The Shot.' Where Silvio postpones his retaliatory shot for six years. He makes his appearance when the hero has married and is happy ... Death did not touch me on the island. I was almost indifferent to it then. It has returned with its shot now, when joy appeared in my life. It waited a long time. Should it be understood that death's shot is retaliatory?

Innokenty's working memory has worsened even more noticeably.

Nastya tells me that constantly, describing situations. And I do see it myself, too.

He loses his train of thought. Catches himself not remembering where he was headed in the apartment.

He doesn't remember anything that's automatic, like did he brush his teeth or take his pills.

I prescribe a heap of pills for him. True, there's little use in them. They're not able to stop the primary thing: the loss of cells.

I've rethought and rechecked everything ten times, with no results. I've buried my nose in publications from the last decade. Nothing.

I've never experienced such powerlessness. It makes me sick. Sick because Innokenty is fading.

Maybe he should be sent abroad? To Munich, for example. I don't think they know anything there that we don't know here, but all the same . . . Another perspective is important, too.

I could say there would be less responsibility on me then, but that actually doesn't worry me. My main responsibility is to him – I'm not afraid of any other responsibility.

There's just one trouble. I feel like we don't have much time for all the decisions. Zeit, zeit.[14]

He asked me:

'What's happening to you?'

I said:

'I'm afraid of your death.'

We hadn't said these things out loud until then. Although they had been thought. I lost my filters for a minute. He's the only person close to me, the only one I can complain to. And now that close person is leaving. And the only thing left is to complain to him. I acted horribly.

I started crying and nestled up to him.

'Forgive me for talking like that about death. That fear has eaten away at me inside and now it's coming out in the open.'

'Well, in the first place, I haven't died yet . . .'

My God, then what can possibly be in the second place?

14 Time, time (Germ.).

354

He was sitting, pale, thin. And my voice wasn't minding me.

He said:

'Death should not be seen as a farewell forever. It's a temporary parting.' He went silent. 'The departed is, basically, outside of time.'

The departed. It sounds like a draft in a tunnel.

'And the one who's staying behind? That person is within it.'

He smiled.

'Well, let that person work on something while waiting.'

So much time apart. It's scary.

It required a lot of effort to successfully contact Zheltkov. I described Innokenty's condition and asked him for help.

Zheltkov started mumbling something incomprehensible. Obviously bored. You see, I, uh, uh, uh, I'm not in charge of medicine . . .

Taken aback, I repeated that consultations abroad and expensive tests are required. In other words, bills will need to be paid. A lot of bills.

But our Zheltkov was in complete, purposeful denial. Unexpectedly so, I noted to myself.

Is this really because Innokenty wasn't even considering Zheltkov's political project?

I told one person in the know about that and he wasn't surprised. He said that if Innokenty had become uninteresting for Zheltkov, then Zheltkov had already genuinely forgotten about my patient. He figured it won't even be possible to get calls through to Zheltkov now.

I expressed cautious doubt:

'Well, a person can't be that shitty!'

'What are you talking about!' he laughed. 'It's easy to be.'

Scheisse . . . [15]

*

15 Shit. (Germ.)

I told Nastya that separation because of death is temporary. I believe in that: anyway, it seems to me that everything is granted according to faith. If you want to encounter someone, you will definitely encounter them. True, I am afraid that's feeble consolation for her now.

I wonder if there will be something to encounter *there*, other than people. Something that does not apparently constitute life's fundamentals but something I feel would be difficult to part with. For example, the crackling of candles on a Christmas tree. How you pinch needles off the tree and carefully draw them to the flame. They give off a coniferous aroma when they burn: it's vivid, like everything with farewells. There is the sparkling of flames in the evening and the extinguished dark, dark mass at night. When you wake up by chance after midnight, your first thought is of the tree. You make your way to it in a nightshirt. You walk almost by feel, most likely by the sound of the barely audible glassy ringing of garlands in a draft. Bare feet freeze on the parquet. You begin warming them once you reach the tree. Alternating your feet as you press their soles to your warm calves. Confetti that had stuck to them drops off. You hear someone has risen to go to the toilet. You press into the tree's broad boughs and dissolve in them. As you wait out the sounds in the kitchen, you slip into cottony drifts at the bottom of the tree and truly do disappear there. Until morning ... It seems that I would even get up posthumously to look at a tree with just one eye. If, of course, the eye is intact.

Well, what else? Let's say: a dish of raspberries on the veranda at the dacha. It swells with light in a diffused ray of sun. An insect with its wings carelessly folded crawls along the edge of the dish. Not a beetle, not a midge, not an ant. You have difficulty naming it, though it's not as if you have never seen it. That happens: you've been running into a person for half your life in the very same place, perhaps in the entryway or at the bookstore, and his face is familiar right down to the finest wrinkle, but his name is unknown. There are constant companions like that in life. When you part with them, you miss them for their low-key, timid appearance, for their folded wings and manner of moving around.

Or, let's say, a fire at dusk. Its reflection has spread along the Oredezh and is no fainter than a moonlit path. The conversation isn't a conversation, only individual words, simple ones, soothing ones. For example: I'll fetch more firewood. Or: the water's boiled. The crunch of a half-decayed branch underfoot. Gurgling water in a pot, sometimes feeble hissing of a log. You want time to freeze like the river by the dam. For it not to grow brighter but not to darken, either. For the red cliffs to remain visible . . . it seems I have already written about those, have I not? Devonian clay. Will that be *there?*

Sometimes I wonder: which of us is the patient, Innokenty or I?

I'm fulfilling his instructions: I'm writing, don't you know, pictures from life . . . I've never done this, and I don't feel I have it in me. I'm used to speaking in terms of diagnoses and prescriptions.

But.

To be honest, I'm liking the writing more and more.

Our cooperative writing is, if you will, an attempt to convey experience to descendants. The same thing mankind has been working on throughout history. It's just that our experience is, let's put it, unusual. That irritated me in the beginning, but I'm okay with it now.

Innokenty, however, conveys more than experience.

Nastya told me he contacted an advertising company on his own and offered his services. She found out about that by chance: they ran across her when they arrived with the contract to sign. She kicked them out on the landing and demanded an explanation from her husband.

And he was sitting in an armchair, listless and quiet. What, he asked, are you planning to live on when I'm not here?

She was silent, tears flowing.

Innokenty himself felt he shouldn't speak to her like that. I think he simply didn't have the strength to choose his words carefully. He spoke directly about what he was thinking.

He doesn't believe in his own recovery. There's no need to say what that means for a patient.

The most horrible thing is that even I can't reassure him.

Pieces of information about Platosha's health have seeped into the press. Personally, I couldn't care less, but he does go outside. He sees the tabloids in the kiosk windows: pictures and headlines, headlines like 'The Experiment Failed,' 'Platonov Is Deathly Ill.' One of the papers bought his MRI scan and published it on the front page. 'Innokenty Platonov's Brain Is Deteriorating.' Nobody even needs to buy any of that, anyway: they see how he walks. How his feet go out from under him, how he holds on to my arm. He doesn't want a cane: he says that would be too much somehow, admitting the very worst. Admitting (I didn't say) the obvious. On the other hand, maybe he's right, though: as long as the obvious hasn't been admitted, it's not obvious.

I showed Geiger the publication with the MRI. He turned as red as a fire engine and rushed off to call someone. Three minutes of choice curses. It all ended with him telling the other party to choke on his own balls. Difficult to accomplish, of course, and I don't know how they responded on the other end of the line. I hadn't expected that from Geiger, but I won't lie: I liked it. Maybe I hadn't seen enough of that in the German guy before.

It's just that, ugh, none of this helps Platosha at all. He has this *idée fixe* now, to earn as much as possible for me and our daughter. He said that since he himself has no future, he wants to provide for the future of those near and dear to him. He said that calmly, as if it goes without saying. The other day he contacted an advertising company, the same thing I, the fool, used to do for him before. I stopped that process right away.

I sense an intense yearning for my unlived years. A sort of phantom pain. I might have been frozen then but I did exist! Which means that's my time, too, and I bear responsibility for it, too. I feel the twentieth century, all of it, is mine, no exceptions. When I watch Soviet newsreels, at times I see myself in the background. Could that really be accidental? No. It is my absence there and noninvolvement in the events reflected there that could be considered accidental.

'Do I understand correctly,' Geiger asked me, 'that it's also permissible to describe those events of your life that didn't happen?'

'Absolutely right. Maybe it only seems they didn't happen. Just like when it seems something didn't exist but it did.'

The main thing is not to overvalue events as such. I do not think they come into being as something internally particular to a person. After all, they are not a soul that determines personality and is inseparable from the body during life. There is no inseparability in events. They do not compose a part of a person: to the contrary, a person becomes part of them. A person falls into them as people fall under a train – and just have a look at what's left of you after *that*.

I ask myself yet again: what should be considered an event, anyway? Waterloo is an event for some people, but for others an event is an evening discussion in the kitchen. Let us suppose there is a quiet discussion in late April, under a lampshade with a dim, blinking light bulb. The sound of automobile engines outside. The discussion itself – with the exception of individual words – might not remain in the memory. But the intonations remain: they are tranquil, as if all the world's serenity entered into them that evening. When I felt like having serenity, I recalled those exact intonations and that exact April discussion.

No, no, I was recalling a discussion at a railway station in the winter, too, but the question is, what year? I suppose it was 1918 or, for example, 1922: I could still have witnessed it in those years. In essence, nothing prevents that discussion from occurring in my absence in, say, 1939. Even so, I did not take part in it, I only listened. But its fundamental quality would not change even if I had not listened: in terms of its degree of tranquility, that discussion is not inferior to what is described above. And in the metaphysical dimension of the phenomenon, the discussion meant only one thing: striving for serenity.

Now, regarding the main thing. Waterloo and a tranquil discussion only seem incomparable at first glance because Waterloo is world history but the discussion apparently is not. That discussion, though, is an event of personal history, and world history is but a small part – a prelude or something – of that. It is clear that under circumstances like that Waterloo will be forgotten, even though a good discussion never will.

Platosha's saying strange things. I've made it a rule to agree with him.

January 1939. A railway station.

Consider it a polar station: snowdrifts to the windows, icicles to the ground.

Four o'clock in the afternoon but it's already twilight.

A yellow light in the window. When frozen, it seems to transform into a large lantern. A lighthouse for those walking to the railway. There aren't many of those who walk: the trains run infrequently here.

A weak bulb burns in the waiting room (let's be blunt: what kind of a room is this?) and that is what fills the window with its light. In the corner is a potbelly stove. Not the greatest interior here, but it's warm. There are footprints of melted snow on the plank floor.

Two people are sitting on a bench, having an unhurried discussion.

The cashier is listening in on their conversation from her window. Occasionally she adds something.

About once an hour, freight trains or long-distance trains rush past the station. Neither type stops here. They drench the window with steam and then their cars or tanks begin clacking monotonously.

During those moments, the chair shakes underneath the cashier. The bench shakes under the two having a discussion, too. They go silent and wait for the train with an emphatically patient look.

On their knees are fur hats with earflaps; they tug at them with fingers reddened from the cold. One's hair is tousled, the other's is the opposite, flattened.

That's how fur hats with earflaps affect people differently.

Why did God resurrect Lazarus? Maybe Lazarus understood something that could only be understood after dying? And that understanding summoned him back to earth. More specifically, he was granted a kindness, a return.

Or maybe there was a grievous sin on him that could only be corrected while alive and he was resurrected for that? Only it is unlikely a person like that could carry a grievous sin.

It is known that Lazarus never smiled after his resurrection. Which means earthly matters could no longer evoke emotion by comparison with what he saw *there*.

I saw nothing when I was removed from life. Then again, I did not die.

1958. A summer morning on the Fontanka River. The sun hits window panes and rushes to the river at a sharp angle. A yardman in a white apron is spraying the granite embankment with water from a hose. When he presses a finger to the end of the hose, he increases the water's pressure and it polishes the grainy pink surface with a hiss. A yardman's task is not as simple as it may seem, and it does not lack for danger. The yardman lets go of the end of the hose and looks absently at his red finger. Then he looks at the water and its weak-willed flow. He shakes his head. He presses the end of the hose again and now he's spraying, undistracted. He shifts the stream from the sidewalk to the granite parapet and, further, to an ornamental grating. The metal transforms the stream into a million mist droplets and they turn into a rainbow in the sun.

An automobile – a Pobeda with its top down – drives along the freshly rinsed roadway. The wheels make a soft, damp sound and small watery crests form behind them. A woman with light-colored hair, wearing glasses, is behind the wheel; she's smiling. Alongside her, on the front seat, is a folder fastened with a tie. A professor. It's very likely the woman is a professor. She's driving to the university or, let's say, to the public library. The morning is greeting her with a coolness that streams, unhurried, out of dark, high-walled courtyards. It's damp in the courtyards, summer is only at the top stories of the buildings, where flower pots are placed in open windows. Below is cold and mud. I'd have liked to add 'and snow' but that would not be correct. There is only cold and mud.

In thinking about how to provide for the future of my family, I catch myself realizing I will not witness what happens to them. There is already no place for me in that future. The only way out is to transfer my *I* into them. Or for me to enter their *I*. I am not ruling out that, during the course of our common motion, we will meet in the middle and our *I* will become common to all of us. Nastya and I need to work out some common views and assessments of situations, inasmuch as my remaining time allows that. We need to at least reach positions on the most crucial things, so the absence of one of us will not be noticeable. So the one who is absent will feel comfortable that decisions will be made in the only proper way.

*

I was stunned today.

When I stopped by at the Platonovs' this evening, I saw a drawing by Innokenty. A portrait of Zaretsky.

I don't know precisely what to call the technique, I suppose it's a charcoal drawing. Something softer than a pencil.

The contours break off in some places; in others they dissolve, somewhere unnoticed, in the paper.

A figure bent over a table. Splayed fingers ruffling hair.

On the table are a bottle and a glass with vodka at the very bottom. A piece of sausage with the end bitten off.

There's not even a shadow of caricature in the portrayal. Either in the face of the sitting man or in how he's propping up his head or even in the bottle and sausage. The drawing is deeply tragic.

The sitting man is mourning something (perhaps his own life) and the vodka and sausage are his only witnesses. The facial features are refined. The shoulders are hunched.

As long as he's silent, his appearance is elevated, perhaps as it was intended to be. Zaretsky is silent. His bleating, his ugly words, aren't heard.

And you think: the thoughts he's immersed in are lofty. And the sausage is just an austere necessity. A requirement for the body.

He's not looking at it. The focus of his gaze is somewhere beyond the boundaries of that room, maybe beyond the bounds of the visible world in general.

That drawing would have stunned me even if I hadn't known anything about Zaretsky. But I do know, so the drawing stunned me doubly. It liberates Zaretsky. It delivers him from his horrendous role as a maggot.

That drawing is a straw that Innokenty and Nastya and I can grasp at. It turns out that the mysterious blockage for Innokenty's artistic work has lifted. He can draw again. And how he draws!

In terms most familiar to me: some group of cells has been

restored in him. For now, 'how' and 'why' are questions into the void. I'm stating a fact, not attempting to explain it.

Platosha is a genius. That amazing portrait that Geiger and I saw ... I wanted to say something about the portrait and then suddenly remembered and realized, just in time, that it would sound pathetic. No matter what, it'd be like retelling *War and Peace* or, say, humming the Fortieth Symphony. I'll just say one thing: only yesterday I hated Zarestky because of my grandmother's stories. But I've forgiven him after that portrait. Almost forgiven. As Platosha drew him. There's one weak spot in what I'm saying: I'm his wife. What wife's husband isn't a genius in her eyes? I'm feeling an intense urge to not be his wife for a minute and tell the whole world that Platonov's a genius. But it just wouldn't work out to not be his wife. He and I are one flesh and one spirit.

Platosha has no strength. He goes out less and less, and he's usually lying down when he's at home. He watches television. Or writes. Sometimes he has fits of fear. He's terrified he'll die soon. Or terrified he'll die in his sleep without saying goodbye to anyone. The floor lamp is lit more and more often in our room: darkness seems like a harbinger of death for him. When we go to bed, he asks me to give him my hand; he squeezes it and that's the only way he can go to sleep. More than anything, he's afraid Anna and I will be left without help. He already sees us as orphans. I go into the bathroom, shut myself inside, and turn on the water, both hot and cold, full blast. Our pipes wail from the heavy pressure. And I wail, too.

I am reading the *Primary Chronicle*. The chronicler recounts year after year. He says: In this year since the creation of the world there was this, in the next year there was this. And in this year 'nothing happened.' Those years are called *empty*. Years in which there was nothing. At first I racked my brains: why refer to these years?

Then I realized: these people feared losing even a small particle of time. Those who lived for an eternity especially appreciated time. And not even time so much as its continuity, the absence of holes. Maybe they thought that genuine eternity only advances after time has been lived carefully. I have felt that, too! I knew I should not release from my life those decades when I was frozen. And I was not mistaken.

Basically, life collapses into pieces, although I am attempting to tie them together. It collapses and then ceases. *Keep thy mind in hell and despair not.* Everything that I think about immerses my mind in hell, which is despair itself.

I managed to arrange testing for Innokenty in Munich. Actually, I didn't, my former patients did.

The issue isn't so much about the necessary sum as the impetus. Only now am I really admitting to myself that the organizational problems were a pretext to some degree.

Is this sort of trip necessary? I don't have inner certainty about that even now.

Based on the data I've sent, they're not ruling out surgical intervention, though I don't consider that useful.

I carried out Innokenty's regeneration, step by step. Does anyone know the state of things better than I?

On the other hand, maybe that knowledge is impeding me now? Maybe a fresh view is exactly what's needed under the circumstances?

Finally, is it possible that what's called 'emotional attachment to a patient' is preventing me from making a correct decision now?

I'll tell him about Munich just before the trip itself. There's no need to tell him earlier. He and Nastya are already on edge.

1969. A May Day demonstration. The morning air is cool. The afternoon air is, too, however: after all, it's not yet summer. Thoughts about temperature are brought on by a foam medical thermometer of gigantic proportions: two people are holding it. It shows 36.6, obviously not the air temperature. Whose temperature, one might ask, is it showing? An unknown giant's? The entire demonstration's? Judging from the inscription – 'The Country of Soviets' – 36.6 refers to the country. One of the demonstrators says the country is hopelessly sick and its temperature is being taken using a thermometer with the temperature drawn on. He's speaking in an undertone, as if only to himself. No, truly only to himself.

Flags of various colors, but predominantly red, flutter in the wind. There are portraits of the leaders of the party and the government (not fluttering). Those in attendance are standing in their educational institutions' columns, the First Medical Institute, for example. They're awaiting a command to start moving. Someone takes a flask from a jacket pocket.

'Cognac. Want some, Marlen Yevgenyevich?'

'Why not?'

His lips envelop the flask and he takes several large swallows. He exhales loudly, wipes his mouth, and latches on again. The sharer saddens. He had not expected his flask would be used as a pacifier. He's afraid the cognac will lose some of its qualities after Marlen Yevgenyevich's lips.

'Polina, have a drink?'

He'd probably be able to touch the flask's opening again after Polina.

'No, thanks,' says Polina.

And she usually drinks. She must have also seen how unappetizingly Marlen Yevgenyevich was drinking.

The column slowly begins moving. First the thermometer, then the flags and portraits. It flows along Lev Tolstoy Street like spilled preserves. It merges with other columns on Kirovsky Prospect, entering the overall rhythm and overall joy. Essentially, the joy arises from the rhythm. From the large accumulation of people. Of course, on the whole there's nothing to be glad about.

Nothing to be glad about.

1975. Alushta. A sand beach. The writer of these lines is contemplating a watery surface. Boats, trawlers, and some sort of huge, extended vessels; we'll just call them tankers. They are so far away they are no longer audible, and their maneuvers are reminiscent of silent film. Or the rocking of plywood vessels along stage scenery. They travel strictly along the line of the horizon, not deviating from it, either upward or downward.

There is a mat lying between me and the sea. It's spread half-facing the sea, taking into account the location of the sun. A girl sits on the mat as I follow the horizon. A young girl, about sixteen. She has just come out of the sea. The sea continues flowing from her hair, which is drawn into a ponytail. The moisture on her skin is like rain on freshly laid asphalt: each drop is separate. That may not be a poetic comparison but it is exactly what first comes to mind. The laying of asphalt made a big impression on me back in its day.

She removes a paper cone from her beach bag. It holds cherries. The swimmer girl settles in with her legs crossed and her back to me. The line of her spine, shoulder blades, and knees is like a grass-hopper's. When Nastya glances over my shoulder at this text, she notes that a grasshopper is an invertebrate. I tell her she is simply jealous. Nastya agrees and kisses the top of my head. I leave the part about the grasshopper in.

The spectacle arouses thirst. I take my wallet and go to the beach vending machine. Water with syrup (3 kop.) is unsuitable in this case. Only simple carbonated water (1 kop.) can be drunk in these circumstances. It slops into the cup with a snort and churns. Small bubbles rush upward and burst with microscopic sprays – transparently (an apt description) hinting that the water in the machine is cold.

The hint, however, is false: the water is not cold. But this is better than nothing, indeed in 1911, when I was here the last time, there was no vending machine at all, and it was not only vending machines that were lacking. I should say that everything has changed a lot here. What has remained is the great joy that the beach gives. You experience it with the mere thought of the beach. And you still experience that joy even when you understand distinctly that you no longer have a place on it and that far less pleasant things await you.

1981. Leningrad, Kupchino district. Heatwave.

Birthday party in a prefab apartment building.

It's best not to enter a Petersburg prefab apartment building during a heatwave. Actually, it's best not to live in one at all.

A Petersburg heatwave is sticky and humid. It's a total oven in a prefab building and it's impossible to air out. And everybody's stuck together in a crowded space.

You don't feel like drinking at birthday parties like this. Well, except maybe cold beer. You truly do begin with beer and end with you know what. Schrecklich.[16]

'Have some Olivier salad. And here's herring under a blanket of beet.'

'Just the word *coat* right now . . .'

Laughter in the room. An Okudzhava song is playing.

'I insist that everyone have something to eat.'

It works out that everyone just drinks.

'Sery, I'm going to sign you up for karate. Obviously not today.'

One of the guests reaches for the vodka, to say a toast. You can see the side of his shirt is damp.

He stands so he can pour for the people sitting on the opposite side of the table. Now it's revealed that his back is wet, too.

---

16 It's awful (Germ.).

After he straightens up to speak, it's clear to everyone that his belly's damp as well. If he'd sat there without crowing, nobody would have noticed a thing.

'Hold Sery's head over the bathtub. Someone really should sit with him and hold his head so he doesn't choke on his puke.'

'It's called *aspiration of vomitus*.'

'You hold his head, then, if you're so smart.'

'I'm smart?'

'No, not you. I was joking.'

A half-hearted fight starts. Everybody rushes to separate the scufflers. They don't resist.

Platosha is getting more and more incomprehensible. He requested that Geiger and I describe – no more, no less – Zaretsky's death. I started objecting, saying we didn't see that death, how can we describe it. Platosha's response: there's a lot you didn't see but somehow you're describing it all. He waved it off: fine, no need, I was just proposing it. Geiger signaled to me, unnoticed, and I bit my tongue. Zaretsky's a significant person for Platosha: everything started with him. There's a reason he drew him.

I wasn't thinking when I objected to Platosha. To be honest, no, I don't understand exactly what our descriptions are needed for anyway but since it seems important to Platosha, the question is retracted. I'd describe something for him every day – demonstrations, parks, weddings, murders – if only he could recover.

Today I found out that I need to fly to Munich in a few days. I found out by chance, after receiving an express-delivery package from a Munich hospital. I immediately telephoned Geiger, who had arranged the matter. He explained that he kept quiet about my trip because he didn't want to worry either me or Nastya prematurely.

I'm agitated. It works out that I will be flying alone. Geiger is fighting with the Ministry of Health over his clinic now and needs to be there every day. He'll fly to Munich, but only for one day, for the concluding consultation. As far as Nastya goes, the doctors insist she not travel anywhere. They say it could end badly. Despite the recommendation, she has resolutely made up her mind, but I won't allow it.

It's terrifying for me to go alone. I'm not letting on, but it truly is terrifying for me. One time when I was a child they brought me to the hospital with an appendicitis attack. The white corridors scared me and the smell of medicine scared me, but what drove me to genuine despair was that my parents were not allowed in the operating room with me. I was wheeled away on a stretcher and I twisted around and looked back at them, a doleful pair waving to me from somewhere in the depths of the corridor. I melted into tears, both from my sudden solitude and from endless pity for them, too, because I knew their orphanhood was more acute than mine. So as not to aggravate their suffering, I did not allow myself to howl out loud but my tears flowed so abundantly that they perplexed even the nurses, who had seen everything.

That picture flashed in my memory like a blurry dot, like some light in the fog, and then suddenly appeared in all its harshness. Back then, in childhood, my departure was not yet a departure and I again met with those dear to me. Only God knows where my movement through a corridor will carry me this time. When Geiger came to see us in the evening, he mentioned, speaking quickly, that they might 'open up that little skull of yours.' 'Little skull of yours' and his careless tone speak to his having rehearsed that phrase.

1923. March.

Zaretsky, a person who has finished working his shift at a sausage factory, is getting ready to go home.

He safely makes it through the guardhouse with a sausage in his trousers. The sausage is hanging on a string right next to his genitalia and is not visible to the guards.

Zaretsky's genitalia (this is discovered at the morgue) are small, thus the sausage has ample space.

Zaretsky's elder contemporary, Freud, would have considered this incident of theft to be unconnected with the stomach. Who knows, maybe the victim truly did feel more confident with sausage in his trousers. Maybe his self-esteem improved.

At any rate, it's uncomfortable to walk around with sausage in your trousers. The sausage constrains movement. It could, in the end, simply tear off the string. Come out of his trousers in front of everyone.

Someone carrying sausage in that manner is taking a risk and Zaretsky understood that.

After walking a fair distance from the factory, he usually went down to the Zhdanovka River. Unfastened his trousers and untied the sausage. Went up to the embankment again, sausage in hand.

A person with sausage always attracts attention in Russia, but especially in 1923.

From here on, there are various possible scenarios.

Someone had begun keeping an eye on this sausage-factory employee. They could have already been waiting for him by the river on that fateful day. Standing behind a tree, say, a weeping willow. They quickly grabbed Zaretsky's sausage when he took it out.

What happened from there? Chance asserts itself here.

They might have pushed Zaretsky so he hit the top of his head on a sharp rock. That's what investigator Treshnikov, who didn't know about the sausage, surmised. Of course those same characters might have hit Zaretsky with that rock – I don't think they were great philanthropists.

The question arises, however: why did they want to kill him? After all, the victim couldn't have even complained about the loss since the item was stolen in the first place.

The second scenario.

Rivers draw social dropouts. Lots of various riffraff hang around on the riverbanks.

Someone among the Zhdanovka dropouts notices Zaretsky. The sausage maker's galoshes slosh in the wet snow, which attracts attention. The bank of the Zhdanovka in March is not the sort of place to take a stroll. It's clear to an attentive person that the man sloshing in the snow has not come down here at random.

Prepared for any development of events, the observer noiselessly follows Zaretsky. He follows him out from behind the suppositional weeping willow. He still doesn't know *what* exactly Zaretsky has schemed up, but sees a victim in him.

He has a knack, the instinct of a hunter. Speaking in contemporary terms, he's a scumbag. He'll kill without thinking about practicability. He'll kill because it's possible to kill. He'll look at the manipulations with the sausage (he's accustomed to not being surprised), raise the rock, and lower it on the back of his client's head.

He eats the sausage as he watches the death throes. He melts into the dusk.

Geiger wrote about Zaretsky's murder and Platosha asked him to read it aloud. Geiger, who has banned the word 'no' with regard to my husband, began reading. I was watching only Platosha. He listened calmly to the strange description he'd ordered and though I thought it had sufficed for him, it turned out that, no, it had not. And that's what he said: it did not suffice. He didn't explain why. It seemed to me that Geiger was a little annoyed and that *his annoyance* regarding Platosha's strange request somehow even appeared to be unexpected. Maybe Geiger was annoyed that it was a strange request and he had fulfilled it. And then, there you go: it didn't fit.

Geiger said to me:

'Well, then you write about that death.' He turned to Platosha. 'Or you?'

Platosha answered:

'Good, I'll try.'

I nodded.

I think we're all truly close to lunacy.

And also: Platosha's flying off to Munich tomorrow. And he's not taking me with him.

Geiger could not manage the seemingly simple matter of writing a description of Zaretsky's murder. It works out that's not such a simple matter. We'll see what Nastya writes. She told me yesterday that I'm not fighting for my recovery. Maybe tiredness is the reason here, I don't know. It is hard to sense the acuteness of a feeling – any – for long. It seems to me that one tires from even fearing death. In the end, something sets in, taking the form of indifference for some and tranquility for others.

I am losing my strength and memory but not experiencing pain and in that I see that mercy has been presented to me. I do know what suffering is. It is terrible, not because it torments the body but because you no longer dream of ridding yourself of pain: you are prepared to rid yourself of your body. To die. You simply are not in a condition to think about matters such as the meaning of life and you see ridding yourself of suffering as the only meaning of death. When an illness's symptoms are mild, that gives an opportunity to think everything over and prepare yourself for anything. And then those months or even weeks issued to you become a small eternity and you stop considering them a short period. You cease comparing them with the average life expectancy and other silliness. You begin understanding that there is an individual plan for each person. What does average life expectancy have to do with anything . . . ?

Tomorrow I go to Munich. I place no big hopes on this trip but I am glad for it in some sense. We're all truly tired and we need to get some rest from one another.

*

Today we saw Innokenty off at the airport. I'll fly to Munich in a week.

Second day without Platosha. It feels empty. Now I can cry as much as I want – nobody sees – but there are no tears. It turns out you need someone's presence for tears, even if you think the person doesn't notice anything. I went to an evening service and I did have a cry there. It's good it was so dark; nobody could see anything.

Platosha sent me an email this morning. He writes that they welcomed him well and showed him the city. They went for a walk in the English Garden during the second half of the day. He liked the garden best of all because – even with the fallen leaves – it reminded him of places in Siverskaya. After that, Platosha described the Siverskaya forest in late autumn, in detail. Sharp air smelling of mold, a brook between the trees, crows on branches. Those birds, he wrote, love thin branches, so they can sway. I hadn't noticed that but it's true, that's exactly what they do: come to think of it, do crows have many pleasures? It's both hilarious and touching: Munich fits into five lines and the rest is Siverskaya. There's a question at the end: did I describe Zaretsky's murder? I thought he'd forget with everything going on now, but he didn't. I'll have to get going on it, I promised after all. I don't feel like it.

They showed me Munich. A beautiful city but its heart beats indifferently. I had never been to Munich and nothing resonates for me here, neither the aromas of its shops or the greenery or the beautiful cars. All of that came about and developed without my participation, with the exception, perhaps, of the English Garden, which reminds me of childhood. Even on the day I arrived, it occurred to me that this visit is seemingly in vain. It's difficult to explain, but that's the exact impression that has formed.

Later I had my first meeting with the doctor, Professor Meier. My initial thought: my German doctor is better. To the question 'Wie geht es Ihnen?'[17] I answered 'Ich sterbe.'[18] My answer reflected the notes Geiger had sent, my overall general state, and, of course, Chekhov; Dr Meier had but the vaguest notion of all that. He muttered 'Noch nicht,'[19] and we communicated further with the help of an interpreter: my grammar-school German ran out there.

While conducting my initial examination, Professor Meier became absorbed in papers for a long time. A half-hour, perhaps longer, passed. Paging through my medical history (which Geiger heroically translated into German!), the doctor kept wetting his index finger with saliva and chewing at his lips. Sometimes he scratched his nose. Then he raised his head and said:

'Expect no miracles from our clinic. That's so there are no misapprehensions. We will do all we can.'

I felt that I was smiling broadly, showing all my teeth:

'But it's miracles I came for . . .'

'Miracles, that's in Russia,' said Meier, his gaze growing sad. 'There you live by the laws of the miracle, but we attempt to live in conformity with reality. It's unclear, however, which is better.'

'*When God wishes, nature's order is overcome,*' I said, expressing my main hope, but the interpreter could not translate that.

She asked me to clarify what I had in mind.

'Tell the professor that he's completely right. There is something to think about here.'

I walked along the clinic corridor and pondered how – when things are located within the bounds of medicine – it is better, of course, to trust Germans. But my case went outside those bounds long ago. So why am I here?

17 How are you? (Germ.).
18 I'm dying (Germ.).
19 Not yet (Germ.).

*

Innokenty just told me he's returning to Petersburg.

He was calling from the hotel, where he'd stopped for his things. He'll head to the airport from there.

He requested that I not tell Nastya about his return. He doesn't yet know if he'll succeed in buying a ticket for the soonest flight and he doesn't want to worry her. The main thing is he doesn't want her to talk him out of it. And I have to take that as automatically applying to me, too.

I didn't talk him out of it. I just said I'd meet him at the airport.

He didn't explain his action at all, but what kind of explanations could there be, anyway? He said only that an understanding of the matter only came to him in Munich.

Well then, it's good that an understanding came to somebody. Me, I don't understand anything. I don't even know if intervention from the Munich doctors would have been useful.

I know one thing: I offered him that opportunity. And he made his choice.

I'm writing by hand for the first time in several months. That isn't at all simple: my hand doesn't move well. Geiger calls this 'problems with fine motor skills.' I'm writing and not typing because it turns out it's forbidden to use a computer when a plane is landing. The word *landing* contains its own overstatement. A half-hour ago, they announced that the plane's landing gear won't extend. We cannot land.

I'm writing because I need something to do. Some people are looking out the windows. They might not have looked, but they were ordered to open the shades. In the event of an emergency landing, the eyes would not need to waste time acclimatizing themselves to natural light. Some people are crying, but it's better to write. I think paper is more reliable than a computer. Unlike a computer, paper would not be destroyed when hitting the ground. True, it can burn.

The airplane is using up fuel so that doesn't happen. There have already twice been commands to press your head against the seatback in front of you, then twice the plane made a landing approach. After flying over the runway, it smoothly rose into the sky: yet again, the landing gear had not extended.

I am in a window seat in one of the airliner's last rows. To my right is an elderly German with a white band above his collar. I know it denotes his belonging to the clergy. He asks with a mild German accent:

'How many of us are flying here, about three hundred people?'

'At least,' I answer.

His line of thinking is comprehensible but I don't want to follow it. I turn away, toward the window. Petersburg is under the wing, but not the slightest sign of landing gear. From time to time, a crew member approaches a window but sees the same things I do: the lines of Vasilyevsky Island, the cupola of St Isaac's Cathedral, and the spire of Saints Peter and Paul Cathedral. It is a rare city that can present such beauty for a last moment.

The airplane's captain comes out of the cockpit and addresses the passengers using a microphone. He says that landing-gear failure is a common occurrence in aviation and nobody has died from that yet. His appearance radiates calm. The first bars of *The Seasons* sound in the speakers. The stewardesses appear in the parallel aisles at the same time. They are no longer smiling like at the beginning of the flight but panic is not noticeable on their faces, either. The captain (his uniform brand-new) walks through the cabin, unhurried, and disappears behind the curtain in the tail of the plane. My neighbor looks at the stately Russian beauties with fascination as they pour mineral water to the music of Tchaikovsky. Danger intensifies the perception of beauty.

Behind me are the sounds of stifled sobs and brief slaps. I turn around. Through a gap in the curtain, I can see one of the stewardesses sitting on a fold-down chair and sobbing; the captain is smacking her cheeks with his hands. His unhurried movement into the rear compartment had a very concrete mission.

In a parallel row, someone is throwing up.

My hand can already barely trace out letters, they're becoming ever smaller and more crooked, I need a brief rest. And yes, this is important, I promised to describe Zaretsky's murder. There doesn't seem to be much time before landing.

The landing gear on the Munich plane is jammed. They just announced that at the airport.

I'm terrified.

I'm trying not to think about anything.

I have my journal with me and will simply describe what I see. I think Innokenty would act exactly the same way.

One thing is good: Nastya doesn't know what's happening. She doesn't even know Innokenty left Munich.

People who are here to greet passengers are standing around in tears. The peculiar stillness of those preparing themselves for tragedy. A draft rustles the cellophane on bouquets: little by little, the flowers are acquiring an ominous meaning.

They're setting up the first TV cameras in the concourse and outside.

The horrible thought flashes that in some sense a catastrophe for a sick person is ... The thought is horrible in its wrongness.

Psychologists are showing up in the concourse. They immediately determine who needs help: really, you don't need to be a psychologist for that.

They don't approach me. I'm writing and they know that those who write are fully within psychological norms.

A TV broadcast from the airport pops up on a huge screen. Television is harsh. It's supposedly impassive in recording what happens, but the harshness is in that impassivity.

Existence is bifurcated. There are people with bouquets here and the exact same ones are on the screen. I see myself. There's a psychologist next to me hugging a client on the screen, stroking her spine every so often. Strange, I hadn't seen them.

I turn around: yes, they're standing here. The client is absent-mindedly crying on the psychologist's shoulder. It's not yet clear if she needs to cry: this might yet all work out.

The airplane: a camera zooms in on it. A huge structure, taking up the entire screen. An opera house, ice palace, or water park, not just an aircraft. The embodiment of the idea of what is grandiose.

It's not flying but hanging. Posing for the camera on the border of the landing field, in ripples of molten air.

It approaches for a landing. Descends.

Rushes over the landing strip.

We see the landing gear hasn't extended again – don't land! Don't land . . .

A mutual scream.

The airplane gains altitude and departs for its next lap.

I figured out a long time ago that Platosha killed Zaretsky. With him so far away now, it's easier for me to write about that. Of course my grandmother threw me off track with her *I put out a contract*, but not for long. For some reason, I simply hadn't considered whom she had the contract with. Meaning: whom she told. When they arrested her father – my great-grandfather – she told Platosha that under no circumstances should he kill Zaretsky. It was difficult not to understand that request. I think the idea had crossed his mind anyway, but what was left for him after what she said?

I don't picture the murder itself very well. I won't fantasize: it's all too serious. I've wanted many times to talk with Platosha about Zaretsky but just haven't dared. Since he doesn't speak about it, I thought I shouldn't, either. Now, though, maybe I will. After all, it's for good reason that he approached Geiger and me about Zaretsky: it was a request about something bigger.

And Geiger, by the way . . . For some reason, it seems to me that he had a hunch about it all, too. Maybe even before I did. But he's keeping quiet, keeping quiet.

Lord have mercy. I told the priest: so I repented in confession that I once killed a man but I feel no relief. The priest responded: you asked forgiveness from God, Whom you did not kill, but perhaps you should ask forgiveness of the one you killed? My God, what can I say to the one I killed? And will he hear me from there? So I came home, took the murder weapon, and went to the scene of the crime. When I arrived there, I said: forgive me, servant of God, Nikolai, that I killed you with a statuette of Themis on a March evening in 1923. Maybe you have been waiting for those words since that same year and I just have not uttered them – I simply did not think that was possible.

Then I went to the cemetery. I took Themis with me and spoke again with Nikolai, servant of God. I asked separate forgiveness for Themis: it seemed to me when I was killing that I was restoring justice, though what kind of justice could we be talking about here? It's sheer injustice. And I even thought that up about justice later: I initially made my choice of Themis for a completely different reason.

My fingers were an ideal fit for the statuette. It seemed as if the figure had been sculpted in an odd way, for a hand to grasp: only the scales were a hindrance. After they had broken off, though, Themis's raised arm became a natural support for the hand. And so the bronze goddess of justice became a handle and her marble base a hammer. The statuette, which had previously been used for exclusively peaceful purposes (primarily nuts) was suddenly transformed into an instrument of retribution. As I walked along the Zhdanovka River, I felt at the statuette inside my jacket and it was as cold as an axe.

I waited for Zaretsky behind a bush. Not behind a weeping willow as Geiger fancied it, but behind a spreading bush that I don't know what to call. I had to wait longer than I had presumed after my study of Zaretsky's movements: something had likely delayed him. That only played into my hands: it was growing ever duskier. And what if he had not come then: that thought had ripped at my consciousness so many times! If the matter had been postponed, it might not have taken place: it's possible to gather your strength the first time, but it is already difficult the second.

The matter was not postponed, though. Zaretsky appeared so unexpectedly that I barely managed to duck down behind my bush. I don't know what, exactly, delayed Zaretsky but his face was sad. Just as sad as how I recently depicted him in my drawing. It was the face of a human, not a reptile. If his face had remained like that, maybe everything would have taken a different turn on that March evening. But his human face gradually crumpled and slipped like an old mask, through which its previous features showed. He began unfastening his trousers. I looked around; there was nobody in the area.

As I came out of my hiding place, I thought that he had informed on Anastasia's father with this face. That imparted strength in me. Coming here, I had feared that I would not be able to strike at the critical moment. That – in the literal sense – I could not raise my hand against him. Nothing of the sort. I took several steps in Zaretsky's direction, sensed how nicely the statuette lay in my hand, and struck almost without swinging my arm. A dry, almost wooden, crack sounded. Zaretsky fell without turning. Without seeing me.

I leaned over him. He was lying on his back. His legs were bent at the knees and shaking very slightly. The sausage was sticking out of his unfastened trousers. Overcoming my disgust, I tore it off and tossed it into the Zhdanovka. Two ducks swam over to the splash. They watched the rippling circles with regret. And I seemed to switch off. Unhurried, I made my way up from the river and plodded off along the embankment, leaving Zaretsky amid the dirty snow and rocks.

I returned home. Anastasia and I drank tea and sat in armchairs in her room. The clock ticked; we stayed silent. It is good to stay silent to ticking. I began thinking everything that happened on the Zhdanovka was a dream. But time went on and Zaretsky was still not there. And then I realized it was not a dream. That it was the most genuine reality. Life. Or rather, death.

'I wonder why Zaretsky's not here,' said Anastasia.

'He'll show up!' I said, my voice cheery.

'And what if he doesn't?'

Anastasia smiled, barely noticeably.

If only she had known how much I hoped he would show up. Horrifying and bloodied, just so long as he came.

But he did not come.

Fire trucks started driving out on the field.

They're lining up along one of the landing strips. Meaning that's where they'll land the unfortunate airplane.

A shot taken from a helicopter: a column of ambulances moving along the highway toward the airport. A half-kilometer behind is another column.

I suddenly thought: what an ancient name, ambulance. It was preserved among all the losses.

I decided to work on descriptions but turned on the TV for some reason. There's live coverage about a plane from Munich. Now I feel on edge: Platosha could have easily ended up on it. Firemen are unwinding hoses on both sides of the landing strip. I think: those people sure do take risks! They might have to douse a burning plane.

I recall how little Platosha wanted to be a fireman, too. Danger had already captivated him back then and he was already crying then, thinking about these people's tragicness and grandeur. About the struggle between life and death, where death takes on the contours of a blazing beam or a gunpowder magazine. Or an airplane coming in without its landing gear.

Ambulances are driving out on the landing field. Doctors get out of them; there are white stripes of lab coats under jackets they've thrown on. Just the sight of those stripes makes you feel faint because they remind you of the body's suffering.

Some aviation expert is speaking on TV. He says they made a decision for a 'belly landing' so they're preparing the strip now. The idle chatter of someone off-camera is irritating. If you're so smart, then explain why the landing gear didn't extend or – even better – make it so it does. If you can't, then be quiet.

He's quiet.

They show the plane. It's already set a course for descent.

A close-up of the firemen. They're watching where the plane should appear from, unable to look away. There are gleams on their faces, from the blinking lights. They raise the muzzles of their fire hoses on command. Foam begins spurting out of them.

Why are they showing all this?

I live with this recollection and it will remain with me until the end of my life. Inasmuch as the end might come soon, I suppose it will apparently remain after my death, too. All the events and all our recollections about them will meet there. If the soul is eternal, then I think everything connected with it will also be preserved: actions, events, and sensations. Perhaps in some other, withdrawn, form or maybe in a different sequence, but it will be preserved because I remember the inscription on the famous gate: *God preserves all.*

I touch my neighbor's shoulder:

'What do you suppose? The blow that I inflict on someone close to me – should it come before I ask forgiveness for it? Is that the sequence for these events?'

Faint surprise appears in his eyes.

'How can they exist otherwise?'

'Just now I thought that they can. Genuine repentance, after all, is a return to the condition before the sin, a sort of way to overcome time. The sin does not disappear, though, and it remains as a former sin and – you won't believe this – as a relief because it was repented. It exists and is destroyed, simultaneously.'

My conversation partner places his hand over mine, which is lying on the armrest, and squeezes it firmly. There are tears in his eyes.

'I didn't understand a single word of what you said. But for some reason, it seems you are correct.'

The airplane has set a course to land. Innokenty, my friend, hold on.

'Why is it you keep writing?'

'I'm describing things, sensations. People. I write every day now, hoping to save them from oblivion.'

'God's world is too great to count on success with that.'

'You know, if each person were to describe his own sliver of that world, even if it's small . . . Although why, really, is it small? You can always find someone whose field of view is broad enough.'

'Such as?'

'Such as an aviator.'

What luck that Platosha's not on that plane.

Take the statuette of Themis. It's hard to imagine my childhood without her, she accompanied the most vivid moments. I didn't yet know what sort of instrument I was preparing when I broke off her scales. But it turned out my childhood prank was part of a drama that unfolded years later on the bank of the Zhdanovka River. I want to say that there are no fundamental or nonfundamental events and everything is important and everything is put to use, whether for good or bad.

An artist drawing life in the minutest details understands that. No, he is not in a position to reflect certain things. When drawing a flowerbed in a southern city, he supposedly cannot convey the aroma of flowers on a July evening. And he cannot convey damp stuffiness after a rain, into which that aroma dissolves so you could drink it. But there is an amazing moment when a picture begins to smell fragrant. Because genuine art is an expression of the inexpressible, without which life is not complete. Striving for fullness of expression is striving for fullness of truth.

There is something that remains outside the bounds of words and paints. You know that it is there but you just cannot approach it: there is a depth there. You stand at the surf and realize you will need to walk differently in order to go further: you cannot rule out walking atop the water. Because, for example, when saying 'my childhood,' I am not explaining anything at all to my future daughter. In order to give her any notion of that at all, I will need to describe a thousand various details, otherwise she won't understand what composed my happiness.

In that case, what awaits description? Well, of course there's the wallpaper over the bed – I still remember its flowery pattern. My finger slides over it in the evening, in the minute before slumber. The clang of the chamber pot lid is as piercing as that of orchestral cymbals. Among sounds, a bed squeaking – at every move I make – is also memorable. A hand caresses its shiny cold railing, entwines with them, bestowing its warmth upon them. It slips down, groping at the folds of the linens and resting against the knee of my grandmother, who sits by the bed. I examine the chandelier and its spidery shadows. It is bright in the center of the ceiling but there is darkness in the corners. On the cabinet, Themis holds her scales, radiating justice. My grandmother is reading *Robinson Crusoe.*

Translator's Note

One of the joys of translating Eugene Vodolazkin's work is the opportunity to correspond with him about the novels, both his original versions and my English translations. As with *Laurus*, Eugene answered questions about *The Aviator* along the way, read my translation, and offered comments and ideas, all with his usual humor and warmth. Working with him is just plain fun. Of course another joy of translating Eugene's novels is reading them for the first time, something I did electronically for *The Aviator* because I simply couldn't wait for a printed book. I hope other readers will be as surprised as I was when I learned what prompted Innokenty's initial hospital stay.

Translating bits and pieces of quoted texts from other authors always raises the choice of either translating them myself or borrowing phrases and lines from other translators' work. I tend to opt for the latter and acknowledge my colleagues' translations if I find translations that fit the tone of both the original quotation and the novel I'm translating. Alan Shaw's translation of Alexander Pushkin's *Feast During the Plague* has now helped me out with two books, for which I thank him, and Bernard Guilbert Guerney's translation of Nikolai Gogol's *Dead Souls* line about fast driving felt just right, even after inserting Eugene's parenthetical addition. Katherine Young, a poet and fellow translator, didn't mind my borrowing a phrase from her translation of Mikhail Lermontov's lovely poem 'Alone, I set out on the road.' Kate also offered her help with the stanzas of Alexander Blok's 'The Aviator' that pop up in Eugene's *The Aviator*. Blok is diabolically difficult to translate and I'm no poet, so it's thanks to Kate that these English-language stanzas read like poetry. She also helped me with Nikolai Leskov's verse.

A number of books offered me options as I searched for specialized vocabulary for aspects of Soviet prison camps in general and the camp on the Solovetsky Islands in particular. Two were especially helpful: Danzig Baldaev's *Drawings from the Gulag*, translated by Polly Gannon and Ast A. Moore, and published by Fuel in a bilingual edition; and Thomas P. Whitney's translation of Aleksandr Solzhenitsyn's *The Gulag Archipelago*.

The Aviator is my third translation for Oneworld and I couldn't be happier to work with Juliet Mabey and her team again. I'm eternally grateful for Juliet's editorial suggestions, ongoing interest in contemporary Russian literature, and warmth. I always look forward to reading and responding to comments from copy-editor Will Atkins, whose precise and patient queries about my word choices and the sense of the Russian original push me to keep improving my translation until the very last draft. I'm also very grateful to proofreader Helen Szirtes, whose meticulous reading resulted in queries that drove me to make further changes in the text. Between production head Paul Nash and assistant editor Alyson Coombes, every person, every detail, and every deadline stays on track during the translation process.

Finally, huge thanks to my colleague Liza Prudovskaya, who read a draft of *The Aviator* and checked it against Eugene's original, making numerous comments, saving me from dumb mistakes, and answering my multitude of questions about vocabulary and tone. Liza's answers help me tremendously with individual word choices, and global decisions about translating narrators' and characters' voices.

Lisa Hayden

Oneworld, Many Voices

Bringing you exceptional writing
from around the world

The Unit by Ninni Holmqvist (Swedish)
Translated by Marlaine Delargy

Twice Born by Margaret Mazzantini (Italian)
Translated by Ann Gagliardi

Things We Left Unsaid by Zoya Pirzad (Persian)
Translated by Franklin Lewis

The Space Between Us by Zoya Pirzad (Persian)
Translated by Amy Motlagh

The Hen Who Dreamed She Could Fly by Sun-mi Hwang
(Korean) Translated by Chi-Young Kim

The Hilltop by Assaf Gavron (Hebrew)
Translated by Steven Cohen

Morning Sea by Margaret Mazzantini (Italian)
Translated by Ann Gagliardi

A Perfect Crime by A Yi (Chinese)
Translated by Anna Holmwood

The Meursault Investigation by Kamel Daoud (French)
Translated by John Cullen

Minus Me by Ingelin Røssland (YA) (Norwegian)
Translated by Deborah Dawkin

Laurus by Eugene Vodolazkin (Russian)
Translated by Lisa C. Hayden

Masha Regina by Vadim Levental (Russian)
Translated by Lisa C. Hayden

French Concession by Xiao Bai (Chinese)
Translated by Chenxin Jiang

The Sky Over Lima by Juan Gómez Bárcena (Spanish)
Translated by Andrea Rosenberg

A Very Special Year by Thomas Montasser (German)
Translated by Jamie Bulloch

Umami by Laia Jufresa (Spanish)
Translated by Sophie Hughes

The Hermit by Thomas Rydahl (Danish)
Translated by K.E. Semmel

The Peculiar Life of a Lonely Postman by Denis Thériault
(French) Translated by Liedewy Hawke

Three Envelopes by Nir Hezroni (Hebrew)
Translated by Steven Cohen

Fever Dream by Samanta Schweblin (Spanish)
Translated by Megan McDowell

The Postman's Fiancée by Denis Thériault (French)
Translated by John Cullen

The Invisible Life of Euridice Gusmao by Martha Batalha
(Brazilian Portuguese) Translated by Eric M. B. Becker

The Temptation to Be Happy by Lorenzo Marone
(Italian) Translated by Shaun Whiteside

Sweet Bean Paste by Durian Sukegawa (Japanese)
Translated by Alison Watts

They Know Not What They Do by Jussi Valtonen (Finnish)
Translated by Kristian London

The Tiger and the Acrobat by Susanna Tamaro (Italian)
Translated by Nicoleugenia Prezzavento and Vicki Satlow

The Woman at 1,000 Degrees by Hallgrímur Helgason (Icelandic) Translated by Brian FitzGibbon

Frankenstein in Baghdad by Ahmed Saadawi (Arabic) Translated by Jonathan Wright

Back Up by Paul Colize (French) Translated by Louise Rogers Lalaurie

Damnation by Peter Beck (German) Translated by Jamie Bulloch

Oneiron by Laura Lindstedt (Finnish) Translated by Owen Witesman

The Boy Who Belonged to the Sea by Denis Thériault (French) Translated by Liedewy Hawke

The Baghdad Clock by Shahad Al Rawi (Arabic) Translated by Luke Leafgren

The Aviator by Eugene Vodolazkin (Russian) Translated by Lisa C. Hayden

Lala by Jacek Dehnel (Polish) Translated by Antonia Lloyd-Jones